Madame President

Marguerite Williams & Jon Guttman

authorHOUSE

AuthorHouse™
1663 Liberty Drive
Bloomington, IN 47403
www.authorhouse.com
Phone: 1-800-839-8640

© 2012 Marguerite Williams & Jon Guttman. All rights reserved.

No part of this book may be reproduced, stored in a retrieval system, or transmitted by any means without the written permission of the authors.

Published by AuthorHouse 2/12/2013

ISBN: 978-1-4685-5534-9 (sc)
ISBN: 978-1-4685-5535-6 (hc)
ISBN: 978-1-4685-5536-3 (e)

Library of Congress Control Number: 2012903130
Cover design: Mervil Paylor Design
Copyright by: Marguerite Williams and Jon Guttman, 2012
All rights reserved

Photography by Picture Elegance

This book is printed on acid-free paper.

Because of the dynamic nature of the Internet, any web addresses or links contained in this book may have changed since publication and may no longer be valid. The views expressed in this work are solely those of the author and do not necessarily reflect the views of the publisher, and the publisher hereby disclaims any responsibility for them.

This book is dedicated, with gratitude and love, to Lewis and Bill, without whose support our dream of writing Madame President would have died aborning.

Prologue

February 22 dawned bright and clear, with the monuments and the White House in sharp relief against the cold, blue winter sky.

By day's end, President Kate MacIntyre was in a mood to celebrate. Her State of the Union address had been well received by both the House and Senate and her approval numbers were off the chart. After the trauma of winning her first term by a squeaker, these numbers were vindication.

During her speech, she looked into the gallery and saw her husband, Deacon, along with her children and grandchildren. Kate couldn't suppress a smile. They were an eclectic bunch, and what was Deacon's mother thinking with that name? He couldn't be less like most deacons she knew. This day was filled with joy and promise, for her and her country. The people had spoken. They wanted her brand of government – with some ideals intact and legislation centered on the people. Damn, those were sweet thoughts.

There in the audience were her Supreme Court justices, her Joint Chiefs of Staff, and her Cabinet. For the first time in four years she had an overwhelming mandate and she planned on using it. She turned and smiled at Vice President Harris Franklin, III. He grinned back. Kate hoped that one day this would be his night. Kate liked Harry, and she would campaign for him vigorously when the time came. He was a proper Connecticut Yankee, reared in a small coastal city, and he, too, loved the outdoors. Harry got along fine with the President and discovered that they shared more in common than not. Maybe it was fly-fishing or maybe their mutual addiction to tobacco.

The applause and standing ovations were plentiful, and she carefully built to her two potentially controversial policy initiatives. Her advisors had suggested she wait until after the State of the Union to announce them, but she wanted to move ahead. Kate was tired of false starts and past failures in healthcare reform. At the least, the country needed a comprehensive prescription plan. As for marijuana, who all didn't inhale at least once in their lives? Marijuana prohibition used too many resources for something that was less harmful than alcohol, in her thinking. It was time to decriminalize it in order to save lives through reduced violence and quality control. Taxation of the nasty stuff would be an added benefit.

The audience didn't freeze entirely when she finally said the words "decriminalize marijuana" and a few brave souls, mostly from the states bordering Mexico, even applauded. That was enough for tonight.

After making the congratulatory walk through the halls of Congress, Kate entered the limousine with her handsome husband and took his hand. She leaned her head on his shoulder and felt the knots in her shoulders melt away. He breathed in her scent. He could never remember the name of the perfume she wore, but it was as much a part of her as her Texas accent. A thought flitted across his mind. All the passion she brought to bear in leading this country, she gave to him when they were alone together. Her kiss still knocked him off his pins.

The Vice President, young and smart and absorbing all he could from the President, followed his wife into their limousine. She had the looks that turned the heads of all men, regardless of their politics. But she was not just a looker. Amelia had a lawyer's keen intelligence and a writer's observational skills. He relied on her insight and would need it if he were ever to lead this country. The motorcades separated as soon as they left the Capital parking garage, taking their occupants to their own residences.

Kate and Deacon felt the explosion before they heard it.

The flames and black smoke that filled the night sky were a mile away. Their heads snapped back as the limousine sped up to almost 100 mph. From the front seat, the words came back to them, "Cowgirl and Roper, on way to White House. ETA one minute. What is the status of Seagull? I repeat, where is Seagull now?"

The two-way radio crackled. Then silence. Finally, "Bring the President to the bunker. The Vice President's limousine has been attacked."

Once they stepped off the elevator into the underground tunnel leading to the White House, Kate headed directly for the Situation Room, despite protestations from security.

Essential personnel had already gathered. Several aids stood in a circle with their backs to her, shielding her while she tore off her Ralph Rucci suit and dressed in more practical clothes her assistant brought her. Reports poured in, but they were chaotic and incomplete. Fraught with worry for Vice President Franklin, she paced the length of the oversized conference room.

Finally, after interminable minutes, the head of her Secret Service detail, Ezra Jefferson, entered the room. He walked straight to her and they stepped aside. "The Vice President is at Walter Reed. He's in critical condition with severe brain injuries. They don't expect him to live through the night."

"What about Amelia?"

"Miraculously, some broken bones and lacerations. The Vice President and his driver bore the brunt of the explosion."

"Is the driver alive?"

"No, Ma'am."

She recoiled. "The other agent in the car?"

"He's in stable condition."

"Who is with Amelia?"

"One of our full details and the hospital is in lock-down."

"And their children?"

"Already on that. Mrs. Franklin requested that they be with her at the hospital, at least for now."

"I want to be with the Vice President."

"You can't leave until we know the situation is under control."

"Maybe you didn't hear me. I'm going to see Harry now."

Jefferson flinched at the President's retort. As he was about to bark out some orders, his phone rang. His face remained a mask. But Kate saw the anguish in his eyes.

He said, "I will tell the President."

"Tell me what, Ezra?"

Jefferson looked at his shoes. Shiny and black. Such an odd thing to notice when he had to inform the President of something so terrible.

"Vice President Franklin died three minutes ago."

Before she could react, he added, "Madame President, there's something else."

She felt swamped by dread but squared her shoulders and met his eyes.

"The Vice President wasn't the only target tonight."

"What the hell do you mean?"

"We found an IED on the route you were taking back to the White House. By the grace of God, the trigger mechanism failed. The sons of bitches were going after both of you."

PART I

Amendment 25 · Presidential Disability and Succession · Clause II

Whenever there is a vacancy in the office of the Vice President, the President shall nominate a Vice President who shall take office upon confirmation by a majority vote of both Houses of Congress.

CHAPTER 1
Tuesday, February 22
NYC · 8:30 PM EST

Roger walked into the Waldorf Towers as the State of the Union address began.

The President's Chief of Staff should have been at the Capital. "Dammit," he muttered, but Kate had concurred this meeting couldn't wait.

When Emilio arrived thirty minutes later, Roger was in no mood for social niceties. Not even with one of his closest friends.

Roger studied the man before him, a man he'd known since West Point. Shorter than Roger by five or six inches, Emilio still appeared to be taller than average. And while his complexion was dark, the Castilian blood shone through with eyes so blue that most people assumed he wore contacts. With Roger's red hair, they made a colorful pair.

After graduation, with a Presidential waiver for Emilio, they both qualified for Ranger training and served together across the globe, including Iraq and Afghanistan. Funny thing about that kind of service, Roger thought. What better way to get to know a person? He knew that he could trust Emilio with his life. He had many times before. Best friend seemed such a trivial way of saying what Emilio meant to him.

When Emilio called him earlier in the day, the note of panic in his voice was unmistakable.

"Roger, I need to see you as soon as possible."

"What's so urgent?"

Not on the phone. When can you come to New York?"

"Uh, maybe next week sometime."

Roger heard silence on the other end of the line. "Are you still there, Emilio?"

"Can you come tonight?"

"But it's the State of Union."

Roger stopped. Emilio would have known that. "What is it, Emilio?"

"Roger, please. I wouldn't ask if this weren't important."

Roger glanced at his watch. "Okay, I hear you. Kate and Deacon keep a suite at the Waldorf Towers that no one knows about. I'll make arrangements to slip away for a few hours. Can you be there at 8:30?"

"Of course."

"Go to the front desk and ask for Mr. Rancher's suite. I'll alert them that you're coming. See you at…" Roger didn't get a chance to finish. The line was already dead.

Emilio hadn't stopped for a handshake when Roger opened the door. He strode across the large living room, found the well-stocked bar, poured himself two fingers of Glenlivet and plopped onto the sofa.

"Yes, and hello to you too. Please make yourself at home."

Emilio's dark face flushed. He shrugged and kept drinking.

"Geez, man, can you at least tell me what was so important that I had to miss my mother's State of the Union?"

Emilio poured another glass and suggested that Roger take a seat.

"As Mexico's Permanent Deputy Ambassador to the UN, I overhear many things. Most of it is drivel. Your CIA probably knows it all anyway. But a piece of information has come my way that you need to act on immediately."

"What information? What the hell, Emilio?"

"Roger, there's going to be an attempt on the President's life."

"President Castillo?

"No. Jesus, Roger. Your President."

Roger leapt up. "Kate? President MacIntyre? What the fuck are you talking about? When? How? This is crazy."

"I do not know the details."

"Emilio, that's bullshit! You can't drop a bombshell like that and not give me anything to go on. What's your source on this?"

"My father."

Roger gasped like he'd been sucker punched. Now it was his turn to walk over to the bar. His mind whirled. Kate? He wanted to kick something or someone, but he had to think straight.

He knew who Emilio's father was and this couldn't be ignored. His first instinct was to call in his security detail and alert the White House, but he needed to press Emilio a little harder. When it came to Emilio's father that might not be easy. The de Franco relationship was complicated, to say the least. Roger searched his mind for details about the family.

Federico de Franco was a much feared but also revered person in Mexico, depending on one's dealings with the man. The son of Juan Carlos and Lucia de Franco, he was the head of Mexico's largest bank, Banco del Republico, and was also the largest stockholder in the Mexican pharmaceutical giant, Pharma de Mexico.

According to Emilio, Federico had been abused psychologically and physically as a child by his father. The cycle would have continued but for the tragic death of Emilio's mother, a young maid in his grandparents household. Officially she died during childbirth, but according to Emilio's grandmother the circumstances of his mother's death were never fully explained. No death certificate, no hospital report, just forged birth certificates for Emilio and his twin sister Martina, a marriage license inserted in the official record and Federico banished to Europe.

Juan Carlos and Lucia raised their grandchildren as their own. Lucia was ever thankful that her husband became such a model grandparent after the cruel, often brutal, way he had treated Federico.

After Federico studied at the Sorbonne and then at the London School of Economics, he realized, early in his banking career, the lucrative nature of the drug business and money laundering. A natural intellect and temperament for business, and a tightly controlled sadistic streak, made him well suited for the illegal side of banking. Soon he found himself living two lives - respected banker and scion of one of Mexico's most prominent and wealthy families, and drug lord, head of one of the largest cartels in Mexico.

If men like Federico were ever placed on the Fortune 500 list, he would be one of the three or four wealthiest men in the world. But it was never about the money for him. It was his insatiable need for power and his total hatred of his father. He was incapable of feeling much of anything, though he was certain he loved his children, in his own way. The fact that he had sired two children was a quirk of nature to him, and he had made certain with two little snips that it wouldn't happen again.

Roger had to separate what information arose from drunken confessions at college or from intelligence briefings. "You must know something, goddammit. Or you wouldn't have insisted on meeting me here. What did your father tell you? And how is he involved?"

Emilio steadied his gaze and began to talk. After fifteen minutes of listening without interrupting, Roger was convinced that he knew all that Emilio knew and that the information was credible.

Roger sorted through his wildly careening thoughts. He needed to alert the Secret Service before he did anything else and he needed to get back to Washington ASAP.

Fred Montgomery, the head of his security detail, as if a mind reader, flung open the door.

The ashen-faced Montgomery entered the room. "Mr. Dunham?"

"Yes, Fred."

"Ezra Jefferson needs to speak with you immediately."

A shot of adrenalin made Roger's fingers sweat. He took his agent's phone.

Montgomery looked at Emilio. "I will escort your guest out."

Roger held up his hand and spoke into the phone. "Yes, Ezra. Do you want my code?"

"Yes, please."

"Veritas."

Jefferson continued. "Sir. There was an attack on the President's car."

"Oh my God, is she…"

"She's fine. The IED didn't detonate."

Roger fell back onto the couch. Emilio looked from Montgomery to Roger.

"Thank God. Where is my mother now?"

"In the White House situation room. But there's more. The Vice President's car was also attacked and…it's bad, sir. He died 13 minutes ago. His driver was also killed in the explosion. That's pretty much all we know as of this moment."

"Where is Deacon, I mean the First Gentleman?"

"With the President."

"Can you patch me through?"

Ignoring Roger's request for the moment, Ezra continued. "You need to leave New York now. A plane is waiting for you at McGuire Air Force Base. We should have you back at the White House in less than two hours and the President will call you once you're wheels-up. One more thing, while the news of the Vice President's assassination has started to leak out, no one outside of those in the situation room and the Secret Service knows that the President's car was targeted."

Roger handed the phone back to Agent Montgomery. "Fred, did they tell you what happened to my mother and the Vice President?"

"Yes, Mr. Dunham. We need to get moving."

Roger stood and looked down at his right hand. It was balled into a fist and his nails dug into the flesh of his palm. He remembered that Emilio was still in the room. The look on Roger's face made Emilio shudder.

"You son-of-a-bitch. It's already happened…"

"Oh God. Is your mother…"

"She's alive, no thanks to you."

"What the hell does that mean? I'm here tonight to try to…"

Montgomery cleared his throat. "Sir, we have to leave now. Mr. de Franco, there is an agent in the hallway. Please follow him out."

Roger reached out and held Emilio by the elbow. "Emilio, I'm sorry. You should know that the Vice President is dead.

"Fred, give the ambassador and me one moment." The agent started to protest but Roger shook his head.

"Emilio I realize that this may become dicey for you. Between the Mexican Government and your family you may be forced to make choices that will compromise our friendship." "I'm aware, as you Gringos say, that I may find myself between the proverbial hard rock and tight spot, but to hell with protocol. How can I help?"

"By meeting me at the White House first thing tomorrow morning."

With that Roger turned to leave.

Emilio called out to Roger's retreating back. "You know that I love your mother, don't you?"

Roger turned and stared at Emilio. Did Emilio love Kate? He sure as hell hoped so. But why didn't Emilio get to me sooner? "I know, Emilio. See you in Washington."

CHAPTER 2
Wednesday, February 23
Washington, DC · 3:00 AM

The closer Roger got to the oval office the faster his pace became. He pushed the door open so hard that it banged against the wall. The President looked up, startled. She stood and embraced Roger.

"Kate. Madame President." Roger struggled to catch his breath. Names between Roger and the President were a bit like Marty Feldman's hump in "Young Frankenstein" – always shifting.

Roger was one of the youngest Chiefs of Staff in White House history and Kate had taken plenty of hits for putting him in the position. It was worth it. He had never failed her or the country. She looked at him fondly, remembering the frightened boy who came into her life over twenty-five years ago.

She had known him for longer than that. He grew up on the neighboring ranch, and his parents were best friends to Deacon and her. The families did everything together, from Easter egg hunts to Christmas Eve dinners and summer vacations. Roger was the only child of his loving parents, Rob and Marie, and he was a steadying influence on Kate's wilder crew, especially her unruly youngest son, Noah, more affectionately called Butch.

In an instant on a dark, rain-slicked winding road, everything changed. Rob and Marie were gone in a flash. And the nightmare began for Roger. He was strapped in the back seat and the pickup that came out of nowhere, with its drunken driver, pulverized the front of the car and left the 12-year old Roger with two broken legs, cracked ribs, and deep facial wounds. His brain was intact, though, and he remembered everything - the deathly silence from the front seat, the blood he smelled in the air and tasted in his mouth, and his inability to move an inch, crushed by the metal doorplates.

By the time help finally arrived, the truck driver had hightailed it away from the scene, then tumbled into a ditch and passed out. Roger already knew what the emergency rescuers confirmed. His parents were dead. He fell into a nightmare of lights and screams and tumbled down, down into a dark tunnel. When he awoke three days later, the first face he saw was Kate's. She was sitting on his bed, his hand held tightly by hers.

When his eyes flickered open, she looked him square in the face and said, "Honey, you know that your parents are gone. Their hurtin' is over and ours is begun because we miss them so damn much."

Roger nodded and tears plopped onto his chest.

"But you are not alone. You will not be alone. Not ever. Not as long as Deacon and I and our kids are alive and on this planet. Your folks didn't have many kin around here, and that's what we are to you now...kin. You understand what I'm sayin' to you?"

Roger lay still as the eye of a hurricane, while the room swirled around him. He tried to answer. His mouth went dry. Nothing came out.

"That's okay. I'll talk now for the both of us. You're gonna' be okay. Bruised as a squashed up watermelon and sore, but okay. When you get out of this place, you're comin' to live with us."

Hard, coughing, wracking sobs came forth from the deepest place in Roger. He grabbed Kate and held on. His body trembled and his teeth chattered. The sobs came like body blows until he fell back onto the bed, spent. He managed to get out four words to Kate before he returned to the arms of sleep. "Don't leave me, Kate."

She bent over and kissed the one place on his forehead that wasn't stitched up or swollen. "Don't worry, Roger. You're mine now. No power in heaven or on earth will change that."

Sure enough, Roger was hers. He called her Kate, but in his mind, she was momma. When she ran for Town Board of her small Hill Country village, Roger was right there beside her, stamping letters, making buttons on an old contraption that he found at the public library, helping her write her speeches. Her other children took a passing interest in her newfound political life, but Roger studied the issues and helped her dissect and shed light on them. Even Deacon deferred to Roger when Kate was faced with thorny local dilemmas, the kind that let them know that all politics are personal and sometimes they cut deep. But she kept on trying to do the right thing by the most people possible.

Roger's mind fascinated Kate. She loved to watch him seize upon an idea and shake it apart like a cat that catches a field mouse. He got into all the right schools but had his heart set on West Point, and Kate knew he needed to break the cord.

Kate moved up the political ladder while Roger finished his education, graduating at the top of his class. By the time he left the Army Rangers, six years later, Kate was already serving in the State House as Lieutenant Governor. Roger spent the next three years at Harvard Law School, though he never wiped the Hill Country dust entirely off his jeans, and Kate bided her time in Austin. He even found time to complete an advanced degree in economics.

Finally their career paths crossed. Roger insisted and Kate protested. "Honey, wait a minute now. You have an offer from a top firm in New York. Don't pass up that opportunity. I'll do fine if you let me call you every now and then for advice."

"Kate, I want to come home and help you with the race."

"Help me with this piddling race for Governor? What was I thinkin' anyway? I'm not cut out for this crowd. And the experts aren't giving me a snow ball's chance."

"You are cut out for it. Texas needs you. Let me help you. I can get back to the law firm any time."

Kate relented and the game was afoot.

"Madame President. Madame President." Kate heard Roger's voice as though over an intercom. Her gaze cleared and she saw him looking at her in a concerned and quizzical way. She almost laughed.

"My God, Roger, my mind was a thousand miles away."

Kate motioned for him to join her on the couch. She patted his knee and waited.

Roger laughed. "Let me try again. Thank God you're okay, Kate. Thank God."

"Yes. But we lost Harris, Roger. They took him from us. This cannot go unanswered."

Roger betrayed his emotions around one person, the woman beside him. He narrowed his eyes. "It will not go unanswered, Madame President. Let me tell you about New York. Emilio may have provided us with one heck of a lead."

"What on earth did he have to say?"

"Briefly, he informed me that there might be an attempt on your life. The Vice President wasn't even mentioned."

"And how did he come by this information?"

"His father. The problem is that Emilio doesn't trust his father or his motives."

"Why?"

"According to Emilio, in addition to his father's legitimate business holdings, de Franco is also the head of the most powerful drug cartel in Mexico."

"But Roger, we already know this."

"Yes, but Emilio didn't know that we had that information."

"Still what would Federico gain by trying to warn us if he were involved?"

"Kate, I'm not sure, but here's the kicker. Emilio's father claims he is being set up by Hezbollah."

"Hezbollah. That's crazy. Besides they've never been particularly squeamish about taking credit for acts of terrorism before."

"No, they haven't, and there's the rub."

"Well, any ideas?"

"I gave this some thought while I was flying back from New York and I think there is a plausible explanation. Hezbollah has long relied on Mexican cartels to transport Middle Eastern heroin into the States. And de Franco is suspected of being the prime mover behind the cultivation of poppies and processing of heroin in Mexico. If Hezbollah is starting to feel squeezed by de Franco, they might want to get him out of the way.

"And if they can't get to him directly, what better way of eliminating him than to have the Great Satan Uncle Sam do their dirty work for them."

"It always seems to get down to business, doesn't it? But wouldn't this be extreme even for Hezbollah?"

"Not necessarily, Kate. From their perspective, it might look like a win/win situation. They get us to take out Federico and then they get bragging rights for killing the President and Vice President of the United States."

"True, but let me point out one other possibility. What if de Franco is trying to use us to eliminate his competition? Seems like the sword cuts both ways, doesn't it?"

CHAPTER 3

WEDNESDAY, FEBRUARY 23
BEIRUT, 10:00 AM · EASTERN EUROPEAN
TIME (EET) (3:00 AM EST)

Ice, an unusual occurrence in Beirut, coated a ground strewn with bricks from bombed out buildings. The Israelis had tried, unsuccessfully, to bomb Hezbollah into smithereens years earlier and much of Haret Hreit was still in ruins. The local government was unwilling or unable to collect the taxes needed for even the most rudimentary repairs, and it was left to Hezbollah to pick up the slack.

And that was, ostensibly, the pretext for this morning's meeting of the IRSO. Officially, the Islamic Resistance Support Organization or *Hay'at Da'am al-Muqawama al-Islamiya fi Lubnan,* is a charity set up by Hezbollah to support a wide array of social programs. Unofficially, it operates as Hezbollah's Treasury Department, financing the organization's military wing, jihadist activities and terrorism.

They met in the chairman's office, hidden behind the walls of posters of IRSO's legitimate charitable works. The room was dense with acrid smoke from the ever-present cigarettes and sunlight struggled to filter in through filthy windows. In the front offices, telephones rang and secretaries laughed amiably, belying the dual nature of their work. The building was nondescript, the partially rebuilt remains of an old post office. The sidewalks were nearly empty, except for a few staggering beggars and dissolute young men. The street was quiet.

Sheikh Nasrallah, the head of Hezbollah, entered the IRSO inner office and directed his ire at Talal El-Hussen, the chair of IRSO. "So, what is so urgent that I drag myself half-way across Beirut?"

El-Hussen, a short, stocky man with a thick black beard and eyes like dense marbles, immediately stood before the Hezbollah leader. "Eminence, you have seen the news on Al Jazeera. The infidels' Vice President is dead."

"Praise be to Allah, but what does that have to do with us?"

The other person in the room, Abdel Salam, the Vice-Chairman of the IRSO and El-Hussen's second-in-command, raised his eyebrows and glanced at El-Hussen. *Sheikh Nasrallah doesn't know?*

But before Salam could speak, El-Hussen interjected, "Sheikh, we have much to discuss."

"Discuss? You leg of a chair, you idiot, are we involved in this somehow? Tell me now." Nasrallah was a big man who had gone to seed. His once muscular frame now sagged on his bones like the sails of a becalmed ship. But his face retained the animal ferocity for which he had long been known. And that face was now a mask of rage, with accusing eyes darting between Salam and El-Hussen.

"Tehran felt it best not to compromise you until the operation was underway."

"So now the Ayatollahs are running Hezbollah, not me?"

"No, Eminence, of course not. Please let me explain and you will understand why I did not bring this to you until now."

"Talal, not a word. This is your shit and I am not going to step in it. Whatever you have done, by the beard of the Prophet, it had better work, or else your life won't be worth a rat's foreskin. And I don't give a damn what your friends in Tehran have to say."

"Believe me, Sheikh, on the grave of my father, it is well worth the risk."

This little piece of theater was El-Hussen's idea and Sheikh Nasrallah had readily agreed to it. In case the walls had ears, better to lay the plan at Tehran's feet than theirs. Of course, if the operation were a success, Hezbollah would claim all the credit and receive all the praise.

Once Sheikh Nasrallah had left, El-Hussen turned to a shaken Salam and asked for an update.

Salam was a hard read. A diplomat by profession, he had sculpted and sinewy good looks, but was effete in nature. As a member of one of Lebanon's wealthiest families, he believed in the cause but was loathe to get his own hands dirty. That's why growling dogs like El-Hussen were kept around, for all the unpleasantries of life.

"Well, of course, only one device detonated, but even that may be to our advantage."

"How so?"

"Since the signature of the device was meant to trace back to our Mexican friend, de Franco, I assume that the Americans, who now have an unexploded IED, will be able to track down the source of the components all the sooner."

"True enough, Abdel. But I am still not happy that one of the devices didn't detonate. Do we have any reason to believe that it was interfered with?"

Salam responded after careful thought, "I cannot answer that with any certainty. We haven't been able to reach Michel. He was supposed to check in with his contact over 24 hours ago, but still no word."

"Michel knows how to take care of himself. I wouldn't be too concerned. Just yet."

CHAPTER 4
WEDNESDAY, FEBRUARY 23
SANTA MARIA DEL ORO, MEXICO · 1:00 AM
AMERICAN CHIHUAHUA CENTRAL STANDARD TIME (CCST) (3:00AM EST)

Michel was a far cry from Beirut or his office at Valentine Pharmaceuticals in Denver, with its books and plants and colleagues coming and going. He was languishing, drifting in and out of consciousness, in a dank cellar, surrounded by the smell of death and suffering, blood and waste, somewhere in the Sierra Madre Mountains of Mexico. A rat ran across his foot. The chair in which he was strapped was wet with his own urine.

Michel Hayek didn't look Lebanese. As a matter of fact, he could and often did pass for Scandinavian. His deep blue eyes and sandy blond hair probably derived from some violent Crusader act of lust 700 years earlier. His family was Maronite Christian.

Michel remembered the first time he'd seen the Sheikh's wife, after he'd been orphaned by the Israeli raid on his village. Nada Nasrallah, a nurse by training, was volunteering at the Red Crescent facility where Michel had been taken. Childless herself, it was love at first sight. Sheikh Nasrallah initially objected because Michel was a Christian, but soon came to accept him as if he were his own son.

Michel believed in nothing and no one, other than his adored new mother and his adoptive father, whom he worshipped.

At an early age, Michel had shown an aptitude for science and sports, and the Sheikh and his wife encouraged those interests, Nada as a mother nurturing a child, and Nasrallah always with a more selfish agenda. Michel attended one of the most selective private schools run by IRSO, but at Nada's insistence, also attended a Maronite parochial school three days a week, until he graduated from both with honors. For three summers, while school was out, Michel had been sent to a special summer camp in Iran that offered training in more than the usual camp activities.

He was captain of his Maronite school's soccer team and, if he hadn't been accepted into MIT, he was accomplished enough to have joined Lebanon's National soccer team. He studied molecular biology and in five years completed undergraduate and graduate schools, earning his PhD.

After graduation, Michel took a job with Valentine Pharmaceuticals, as well as an appointment as a visiting Professor at Beirut Arab University. His job was structured so that he would be able to teach one semester each academic year.

An unexpected result of his research and writing was that he had actually become absorbed by his field of molecular genetics. He believed that studying the structure and function of genes at a molecular level would yield real breakthroughs in the treatment and prevention of disease. And his work had already produced some dramatic results. Though the Sheikh initially encouraged Michel to pursue this career as an unassailable cover, Michel discovered a passion and talent for it that transcended pretense.

Michel was a covert agent in the classic sense. With impeccable credentials and a global reputation, he was able to travel the world without suspicion. Over the years Sheikh Nasrallah had come to rely on Michel for the most sensitive of missions. Michel didn't ask extraneous questions and had never failed the Sheikh. That is until now.

Why he was alive was a mystery to him. In spite of all the movie portrayals of agents standing up to absurd amounts of torture, Michel knew from the start that it was a matter of time and the sophistication of the torturer before everyone talked. Michel had lasted a few hours.

Suicide bombers were one thing. You took your finger off a button and, poof, you were being comforted by your 72 virgins in Paradise. But torture was something else, no matter how much you believed in the cause.

The sound of boots stirred Michel from his thoughts.

"Michel, it's time for another chat."

The sight of el Escolar, who had been playing whack-a-mole with him for days, instantly soured Michel's stomach and he vomited.

Escolar smiled a sad smile. "I'm sorry your dinner didn't agree with you, but I have news, my friend. The first part of Talal's plan has succeeded, at least in part. The Vice President was eliminated, but the President survived."

Michel's mind raced. The targets were the President and Vice President of the United States? That was Talal's plan? Did one of the devices malfunction? I checked the IEDs myself, right here in Santa María del Oro.

"You have nothing to say about this, Michel? I am disappointed at your silence, but I can see in your eyes that you were truthful with me. Indeed, you did not know the targets."

Now a taunt, "I guess the Sheikh didn't trust you with that information."

Michel whispered, "I have something to tell you."

Escolar leaned forward. "Yes?"

Michel gathered his spit and fired it at the other man's eye. It hit its target.

Escolar straightened back up and laughed. "So, my little mouse has nothing left but spit?"

Michel prepared himself for the blow that was sure to follow, but the unexpected ring of a cell phone broke the unbearable tension in the room. Escolar stepped away and answered, beyond Michel's hearing.

Michel looked at his bleeding hands as questions clouded his mind. How had this man discovered my involvement? And why did he not warn the Americans, if he knew about the assassinations? He could have stopped them. Instead he kept the information to himself? Something wasn't adding up.

He remembered finishing his lecture in Mexico City on non-classical gene therapy, and then driving a rental car to Santa María del Oro to pick up the apparatus for the IEDs. Later, he crossed the border at Presidio, avoiding the more heavily scrutinized crossing at El Paso, and drove to Washington. Once in DC, he had a lecture scheduled at Georgetown the week before the State of the Union address. He made contact with a member of the Arab Student Alliance and handed over all of the IED components. He had no idea who or what the targets were because Hezbollah always compartmentalized operations. He was a courier on this mission; he didn't expect to know the ultimate purpose.

Later Michel caught a flight back to Mexico City, planning to finish his business in Mexico and take a well-deserved week of vacation before returning to Denver. He remembered getting into a cab at the airport but nothing else until he came to in this cell two days ago. He focused on the sound of his own screams in order to remain conscious. Escolar had two men with him at all times, until this encounter. They held his arms and feet. They threw cold, fetid water in his face. But it was Escolar who administered all of the pain.

Michel hung his head to look at his naked body. His nipples were scorched and bleeding and his testicles were the size and color of rotted plums. The burn marks all over his body were already starting to scab over. Michel couldn't understand why the man kept on and on, long after all the words and confessions had been uttered. Of course, Michel soon realized that it was for sheer pleasure. During the most intense infliction of pain, Escolar would stop, throw his head back, close his eyes and sigh deeply, as though in the arms of a lover.

As Escolar turned back into the room, the sound of his conversation reached Michel. He raised his head and tried to focus on Escolar's words. "Yes, my son. You know everything that I know. But I believe that there is someone who might be of great interest to the Americans."

He turned and smirked at Michel. "As soon as I interview him, you will be the first to know, Emilio. I promise."

CHAPTER 5
WEDNESDAY, FEBRUARY 23
NEW YORK CITY · 3:00 AM

Emilio stood at the tall windows that lined his 64th Street townhouse. He looked down through the filtered lamplight on trees that were still bare of leaves and sidewalks that were slick with ice from the most recent storm. His den on the fourth floor was his sanctuary from the city, and he had filled the comfortable room with paintings and sculpture from prominent Mexican artists. He had always lived beyond the means of someone his age, and his townhouse between 1st and 2nd Avenues was no exception.

He snapped the phone closed after speaking with his father. As strained as their relationship had been for many years, his father's voice seemed more distant than ever, as though he were talking from inside a deep cave. Emilio learned a long time ago not to trust his father, but now he needed him. Damn it all, he didn't like depending on the old son-of-a-bitch for anything, much less the life of the President of the United States.

He looked one more time at his phone, wondering if it would bite him, rather than merely ring, waiting to hear from a person who might direct him along this now treacherous path. For the good of two countries, he had to get this right. He had been torn between the countries since attending West Point, loyal to both, seeing the flaws in both, but also seeing that each was intrinsically important to the other. It was maddening how few people in his world understood that.

He walked to the bar and opened a bottle of single malt scotch. He needed to feel that burn in his throat, but the phone rang. "Emilio, my friend, are you alone?"

Emilio stood straighter. "Yes, President Castillo. Thank you for returning my call. I am sorry to disturb you at home at this hour, but circumstances…"

"Of course. Do I understand correctly that this is your secure line?"

"Yes."

"Please tell me what is so urgent. Does it have anything to do with the events in Washington of a few hours ago?"

"I am afraid that it does, Mr. President, and I am in possession of some information that is extremely sensitive."

"Go on."

"This is difficult for me to say, Mr. President, but I fear that my father is somehow involved in terrible things."

"Yes? As he has been for many years."

"You know of my father's secret life?"

"Emilio, this life of his is not a secret. All that his money and influence have bought him is a degree of discretion."

"Still…I thought you were friends."

A dry laugh and then, "Friends? We have an understanding. Truth be told, right now Los Rojos is my biggest headache. I think the idiots have placed themselves at the service of Hezbollah. But what is it that you wish to tell me, Emilio?"

Emilio decided that there was no good way to say these things; directness was essential. "My father claims that he is innocent, that he is being set up by agents of Hezbollah to take the fall for the assassination of the Vice President."

"Your father is many things, but innocent is not one of them. At any rate, what is the basis of his claim that Hezbollah is pulling the strings?"

"All he would tell me is that he has found a source to prove that Hezbollah was behind the assassination."

The President weighed his next words. "Hezbollah has become a major player in Mexico's internecine drug world. But the Americans won't make a distinction between Hezbollah and de Franco heroin. We need to proceed with care. One false step or overreaction on our part could have unimaginable consequences."

President Castillo knew that he needed someone to trust. Tensions would inevitably arise between Mexico and the U.S. from an assassination traced back to Mexico. He believed that Emilio was the right person to communicate with the American President for him. Mexico's ambassador to the United States had a possible affiliation with the cartels. He mentally kicked himself for not yanking that jackass sooner from the position.

"Emilio, you are close to the President's adopted son, Roger Dunham, correct?"

"Yes Sir. In fact, Roger is expecting me at the White House this morning."

"Oh?"

"Yes. I spoke to him earlier this evening with the information that my father gave me."

"What exactly did you say?"

"That my father warned me that there was a serious threat to the life of President MacIntyre, and that it would be soon."

"Santa María. The President was also a target? And you had this conversation before the Vice President was killed?"

"Yes – only minutes before."

"Then it would appear that your father is either prescient or involved. But either way the risk to Mexico has grown geometrically."

Emilio had already thought about this. "There is another possibility that would mitigate our risk. Perhaps he is telling the truth. Perhaps he did discover something about a Hezbollah plot, but nothing specific. And perhaps he is being set up, as he insists. And, Mr. President, you should know that the Americans are not going public with the information about the unsuccessful attack on President MacIntyre."

"A reasonable precaution under the circumstances."

Castillo was certain about one thing. If either Hezbollah, with its presence in Mexico, or de Franco were involved in this plot, Mexico would be the loser. The wrath of the United States would somehow be directed toward Mexico.

"You said that Roger wanted you at the White House?"

"Yes, Mr. President."

"Well, Emilio, so do I."

"Sir?"

"For better or worse, my boy, you have been selected by the fates to be Mexico's man on the ground in Washington. Trust is a rare commodity. Tell the American President anything that is helpful. I will speak with her myself, of course, but she needs to know that you are someone on whom she can depend.

"Emilio, it is sometimes difficult to be an honorable man, a patriot. You must set your family loyalties aside for the good of two countries. Can you do that?"

Emilio nodded to himself, "I can and I will." *Unless it hurts Martina.*

CHAPTER 6

Wednesday, February 23
Washington, DC · 7:30 AM

Kate stuck her head out of her office. She practically tripped over Ezra and looked up at him and smiled. He stood at attention and weakly returned her smile. She shrugged her shoulders as she glanced up and down the hall. No one simply walked. Everyone ran in what appeared to be fourth gear. Not much eye contact, she noticed.

Her personal secretary hurried over. "Do you need something, Madame President? Coffee? Some toast? You need to eat something and rest a little." It was 7:30 in the morning. Had the President eaten anything since the terrible events of last night?

"No, Rose. I was getting the heebie-jeebies in my office. Sometimes, it can be a little too quiet. My office used to be my kitchen table with kids and dogs and ranch hands slamming doors and coming and going. I seem to think better with a little commotion." Kate sighed. Not any more.

"Well, Madame President, if it's commotion that you want, keep standing in the doorway. Or I can let in all the people who've asked to see you. Of course, we cancelled all your appointments for the day. You can see the Boy Scouts from Minnesota some other time."

Kate laughed. "I know that Roger is my gatekeeper right now. We need to get the schedule going. Where is he?"

"He was here a moment ago. Took a call and wandered back to his office. I'll find him and send him in."

"Thank you, Rose. One last thing – has Barbara, I mean, the Secretary of State, landed yet?"

Barbara Jordon Lowery, the Secretary of State and one of Kate's closest friends, was on yet another peacekeeping mission to the Middle East when her flight was diverted by news of the events of last night.

"I'll check with State and get back to you in a moment."

Roger knocked and then entered the Oval Office. Kate had left it much the same as previous presidents, but she had added some subtle feminine touches. Softer flower arrangements, better lighting, buttery yellow paint, and original oil canvasses of bluebonnets by Julian Onderdonk on loan from the National Gallery of Art. Some of her close friends actually knew that she had been named a Bluebonnet Belle at the University of Texas, but she didn't talk about that much.

"Roger, any word from Emilio yet?"

"He called. He'll be here within the hour."

"Well, let's get on with the day until then. State has already put together a call list so I can start to reassure our allies. And Speaker Sandermann called to inform me he'll be heading up a Congressional Investigative Committee and wants to see me as soon as possible. You'll need to put together a list of potential Hill blowhards to placate him."

Roger pulled out a piece of paper from his coat pocket and unfolded it. "Already on it. I've contacted the people we want to oversee the official investigation of our failure of intelligence last night. Everyone said yes, without hesitation. I've still got 'til noon for the other list, right?"

"Even that old goat, Senator Harwood?"

Roger nodded.

"Good. We need him to be inside the tent on this one."

"Homeland is here for your morning briefing. The Directors of the FBI, CIA and NSA will be here in about an hour. That's what I was coordinating when you sent for me. After we speak with them, the Secret Service Director…"

"Clint Hollingsworth is a good man but right now he's acting like a dimwit. He wants me to cancel all public appearances, and go into lockdown mode until we get to the bottom of things. I told him, in no uncertain terms, that the President of the United States will not be intimidated."

"Yes, ma'am. Anyway, he needs some time with you as soon as possible. As to Preston, excuse me, I mean the Speaker, I think that you will have to make time to see him this afternoon, but, for Pete's sake, don't trust him."

Kate gave him a sideways glance. "Let's not be so hard on the Speaker. He is next in line for the time being and we may need his help."

"I know, I know. But he was such an asshole at the convention…"

"Water under the bridge, Roger. Who's next?"

"Well, Dickey wants to talk to you about tonight's address. Says he'll need at least 30 minutes of your time to polish it up."

"Have you seen his first draft?"

"Yes, it's rough. I'll work on it with him before you see it. The intelligence has to catch up with it throughout the day."

"I assume no trouble getting the networks?"

"Not hardly."

"Okay, what about Ford Lowery? As my chief political strategist, not to mention the husband of the Secretary of State, he's going to have a lot to say on the VP nomination. I need the short list by noon and an even shorter list, fully vetted, first thing tomorrow morning. No surprises. No tax dodgers, no nannygates, and no hookers. I want some diversity on that list, dammit. We need someone who can be confirmed quickly. It's the one way our country can heal. And the sooner Sandermann is two heartbeats away from the Presidency, the better."

"Amen to that. Back to Ford. He's also been trying to get into your office for hours…"

"Who hasn't?"

A loud knock interrupted them. Whoever rapped that hard on the door meant business. Roger stood as Gabriel Sanchez, the Director of Homeland Security, entered the Oval Office.

Sanchez extended his hand to the President. "Madame President, I am most relieved to see you after the harrowing events of a few hours ago. I apologize for breaking into your conversation, but these pictures couldn't wait."

He held out a sheaf of papers filled with high-resolution images taken by the latest Keyhole-class satellite.

Kate studied them, trying to make out the blurry details. "Explain."

"From the looks of it, units of the Mexican army are merging on the Texas border."

"That's crazy."

"And that's why I'm here."

Roger walked around her desk to look at the photos. He uttered a low whistle.

"What do you know for sure, Gabriel?"

"Madame President, we know very little. Initial estimates make it out to be at least 50,000 men in uniform, clustered in five different locations along the border."

"What are they doing?"

"There have been incursions, but we thought that those were related to the drug cartels. The thing that troubles me the most is that we can't determine if these are real troops or cartel."

"You mean to tell me that we don't have the assets on the ground to know the difference? For God's sake, Gabriel, this is unacceptable. How are we going to find out, and find out within the next few minutes?"

"Unfortunately, getting hard intelligence from the ground will be a matter of hours, not minutes."

Kate knew her Mexican history. "Most of the northern border of Mexico is controlled by the cartels. Their government has looked the other way for years. We've asked them to rein in the cartels, especially now that the incursions are a daily occurrence."

Roger wondered aloud, "Is it possible that the Mexican Government has finally decided to police its own border?"

Gabriel took a long minute to compose his response. "Possible, but I doubt it. Normally there would be some sort of coordination or, at least, communication with Defense and, according to Edgar, no one from the Mexican Ministry of Defense has been in contact."

Edgar Frazier, SecDef, was another of Kate's friends from Texas days. His mane of silver white hair belied an athletic prowess of a man half his age, and he kept his tall, lanky body in superb condition. One feature in particular almost preordained his appointment. His eye patch - America's own Moshe Dayan. Deacon's arm-twisting finally convinced Frazier to take a leave of absence from Hibodyne Nano Technologies. The behemoth Defense Department was still recovering and reorganizing from years of unrequited wars in Iraq and Afghanistan and needed a strong hand at the helm.

"Madame President, I wonder if there is any correlation between these photographs and the events of last night."

"That's a leap, Gabe."

"I am the head of Homeland. You pay me to make leaps. And I don't believe in coincidence. Huge movements of men in Mexico at the same time our country is attacked at its seat of government?"

"Okay, maybe not such a leap, if this is all about drugs. But why change the balance right now? What purpose does it serve? After all, they get their drugs through a border that's an open spigot and they get their money back out. They are unstopped and unstoppable because of our country's insatiable appetite for drugs."

Gabriel's brown face lost all trace of a smile. "We've run every conceivable scenario, Madame President. If we legalize marijuana, as you announced in your State of the Union address, then we'll take away a profit center from all the suppliers, dealers and transporters who operate out of Mexico."

Roger interrupted, "But the people who attacked the President and Vice President couldn't have known that because she said it for the first time last night."

Gabriel sighed. "Think about it. They could have known if there were leaks. This is Washington where talk is everybody's stock in trade."

Kate stopped them. "I don't believe that there was a leak from this office. Everyone on my staff who was involved in the speech is trustworthy. They wouldn't have done that."

Roger grimaced at Kate. "Pot being legal? I'm sure that there were people who heard a hint of such a thing and tweeted to a hundred of their closest friends."

"But, Roger, that's different. Those are young people who bear me no ill will. The bastards who killed Harris had nothing but evil in their hearts. It's hard to fathom that someone would try to kill us over a change in our marijuana policy. It's laughable."

Gabriel asserted, "Let's not forget one other possibility. Hezbollah operates out of Mexico in force. It's their pipeline for heroin into the United States and acts as one of their largest sources of revenue. They have openly announced that they want to stab the 'infidel' in its heart. I'm afraid that's you."

Kate exchanged a look with Roger. She had to talk with Emilio first. She had to know what his father believed about Middle Eastern involvement. "For now, Gabe, can we stay focused on Mexico? I need that firsthand intelligence from the border."

"All right, then. As a precaution, Madame President, I think you might want to contact governors of the border states to tell them that you will be signing an executive order to federalize the National Guards in Texas, Arizona, New Mexico and California. Perhaps it's time to add President Castillo to State's call list regarding the assassination of the Vice President, and then we could begin a conversation about border activities."

Roger interjected, "We've already raised our forces' status alert. Do you think we should raise it another level?"

"That might be a bit premature, Roger. What do you think Gabe? I don't want to antagonize Mexico. My God, we're not at war with them. At least not yet."

Kate and Deacon's ranch was about 100 miles from Piedras Negras,

Mexico and she had long felt that the destinies of the two countries were inextricably linked. Like many Texans, she felt a part of the Mexican heritage of her native state.

"Rose," Kate almost shouted, "get me the Mexican Ambassador on the phone right now." And as an after thought, "Sorry. I meant please."

"Understood, Madame President. No time for niceties today."

"Roger," the President studied her Chief-of-Staff's face, "you have that look on your face. What are you thinking?"

He paused to consolidate his random thoughts. "Madame President, should you not first call President Cas--"

"I realize that diplomatic formalities would have me first call him directly, but I cannot do that until I know more about what's happening on the ground at our border. I need to buy us some time."

Roger paused. "We don't have a lot of time. We are at war with the cartels. I believe that calling up the National Guard is a reasonable next step that should be done sooner rather than later."

Kate shook her head firmly. "Every small action of seeming insignificance can have catastrophic consequences now. Before we do something so overt, let's give ourselves as much time as possible. Let's react, but not overact. We must come to understand the forces at work here before making a decision that escalates tension. Roger, could you have State put together a briefing paper on the stability of the Mexican government?"

She slumped into her desk chair; the shock of last night was wearing off. "I would kill for a cigarette."

Sanchez pulled one from the inner pocket of his coat. "No need for murder, Madame President. Here."

"I knew I could count on another closet smoker to save the day."

"I think that's why you gave me this appointment, Madame President. Probably more than my knowledge of Homeland, you know that I have the ability to smuggle cigarettes in to you, day or night."

"Gabe, I feel certain that your lending me a cigarette under these circumstances keeps the homeland more secure."

CHAPTER 7
WEDNESDAY, FEBRUARY 23
WASHINGTON, DC · 9:30 AM

Little known to the public, the President had a private space next to the Oval Office. On tourist maps, it is called the Study, but most modern presidents have used it for their real day-to-day work. It is here that their own comfortable furniture and pictures surround them. President MacIntyre had the room painted a robin's egg blue, and hung her beloved bluebonnet paintings on every wall. She felt at home in this room, and fiercely protected herself from unwanted guests. Today, her guests were entirely wanted.

Roger and Emilio sat on the small blue, green and yellow striped couch and faced Kate, who held court at her desk, with her chair turned toward them.

"Emilio, Roger tells me that you received this vague information about the assassination from your father."

Emilio automatically stood, and caught himself. He sat back down. "Yes, Madame President, but I am afraid that my father is holding something back."

"What makes you say that?"

"When I spoke with him last, there was something in his tone. Some hesitancy, which is unlike him. My gut tells me there is more. He is nothing, if not forceful. He mentioned a 'source'. We have to interrogate that source and hear it for ourselves. I do not trust him. We cannot believe his interpretation; it's too important. His life has brought shame on my sister and me. And on my country."

Kate felt a surge of sympathy for the young man before her, for whom honor was a way of life. "That reminds me. How is Martina? I saw your sister last fall at a fundraiser, and she was more beautiful than ever. It appeared that her marriage to David Valentine has been a good thing."

Emilio shrugged. "I suppose so."

Kate chose to ignore that obvious opening and returned to Emilio's father. "We should, at face value, be grateful that your father tried to warn us, Emilio. But we are going to need confirmation if we are to trust his intentions. And, yes, we need to interrogate his source. I am afraid that you may be our only means to that end. Would you be willing to talk to your father sub-rosa…and in person?"

Roger interrupted. "Mother, do you realize what you are asking? If Emilio is going to put himself in harm's way for you, then I'm going, as well."

"When a kosher pig flies by this window, Roger, and this is not a subject for discussion. I need you here." Kate stood and looked out that very window, as if for verification.

She turned back to the men. "Emilio, are you up for a trip to Texas and then on to the Sierra Madres?"

Emilio joined her at the window, hoping to put into words his feelings for her and her country in such a way that she would understand how much he meant the word 'yes.' But before he could answer, Rose opened the door into the room. "Please forgive me, Madame President, but there is an urgent call that you will want to take."

"Who is it?"

"It is Ambassador Juarez."

Emilio sucked in his breath.

Kate looked at Roger and he nodded. "Rose, the President will take the call in here."

After Rose left the room, Emilio blurted out, "Be careful. Juarez cannot be trusted."

Kate picked up the phone on the second ring. She remained standing by the desk. "Hello, Mr. Ambassador."

"Madame President, thank you for taking my call. I have been so concerned about your well-being after the traumatic events of last night."

"I appreciate that, Eduardo." Kate wondered why he would be concerned about her 'well-being'. Did he know something about the second IED? All right, Kate, keep the paranoia in check.

"Your State Department contacted me about the troop movements along our shared border. Madame President, I must assure you that there is nothing dangerous or unusual happening on the border. Perhaps it is some kind of drug interdiction or simply a continuation of President Castillo's policy of confronting the cartels and eliminating them. I assure you that if anything important were happening on the border, I would know about it."

Like hell you would, Kate thought, but said, "I certainly hope so."

Kate knew that Castillo didn't trust Juarez any further than did she. She knew what Secretary of State Cordell Hull felt like when Japan's Ambassador Nomura came to him and handed him a piece of paper breaking off negotiations for peace. What Hull knew that Nomura did not was that diplomatic negotiations were being bombed into oblivion at Pearl Harbor at that very moment. For Hull, an old school diplomat, Kate knew that it must have been one of the most difficult moments of his long career, having been instructed by President Roosevelt not to say a word to Nomura about the attack.

Kate sighed. This was a classic case of closing the barn door after the cows are out. She wished that she could unleash a string of expletives but, like Hull, was constrained from doing so.

"Thank you for calling, Eduardo."

"I have the greatest respect for you, Madam…"

Kate clicked off the line. That was quite enough of him.

She glanced at Emilio and saw the pain on his handsome face. Not much she could do about that.

He left the window and stood tall and unwavering in front of her. "Yes, Madame President, he is a pitiful excuse for an ambassador. Many believe that he is in the pockets of the cartels and has been for years. But I do have faith in President Castillo. He needs the opportunity to act promptly, if anyone in Mexico had any involvement in the murder of Vice President Franklin. Please, Madame President, give him the chance."

"I understand Emilio but I fear it may be in your hands, not his, as to how this will unfold. Perhaps you should give me the opportunity now to speak with my Director of Homeland Security and Secretary of Defense. I believe that both men are waiting to see me. Thank you for being the friend I always knew you to be."

Roger walked out with Emilio and passed Gabriel and Edgar in the hallway, both looking grim. "I will join you in the President's study in a moment."

Both men started to respond to Roger, but Edgar was insistent. "Is Barbara going to be joining us?"

"No, her plane hit some weather and is still sitting on the tarmac in Newfoundland."

Gabriel, not a close admirer of the Secretary of State, could barely refrain from smiling. "Well, I guess she must be burning a hole in the ice shelf."

Gabriel and Edgar's heads were bent in quiet conversation as they walked away to join the President.

"Emilio, I know this is rough. I will be back in touch with you this afternoon. I won't keep you out on a limb."

"I'm a big boy, Roger. But thanks for the concern. My country, my father, my problem."

"Our problem. And rest assured, that despite what the President says, if you're going to Mexico for the United States, so am I."

When Roger shut the door behind him, Gabriel and Edgar were talking at once. Roger held up his hands and asked them to start over for his benefit.

Kate reiterated, "The entire intelligence and law enforcement communities are focusing on the assassination. I need for the two of you, in a highly controlled way, to assess the military situation on our Texas/Mexico border. I want hourly intelligence updates about that and about the assassination. Army has its own intelligence department, as does State, the CIA, Homeland, Defense, NSA, and god knows who else. I will rely on you two to specifically work with me, distilling the information as it comes in."

Anticipating a response from Homeland, Kate added, "I know, Gabriel, Homeland Security is supposed to coordinate all intelligence and filter it up to me. But I don't want any pissing contests here, and Defense is the one bailiwick not under your aegis."

The men, still standing, looked at one another. Gabriel said, "Not a problem, Madame President."

"Oh, and Gabriel, once Secretary of State Lowery thaws out from Newfoundland and is up to speed on all of this, I expect you and she to play nicely."

Kate continued, "What I'm about to share with you goes no further than this room. If that's a problem, you are going to have to live with it for now. We have information that leads me to believe that it is not Mexico, or the drug cartels to be more specific, that are behind the assassination. But we are not certain of our source…"

"Our source? Who would that be?" Edgar did not like the feeling of events spiraling away from him.

"Okay, fellas. I know that I have to trust somebody here, and you are my somebodies. The clock is ticking. The more information that comes in about the unexploded device, the more it appears that there is Mexican involvement through the cartels, right? But if our source is correct, that may be a well-placed red herring."

"Please, Madame President, who is the source?"

She made her decision. "He is the father of the man that you passed in the hall."

Gabriel said, "You mean Federico de Franco? I thought I recognized his son, Emilio."

Kate was impressed. The man did his homework. "Yes. And Emilio brought word from his father that there is a source in Mexico who might be involved in the plot."

"Do we trust Emilio?"

"I'm not sure we have a choice. Either we trust him, buy some time and certainty, if there is such a thing, or I risk bombing the wrong country to smithereens. And, yes, I do trust him."

Edgar questioned, "But if not Mexico or the cartels, then who?"

"Hezbollah." She spit out the word.

"Oh shit. If that's correct, then we're on the wrong track with all our planning. Our response has all been aimed at Mexico. Now, you're saying it's the Middle East?"

"I'm not saying that, Edgar. I am saying that Emilio brought us this plausible possibility, and did so to Roger moments before the bomb went off. This rush to judgment about Mexico might be how we are being played."

Edgar pressed on, "Forgive me, Madame President, but Hezbollah's involvement seems pretty far-fetched. Can we really trust the head of Mexico's most powerful and dangerous cartel?"

"At this point, we can't trust anything, but look at our behavior over the last ten hours. It does seem a little too pat, doesn't it? All I'm saying is that I need as much intelligence as y'all can give me, and I need it in real time."

Gabriel held up his hands. "But that's why you have us, to evaluate the intelligence before we bring it to you."

Roger almost laughed. He knew what was coming.

"I am not going to sit by and let mistakes of this magnitude happen during my administration. My ass was almost blown up last night and this country lost one of the best leaders it's ever had. I'm fightin' mad. You can bet that we're gonna' smash whoever did this. But, by damn, we are going to smash the right people.

"Gabe, where are those cigarettes? Leave the pack. I'll pay you back later."

She tilted her head back and inhaled like it was her last breath on earth. She blew the smoke out slowly.

CHAPTER 8

Wednesday, February 23
Washington, DC · 2:00 PM

Preston Sandermann looked up from the bowl of she-crab soup he was savoring. The front door of his elegant Georgetown house had flown open and Valerie stormed in. He groaned inwardly. The Speaker had come home to escape the bedlam on the Hill and Valerie always brought her own brand of bedlam with her. But he put his spoon down and looked at her with a forced smile.

"Preston, you're home? Shouldn't you be on Capital Hill banging your gavel or something? The country's going to hell in a hand basket and you're eating soup?"

"I'll go back in a few minutes, dear. I needed to clear my head."

Valerie Sandermann paced the room. Her tall, athletic body was pressed forward as though facing a stiff wind, and her high heels made a loud clicking sound on the parquet floor. "My God, doesn't anything ever get to you? The Vice President's been assassinated, Secret Service are swarming all over the front yard, the government's in turmoil and my husband comes home to clear his head and eat soup."

"It tasted pretty good actually."

"I guess it did, since you put it in your grandmother's Royal Crown Derby."

"Coming from you, I'll take that as a compliment. Would you like some?"

Sandermann stopped suddenly. He really didn't have time for this shit today. Nobody could get his goat like Valerie. Why was that? So what if he were reared to have good manners and fine things, despite the family fortune having long since been squandered by his wastrel father. His pedigree was top shelf and was the reason she married him in the first place. Oh yes, a marriage made in Heaven. His mother got the family coffers restocked and Valerie's father got connected to one of the most prestigious – albeit poor – families in America.

"Valerie, sit down. You're making me dizzy. You seem to have something on your mind. Do you need me for anything?"

Valerie waited for Preston to pull out her chair, but finally did it herself and plopped down with a huge sigh. She put her elbows on the table and rested her head in her hands. "First of all, what's with the Secret Service? One of their agents actually followed me to the powder room. Is all this beefed up security really necessary?"

"According to the Presidential Succession Act of 1947, it is. Until a new Vice-President is confirmed, you're stuck with me, the proverbial 'man who is a heartbeat away from the Presidency.'"

Valerie's eyes took on an unnatural gleam. She could never hide her ambition for her husband. She wished he were as driven.

"Oh, of course. But I imagine our dear neighbors won't like this one bit. Their manicured flower beds may get a bit trampled."

Valerie actually didn't give a whit about the neighbors. Granted, she loved the beautiful townhouse, with its carved limestone entry and blood red brick façade. She entertained like Washington's newest Pearl Mesta, taking advantage of the octagonal screened-in porch in the cooler fall months for rounds of whiskey sours and Manhattans – she was a bourbon girl – surrounded by a garden that had been featured in *Architectural Digest*. Her household cooks were far better in the kitchen than any caterer, so her food was not duplicated at any other event in a city known for the grandeur of its events. She brought her western need for comfort to her husband's eastern sensibility and created a space that was both inviting and impressive, not too stuffy, but filled with priceless art, oriental rugs and furniture. She had a way of making people feel relaxed and challenged at the same time, and she made sure that no one would ever accuse her of being a pushover. She wanted to be a woman of substance.

For a brief moment, Valerie allowed herself to remember the convention four years ago, when her husband lost the nomination to that woman by fifty votes. Fifty votes. Preston didn't have the balls that Kate had exhibited. Kate stole the nomination out from under Preston's aristocratic nose, pure and simple, with political machinations that would make Machiavelli proud. Valerie was the one who saw it coming and none of Preston's toadies would listen to her. He married her because she was a political animal and then ignored her. Idiot. Preston had been able to move on. Not Valerie. And all those nice Secret Service men, now outside her door, with their broad shoulders and guns and walkie-talkies reminded her of what they had lost, perhaps.

"Well, we'll try to minimize their inconvenience. But the country has suffered a real blow, Val. Everyone has to pitch in."

"Don't be sarcastic, Preston." She relented and took his hand. "How are you holding up? You seemed to be on every channel for the last few hours."

Sandermann was startled by her sympathy, but he still responded to her affection, however rarely she manifested it. He looked at her perfectly oval face and smooth skin and marveled at her beauty, all without the surgeon's knife. She also had the political instincts of a backroom pollster, which had come in handy to him more than once.

"The news buzzards are circling, that's for sure. They don't know much, so they're desperate to fill the vacuum. If I bothered to read blogs, I'm sure they would say that everyone from the pharmacist at the corner drug store to Judge Crater is a finalist for the VP slot. All I can do is try to sound calm and reassuring. That's what the President has asked of me so far, and I will do as she asks. I think that I can safely say that the only person not on her short list is I. Besides, I don't want the damn job. I have more power as Speaker of the House than the Vice President could ever dream of having."

"Preston, isn't it a little soon to be putting together lists? My God, Franklin hasn't been dead a day yet. What's the rush? Are things really that uncertain?"

"Don't kid yourself. Her advisors are probably on their fifth revision. She has to move fast, Val. The country needs resolution. The sooner the better."

Valerie nodded. Her gaze looked past Sandermann into some indeterminate future.

Sandermann stood and gave his wife a kiss on the top of her naturally blond head. She jumped. Then laughed. "I'm sorry, Preston. I guess I'm a little nervous. What should I expect from the Secret Service now? And do I really need someone following me around where ever I go?"

"Need? Probably not."

Valerie took note of the word "probably" and for a moment felt slightly sick.

"I know that you can take care of yourself, what with being raised with a gun in one hand and the horse's reins in the other, like any good Rocky Mountain girl. But here's the way it's going to work until the new VP takes office. You and I both get 24/7 protection. It's the law. Period."

"That means you have to be careful, Preston. You may not be on her short list. But you are on mine."

"You make it sound a little like I'm a sack of potatoes on your grocery list, but thanks, I think. By the way, where were you this morning?"

Valerie tossed her head back and gave him a dazzling smile. "Well, my darling husband, you'll never guess who called me and asked me to come by his office."

"Okay, I'll bite. Who?"

"Roger Dunham."

"Excuse me? Roger Dunham?"

"Yes. Close your mouth, Preston."

"But why would he call you, Valerie?"

"It's kind of funny actually. Seems mommy dearest is pretty much chain smoking after the events of last night and…"

"Well you might be, too, if someone had placed an IED under your car."

"Preston, did you say what I think you just said?"

"Oh shit. You didn't hear that. Not a word. Do you understand me? Not a word about it to anyone. Valerie, I mean it."

"So they tried to kill the President as well? I'm so sorry. Thank God she's okay."

Preston thought he heard some insincerity in her voice. "Now Valerie…"

Valerie waved off the predictable lecture to be nice. "Well that does, indeed, explain the smoking."

"But not why Roger asked you to the White House."

"Oh, nothing really. He needed a favor."

"And what sort of favor would Roger Dunham be asking of you?"

"He wanted to know if I could get my hands on the new anti-smoking patch that the FDA approved from Valentine Pharmaceuticals. Didn't want to wait until April to acquire them."

"Are they really that good?"

"Better than good. They have over a 98% success rate and take two weeks to work. Father is thrilled."

The father in question was David Valentine, the Chairman of the Board of Valentine Pharmaceuticals and its largest shareholder. He was the grandson of the founder, but he had taken what he inherited and made the most of it. Valerie and her father had a wary relationship because of his second marriage to a woman half his age, and Valerie never felt she had won her absent daddy's approval. She sat on the Board of Directors and took the work seriously because Valentine Pharmaceuticals would one day be hers. She tolerated the trophy wife, Martina, to mollify her father. Besides, Martina de Franco was an heiress in her own right and didn't need Valentine money to be a good shopping buddy for Valerie.

"Val? Valerie? How is a 98% success rate possible?"

Her eyes refocused on Preston. "Some sort of molecular re-engineering is all I know."

"Didn't you tell me a few months ago that there was some problem with the prototype during the initial testing phase?"

"It was a minor detail that was dealt with early on. Anyway, I told Roger that I might be able to snag one off the assembly line when I'm in Denver tomorrow."

"Denver?"

Preston came back to the antique mahogany table, made in Charleston over two hundred years ago, and sat down. She had his full attention.

"Oh Preston, don't you remember I have a board meeting there in the morning? I told you. It's okay. I know you have a lot on your mind. Father is sending the company jet to pick me up at the crack of dawn. But really, Preston, can't you give me some idea of the person you think she's going to select?"

"Val, this might not be a good time for you to leave Washington. The Secret Service will most assuredly protest."

Valerie laughed. "Pres, my father's security is at least as thorough as the government's. He's already on the case. The company headquarters is a fortress. Now it will be like a bunker. They don't need to worry about me."

She took both of his hands in hers and held them firmly, the muscles in her arms standing out in well-defined cuts. "Now, tell me who you think she will choose."

"Okay, if I were to venture a guess, I'd say the junior senator from North Dakota. He is a known quantity and easily confirmed."

"David Richter? That doesn't make any sense. Who picks a Vice President from North Dakota? There are more voters on this block than in that whole state."

"I might remind you, Kate doesn't need any more votes. She was re-elected this past November in a landslide. A landslide that gave me the largest majority a speaker has had in over a generation."

"How long do you think the confirmation hearings will take before he or she is confirmed?"

"If it is Richter, not long at all. He was in the House for four terms before being elected to the Senate, and he's well-liked on both sides of the aisle."

"Which means he hasn't managed to offend anyone, right?"

"Basically. Anyway Kate asked me and the Senate majority leader if we would be able to fast track the nomination once she made her choice."

"Why the rush? The VP doesn't really do all that much except wait for a phone call and attend state funerals. Dick Cheney saw to that. After him, no President wanted to endow the second-in-command with so much authority." Valerie's voice had the distinct tone of resignation.

"Be that as it may, if it's Richter, I'd guess two, maybe three, weeks at the max."

Preston stood and turned to leave. The tone in Valerie's voice stopped him.

"Please be cautious, Preston. If something goes wrong, it will be your ass on the line."

CHAPTER 9

WEDNESDAY, FEBRUARY 23
WASHINGTON, DC · 8:00 PM

Kate wracked her brain to find a way to start the address with something other than "My Fellow Americans." It was so LBJ. But it revealed her personal loss and the comfort she sought in calling upon her countrymen in a time of crisis.

"My fellow Americans, I speak to you tonight with a heavy heart but also with a keen sense of purpose. The cruel assassination of Vice President Harris Franklin III…"

Kate paused on each syllable of Harris's name to emphasize her own deep pain.

"shall not and will not deter us from…"

Here Kate's speech writer had to be careful, because almost 300 million Americans and probably billions more abroad would hang on the next few words, looking for any indication of a motive for the killing.

"accomplishing the programs, both domestic and foreign, that you overwhelmingly sent us back to Washington to complete. There is no terrorist, no assassin, who can break our will or keep us from fulfilling the work we have started, the work in which we believe and the work on which we base our lives.

"We will continue to seek peace abroad, engage with countries in every corner of the world to achieve understanding, and assert our role in the world as the guardians of democratic values, human rights, and respect for all nations, especially those nations that seek peaceful solutions to global problems."

Kate wanted to hit the right note of determined reassurance. She did not want this to be a policy speech, but rather an affirmation that the country will endure and that the Executive Branch is not in disarray. However, Kate also needed to say, for herself, as much as anyone else, that her Vice President's death would be avenged. What had to remain unsaid tonight was the fact that she was also a target. She looked straight at the camera and did not blink.

"We will seek out the cold blooded killers of Vice President Franklin, and we will bring them to justice."

The ice water that sometimes ran through Kate's vessels showed how determined she was for a righteous resolution. She rose slightly and leaned on her desk. This movement caught the cameraman off guard, but he quickly compensated.

"Now, to the person, people, or governments who did us harm, who stole from us our Vice President and my friend, do not confuse our respect for the rule of law with our determination – no, our absolute certainty – that we will find you and bring you to justice. Hear me. I will bring to bear every resource of the United States of America in this quest. You will stand before me and every citizen of this country, and you will receive our judgment."

Kate stood up straight and tall. She pointed at the camera and looked through it to the people she knew were watching at this moment.

"You will not escape your fate."

CHAPTER 10
Thursday, February 24
Denver · 9:00 AM MST

Valerie put down the Washington Post, tired of the headlines and editorials that praised the President's speech. Blah, blah, blah, she thought, as she gazed out the window of the Lear Jet at the high, grassy plains of Denver. Valerie saw the brown farm fields, silos and pastures give way to suburban neighborhoods with big houses, small lots and few trees. Highways stretched for miles, unimpeded by the ripple of a green hill or dale. The Mile High City was as flat as a Kansas cornfield. It happened to be at altitude.

The flight attendant approached Valerie and waited for her to look up. She had been the target of Mrs. Sandermann's sharp tongue more times than she could count and didn't want to interrupt her reverie. Finally Valerie noticed her. "Yes, Megan. Do you need something?"

"No, ma'am. The captain wanted you to know that we are going to land in a few minutes and we expect the usual updrafts from the mountains. He requests that you fasten your seatbelt."

Valerie sighed with displeasure but complied, after first turning to the head of her Secret Service detail. "To be clear, Mr. Thompson, my father will be providing my security at the corporate offices."

"Thank you, Mrs. Sandermann, but we are charged by a higher authority than your father to stay with you."

"That's fine. But please let Valentine Pharmaceuticals take the lead. Humor me for my father's sake. I know that you have jurisdiction. Just be subtle."

The last thing Valerie wanted right now was the distraction of a pissing contest between competing security details. Boys!

The Lear Jet flew past the monstrous Denver International Airport and touched down with its well-known gentle bounce at a private landing strip of the Rocky Mountain Metropolitan Airport, nine miles northwest of downtown Denver. The Valentine Pharmaceuticals headquarters was located nearby at the Interlocken Business District of Broomfield, with easy access to Interstate-70, but far enough away to be entirely private.

The security detail from ValPharm was waiting for them on the tarmac. Valerie counted three large Suburbans. Men dressed in ubiquitous black suits with narrow black ties and white shirts hurried aboard and whisked her to the waiting helicopter, with her new Secret Service detail sprinting to keep up with them.

"Good morning, Mrs. Sandermann. Hope you had an easy flight. I'm Foster and I'll be in charge of your security while you are in Denver."

"Excuse me. I am Brad Thompson, and I will be in charge of Mrs. Sandermann's protection on behalf of the President."

Foster's face turned red. He realized that he would have to be a bit more politic than he was used to. "Sorry, forgot my manners. I'm Doug Foster and Mr. Valentine assigned me to, well, to supplement Ms. Valentine's, I mean Mrs. Sandermann's security. Of course you are in charge." Political bullshit.

The short flight took five minutes to the rooftop helipad, and Valerie emerged with the explosion of power she felt whenever she was this close to the Front Range of the Rocky Mountains. The ground was hard and the air frigid, precisely the way she liked it. Her lungs opened up and her skin tingled.

This board meeting was important, following up top-secret revelations about the patch that occurred last July. Six of the 2,500 people in the phase II test group had died from heart failure, so the company immediately went into overdrive to find the cause. They discovered an unintended gene mutation, corrected it and then very quickly covered it up. Valentine Pharmaceutical had too much riding on the "patch" to do otherwise.

The subsequent test groups in phase III had suffered no ill effects and the efficacy had been an amazing 98.9% success rate.

FDA approval was tantamount and, once received after the phase III test results were in, an April release date was secured. Fortunately for Valentine, the FDA still hadn't instituted its long ballyhooed data auditing system for drug trials by the pharmaceutical industry. Manipulation and suppression of inconvenient raw data was still a fairly tame process. However, keeping the results under wraps in this world of whistleblowers was another story. Three people in the room for today's meeting would be aware of any problem: Valerie, her father and the chief researcher on the project. This meeting was to be a triumph, the next great money-printing machine for the company, much like Valium had been for Roche.

Valerie strode toward the enormous building's rooftop entry. Designed by Jan Bloch, a master student of Louis Kahn, the building had sweeping views west to the Front Range. Kahn's sense of design was a favorite of the Valentines, beginning with the nearby family home built by David's father. Brilliant red and orange sunsets painted the windows, with the snow capped mountains in relief across the open plain.

With a nod to Richard Meier's grand architecture of the Getty Center, Bloch chose cleft-cut, sienna colored travertine marble for the exterior and used curvilinear design elements along the roofline, repeating and acknowledging the tan shade of the mountains beyond and the sinewy shape of their peaks. Interior light in geometric shapes descended onto the terrazzo floor from dozens of skylights in the vaulted atrium ceiling. A dazzling array of plants, from succulents to tropicals, caught the sun and grew into the space.

She glanced at her watch as she entered the elevator. It was 9:50 AM. The meeting would begin at 10:00 sharp, if she knew her father. She was dressed for the occasion in her favorite black Armani suit – understated but with the perfect drape of jacket and slacks. She wore her South Sea black pearls on her white silk blouse, and her favorite Hermes scarf, with its ocean theme from a few years ago. High heels from Manolo, but not so high as to make her tower over the men, and a Chanel alligator bag completed her look. It was an ensemble to be envied, but did not appear overly fussy or planned.

The hallway outside the boardroom was paneled with wood imported from some of the most beautiful chateaus in Europe, and it housed one of the largest corporate art collections in America, the world perhaps. But Valerie had no time for art appreciation this morning.

Before entering the room, she turned on her heel and addressed both sets of her security detail. "Look folks, do whatever you have to do to play nice. But you will stay in the hallway; I can handle it from here."

Valerie walked into an almost full room, her erect and broad shouldered frame a mirror of her father's. David Valentine was bent over reading from his briefing book, his ebony hair shining in the sun coming through the bank of windows to his right. He felt Valerie's presence before he saw her, and looked up from his seat at the head of the long, Russian walnut table. He rose to greet her with a formal kiss on each cheek. Valerie briefly wondered if he had become so cosmopolitan because of her stepmother, Martina.

"Daddy, you look well."

"As do you, Valerie. How is Preston handling all this newfound attention?"

"He is sad about the Vice President's death. Apart from that, he is trying to do what the country and the President need of him." Discretion was her shield in dealings with her father.

"Ah, yes. Good for him. A company man, after all. You might as well find your seat now."

In a much lower voice he added, "Let's get this cluster fuck started."

Cosmopolitan? Valerie corrected herself with a half-smile. Her father was still the rugged Coloradoan she loved in spite of his Euro-trash second wife. And speaking of Martina, Valerie noticed her seat was empty.

As if on cue, the raven-haired beauty came in and greeted Valerie with a friendly smile and an actual hug. No air kisses from Martina. She was too earthy for such insincerity. Educated at the Sorbonne at her father, Federico de Franco's insistence, she stayed on in France and partied until she grew weary of it. Then she met David Valentine and fell hard for him, even though he was twice her age. She grew to genuinely care for her husband's daughter and tried to be her friend. Valerie was resistant, but she did understand some of what her father saw in Martina.

When Valerie was 12 years old, David left his wife, Helen, and in so doing, left Valerie. David had been suffocating from years of Helen's craziness and would have sued for custody of Valerie if his lawyers had predicted any chance of winning. The courts back then almost never granted custody to the father. It was one of the few instances where wealth and privilege didn't play into the equation. No one knew how she had suffered under her mother's torment. She spent the rest of her teenaged years resenting her father for abandoning her to what she referred to as her psycho mom. David had been extremely generous to Helen in the divorce, putting her up in a 200-acre ranch, and seeing Valerie as much as his busy schedule would allow. As an adult, Valerie never visited her mother and was relieved that the devil woman preferred to live in splendid isolation.

David met Martina de Franco years later and found a formidable woman who was smart by any standard measurement, and who also had the rare gift of insight into people. She protected David from those who wanted to separate him from his money, and she helped him cultivate a group of friends that were unlike any he had experienced before. They traveled and enjoyed art, supporting fledging artists wherever they found them. Most people didn't know the fortune behind the woman, who never used a dime of David's money for her own purposes. She was not to be trifled with, and David enjoyed standing back and watching the fireworks when someone was foolish enough to do so.

A sudden whiff of strong cologne and a tap on the shoulder broke into Valerie's thoughts. She turned and offered her hand before a peck on the cheek could be proffered.

"Dr. Ellison good to see you looking so well."

Of the group of board members now present, this one in particular fascinated Valerie, the good Reverend Hyler Ellison. He looked more like Ichabod Crane than the usual florid televangelist, and his Adam's apple bobbed up and down when he spoke. Valerie tried not to stare at it, and looked down instead, catching sight of his Patek Phillipe. She wouldn't watch his television show even if threatened with a non-anesthetized root canal, but she recognized that his operation was a cash cow and, thus, he was powerful in his own right. He was a tad too unctuous for her taste.

Ellison, who had undergone recent knee replacement surgery, held her hand before she could remove it. "I feel like a kid again, Valerie. It has given me a new lease on life, especially after the physical therapy was finished."

Valerie pulled away and moved toward the table, but said over her shoulder, "Good, Dr. Ellison. That's great news. No limp, either."

He followed her. "Please call me Hyler. And, no, the limp is gone like yesterday's news."

Before she had to think of something else to say to the skeletal preacher, her father saved her. "Ladies and gentlemen, if I could call the meeting to order. We have a full agenda and need to get started."

Martina laughed to herself at Valerie's obvious discomfort with Ellison. And she was glad that it was Valerie who had to deal with him today.

Valerie noticed that Michel Hayek was absent. He was not a member of the board but he was the lead scientist on Valentine Pharmaceuticals anti-smoking program and usually attended these meetings. Her first thought was that he must still be in Beirut teaching at Beirut Arab University. An annoying, but necessary concession on the part of the company to lure him in the first place. But hadn't she read that Michel was lecturing at Georgetown University last week? If so, why wasn't he here? She would miss him. She had come to appreciate, even look forward to, the finer points of his nature.

Last summer, with most of the research behind them, Hayek had requested an extended leave and handed over management of the program to his number-two researcher, Jackson Baines. And it was Baines who had discovered the cause of the anomaly and informed David and Valerie. Jackson was a decent substitute for Michel, to Valerie's way of thinking, both in his discretion and as a piece of eye-candy; in fact, he bore a strong resemblance to Michel in his build and coloring. He was a few years younger than she and looked far more like an old-fashioned matinee idol than a science geek. But Baines appeared more nervous than usual today and Valerie wondered why. He was going to explain to the group that everything was on schedule, the initial production run of the small blue box was zooming along, marketing was already hyping the greatest medical breakthrough since aspirin and there were no foreseeable glitches for SST – the branded initials standing for Stop Smoking Today.

"Ladies and gentlemen, I am pleased to announce that we have final confirmation from the FDA of an April 1st release date for SST. Our revolutionary drug will change the face of addiction forever." *Not to mention what it will do to our stock price.*

The board members broke into enthusiastic applause and David's usually impassive face creased with a broad smile. Valerie looked at him in wonder. *Revolutionary is one word for it. But scientific breakthroughs will get you only so far. The genius of influence and deal making, as well as a little statistical legerdemain, are probably more like it.* At that moment, an unexpected thought crossed her mind and she tried to tamp it back down, but it had the intoxicating taste of forbidden fruit, the longing for which would not go away. She shook it off.

She caught Baine's eye and gave him an encouraging smile. But for him, it felt more like being examined by a she-wolf who was looking at her dinner.

CHAPTER 11
Thursday/Friday, February 24/25
Denver • Early Afternoon

After the lunch break, the board entered into a protracted, heated conversation about the President's State of the Union address, with its mention of legalizing marijuana.

Though David believed that government should stay out of everyone's business – the less government is more point-of-view – he realized that there was something bigger here for his company's bottom line. He started the free-for-all by saying, "Whatever you believe about the efficacy of marijuana use and whether it should be legalized or not, there is an inescapable financial implication for this company."

The room erupted. The good reverend argued that the company should come out strongly against legalizing the dirty weed. "My heavens, don't we have any principles at stake here? Isn't it the gateway drug? Doesn't it hurt people, especially teenagers? We must oppose this, as individuals and as a company."

David let him go on briefly, half expecting him to stand and ask everyone to circle up and pray. Finally, Valentine's CFO interrupted and said, "Wait a minute. We should be asking other questions. Like, can we make money from this? Aren't we obligated to do so for the sake of our stockholders?" *And my 401K?*

"For God's sake, man, do you really believe that we should not be guided by any moral imperatives?"

"Sure, Reverend, but I do believe that we are primarily in the business of making money. And you shouldn't doubt for one minute that all of our competitors are having this same conversation about how they can make money on this initiative."

David held up his hand. "Folks, we cannot solve the marijuana debate today. You just needed to start thinking about it and how our industry should respond. But we should also talk about the President's prescription plan."

Valerie hesitated, knowing that she had a serious conflict of interest here. Preston and his fellow Democrats would most assuredly support this sacred cow of the Party platform. However, her corporate hat won out and she ventured a question. "Is there any reason that we should support it? Doesn't it inhibit fair trade?"

David smiled at his greedy little girl. "Officially, we would take that position. But within the walls of this room, let's be honest. The drug plan is like 365 days of Christmas for us and our pharmaceutical friends."

Ellison looked stunned. "What are you talking about?"

Martina jumped in and her husband turned to her and nodded. "Reverend, as David said, it won't benefit us. It will benefit the entire industry. Most of you know that I come from a pharmaceutical family myself, and I can tell you that my father's firm has studied every metric applicable to this issue, and they all result in the same answer. If we sell more pharmaceuticals, we make more money. Period."

Ellison rubbed his hands together, as if before a feast of fatted calf and slaughtered lamb. "I see. And if the country has more patients who can avail themselves of healthcare, more patients will see more doctors. The doctors will then prescribe more drugs because patients will now be able to afford them."

Martina smiled.

David continued. "Don't forget, America now spends more than $300 billion dollars a year on prescription drugs. Imagine how much that number will grow with universal drug coverage. So, we threaten opposition to the plan, as we did back in '09 with Obama's healthcare overhaul, and the government gives us an $80 billion bribe to go along with something that was good for us to start with. Beautiful equation, don't you think?"

The entire room murmured in agreement. Baines, however, was not engaged in the board dialogue. He was too distracted by Valerie's invitation to have drinks after the board meeting. He was used to the interest of women of all ages, but this woman was the daughter of his boss, and, oh yes, the wife of the Speaker of the House, potentially disastrous territory for him. *She was awfully beautiful, though.*

His Blackberry buzzed against his hip, rousing him from his daydream. He slipped it out of his pocket and glanced down. Sure enough. It was Valerie texting him the name of the restaurant and the time of their dinner reservation. Gaetano's. 8:00 PM. *Good choice.*

Baines realized with a start that David was dismissing the group and he hurriedly closed his PDA and gave his full attention to the man who paid his salary. "Thank you for your time today and for your continued dedication to the well-being of Valentine Pharmaceuticals. We'll be in touch and will see you, as always, in three months."

The board members applauded, a first. Baines suppressed a smile. David had a way about him, and so did the daughter. Baines took a mental count of the soaring value of his stock options, once the patch was introduced to the market. Michel could not have chosen a better time to be in Beirut.

Ellison returned from the restroom, passing several groups in lively conversation. He saw Valerie, David and Baines at the far corner of the room and walked toward them to say his goodbyes. They were too engrossed in each other to see Ellison approach, and he caught some words that gave him pause.

"You'll keep your mouth shut…stock options…mitigate your guilty conscience."

Ellison stopped in his tracks. What in the world was David saying? He craned his neck toward the group.

"Yes, I know…six deaths… an unforeseen and almost implausible co-agent. Of what consequence are they in light of the hundreds of thousands, probably millions, of people who will truly be helped?"

"Of course, Mr. Valentine. And I certainly appreciate your generosity… but…"

"But nothing, dammit."

Valerie touched her father's arm and glanced in the direction of Ellison, who was trying to look occupied with assembling all his papers and his briefcase. *Co-agent, that's the first I'm hearing of that.*

The angry look on David's face transformed itself, as if by magic, into that of the hail-fellow, well met. "So, Hyler, are you on your way back home or are you traveling to another stadium revival?"

Ellison laughed. "Neither, really. First to DC for a prayer breakfast with the President on Sunday, and then I'm joining Beryl for a long delayed vacation at our house on St. Bart's. It is a perfect time of year to be there, and the children will be joining us."

David was a little surprised that Dr. Ellison would be on any invitation list, even for prayer, by this President. *But I guess after the event of two days ago, she might feel the need to cover all bases.*

David clapped him on the back. "Well done, Hyler. And since you're joining Val in the morning for a tour of the plant, let me arrange for the company helicopter to get you to your plane."

"Much appreciated." Ellison walked away, still not sure what to make of what he'd overheard.

David turned back to his daughter, seeing that Baines had already slipped away. "Valerie, are we still okay with Baines? We can't afford any complications."

Valerie nodded. "I think so, Father. But I'll be even surer after dinner."

"Well, be damn sure."

Baines arrived at Gaetano's and was seated with time to spare. One did not keep Valerie waiting.

A regular at Gaetano's, he was bemused by Valerie's choice of dinner venue. The restaurant was dark, and the long wooden bar gleamed under the light through lead glass dividers. It was in the northwest quadrant of Denver, an easy drive from Broomfield. It had occupied the corner of Tejon and 38th since 1947, where three notorious Italian brothers of the Smaldone family once held court for the famous and feared of Denver mobster society. *Just not the sort of locale that he would have pegged her for.*

The new owners had kept the interior, and the food, authentic, and Baines thought that the Gorgonzola rib eye was the best steak in Denver. He spotted Valerie on the sidewalk, through the large English 'G' etched on the tall windows and tapped on the glass to get her attention. She was beautiful in a short, black dress that showed off slim ankles and the lean figure born of being a tennis standout.

"Valerie."

"Jackson." She approached him with a languid, sensuous walk and his heart rate increased exponentially. He stood to pull out her chair and she leaned into him, lingering a bit long for a simple, friendly hug.

Jackson immediately noticed her espying the empty wine glasses. He had half thought to order before she arrived but knew better than that.

As if reading his mind, Valerie's first words of conversation were, "What wine should we have tonight?"

"I thought we could start with a nice Brunello di Montalcino."

"Do they have Biondi-Santi? Preferably reserved?"

"I believe so. Let's find out. Would you also like some calamari?"

"Sure. But not as much as the Biondi-Santi."

The wine steward was pleased to be able to confirm that they did have several bottles of the 1978 Brunello, but no longer could get the vaunted 1985. They agreed on the '78 and knew it had to breathe for a while. They weren't in any hurry and took their time with two martinis each, dry, no olives. When the wine arrived, with the right amount of flourish, Baines deferred to Valerie to taste it.

She flashed a huge smile after the first swallow, savoring the hints of blackberry and black cherry, with a finish of chocolate and violets. "Father insisted that I live and work in Europe for several years after college, mostly to help me escape my mother." She stopped suddenly and held up her hand. "Sorry. I didn't mean to go there. Anyway, I chose Tuscany and still have many friends in the wine industry around Montalcino. There is no wine that, for me, compares to the Brunello of Montalcino, not even Burgundy."

Baines nodded and didn't know quite what to say. He obviously wasn't going to veer into unsafe territory. "What did you do when you returned to the States?"

"As cliché as it sounds, I joined my father in Valentine Pharmaceuticals. Then, when he found me a proper husband, with all the right political ambitions and pedigree, I married and moved to Washington. But I continued to commute to work, as it were, and here I am today. I tolerate Washington, but Valentine Pharmaceuticals is my life."

Baines glanced around the restaurant and realized that a detail of Secret Service men was keeping Valerie in sight. He shook his head. *My God, what am I doing here with this woman? I really must be crazy.*

Valerie noticed her companion's distraction. "Okay, you saw my security detail, right? Not to worry. They are nothing, if not discreet."

Jackson laughed. "Okay. If you say so."

Valerie took another sip of wine and savored it for a moment before turning the conversation from idle chitchat. "Let's talk about work."

Jackson waited. *Warning Will Robinson.*

"You were quiet at the board meeting today. Is there something more on your mind?"

"I'm not comfortable with our arrangement."

Valerie studied his dark eyes for any sign of a tell. Nothing. "What part of the arrangement?"

"The part about the deaths of six women because of the patch."

"I was aware of the deaths, but not the gender."

"Valerie, six women died because of the patch."

"Again, just women?"

"Yes."

"But wasn't it used by thousands of people?"

"Three thousand, to be exact."

"Isn't it odd that this terrible thing happened to women, and not men? Why did they die? Of what?"

"As you know, we achieved our initial objective. People quit smoking. But there was an unintended genetic mutation around the heart wall of those women. They died of cardiac infarction."

"Why those six? Isn't six a low percentage?"

"Not if you're one of the six."

"Well, what was different about them?"

Jackson sighed. "Valerie, this is really sensitive information. I don't feel comfortable talking about it in public."

Valerie knew better than to push him too far at this point. She needed more from him.

"That's okay. We can find someplace more private after dinner. Let's enjoy our wine and steak now."

Jackson was used to playing the part of the male aggressor and found himself turned on by the role reversal. He began to relax and enjoy the moment.

From the look on his face, Valerie knew she had him. The answers she sought would come later in the evening. Of that she was now sure.

Valerie ordered another bottle of the Brunello and they made small talk about Denver and college and travel for the hour that they took with dinner. The steak was delicious and her appetite was in overdrive from thoughts of after dinner pleasures and revelations.

The next day dawned bright and early for Valerie. She completed her quick tour of the plant with Hyler, and her driver, followed by the ever-present security detail, picked her up at 9:00 AM for the return flight to Washington. She didn't have a headache, despite the wine consumption with Jackson. She guessed her clear head might have something to do with the great after-dinner sex that they enjoyed until almost sunrise. He did not disappoint. All those great looks and good in bed, too. She smiled before she realized it and caught herself, quickly rearranging her face in its usual passive countenance. Apparently, sex and alcohol were still reliable tongue-looseners, and she got the information that she needed from him. A very useful man, indeed.

Who would have thought that the world's most expensive perfume could also be lethal? What a bizarre twist. Some component of the perfume's ester reacted with the patch and caused the heart infarction? Thank God it was such an expensive perfume; otherwise, many more might have died. It was quirky, to say the least, that only six women had the specific and statistically improbable reaction – not instantaneous death, but death coming quickly enough that the researchers didn't catch it.

Valerie was certain that Jackson's brief fling with morality had passed and that he and the information he possessed were secure in the company fold. He would be such a nice diversion from time to time. She ran her tongue over her lips when she thought of their naked goodbye kiss.

Geez, she was glad that she never smoked. But it was too bad about that elegant perfume.

CHAPTER 12
Friday, February 25
Mexico City · 9:00 AM CST

The phone sounded as though it had been shot, rather than merely hung up. Castillo banged it so hard into the cradle that it cracked.

His Chief of Staff opened the door about an inch and peeked in at the President. He whispered through the slit, "Sir, is everything okay?"

"Hell no. Everything is far from okay. It's fucked up beyond all recognition. Wait a moment and we can walk outside. I need to clear my head."

Martín Arroyo slid into the office and said nothing.

President Armando Castillo grabbed his jacket and bolted from the room, motioning Arroyo to follow. As Castillo stormed the hallway, he collected members of his security detail as though they were attached to him by magnets. He hit the exit bar on the French doors and looked back at all those men running to keep up. He had to keep from laughing at them, fumbling to put on their coats and not trip over each other.

He always seemed to think better when he was outside in the beautiful, private pinewoods of Los Pinos. The forest was so dense around the Presidential Palace that even deep in the heart of Mexico City, he could hear no urban sounds, only birdcalls and the breeze through the pine boughs. Even the smog was less toxic smelling here. "Martín, how is it that 50,000 men dressed in Mexican army uniforms, I repeat, army uniforms, have amassed on the border with Texas and I know nothing about it? And yet the President of the United States has this information and called to put my head on a stick."

"Shouldn't we call the Minister of Defense, sir?"

"Maybe we should call the Minister of Cartels. What is going on?"

"Sir, may we back up? You were on the phone with President MacIntyre, right? Do you believe her?"

"Yes, of course. She has no reason to lie to me, especially after the events in her city. My own people don't tell me such things, so I suppose I am fortunate that she tells me about thousands of people moving around in my own country. What the hell is going on here?"

Arroyo started to speak and Castillo held up his hand. "Wait. Before you say anything, I must ask, did you know about this?"

"President Castillo, I have worked for you all my adult life. You know me. I would never keep anything from you, much less something of such importance."

"Okay, then answer my question. What the hell is going on?"

"Sir, let's think about this. It appears, if what the American President says is true – and yes, you have no reason to doubt her – that something big is happening on the border."

"Yes, that's obvious."

Castillo slumped on the nearby bench. His security men stepped forward and he waved them off, shaking his head. "Our recent intel has revealed a great deal of chatter about one of the cartels, probably Los Rojos, moving people around. Could it actually be them, dressed to look like soldiers in the Mexican army? Are they army deserters who came to them in their own uniforms? If so, why have I not received any reports from my intelligence agency?"

Like clockwork, two sober-looking men in dark suits came bounding through the door, followed by more security teams. Castillo looked up at the commotion.

The two men, both from CISEN, the National Security and Investigation Center, came forward, flushed and out of breath. The Director, Juan Marcos and his Assistant Director, Antonio Pasqual stopped in front of the president. Marcos spoke. "Mr. President, we must speak with you immediately. And privately."

Castillo eyed them. "I gather that. Please do so."

They both looked at Arroyo.

"No. He stays."

"But, it is a matter of ..."

"This is not the day to underestimate me, gentlemen. Continue, or I will appoint your successors who understand that I am still the president of this country."

They stared open-mouthed at the man who was known to never lose his temper.

"Sir, we have information that indicates the Los Rojos Cartel is deploying men on our border with Texas."

"Pathetically enough, I heard this moments ago from the President of the United States. Imagine my dismay at receiving information of such urgency from her."

"We only now put this together," sputtered Pasqual, suddenly picturing his head bumping down the garden path, rolling away from the rest of his body, "and without the help of satellites, I might add."

Marcos continued. "About an hour ago, we received confirmation of this movement to the Texas border. By itself, it was surprising enough…"

"Where is General Vilas right now? What does he say about this?"

"President Castillo, we can't find him. According to one of his aides, he is on vacation."

"On vacation? Since when does the Army Chief of Staff take a vacation and I not know about it? Fuck this."

Arroyo's assistant opened the door to the garden and motioned for him. The President's Chief of Staff shook his head, almost violently. The assistant did the same. Arroyo scurried over, about to fire the poor woman, when she leaned over and whispered something to him. He shook his head in disbelief, but quickly walked back to the President.

He whispered, "Sir…"

"Not now, Martín. Tell her that whatever it is can fucking wait."

"Sir, it can't wait. Federico de Franco is holding for you on your private line."

CHAPTER 13

Friday, February 25
Beirut, Lebanon · 2:00 PM EET
(Eastern European Time)

The HB108.287tran was state of the art – a microphone and transmitter that, thanks to nanotechnology, was as thin and translucent as a piece of scotch tape and no larger than the fingernail of your pinky. The brilliance of the device was its ability to automatically mate with any SIM card and immediately interface with the cell phone's antenna. The range was about a mile, but because Hezbollah had concentrated so much of its operations in the Haret Hreik, a mile was all he needed.

Fortunately for Abdel, Talal rarely traveled more than 10 city blocks from IRSO's headquarters and today was no different.

Abdel Salam was no fool. The arcane world of Hezbollah allowed for few missteps. And the one way of assuring his own longevity was to know whatever Talal knew, which Abdel could do from the comfort of his own IRSO office.

Over the past two years he had averted several near misses through the use of this bug, but what he was to learn today was, even for him, an epiphany.

Talal El-Hussen was sitting in the handsome, but simply appointed, living room of the Nasrallahs' apartment, in the Haret Hreik dahieh of Beirut. They had once lived in an elegant home in Ram Bchamoun in the southernmost part of the city. But security needs, after the 2006 war, had finally necessitated the move. The modest apartment had a fraction of the space afforded them in Ram Bchamoun, and it was surrounded by sterile buildings and burned out streets. Nada blamed the Israelis not only for the loss of the home that had been in her family for generations, but for the cramped space that gave the Sheikh easier access to take out his daily frustrations on her.

At least the market pulsed with activity on good days, when the vendors and shopkeepers took over the street, along with people of all ages and stations in colorful clothes and scarves. It was the place where Nada felt most alive.

She entered the room, dressed in a flowing silk dress with her head covered by the traditional scarf, and served them tea and harisi. Her husband had a weakness for the sweet, dense cakes.

Talal spoke quietly. "The situation in Mexico has become more complicated, Eminence. I…"

The Sheikh threw Talal a cold look to silence him until Nada left the room. Though she was smart and well educated – they met at university – Nasrallah kept Nada strictly out of his business.

However, she had confronted him earlier in the day, to no avail, wanting to know Michel's whereabouts. Michel left Beirut without saying goodbye, which had never happened before, and when she called his office in Denver, the secretary told her that Michel wasn't scheduled to return from his teaching assignment in Beirut for another two weeks. Nada nursed an intuition that Nasrallah knew more than he let on, and she feared for her son. Her son. The most important person in her life. No. He was her life.

Nasrallah studied his wife. Still lithe, and with an unlined, olive face, aquiline features and glossy, black hair, she was a classic beauty. The fact that she was taller than her stubby husband was the subject of snickers among his minions, but Nasrallah thought of her as the grand prize in the wife auction. She was a pious woman and after a few unusually cruel beatings, never again questioned his iron will. That, plus her looks that men and women alike envied, was all that he needed of a woman, although he never quite knew what was happening behind those almond-shaped eyes. Of course, she was sad at not being able to give him the children promised by Allah, but he dismissed such emotions.

Nada shut the door softly behind her. But just as the small confines of the apartment offered her little refuge from the Sheikh's rage, it did afford her the ability to overhear.

"You know better than that, Talal. Now, what is complicated? Does this have anything to do with Michel?"

Talal was visibly shaken. "Yes and no. He is now five days past his scheduled contact and none of our Mexican informants have any clue as to his whereabouts."

"Is this all speculation or do you have any facts?" Nasrallah fingered the white cotton cloth of his gellabah, concentrating on Talal's response.

"Michel has vanished, which means, at the very least, our plans have been disrupted. It could even mean that Michel has been compromised."

"Compromised? By what?"

"Not by what, Eminence. By whom. I fear that de Franco may have stumbled onto our intentions. And he is capable of anything."

"How is that even possible, you piece of camel dung? Are you implying that we have a breach in our security?"

Talal paced the room, noisily rubbing his worry beads back and forth in his palm. Nasrallah fought the urge to strangle him.

Talal looked down at the tile floor. "In Beirut, no. But in Mexico…" Talal shrugged his shoulders.

He continued. "Among Los Rojos, General Vilas, and our government contacts, there is not an ounce of honor."

"That is not news to me, you fool. What else is your good-for-nothing stomach telling you?"

"Your Eminence, based upon our original timeline, the Americans should have reacted by now against de Franco. We planted enough evidence to lead a blind donkey to him. Their lack of action is disconcerting. If the Americans don't act soon, the entire coup could be thwarted."

"Then, you brother of a whore, we have even more need to reestablish contact with Michel. We must find out if he has been killed, or even worse, taken. He could put us all in jeopardy. The coup must not be stopped. Mexico's destiny is to be our de facto client state, a stake in the heart of the Great Satan. What are you doing to find Michel?"

A hint of a smile crossed Talal's lips. He hoped that Nasrallah did not see it. This was not the time for that. However, how could he not smile at the advantage that Hezbollah could gain by controlling Mexico through Los Rojos and General Vilas? It was staggering. Perhaps, their Iranian cousins – and the world – would finally give them the credit they were surely due. "The time is of the essence. I believe that we have to send Abdel to Mexico."

Nasrallah roared, "No."

"Hear me out. I know that you do not trust or approve of him, but he was stationed in Mexico for a number of years and we can quickly secure him diplomatic cover. Whatever has happened to Michel, Abdel is the person who can finish Michel's business on such short notice. He has the credibility to meet with government officials and Vilas."

"I still do not like this. Abdel is weak. He will never father a child. I keep him because his family is one of our largest benefactors, and, yes, he is a good organizer and true believer. But there is something not right in him."

Talal had heard this all before. He remained quiet and let Nasrallah rant. It was true. Abdel was not a typical true believer. He was once stationed in Mexico City as a diplomat from Lebanon, and his wealthy family had afforded him a lavish lifestyle. Single, in his mid-thirties, slim and clean-shaven, he worked out six days a week and always had a good tan on his relatively light skin. Talal did not like or approve of him, either, but believed that Abdel had worth to Hezbollah for those very reasons. He could slip in and out of the decadent and spoiled western society on missions for Hezbollah. The irony of that was not lost on Talal. He could never take full advantage of Abdel's skill sets because of Nasrallah's medieval prejudices.

Abdel, still in his IRSO office and more grateful than ever for the HB108.287tran, leaned back in his desk chair and laughed out loud. The chair tipped back and almost fell over. Not right? Me? If they only knew.

"Talal, have you ever let yourself think that there may be a wolf in our own tent? If that is so, then the thing I have always feared most could happen."

"What do you have to fear, Eminence?"

"That we could lose everything if Michel Hayek ever found out the truth of his own family. He must never know that his father was a traitorous fool who worked for the Israeli pigs…"

"Or that it was you who ordered his family killed?"

"Yes, Talal, you dog, and you who carried out my orders by setting up the Israelis to bomb the house next door with its supposed Hezbollah agents. The poor Hayeks were thought to be collateral damage in this despicable act of Israeli intemperance." The words dripped icily off Nasrallah's tongue.

"The Jew lovers got what they deserved. And you showed mercy by taking in the orphaned Michel as your own son."

"And Nada would never forgive me if she knew."

Nasrallah sighed and renewed his imperious tone. "I will give you a little time to fix this. But be quick about it. Your King's gambit requires speed and does put the King in some peril."

Talal groaned inwardly. My King's gambit? Son-of-a-bitch. You have to give the old bastard credit. That's why he's lasted so long. But he's wrong if he thinks he can leave me to die without water in the desert.

The clean-shaven man looked up at the sound of a low flying plane. He slammed the cab door with a resounding thud and strode into the main terminal of the Beirut Rafik Hariri International Airport. Named in honor of the assassinated former prime minister of Lebanon, Rafik Hariri, it was considered one of the premiere airports of the Middle East, second to Dubai. In 2007, then President George W. Bush recognized the modernizing efforts of Lebanon and lifted the ban on air traffic that had been in place since 1985, when a TWA flight was hijacked there.

The man looked around the spotless, white terminal always vigilant. He blended into the crowd effortlessly, innately fading into the background. Only the dead, black marbles that passed for eyes revealed his nature. The one thing that marred his bland features was a vivid, red scar across his right cheekbone that he usually covered with make up. Oddly enough, it was a fencing scar from his college days. What surprise his fellow travelers would feel if they knew his true occupation.

His cell phone rang and he picked it up without speaking. "Jad, are you at the airport?"

"Yes."

"We can speak safely?"

"Yes."

"Talal has spoken with you?"

"Yes."

"Do you have any questions?"

"No."

"Then go with the blessings of the Prophet."

"Insh'allah."

"Insh'allah."

Jad Farrah never had any questions after he set himself on a path. A highly skilled assassin, he never felt empathy or remorse. He carried out orders and was paid nicely for his services. At the top of his game, he was afraid of nothing and no one, not even the infamous Sheikh.

CHAPTER 14

Friday, February 25
Santa Maria del Oro
de Franco's Compound · 9:15 AM CST

"Armando, I must speak with you right away."

On the other end of the receiver there was deafening silence and finally, "Isn't that what we are doing? I took your call, didn't I?"

"I mean in person."

"Not possible."

"Then make it possible."

"Need I remind you of whom you are speaking with? I do not have to…"

De Franco knew that the President of Mexico would not be easily lured away from Los Pinos. He had to be his most persuasive, without revealing too much. "Armando please, if I could come to you I would, believe me. But I have someone in my custody and I cannot risk transporting him to the capital. You must hear what he has to say."

President Castillo remained adamant but there was now a note of hesitancy in his voice. "I can't leave Mexico City right now. You of all people should know that." Federico had caught him off guard and he needed to take a moment to think. "And I must ask, who am I talking with?"

"Excuse me. What do you mean 'who am I talking with'."

"Is this the jovial industrialist Federico de Franco or am I speaking with El Escolar?"

De Franco drew back from the phone. Castillo had cut through the chaff quickly enough. He started to give him a flippant retort but stopped himself suddenly. Who was he, indeed? The businessman patriot who would do anything for his country? Or the head of one of the world's wealthiest and most ruthless cartels?

"In the moment, I don't know how to answer that. But it doesn't matter. What does matter is that I am speaking to you as a Mexican citizen who has crucial information that you must hear in person. I realize that I am asking much of you, at a time when things are confused and chaotic, but this cannot wait…"

"Oh for God's sake, Federico, tell me what this is all about. I have no time to spend on your dilemma. I have dilemmas of my own."

"Is one of your dilemmas the whereabouts of General Vilas?"

"What? How do you know about that?"

"What do you know about the Hezbollah's involvement with the events in Washington?"

"Hezbollah? Washington? You are talking nonsense, Federico. Enough…"

"Stop. Don't hang up. What if I told you that Hezbollah is masterminding a coup against your government, as we speak, and that General Vilas is a key player?"

With that, Castillo walked back to the garden bench and sat heavily. He massaged his forehead as though rubbing away a wasp sting. "Okay, you have my attention. Go on."

CHAPTER 15
Friday, February 25
Washington DC · Late Afternoon

Emilio exploded, "That's crazy, Roger."

"Is that your professional assessment or the Georgetown lawyer in you speaking?"

"Neither. I've got Presidential cover on this, but you'd be acting in direct contradiction to your mother's none-too-vague orders."

"Hear me out. I know that the plan has some holes, but I think it's the way to insure the safety of the President, and perhaps both our Presidents, and the relationship between our two countries."

Emilio paced around the living room of Roger's Watergate apartment. His footsteps echoed on the marble floors, even with the nice rugs that Roger had gathered on his trips around the world. Roger liked his two-bedroom apartment, overlooking the Potomac and onto Georgetown, despite the fact that it was so different from the Hill Country surroundings on the ranch. He knew that this job was temporary, which gave him a chance to enjoy living in an urban environment, knowing that he would go back to the open spaces and scrubby hills of central Texas.

Emilio constantly teased him about his monk-like lifestyle. Roger recognized the truth of that sad fact. He had no time to call his own – chiefs of staff rarely did have that luxury. At least, he wouldn't fall prey to the high divorce rate among top White House staffers since he had no wife. Hell, he couldn't find the time to ask an interesting woman out on a date, much less woo her into bed. Monk-like, indeed.

Roger said, "Could you please stop your pacing and sit back down? We need to concentrate on this."

"What exactly is 'this', Roger? I can't believe you mean what you just said."

"Bear with me. We must have first hand verification of Federico

– excuse me – your father's claims and only you can do that. My mother's right on that point. And, second, if what your father claims is true, we need to get to his source. Assuming the source is still breathing."

"But, Roger, we will have no guarantee of either. Why not allow me to go by myself? After all, I'm probably the reason this has any credibility. It's too much of a risk for you, the Chief of Staff."

"Bullshit."

"Again, this is crazy. I'm more than willing to see my father in person, but if this turns ugly, and believe me it will because everything around him turns ugly, neither of us is in any condition to resume our old lives as Rangers.

"In addition, my father is not stupid. He knows that his call to me has already set something in motion."

"Precisely my point. This will have to involve more than the two of us when we pay Senior de Franco a…"

Roger turned at the sound of the doorbell.

"Dad, Director Sanchez, come in. Emilio is already here."

"Roger, it's Gabriel or Gabe. I mean it."

In spite of being the most powerful gatekeeper in the world, let alone a highly trusted advisor to President MacIntyre, Roger still maintained a humble and understated demeanor toward those in Washington's inner circles, particularly the Director of Homeland Security.

"Yessir. Gabriel. I believe that you saw Emilio de Franco at the White House. Let me introduce you formally." The two men shook hands.

Deacon waited for no such niceties and gave Emilio something like a cross between a handshake, a hug and a pat on the back. "You look good, son. I haven't seen you enough lately."

"Life has kept me pretty busy, Deacon."

Deacon snorted. "Yep. Tell me about it."

As the four men moved to chairs in the living room, Emilio studied Gabriel. He was everything that Emilio had heard about him, with an imposing physical presence despite being less than six feet tall. He seemed to be all muscle and shoulders, with a flat stomach and small hips. Emilio wasn't certain if Gabriel's obvious athletic prowess was the reason he was appointed the chief spook of all spooks, or if it were his Stanford PhD in international political science.

People often underestimated Gabriel's keen intelligence because he looked more like a Greco-Roman wrestler than a brilliant mover of men.

"Okay, Roger. You got us here. What's on your mind?" Deacon was never one to mince words.

"I wish that Secretary of Defense Frazier could have joined us, but he is meeting with the President. Emilio and I have a plan that we'd like to run by you."

Emilio chimed in, "For the record, it's Roger's plan, but it's my ass on the line."

"As you probably know, the President has asked Emilio to go to Santa María del Oro to meet secretly with his father. Emilio is going to determine the truth of de Franco's claims about Hezbollah and find the source of the information. The President tacitly asked Emilio to get this supposed source out of Mexico. It's the only way we can be sure of anything. And the President doesn't like ambiguity."

Deacon glanced over to Gabriel with his head cocked and his eyebrows raised.

Gabriel responded to the unspoken question. "I can confirm that the President did authorize Frazier and me to use whatever means necessary to verify de Franco's claims."

Roger had the in he had been waiting for. "Does that include offering logistical support to Emilio?"

"Probably."

"Why do I sense that there's more, Roger?" Deacon always had a way of seeing right into Roger. It could be unsettling, but Roger was ready to make his case.

"Dad, Gabriel, what we're proposing is an extraction team of Army Rangers, based out of the Hill Country…"

"Hang on. Hill Country? Do you mean the ranch?"

"Yessir, I mean Aguila." Deacon's parents had named the ranch years ago, before Deacon met Kate, a beautiful, auburn haired girl with no political aspirations. And now the name was a double entendre, since the head eagle of the United States lived there.

"We keep the nest private, Roger. You more than anyone should know that. No heads of state. No senators. No press corps. I can't quite believe what I'm hearing."

Roger swallowed hard, but kept going. "I wouldn't even suggest the ranch if the stakes weren't so high, Dad. But Mother – the President – is in grave danger and we have to do everything possible to deal with this threat. There's a time element and a requirement for secrecy that make the ranch, with its size and proximity to the border, the most suitable location. We can launch men and materials from there in a matter of hours. You were a Green Beret. You know how this works."

Gabriel asked, "Hang on. What are you thinking? How many men? What kind of support do you need? Can't Emilio have a private conversation with his father as the President requested?"

Emilio pushed in. "That would be fine, except for one thing. The extraction. The President really needs us to bring the source back."

"Emilio's right. We have to get in and out under official radar. If Hezbollah is truly involved, they can't know this is happening. We have to get to Santa María del Oro from the border without alerting Los Rojos or any of the other gangs. To do this, we have to be dressed as locals with undetectable vehicles. We have to blend in…"

"Son, why do you keep using the pronoun 'we'? What the hell are you thinking?"

"Dad, I'm not thinking. I'm telling."

"But you are Kate's Chief of Staff. How could you possibly think that you could leave her at a time like this? And not just leave, but leave without her knowledge of it. She'll be frantic at a time when she needs to be clear-headed. And Roger, it should go without saying that you would be a high profile hostage."

"Well, Dad, at the very least, she will want me to be in charge of the planning. She will know that I have to be at the ranch, if that's where we decide to stage the crossing. Let's leave it at that for now. Besides, the governor is already screaming bloody murder about the troops on the border. What better way to mollify Governor Douglas than for Kate to send me to smooth things over with him? I need to be in Texas, and I need to get there quickly."

No one spoke. Each man was puzzling through this bizarre situation. The Vice President was dead. The President needed action. The country was in a frenzy. And the four of them were sitting in a Watergate apartment like chess masters, except it was the fate of nations on their board, not chess pieces.

"Okay, Roger. Use the ranch. But please try to keep your ass from getting shot off. That goes for you too Emilio. And make no mistake. Your mother will find out about this and when she does, we will all, that's everyone in this room, have hell to pay."

Gabriel laughed out loud. Everyone looked at him.

"Sorry. I'm here with all you cowboys, and I guess that you just cowboy'd up. Now I know what that means. Okay. Let's hear a little more about how all this might play out. We've got work to do."

CHAPTER 16
Friday, February 25
Washington, DC · White House · Late Afternoon

Valerie's driver stopped at the guard gate before being waved in to the West Wing's entry portico off West Executive Avenue. A uniformed officer came to her door, opened it and ushered her into the lobby, once a much grander space, but now reduced to make room for more offices. Valerie had called ahead and spoken with Rose who assured her that the President would make time for her.

The day had turned cold, with a sharp wind off the Potomac that brought spitting rain. Valerie removed her mouton coat, missing the days when it was politically correct to wear fur. Never mind. The sable was in storage for the day when she was finished with this nonsense.

One of the ever present security details checked Valerie's credentials yet again, with security on heightened alert, and showed her to Rose's office. She took a seat and appeared to wait patiently.

Looking up from her desk Rose smiled. "The President is finishing up a call and will be with you in a moment."

Five minutes went by and then ten. Inside, Valerie was seething at the indignity of being kept waiting. Roger asked this favor of her, after all. It wasn't her idea. She tightly clutched her Ferragamo tote, which readily held the box that she was delivering to the President.

The door to the oval office opened and Valerie, surprised by Kate's sudden appearance, rose quickly to greet the tall, big boned woman from Texas.

"Madame President, thank you for taking the time to see me. Between the loss of our dear Harris and the at…" Valerie cut herself off. She wasn't supposed to know about the attempt on Kate's life. "I mean the situation on the border with Mexico, things must be very hectic around here."

Kate pretended not to notice Valerie's slip of the tongue and allowed

Madame President

herself to be hugged, a gesture that felt oddly cold. "Come in, Valerie. Please. I am sorry that you had to wait. Rose, please give us a few moments. And Valerie, would you like some coffee or tea?"

Valerie was about to answer 'no', but changed her mind. Why not? She should at least give me something to drink for my trouble. "That would be nice, Madame President. It is such a raw day and I am a bit chilled."

"Rose, two coffees would be great. Thank you."

Kate shut the door to the exquisite room and looked at the space all over again. This often happened when she walked into the perfectly assembled office, with its classical geometric shape and comforting familiarity. She pointed Valerie to a love seat and she took the nearest chair.

"Madame President…"

"Valerie, when we are alone together in this room, please call me Kate. No need for such formality in private."

"Thank you…Kate."

"When you asked to see me alone, I became a little concerned. Is Preston all right?"

Valerie laughed. "Oh yes, he is quite fine, going about the business of government. He is in his element."

"Good. Then to what do I owe the pleasure of this visit?"

Rose tiptoed in and left the coffee service without ceremony. Kate poured for both of them and then sat back in the blue tweed, winged back chair.

"Why, Kate. I thought that you would know the reason."

Kate shook her head.

"Roger asked me to come by on Wednesday because he had a favor to ask."

Kate, caught off guard by the idea of Roger asking anything of Valerie, tilted her head in an implied question.

"Well, my goodness, I hope that this isn't awkward for you. But he knows that Valentine Pharmaceuticals has been working day and night on a new quit-smoking patch and asked if I would bring you one of the first boxes off the assembly line."

"Really? Certainly not awkward, but interesting. What do you call this new wonder drug?"

"I know it's sort of corny, but we named it SST – Stop Smoking Today."

Kate laughed. "Yes, a bit corny."

Valerie stiffened.

Kate continued. "I don't smoke so much that I need help in quitting, but I appreciate your kindness. It's not really an issue for me."

"Apparently it is for Roger, Kate. At any rate, the product is pretty amazing. The FDA approved it, of course, and your Surgeon General thinks it's a major breakthrough in public health because of its success rate. And you know how much smoking costs this country. Tens of billions of dollars in healthcare costs annually."

"No wonder Roger was interested. How does it work?"

"I can't tell you the exact science, but I know that it genetically alters the pleasure receptors in the brain so that they no longer respond to nicotine."

"How quickly does it take effect?"

"That's the really amazing part. Fourteen days and you're done."

"So, Valentine Pharmaceuticals hit a homerun with this one, huh? No booster shots? No follow-ups? Side effects?"

"Not particularly. Perhaps a mild stimulation of appetite, but since you need no more than fourteen days on it, without further intervention, that doesn't seem like much of a price to pay."

Kate looked at Valerie's rail thin frame and shrugged. "I guess not. Thank you for helping Roger out with this. Now, how about you? How are you holding up with all of the intensified scrutiny on your family and the security around 24/7?"

Valerie realized that the President was done with the SST conversation so she shifted gears. "It's fine, Kate. I know that it's necessary and I want to support you and Preston."

Kate's phone beeped and she looked at her watch. Yep. The prearranged ten minutes were up and Rose was a master gatekeeper. As Kate began to stand, Valerie hastily inserted a question. "Any hints on your search for a Vice President? It does have some personal meaning for me."

Kate smiled slightly. "I know it does, Valerie. And I like uncertainty about as much as I like shopping for a bathing suit, but I can't give you any information about this right now. We're taking our time. I have shown the preliminary list to Preston. Why don't you ask him?"

Valerie looked at the box in her lap and paused for a moment. Kate waited.

The Speaker's wife seemed a million miles away and then her eyes refocused on the President. "I shall. Well, here is the patch, if you decide to use it. Best of luck with everything, Kate."

That word, luck, sounded strange to Kate's ear, but Valerie was nothing if not strange. She walked the visitor back to the door and opened it for her. As Valerie moved away, Kate called after her. "Thank you, Valerie. Give my best to Preston."

Valerie held her hand up and waved it, without turning around.

CHAPTER 17

Saturday, February 26
Washington, DC · Family Residence · Early Morning

Kate stood in front of the bulletproof windows in her bedroom, soaking up as much sunlight as possible. Deacon was already up and out for the day – to where she wasn't quite sure. But she had enjoyed the quiet in front of the fire, actually taking the time to write in her journal. If there were ever a time in her presidency that she needed to keep track of events and her thoughts about them, it was now. She admired the late President Reagan for being disciplined in this pursuit and she found that it cleared her mind, which had been in ceaseless turmoil for the past four days.

It was still cold out and she dressed in her favorite cashmere sweater and matching slacks in a soft periwinkle. It was comfortable and clung nicely to her fit frame. Like most smokers before her, Kate bid a fond adieu to cigarettes with one last indulgence early this morning. She opened the red box that Valerie had given her and poured over the instructions, which seemed simple enough. No one would notice the patch or that she was not smoking, except maybe Gabriel, and if Roger was that worried about this habit, then she should try it for him, if for no other reason.

Who am I kidding? I need to quit smoking for myself. Okay, I'll start again today. How many times have I tried to do this? Maybe Valerie's company has come up with the answer. How ironic would that be? For me to get any kind of help from that woman...

A knock on her door interrupted her thoughts. She walked over to the fireside table, closed her journal, and tucked it into the nightstand.

"Come in." She was expecting Ford Lowery and Georgeanne Wright, her chief political strategists, this morning. As White House Counsel and Special Advisor to the President, Ford's job was to cull the list of VP possibilities down to two or three. Georgeanne coordinated internal polling for the White House and was invaluable to any political decision-making. And, yes, this was a political calculation as much as it was about good governance.

Kate had done her homework. Twice before in the history of the Republic had this been necessary. And surprisingly enough, Richard Nixon had set out three criteria that described the person she was looking for. "First, that the person be capable of serving as president; second, that the person share the president's views on foreign policy; and finally, that the person be able to work with members of both parties in Congress and be capable of confirmation by both houses."

"Good morning, Kate," and quickly remembering that he was not alone with the President, Ford corrected himself, "Madame President. Here is the list as promised."

"Right to business. Ford, that's one of the things I love about you. I assume that Barbara has finally thawed out from the frozen tundra and will be by later this afternoon."

"Damn right, Newfoundland is colder than a…well, you know. Anyway my wife said she'd be joining you and Roger after lunch."

Turning to the young woman with Ford, Kate queried, "And how are you this morning, Georgeanne?"

"Fine, Madame President."

"Okay then, enough of the social niceties. Let's get to the business at hand. Grab a seat by the fire and help yourselves to some coffee. It's going to be a long morning and I want to put this puppy to bed before lunch.

"Now, Georgeanne, before Ford shares 'his' list with me, why don't you catch me up on the pulse of the country."

Georgeanne fielded many of the calls that were coming in from around the nation, with almost unanimous positive support from concerned citizens. These calls reflected a mirror image of the White House internal tracking polls in terms of Kate's favorability ratings. But Kate was never one to rely on the opiate of poll numbers, and Georgeanne's feedback on real people with real voices was invaluable to Kate in gauging the mood of the country.

Kate smiled at the lovely woman in front of her. Georgeanne had appeared at the Governor's Mansion in Austin, wet behind the ears and with a degree from Texas A&M in political science and a masters in statistical analysis from the LBJ School of Government. What cheek and confidence it had taken that girl to come looking for a job, traits that Kate admired. And Kate figured that if she could forgive her own son, Butch, for choosing A&M, she could forgive this woman. No one was perfect. Time and again, through the years, her instincts about Georgeanne had been right. She had a rational and creative mind, an unusual combination, and she was fiercely loyal to Kate.

"What are the people saying about all this?"

"Well, you have read the polls, of course. But I believe that there is a hidden longing underlying everything. Relief. Anger. Sadness. Fear. It's all there. But the biggest thing people want is the truth. They want to know who did it and how the assassins will be brought to justice. And they want to know that from you. You have to be the one in front of them with the message. They want to know – soon, real soon, who will be your second-in-command. The natural order of things has been disturbed."

Kate listened intently to Georgeanne. Funny. Those were all things that Kate wanted, too. Now it was Ford's turn. She nodded at him.

"The political question of Harris' successor hangs over you, Madame President, your own personal sword of Damocles. It really comes down to two names and I suspect that Deacon won't be thrilled with one of them."

She didn't have to guess what Ford meant. Sure, the Speaker of the House was not popular within her own family, but sometimes the politically expedient solution was best for the country. She had no time to bring someone on board who didn't know policy and the inner-workings of government. Preston Sandermann could be a snob, but he knew where all the bodies were buried and he might be an asset. Deacon was adamantly opposed to him. Kate understood why Deacon might not like the guy, but why did he respond so bitterly to the thought of Sandermann as her Vice President?

Deacon was intuitive. She had always relied on him for the unvarnished truth. But he might not win this argument.

"And, Madame President, that leaves one other name…"

"Hey Katie. Where are you girl? I've got some news."

Kate and her guests looked up at the sound of Deacon tromping into the living quarters. He was the picture of vigor and masculinity, with his Stetson, plaid shirt, and long legs in pressed jeans. Kate gave him a brilliant smile and forgot the outside world for a moment. He always had this effect on her though she thought no one else noticed. Georgeanne suppressed a smile. She liked it for her boss when Deacon was around. It made all their lives easier.

"Hang on, Deacon. Ford, Georgeanne and I have something to go over with you, too. Let me go first, how 'bout it?"

"Okey doke."

He took a chair opposite Kate and folded his hands in a mock attentive way. Kate glared at him.

"Deacon, we have got to talk about my selection for Vice President." She raised her hand. "I know how you feel about Preston…"

"Not entirely, you don't. But I'll leave it at that since, Ford aside, there are tender ears in the room." He grinned at Georgeanne. "Go on."

"We have got to give him a chance, Deac. He is politically savvy and is one of the de facto leaders of our party."

"But, honey, I thought you were seriously considering that fella' from North Dakota."

Ford was always amazed about how this 'Texas cowboy' knew what was coming even before an idea had been hatched.

"Senator Richter, isn't it? Now I like him. Seems like a straight shooter, and you won't always be havin' to check your backside for hatchet marks if he's your guy."

"Funny you should mention him. His supporters are gaining some steam. And I think that Ford was starting to tell me where we stand with him. Go on, Ford."

"Yes, the junior senator from North Dakota has some power behind him. It appears that he has made inroads with big business, even though he's from such a small state, and he has a touch with the person on the street. He would be quick to tell you that he is the man on the street and that he has a finger on that pulse."

"Since he's a widower with two school-age children, he has his hands full and doesn't have the time to get into trouble. But all kidding aside, he's still grieving over his wife's death from cancer and he wants to be hard at work in the Senate and in tending to his kids. By the way, the kids are the most telegenic little guys – an added bonus. He might not let them ever get in front of a camera…"

"Which is his prerogative…"

"Yes, Ma'am. It is. But this guy is the real deal. He loves his family and he does his homework in the Senate. He's a quick study, with no obvious baggage."

Remembering Kate's, or was it Nixon's, three criteria, Deacon added with a confident voice, "He's capable. He agrees with you on foreign policy. And perhaps most important, he can be confirmed quickly."

Before anyone else could respond, Kate, having made up her mind, echoed Deacon's enthusiasm for the Senator. "Well I guess it's bully for Richter. Now, Deac, what was your news?" "Nothing so important or exciting as yours. I need to make a quick trip to Aguila this evening for a few days. But don't fret. I'll be back in time for Harris's funeral."

CHAPTER 18

SATURDAY, FEBRUARY 26
WASHINGTON, DC · SITUATION ROOM · MID AFTERNOON

"**H**ow many times do I have to say no? And not just no, hell no."

"But Madame President."

"Don't you 'but Madame President' me. I'm the President of the United States and I'm giving you a direct order. And Deacon, don't you be looking at me like that."

Kate's mind was swirling. This was supposed to be a meeting with her chief-of-staff, top advisors, including Deacon, Emilio de Franco, Sanchez, Frazier, and Barbara and Ford Lowery to discuss the now designated Operation Eagle's Nest. Kate was always amazed by the Hollywood nature of operation nomenclature. But somehow the conversation had degenerated into a shouting match.

She had chosen the situation room because it was the most secure area in the White House and because their meeting there would be less conspicuous. Also, they would have access to the latest Satellite imagery and on-the-ground intelligence.

Kate had spent the greater part of the last few days in this 5,000 square foot room. Along the walls, lights of dozens of monitors and digital maps cast an otherworldly glow that made faces appear ghostly. All of the participants had an assigned place at the huge conference table and sat motionless. Most had watched history being made in this very place and no one was blasé about it. Every eye in the room was on the President.

Kate tried to dial down the rhetoric. "Roger, I understand why you want to be involved. But you have to understand why I can't allow it. Three years ago you were almost killed during that Al-Qaeda attack at the G10 meeting in Geneva…"

"But…."

"Let me finish. I realize that at the time you were the one member of our delegation with the appropriate skill-sets – your Army Ranger background, your linguistic ability, plus a Masters in Economics – to have facilitated the successful outcome of what could easily have been a national, no, world disaster. This time it's different. We have all the resources of the United States Government at hand. There is not one iota of a reason to put my chief of staff in harm's way. I won't condone it."

Gabriel saw an opening and offered a suggestion. "Madame President if I might suggest a compromise that could actually facilitate the plan we are presenting to you. What if Roger goes to Texas on the pretext of inspecting the situation on the border? Roger can help coordinate the logistics and implementation of the plan from the ranch, which he is more than competent to do, as you so aptly mentioned about Geneva. And I guarantee you that he will be back in DC in time for Harris's funeral."

Frazier added, "And with Roger's background in special ops and politics, he will be invaluable in planning and implementing such a nuanced operation."

Ford spoke up for the first time. "From a purely political perspective, sending Roger to Texas is the right call."

Before Deacon could add a note of support to Roger's involvement, Kate gave in. Sort of. Kate knew she was on the losing end of the argument. Though she had the power to checkmate any argument, and the mother in her would do anything to protect her cubs, as President she would never publicly undercut Roger.

"I still don't see why he can't do that from here, but I guess it will serve to quiet Governor Douglas down. And it would take quite a magician to do a first hand inspection of the Texas/Mexican border from the White House."

"Okay, but only to the border and only to the ranch. Be back here Tuesday morning or all of you can start working on your résumés."

Roger and Emilio had further refined the plan since Gabriel and Deacon gave it the green light yesterday afternoon. They stood and began to lay it out for the group.

Homeland and Defense were already at work supplying them with the logistical and operational support that they would need. Secretary of State, Barbara Lowery, was quickly brought into the loop because the operation would involve a surreptitious entry and extraction, crossing into a sovereign nation, Mexico. The diplomatic ramifications could be disastrous. Secretary Lowery hoped that State wouldn't be called on to do more than issue a statement after the operation had concluded successfully, but she believed in preparing for all conceivable outcomes.

"Madame President, our expectation is that this mission will require the State Department to issue a formal apology to President Castillo for our necessary incursion into his sovereign nation. But now that we are on the subject of Mexico, I think we must discuss the sudden instability of the Castillo regime and how that might affect this mission."

"Good point, Barbara. Any updates on the situation in Mexico, Gabriel?"

While Secretary Lowery was speaking, Gabriel's secure phone began to vibrate. He pushed his chair away from the table, twisted his torso slightly and took a call. Kate waited for Gabriel to turn back around and asked the question again.

"As a matter of fact, yes. This call was from Langley. They picked up a brief conversation yesterday between President Castillo and Federico de Franco. Seems de Franco is asking for a face-to-face with Castillo. De Franco made a clear reference to an asset, or better said, a prisoner, with direct information on Hezbollah's involvement in all of this."

"And you haven't heard this before now?"

"Madame President, I don't need to remind you that everyday the NSA and the CIA monitor billions of global phone calls. Even with our supercomputers, it can take some hours before all the information is analyzed."

"Sorry Gabriel, sometimes I forget that what we see in the movies is not reality."

Low laughter rippled through the room. Gabriel pressed on. "We also now have confirmation that General Vilas has flown the coop, or at least according to our sources in Los Pinos, can't be reached by President Castillo."

"Well, hell. Does this mean what I think it does?" Kate slapped the table and stood with her arms folded.

"Madame President, we can't be certain. But with the movement of Los Rojos soldiers on our border and the sudden absence of the Mexican Army's Chief of Staff, we have to face that this might be the early stages of a full blown coup."

Barbara jumped in and waved her hand at Gabriel. "Don't you think that's a bit of a stretch? Mexico has had a stable and democratically elected government for over 75 years. State's intelligence sources," she added defensively, "are the best we've got. They haven't picked up any indication that there's that kind of change in the wind."

"Okay kids, I told you two to play nice. Barbara, double-check your intel. Gabriel, you do the same. I want to be damn sure that we have the latest possible information on what's going on in Mexico before I put Emilio, and maybe dozens of others, in harm's way."

"Thank you, Madame President, but regardless of the situation in Mexico City, I still must see my father in person. This operation is too important to both of our countries to worry about a possible coup in Mexico City. However, I'm not without resources in that department. Let me also do some snooping around. If I discover any relevant information, I'll share it immediately with Gabriel. After all, I've been instructed by President Castillo to offer you any assistance I can."

"Let's hope that your President hangs on to his position…and his head. He's been a friend to this country."

Kate walked over to Emilio and stood next to him. He turned to face her and then dropped his gaze out of humility. At times like these, he was fully cognizant of her power. She said softly, "I realize how difficult this is for you in personal and professional ways. You know that I appreciate the help more than I could say, right?"

"Yes, ma'am. But it hasn't been as difficult for me as the past few days have been for you and the United States."

She tipped her head almost imperceptibly at him, then walked back to the head of the table, where she remained standing.

"Gentlemen. Ladies. Let's get to it. We need this organized down to the last walkie-talkie and pair of socks. I'll expect hourly updates. And remember, when you circle the wagons, shoot out."

People nodded their heads in unison and began to push away from the table when the President stopped them.

"Oh, and one last thing, I need not remind you of the absolute necessity for secrecy here. This must, I repeat must, be on a need to know basis. Now go."

The room erupted in a barrage of activity – muffled voices calling out orders on phones and aides reentering the room to grab-up papers and briefcases. Within a matter of seconds, the space was empty, except for Deacon and Kate. He looked at her, her eyes a million miles away. He closed the space between them by placing his big, rawboned hand on her back to escort her from the room. As he watched her square her shoulders for the tasks at hand, he thought, yep, heavy lies the head that wears the crown.

But he had no doubt that she was the woman for the job. He had to make damn sure that the bastards didn't kill her before he could get her back to the ranch for good.

CHAPTER 19

Sunday, February 27
Washington, DC · East Room · 9:30 AM

Kate smiled inwardly as she put on the pearls that Deac gave her as a wedding present. From Tiffany's. The boy did good, even as a young cowpoke. Pearls for the preachers. That's what we should call a prayer breakfast.

She hurried down the stairs, accompanied by her daughter, affectionately known as number two child. It never ceased to amuse Kate that the family had taken to that old Charlie Chan routine of referring to each child by birth order. Lucy had flown in last night to sub for her daddy. Deacon had called and asked her to come to the White House a few days before the funeral, while he and Roger were attending to business at the ranch. Lucy knew better than to ask many questions of her father, but she figured that something big was going on for both men to leave her mother in Washington without family. They were a close-knit crowd and didn't want Kate to be without one of them.

Kate patted Lucy's glossy auburn hair that still hung down her back in a thick waterfall. She was a beautiful child who had grown into a stunning woman – Kate thought in every way. She was Phi Beta Kappa from UT, following in her mother's footsteps, Student Government President, varsity tennis player, and as an international studies major, world traveler. Lucy had her pick of suitors and had settled on a man, Bo Anderson. Kate had finally warmed up to him.

Bo was a few years older than Lucy, but that wasn't the issue. Kate wasn't sure that he and Lucy shared the same values. Bo now headed his family's oil business, mostly drilling and refining, and he ran with a fast and loose crowd. But through the eight years of the marriage, Kate witnessed Bo's devotion to Lucy and their two children. He was a wonderful father to their five-year old twins, Joy and Josh. Kate had tried to dissuade Lucy from that traditional alliteration, but even that seemed a sweet thing now. Well, admittedly, there wasn't much that Lucy could do that Kate wouldn't find a way to think was perfect.

Bo ran Anderson Oil with a firm hand – well organized and smart. The business had survived the recent recession when many others in Houston did not. Their home in River Oaks had all the trappings of wealth, but it was warm and welcoming, not pretentious – something else Lucy did right. And Bo's support allowed Lucy to come to Washington without the kids when Kate needed her. Bo never stood in the way of mother and daughter, another reason that Kate softened toward him. Bo's politics might still be a little to the right for Kate's liking, but even there the MacIntyre's family influence had had a mellowing effect. Besides, having the President of the United States as your mother-in-law does have its perks.

Ezra Jefferson tried to stand apart from the remaining few members of the clergy straggling in as he awaited the President to descend the grand stairway. Normally Kate would have taken the elevator with Lucy, but like kabuki, every step that the President takes in public must be scripted. Lucy bolted to him when she saw him and gave him a big hug, which he returned stiffly, while keeping a direct eye on the President. "Ezra great to see you."

Ezra looked at both of them fondly and simply said, "And you. Now, Madame President, the East Room awaits."

As they traversed the Cross Hall, Ezra interjected, "Fortunately, this is your only scheduled event today, so you won't be leaving the White House."

"I know, Ezra. I am easier to corral when I'm inside. Actually, I'm surprised to see you here. It's Sunday, as you said the schedule is pretty light, and you haven't had a day off since, well since Tuesday, I'd guess. Don't you need to catch a break?"

"Actually, Madame President, I am with you for the duration."

"What about Mattie? She surely misses you."

"Mattie knew what she was signing on to when she married me. But I appreciate the concern. Now, shall we go pray?"

"Sure. If both eyes are open."

Kate led Lucy into the East Room, followed by Ezra, and she proceeded directly to her table, shaking hands and extending hugs along the way.

As she was taking her seat, Sy Lippman, her Press Secretary, came hustling over to her.

"Madame President, it's urgent that I have a moment with you in private."

"Now?"

"Yes, please."

His tone left her no doubt that she should go. Kate rose, made some excuse to her breakfast companions and discreetly exited the room with Sy via a nearby door to the Green Room.

When they were alone, he jumped in. "The head of CNN called me, no less, with an urgent request for confirmation. They intend to go live with a story in one hour, and wanted to give us a chance to confirm or deny. But in either case, I don't think we can stop them."

He paused to breathe and Kate asked, "What is this about, Sy?"

"Madame President, I am sorry to have to ask you this before Mr. Lowery gets here, but I have no choice. He told me to come directly to you. Is there something in the events of last Tuesday night that has not been revealed to the public?"

She gave him a hard look and then turned pale. She looked around and was relieved to see Ezra sliding into place nearby. She also was mindful that the crowd must have noticed her absence. *So much for secrets in Washington, but a leak in my own inner circle?* Anger suddenly boiled over her usually calm demeanor. "Sy, tell me directly, dammit, what they have."

"Very little. But enough to go with. According to their source, there was a second explosive device that was intended for your limousine. It malfunctioned. Is this true?"

"Yes. Sorry, Sy. It was on a need-to-know basis, which gave us an advantage with whoever did this. The person or persons wouldn't know what we knew. Obviously, that advantage is now about as helpful as screen doors on a submarine. Dammit, dammit, dammit."

"I don't have much time now. What should I say to CNN?"

"To hell with them. It's my story and by God, I'll be the one to tell it to my country. Sit back and watch."

"But, Madame…"

"No buts. Hang around. Get yourself some eggs."

She glanced back at Ezra to let him know that she was going back into the East Room, not that she feared there were any potential gunmen among all those people of the cloth. His presence gave her a boost of confidence. As he caught up to her, she whispered, "So much for secrets, Ezra."

She regained her poise and gave Lucy a smile to relieve her anxiety, at least for the moment. Rabbi Greenberg made some nice remarks about leadership, faith and prayer, and the place for those things in the halls of government. He then asked the invocation and introduced his friend, Kate. And they were friends.

Kate walked to the podium and greeted her guests. This was one of her favorite traditions, even though politics and religion do not mix easily. Being a woman of deep faith, she prayed regularly to some higher power, but not always at church. She and Deacon found God on the winding Hill Country trails, under the bluest sky most people have never seen. She sought truth in the Bible, especially the Song of Solomon and the Psalms. Or maybe it was Isaiah's wisdom in chapter 40, verse 31, "But they that wait upon the LORD shall renew their strength; they shall mount up with wings as eagles; they shall run, and not be weary; and they shall walk, and not faint."

"To my honored guests, I must tell you that necessity has caused me to set down my prepared remarks and speak to you on a topic of great importance to our country. What I am about to share with you might even make this prayer breakfast more significant.

"On the terrible day we endured last Tuesday, when we lost our beloved Harris, Vice President Franklin to the world, we suffered a tragedy beyond all expression. We have not yet been able to bury our friend and I would have preferred to wait until after his funeral to make this information public, out of respect for the gravity of this loss."

The preachers around the room nodded, as preachers are wont to do.

"However, events have conspired to force me to make this known now, with you. The cowards who took Harris' life had more in mind. The car in which I rode was also a target, but the incendiary device did not work as they intended. I cannot fathom why I was spared and that precious life was taken, but it is not mine to know. All the resources of our country are at work to find and stop the assassins.

"You now know as much as we know, or can confirm. We crave resolution, and our citizens demand it. We cannot share every piece of information as we move forward because we will not help our enemies in that way, but I do pledge to speak to my fellow Americans as events unfold.

"For you and them, I ask for prayers for Harris's family and for our country. We may have lost one of the finest men I have ever known, but we have not lost ourselves and our determination to lead with humility and grace. That is my prayer. I rely on yours."

Stunned silence followed the last echo of her words. As one body, they finally stood and sang "God Bless America," led by Hyler Ellison who came forward to give the benediction. He wrapped his long arms around the President's shoulders and then was joined by Lucy on her other side. Lucy looked at her mother with a combination of terror at this near miss and awe at her strength.

Sy smiled. *So much for the scoop.*

After the singing ended, Ellison's prayer was brief. "Grace and humility, God, for that we pray and long. Give us the strength to abide within your will. In the name of all that is holy and in every way it is expressed around the world, let the people say Amen."

Kate stepped away from the podium and bumped into Ezra, her shadow. "Ezra, would you mind asking Reverend Ellison to join me in the study for a brief moment, after this gaggle of preachers breaks up?"

"Of course."

Hyler rushed into Kate's office and threw down his coat and briefcase on the nearest chair. Kate stood and let him hug her. She was not really fond of the man, but under the circumstances, what could it hurt? She didn't mind thinking of one more person becoming a friend right now. "Kate, Madame President, what can I do for you? Anything you ask. I am horrified at how close we came to losing you, too. Have you been able to speak with your own pastor about this terrible brush with mortality?"

Kate almost snorted. "That man and I aren't particularly close. My fault. Not his. I could never warm up to him."

She pointed to the small sofa for him to sit and she took her usual desk chair.

"Are you telling me that you don't have a minister at a time like this?"

"Well, Hyler, no I don't, not really. But I have friends, Deacon, my family. I'm fine."

Hyler bowed in ironic submission. "All right. I won't press you on this right now, but I'm not done with this conversation."

"Why?"

"Because it's my job, Madame President. You've got your job. I've got mine. But you didn't ask me here to talk about your lack of pastoral counseling."

"Yes, of course. Now that you know more about the extent of the crisis facing us, I hope that I can count on you to help calm the wounded spirits of our fellow countrymen. Many people believe in you. I hope that you will use your own particular seat of power to support all of us through this dark time."

"You flatter me, Madame President."

"No, there is no time for flattery. I know that we have never seen exactly eye-to-eye on, well, practically anything."

Hyler laughed and nodded. He could not disagree.

"But I need you now. The country needs you. Will you set aside our differences and help me keep up the courage of America? And, okay, my courage, too?"

Kate was mortified that a tear flopped out over her lower eyelid and down her cheek. She realized with a start that she hadn't cried since last Tuesday. Hadn't even thought about crying. Geez, she didn't even like this fellow. She brushed away the tear impatiently. No time. No time.

"What do you think? Do you have my back on this?"

"Of course. And you know, we're not that far apart. Inside."

Kate wasn't sure what he meant by that, but she kept her peace.

"And yes. I would be honored to help you in any small way I can. Here is my cell phone number and my home number. Call me anytime when you have suggestions for me...or maybe need a pastor?"

Hyler stood to leave. He decided not to push it.

She helped him on with his coat and they shook hands. As he walked through the door, Kate asked, "You're on the board of Valentine Pharmaceuticals, aren't you?"

He turned back to her. "Why, yes. That's an odd question."

"I wanted to tell you that I am one of your customers."

"I'm sorry."

"Yes, I'm using the brand new, hot off the presses, SST patches in the handy dandy red box. And it seems to be working, Hyler. Maybe all the hype is true. My family has nagged me about this for years, and I am supposed to be the Role Model in Chief."

"You're trying to quit at a time like this, with all this stress? Now, that's impressive."

"Oh hell...I mean heck...Sorry. I've never been one to make things too easy. Anyway, I wanted you to know since you have an interest in the company."

"Thanks, again, Madame President." He paused and considered what to say next. "By the way, I believe in you."

"Dammit, Hyler, do not make me cry again. Git on outa' here."

CHAPTER 20

Sunday, February 27
White House · Early Afternoon

"That dog won't hunt, Doc."

"What does that mean, Madame President?"

"You too? After all these years can't you call me Kate, for God's sake?"

"Okay, Kate. It's probably some post traumatic stress after the attempt on your life. You would call that traumatic, wouldn't you?"

The President leaned back in her chair and rolled down the sleeve of her blouse. "Of course. But I think it's fatigue. I'm having these terrible dreams and my left eye twitches. That's from not getting enough sleep, right? But, whatever it is, I sure as hell hope you don't have to take any more of my blood. Doc, you have the blood-drawing skills of my beagle. Delivering my ten-pound baby hurt less."

"Quit changing the subject. Isn't it about time for your annual checkup? A day at Walter Reed will do you a world of good and will definitely ease my mind."

"Nope. Not now. Too much tumult. My checkup is going to have to wait."

"You are taking the Xanax I prescribed? And you started that new patch, right?"

"Yep, yesterday. You want to see it?"

"That won't be necessary, but I still think you should consider something to help you sleep."

The President nodded. "I'll be fine."

"I don't believe that. Especially after what happened five days ago. And you haven't even buried your Vice President yet. You have a lot hanging over you right now."

Yeah, and you don't even know about the situation in Mexico. "Tough rocks. I'm better. And I have to get back to work now." She waved him toward the door of the oval office.

"Yes…Kate. But the sooner we get a handle on your health, the better for you and the country." He gave her a tiny salute.

Kate MacIntyre raised her black eyebrows and smirked. "I'm exercising. Watching my damn calories. Quittin' smoking. Enough."

She looked back down at the stack of papers on her desk. He knew they were done for the day.

In the brief instant she was alone, she opened her drawer and pulled out a bite-sized Snickers. Calories, my ass.

CHAPTER 21

Sunday, February 27
White House · Early Afternoon

Gabriel entered the Oval Office as the doctor was exiting and gently pushed the door closed behind him. He smiled at the President as she attempted to hide the empty candy wrapper. Candy bars: the nemesis of all ex-smokers. She caught his look and smiled back at him. Forbidden fruit. But he knew better than to comment.

"Madame President, we need to get through your daily security briefing before you meet with the Joint Chiefs."

"Right. So how goes the state of the world Mr. Super Spook?" Kate and Gabriel had developed a unique working relationship. The right amount of banter to ease the tension of global meltdown. Gabriel would parry and Kate would verbally thrust, but by the time the daily briefing was over, much work had been done.

"It's not only the state of the world that concerns me. It's you. Are you feeling okay?"

Pretending to ignore the obvious, Kate's eyebrow raised a smidgeon as she swiveled in her chair. "Fine and dandy like a hard candy Christmas."

"What does that mean?"

"Oh, you men are all alike. If I were a man, nobody would say diddlysquat about my health, but because I'm a woman, a little acid reflux suddenly becomes post traumatic stress syndrome and then that becomes 'why don't you go have a check-up.' Well, I'm fine. Thanks for your concern. Now can we get down to the briefing?"

"Wait. Sorry Gabe, I needed someone to vent at and you were the designated target."

"No need to apologize. Here's the latest intel from Lebanon, and so far we haven't picked up anything that might implicate Hezbollah. But, and I emphasize but, we still are ramping up our surveillance of IRSO headquarters."

"Have the Israelis been of any help? It's been three days since I spoke with Prime Minister Golan, and he promised us the full cooperation of Mossad."

Sanchez didn't have the same knee-jerk reaction to the Israeli Intelligence agency displayed by most of America's Intelligence community. Yes, they were good, very good in fact, but even the "chosen" didn't always get it right. The 2006 war was a prime example of the perfect storm of intelligence failure.

"General Stern is sharing real-time intel with us, but so far they got bupkis. However, he did offer one snippet of information that I found intriguing. Yitzhak thinks there might be a mole buried very deep in the Hezbollah infrastructure, but the problem is the mole doesn't work for the Israelis and they don't know who the handler is."

"Gabe, I don't need to tell you how important this might be. If there is a mole in Hezbollah, we need to know who it is and for whom he is working…ASAP."

"I totally agree, which is why I've made it our top intelligence priority. If this person really does exist and even so much as sneezes, we'll be offering a 'God bless you'."

Kate motioned for Gabriel to remain seated as she rose from her desk and walked over to the door.

"Rose, could we please have a fresh pot of coffee and I'm suddenly starving. How about having the kitchen send up some chicken salad sandwiches."

"Of course Madame President. And maybe a little something sweet?"

"Sure, why not."

Turning back to Sanchez, the President smiled. "There's obviously nothing wrong with my appetite. Where were we? Oh, yeah, is there anything new from Mexico City?"

"Not since yesterday's briefing. General Vilas is still off the grid and according to our folks at the Embassy, nerves at the Presidential Palace are stretched pretty thin. Mickey thinks that State's assessment still holds. Mexico is on the verge of a full-fledged military coup and the timing really couldn't be any worse for us."

Mickey Sanchez, Gabriel's older brother had been the Ambassador to Mexico for six years – a holdover from the previous administration and one of State's best career diplomats. It was a serendipitous piece of good luck that time and circumstance had placed him in the thick of things.

"We are waiting for confirmation on one piece of intel from a CIA operative at our Embassy in Mexico City who was returning by car from a family visit in Texas. He stopped for gas about 100 miles south of the border, near Sabinas, and while stocking up on some Bimbos..."

"Excuse me?" Kate interrupted before remembering that the Bimbos brand was Mexico's answer to Hostess Twinkies. "Sorry, I forgot for a moment."

Gabriel continued without missing a beat. "...overheard two of the locals bitching about having to get the landing strip cleared because some high and mighty Army muckety-muck was flying in later that afternoon."

Kate stood and looked at an old fashioned map of North America that she had pinned on the wall next to the window. She tapped on the Rio Grande that formed the border. "I know this part of the world, Gabe. This could be important...crucial. Even if it's a one in a million chance that places General Vilas with Los Rojos, then we might be able to offer some sort of assistance to President Castillo's government. I want every available asset on this."

"We're already on it. I've ordered our new KH20 satellite to be repositioned. With its enhanced capability and new facial recognition program, we should have something more concrete within a few hours."

Kate was glad to hear that the taxpayers were finally getting a return on their $100 billion plus investment in defense R & D. "I didn't know that the enhanced CCD was operational, Gabe. It could make a real difference.

"But in case, I think we'd better start thinking about troop deployments. At the very least, let's get some Marines positioned to a more forward staging area."

Gabriel nodded. "Already on that, Madame President. Edgar placed two carriers at Norfolk on full battle alert. The USS Eisenhower and the USS JFK, I believe. And as we speak, they are being re-equipped with troop carrier CH-48 transport helicopters. By midnight, we should be ready to set sail, on your order, for the Gulf of Mexico."

"Excellent. But let's not get carried away, pardon the pun, with ourselves quite yet. These are still precautionary measures for the moment."

"Understood, Madame President."

Kate was leery of letting 'the boys with their toys' get too far ahead of her. She, like several Presidents before her, had learned the lessons of Rumsfeld and Cheney. *We're not going to war yet.*

"Okay, where in the Gulf?"

"Off the coast of Veracruz. But still in international waters."

"How quickly will we be able to get an advance force of Marines to Mexico City after I give the order?"

"Two, two and a half hours tops."

"Now, I am giving you the green light on staging the deployment, but only the staging." Kate paused for a moment as she pondered the consequences of the order she had given. "Gabe, there are inevitable political ramifications in this decision. It has to be held as tight as white on rice, or it could do more damage to President Castillo's government than anything done to him by the drug cartels. The potential harm of American marines being deployed to foreign soil, our neighbor and ally, no less, could be catastrophic."

"Yes ma'am. The Joint Chiefs are being briefed in the Situation Room right now and will be ready for discussion when you arrive. I don't think that there's anyone in that room who doesn't know the need for extreme caution and secrecy."

A steward tapped lightly on the door and came in with a serving cart. "Will there be anything else, Madame President?"

"No, thank you, Monroe, except could you please close the door on your way out?" Kate never took the White House staff for granted, many of whom were second and third generation, and offered him a warm smile as he backed out of the room.

The President and Director of Homeland Security spent the next few minutes reviewing other problem spots around the globe. But until this crisis was over, it was apparent that Washington, DC, Mexico and Lebanon had become the center of focus.

After looking at the digital clock on her desk, Kate wrapped things up. "Well, Gabe, we've been keeping the Joint Chiefs waiting long enough for the leader of the flippin' free world." *Me? Whoo boy.*

"So, unless there's some other matter that urgently needs our attention, let's head down to the Situation Room."

"Yes, ma'am. Nothing that can't wait until tomorrow's briefing."

"If you would give me a moment, I want to speak with President Castillo before I face my military men. They're pushing hard for a direct response against Mexico. Or, at the very least, a precision strike against de Franco's mountain retreat. And with public opinion fully on their side, I don't know how much longer and on what pretext I can continue to put that decision off."

Sanchez, already on his feet, offered, "Maybe I can be of some help. Since we can't share the details of Operation Eagle's Nest, though I suspect a few of the chiefs may already have a hint or two about it, let me play the intelligence gathering card and hope that buys us some more time."

"Remember Gabriel, while we are a democracy and the military is subject to my final decisions, we are also a political organism and feelings are running high. Reports of incidents against Mexicans, citizens and immigrants alike, have escalated exponentially since I was forced to go public this morning with the news of the attempt on my life."

One small, oatmeal cranberry cookie later, Kate was on the phone with President Castillo.

"Armando, I realize that you are under a great deal of pressure right now. I don't want to place any additional burdens on you, but you must realize that my government cannot delay indefinitely reacting to the intelligence we have at hand. Do you have anything new to share?"

President Castillo had taken the call in his office. It might be early Sunday afternoon for him, but it seemed that many of the world's leaders were in their offices today.

He had to make a decision and do so rapidly. "Kate, one thing. De Franco contacted me and he wants me to meet with him, privately, at his home in Santa María del Oro. De Franco maintains that he has captured a Hezbollah operative who can confirm his claim of innocence in any involvement of the events last Tuesday. Speaking of which, let me say how grateful I am that you were spared. More than words could express."

Kate needed to respond carefully here. She already knew about the meeting but didn't want to reveal that to Castillo. Furthermore, she still needed to be sure that de Franco wasn't playing her. There was also the possibility that a handful of Mexican government officials might have played a role in the assassination.

Looking out the window towards the Rose Garden she responded with a redirection. "Thank you, Armando. I wonder…do you have any idea where General Vilas is at the moment?"

"No, and you must appreciate my position. If I leave the capital, even briefly, and the General is fostering a coup, that could play right into his hands."

"Armando, do you have a choice? We must have confirmation of de

Franco's innocence or guilt, and we must know to what extent Hezbollah is involved. I can't hold my people off indefinitely."

Kate let that implied threat sink in before continuing. "However, I might have one piece of helpful information for you. We are waiting for verification, but we think that we may have found your General Vilas."

"Kate, if that can be confirmed, the whole situation in Mexico City would become more manageable."

No head of state ever wants to share his own government's instability with another head of state, but Armando resigned himself to being as forthright as possible. "You certainly know from your Embassy that rumors of an impending coup are rampant. My intelligence people tell me that I've got about four or five days, a week at the most, before this all blows up."

Kate thought that she heard a crack in Castillo's voice. Must be bad. "Two things. If Vilas is behind this instability, and I don't doubt for a moment that he is, and if Los Rojos cartel has aligned itself with him, then my country could be teetering on the brink of collapse."

Kate said, "I am sorry, Armando."

"Furthermore, if Hezbollah is the puppet master, I'm not sure that I will have enough support within the Army, and even with my own people, to prevent a bloodbath."

"Armando, we will do all in our power to see that the unthinkable does not happen. But for the sake of both of our governments, I think you must find a way to slip out of the capital and meet with de Franco."

Castillo sighed deeply into the phone. "I agree, but it's not going to be easy."

"I've instructed Mickey, I mean Ambassador Sanchez, to provide you any support that he can. This is an internal affair for a sovereign state, so we will tread lightly. We don't want our involvement to hurt more than it helps. But please allow us to overtly or covertly assist you in any way we can."

"Thank you Kate. It can be really lonely at the top sometimes."

"Tell me about it." She decided to keep mention of the Carrier Groups to herself for now. She wished that she could reveal it to Castillo, but she had her own government to think about.

The conversation had gone on longer than Kate expected and she still had the Joint Chiefs waiting. After that the "Assassination Task Force" would be meeting in the Situation Room to discuss any new information or theories.

And how could she forget that she had to meet with Ford and

Georgeanne for a final discussion before calling Senator Richter and offering him the Vice Presidency.

Good thing I have the constitution of a pack mule she mused to herself as she hurried out the door of the oval office, met up with Ezra, and headed to the elevator that would take her to the Situation Room.

CHAPTER 22

Monday, February 27
Sabinas, Mexico · Late Morning

A dry wind blew across the arid landscape and General Vilas covered his eyes with his right hand as he stepped off the small Gulf Stream. His left arm hung limply by his side, from old nerve damage sustained in a land mine accident during a training exercise. He could never quite believe that he lost the use of his arm from mere training.

In his early 60s, his hair was still mostly black and his solid frame had not gone to seed, as had so many of his fellow officers. The European conquest left its genetic imprint on his skin, which was a light cocoa color and mostly unwrinkled. From a long line of military men, he had ascended to the top of the Mexican army by dint of hard work, a complete education, including a fellowship at the U.S. Army War College, and well-placed supporters from his wealthy father's sugar refinery empire.

He hadn't so much chosen the military as it had chosen him. His older brother assumed the reins of the family business, as primogeniture dictated, and that left the army for Antonio Vilas and the priesthood for his youngest brother. Vilas shook his head at the thought. They were such a cliché.

But a military career wasn't enough. He felt a personal calling to raise Mexico from decades of torpor and corruption. Years ago, he turned to the man standing beside him to help him in assembling the machinery necessary to achieve real authority, not the kind of toothless influence afforded to the military from a civilian government.

A strong gust of wind jostled Vilas' hat and it blew off his head. Before he could bend over to pick it up, the man who came to meet him scooped it up and offered it to him in one graceful motion. Vilas yanked it back and dusted it off. "Thank you, Adán. I detest this god-forsaken location. Does this wind ever stop? The landing was a mother."

"No, General. The wind is as constant as your reference to it. It is one of the many things that makes me return here year after year. You see a desert, barren and lifeless. To me, it is sanctuary. We are approximately 105 kilometers from Piedras Negras, with a few larger roads between here and there, but mostly gravel trails, cut through the foothills. No one can approach from any direction without my knowing. The winter cold and the summer heat have such extremes that few can endure it and hide from me. This is my tower onto the world."

"You make it sound so poetic, Adán. I will, as always, have to take your word for it. I do not intend to stay here long enough to test your proposition. I must return to the base at Zumpango before my absence arouses further suspicion. My adjutant, Colonel Montoya, has been fending off calls from the offices of the President and the Ministry of Defense all weekend. The cover story of my being on vacation can't hold indefinitely. I'm amazed that the incompetent Castillo hasn't demanded my court marshal yet. But my more pressing problem is when will our guest arrive? I thought that he was to be here before now."

Adán Guerrera peered out to the road that was little more than a cart path. The General studied him, fascinated by the man's beauty. How could a man so cruel and without soul, the brutal head of the most brutal cartel, be such an Adonis? When Guerrera walked into a room, men and women looked at him appreciatively, with his perfectly proportioned body and sinewy bearing. His face had what artists had studied for years – the classic ratio between eyes and nose and mouth, a golden triangle.

Guerrera trained his tawny eyes on Vilas. "He is close at hand. Patience, General."

"Fuck patience. Why didn't you fly him in and have him land at your runway, as did I twenty minutes ago?"

"Because there has been a change in personnel."

"What the hell…you are just now telling me this? You damn well better start from the beginning and tell me what would cause us to change anything of our plan at this late hour."

"Please come inside and we will have something to eat and drink. And then we will talk."

Vilas reluctantly followed Guerrera into the hacienda, if one could call it that. It was more like a castle on the Rhine, but one built in Moorish architectural style. The vast great room was like a scene from Arabian Nights, filled with lush chairs and sofas, along with priceless rugs from

Iran and Turkey. It was hard to keep one's bearings in the ever-changing landscape of Guerrera's life.

As if wished on a magic lamp, a half-dozen servants appeared, carrying food and drink to the two men. Vilas' stomach growled at the aromas of steak from the grill, sautéed onions and peppers, roasted chicken, shredded barbecued pork, and fresh poached tilapia. He relented and took a plate piled high with sumptuous dishes from other international cuisines. No tamales here.

Vilas talked with his mouth full, which Guerrera found disgusting but had to tolerate, for now. "A change in personnel? This better be good."

"I would have informed you earlier but you did not pick up your cell."

"I always turn my cell phone off when I fly." *You never could be too cautious.*

"Perhaps, that was for the best, since I wanted to talk to you in person. It appears that Hezbollah's initial contact person has fallen off the radar screen. They don't know where he is and neither do we."

Vilas threw down his fork. "Disappeared? Are you telling me that he could be in the hands of someone we don't know and spilling his guts? This could put the whole operation in jeopardy. How can you sit here and pretend everything is okay? Do you think I'm an idiot? That decent food will distract me?"

"General, I think no such thing. What I can tell you is that Hezbollah has already dispatched another agent. Other than a few hours of inconvenience, we will not miss a beat."

"You may have a few hours to waste but I must return to the capital immediately." Vilas stood up from the table and started to turn when a voice growled at him as though rising from the bowels of hell.

"General sit down and eat."

Not used to being spoken to in this manner, he almost went for his sidearm, but something in the timbre of Guerrera's voice made him think twice. He sat back down.

"When will this new agent arrive? We are running out of time, if all is to go according to plan." Vilas paused and gave added weight to his next words. "'Though we have heard of stupid haste in war, cleverness has never been associated with long delays.'"

Guerrera suppressed a groan. The General was known to quote liberally from *The Art of War*. Guerrera had been waiting for this day's reference.

"Oh yes, General. Sun Tzu, right? We will not delay by much. The agent missed his connecting flight to Sabinas and you had already taken off."

Guerrera, aware of the look of annoyance in the General's face, attempted to assuage him, "Be assured, Antonio, he will be here by tomorrow. In the meantime, we have much to discuss. Why waste this fine meal my kitchen has prepared?"

"What of their missing agent?" The General barked. Guerrera chose not to be offended.

"Our friends in Beirut have told me that they are dealing with him. I believe them. He will not be a threat to us."

"I wish I could be as confident of that as you. However, now I am equally worried that the Americans haven't taken the bait yet. We must determine why they haven't acted against de Franco and what their next moves might be. Do we have any way to assess events for ourselves?"

Guerrera was also used to the General's non-sequiturs. "You are right to be concerned about the lack of American response, Antonio. I do not have any more insights than you do. Perhaps, we should delay our plans. To use an American phrase, at this point there is no harm, no foul for us. We can still back down and be successful another day."

Vilas threw down his fork, which bounced off the table and onto the tile floor with a clank. "We've come too far. 'Rapidity is the essence of war: take advantage of the enemy's unreadiness, make your way by unexpected routes, and attack unguarded spots.' We must move forward. Our enemies on both sides of the border are in a state of confusion. We will never have this much advantage again."

A young girl of about 16 ran in at the sound. She was the one who drew the black bean because all the servants knew that their patrón was in a foul mood. As she leaned over to pick up the fork and then the plates of food, Guerrera shot an arm out and around her waist. He brought her close to him and scratched her face with the sharp nail of his index finger, causing a red welt to form. Blood trickled across her cheek. At the same time, he lifted her white skirt and pulled down her panties and spun her around to face the General. "See who I bring to my desert castle, General? Isn't she beautiful and pure? Look at her milky skin and her mysterious dark hair. I have been assured that she is a virgin. I had intended to save her for myself, but she is yours – a nice way to kill some time, don't you think?"

The girl bowed her head, shiny black curls hanging down to her waist, and she tried to bring her arms around to cover herself, but Guerrera had her pinned. She couldn't move and dared not cry. She knew the scars that covered the once pretty face and body of the last girl who had been sold to this monster and who had fought back. Drugs were not the only things he trafficked in. Guerrera's face lost all of its perfect contours, the beauty fell away, and in an instant his eyes exposed the roiling evil inside.

Vilas realized that this seemingly charming man was capable of anything, that he was a sociopath. Vilas was a soldier's soldier, trained to kill. He had heard tales that Guerrera was a savage, and knew for himself that he beheaded fifty border federales and then catapulted their bloody heads over the Rio Grande into Texas. Vilas had a sudden chill, like a cold hand had reached out to him from the grave. He had made the decision to work with this mad man; now he would have to live with the consequences.

Vilas softly declined the offer, not wanting to jab a cobra poised to strike. "I would rather continue our work, Adán. Please send the girl away. She is a distraction that I do not want or need right now."

Guerrera threw the girl aside and pushed her with his boot. She caught the General's eye as she pulled herself up from the floor and patted down her skirt, and thanked him with a terrified look.

Guerrera's face returned to its calm mask, as though it was another person who had demonstrated that the girl's life was essentially over. Guerrera didn't argue with Vilas. He decided to be gentle with him. But his patience was running thin. "I understand that there are many pieces in play. Our friends in Hezbollah have sent us a new man. We have to hear him out. That's all we can do for the next few hours. Assuming Hezbollah can convince us that the American delay is not important, I agree that there is no need to alter our strategy."

General Vilas, not assured of Guerrera's true feelings, chose his words carefully. "This American President is not always predictable, making her dangerous. Hezbollah's plan is predicated on Washington's response. Perhaps, and I'm saying perhaps, they might be looking for some verification other than the trail left by Hezbollah. The Americans are faced with two realities. One is that they will bomb the hell out of de Franco, which would be a public spectacle. The other is that they silently rid themselves of de Franco, leaving no trace."

Guerrera nodded as Vilas continued. "And either serves our purposes. Washington is off balance because of the assassination of their Vice President – Mexico City because of rumors of instability in our capital and our diversionary movements on the border. I suspect, with 50,000 of our men, and the ruse of tequila incited drunkenness causing havoc and terror, neither President Castillo nor President MacIntyre has a clue as to our real purpose.

"And once de Franco is neutralized, we can start shifting our forces to the capital for the takeover."

"General, I may have underestimated you."

"Many have, Adán, and have lived to regret it."

CHAPTER 23
Monday, February 28
Washington DC · Speaker's Office · Afternoon

The formal minutes of the meeting to consider the confirmation process for the new Vice President read like a who's who of Capitol Hill.

In attendance were:

Preston Sandermann III, the Speaker from Georgia

Congressman Ed O'Reilly, House Majority Leader from Illinois

Congressman Blair Boone, House Minority Leader from Tennessee

Senator Chester Harwood, Senate Pro Tem (89 years old) from Missouri

Senator Daniel Cooper, Senate Majority Leader from New York

Senator Lawrence (Larry) Shepard, Senate Minority Leader from Louisiana

Paula Wolfson, the Speaker's Chief of Staff

Daniel Katz, Senator Cooper's Chief of Staff

Actually that's all the minutes read. None in attendance wanted any record of this meeting, other than the necessary prerequisite of when, where, why and who.

"What's the goddamn rush?" demanded Senator Shepard of Louisiana. The Senate minority leader wasn't known for his political subtleness or drawing room language. And his eccentric habit of pacing back and forth was getting on everyone's nerves.

The office of the Speaker of the House had a window that pulled people to the view. It was on a direct line to the Washington Monument, as though the Speaker and that famous obelisk were attached by a magical power held by both. A suite at the front of the building, it was one of the few offices still remaining in the Capitol, and it was one of those sacred places in Washington. Preston held his meetings there whenever possible. He liked to think of one of his heroes, Sam Rayburn, moving around that same room. In outward appearance and habits, he couldn't have been more different from Sam, but they were cemented together by beliefs and by office.

A fire warmed the larger room of the two in the suite, making the sand colored walls appear a shaded gold. Those in attendance sat in comfortable chairs arranged in a semi-circle facing the neoclassical mantelpiece and marble hearth. The room itself seemed to have a soothing effect on people, making for more productive meetings. It was this room, in this building, facing that view that Preston Sandermann loved most of all his various dwellings. He had earned it. It was a gift from the citizens of this country, not his father and not an exactitude of his wealth.

"Seriously Larry," the Speaker interjected, "can't we keep the 'gds' to a minimum. And could you please find a chair. The President wants this confirmation process to be as thorough and judicious as we do. All she's asking is a little consideration on our parts in terms of expediting the process."

"Expediting the process? Good Lord she sends down her nominee yesterday, a Sunday need I not remind you, and expects us to vet, confer, advise and consent, and do so in two weeks. This ain't my first rodeo. My caucus won't go for it – no way, no how..."

"Oh, Larry, don't get your panties in such a wad," chimed in Blair Boone. "I don't think we should stretch this out any longer than necessary. After all, Harris is dead, the President almost had her ass blown off, and we may have a border war in the making. I don't know, but unless the vetting turns up something untoward, I think we can show the President some consideration."

"Well spoken, Blair. In times of national crisis, politics should have no role." Harwood had little or no use for the Senate Minority Leader, but the House Minority Leader was something else. They played in a weekly poker game and both enjoyed their bourbon.

"If I might have everyone's attention." Preston wished he had his gavel to get the room to quiet down. "The house leadership, both parties I might add, has come up with the following time line for confirmation of our good friend Senator Richter.

"Paula, if you would be ever so kind as to hand out the list to everyone, I would be appreciative."

Paula Wolfson, from an old Charleston Jewish family, had been working for Preston since his first congressional campaign and was now his Chief of Staff. Being a southerner herself, she appreciated the Speaker's courtly language, even when it attached itself to a cuss word or two. "Of course, Mr. Speaker."

"As you can see…"

As Paula began her recitation, the Speaker's mind raced back to a conversation he'd had earlier that morning with his wife.

"Why is this such a problem for you Valerie?"

"Preston, I don't get the rush. Maybe it's my womanly intuition, but I think the President is pushing you all too hard on this confirmation process. Perhaps, and I'm saying perhaps, there's more to David Richter than meets the eye."

"Oh Valerie, that's bullshit and you know it. He's probably the most scandal-free public official in Washington." Preston pushed his glasses back up to gain better focus on Valerie. "Is it something personal? Is there something here I should know about?"

Valerie had to tread with care and she knew it. "No, my love, it's like I said the other day. I don't trust that woman and if something does rear its ugly head about this nomination, it's your ass in a sling. If the public perceives the process was flawed, they will blame you not her."

"One second, partner," Senator Shepard interrupted Paula and brought Preston back to the moment, "I don't remember being consulted on this. Were you, Cooper?"

Preston was done with being patient. "Had you answered your cell phone or checked your e-mails, or even checked in with your Chief of Staff for that matter, you would have seen my urgent calls to try to reach you. I did finally speak with your wife and she had no idea where you were off to. So, unless you'd like to give us a detailed breakdown of your whereabouts for the past 24 hours, I think you might tone it down a notch or two."

The Senate Minority Leader's reputation for having an eye for the ladies preceded him and he sheepishly backtracked. "Well, this all looks fine to me. I guess, unless the FBI comes up with something, we should be able to hold the final vote no later than let's say the 12th of March."

Ed O'Reilly said, "Coop, some of us may need to refresh our memories as to which committees are handling this and why?"

Coop, as he was known to one and all, turned his head away from Senator Shepard and whispered something to Daniel Katz, his Chief of Staff. Katz culled through his portfolio and pulled out a memo that Preston had sent over in regard to this very question.

Senator Cooper responded. "We didn't have a lot of precedent to go on here, did we Preston?"

"No, Coop, we didn't. Please give us what precedent we do have."

"Not a problem. Seems as though the 25th Amendment's second clause concerning the naming of a new Vice President has been applied twice before in the history of the Union. And both times were back-to-back, in the 1970s."

"Wait a godda…I mean, wait a minute. I was in the House back then. We don't have to rehash those circumstances, do we?"

"Humor us, Larry. We haven't been around as long as you, with the exception of Chester here, and these are such important details. You lived it, but it's ancient history to some of us."

"Who you calling ancient?" The room went silent until Larry laughed at himself. "All right, all right. Press on, Coop."

"Actually, Larry, I was going to ask Daniel to do the honors."

"Sure, Senator Cooper. When Vice President Agnew was forced to resign, President Nixon became the first President to make use of the Amendment, which had been ratified six years earlier. In 1973, Nixon nominated Gerry Ford, at the time the distinguished Minority Leader of the House, and his confirmation took about two months. The second time the Amendment came into play was in 1974, right after the aforementioned President Nixon was himself forced to resign. President Ford, in August of 1974, nominated Governor Nelson Rockefeller of New York to be his Vice President. And Rockefeller was confirmed in December of that year.

"The first time around neither house had any experience in handling the legislative responsibility conferred upon them by the 25th Amendment. It took the leadership a few weeks to decide which committees would handle what. The Amendment simply tells us that we need a simple majority vote in both houses to confirm. The amendment doesn't even mention a swearing in. I guess we do that for form's sake."

"Daniel, if I may jump in for a second?" The House Majority leader spoke as he sat up from his usual slouching posture. "You'll note that precedent from the 70s now calls for the Judiciary Committee in the House and the Rules and Administration Committee in the Senate to handle the nomination. And the Speaker and Senate Majority Leader have told us that they see no reason to change precedent."

Madame President

"Indeed not." Preston added emphatically.

"There is another relevant detail." Daniel had everyone's attention. "Back in the 70s it was the vetting process that took the most time. In Ford's case, it took six weeks or so because he was a member of the "club" and well liked on both sides of the aisle, but Rockefeller was a little more problematic. Between his great wealth, corporate ties, and…" here Daniel paused to find the right words, considering the eccentricities of those in the room, "his personal life, the vetting took almost four months. Stories abound that Rockefeller actually told the President that he should withdraw the nomination. But Ford stuck with him. And by all accounts, Rockefeller served his country well.

"And since Senator Richter is a widower with two young children, not a man of great wealth and liked by practically everyone, the vetting process should be relatively neat. Also, I'd like to remind you that we didn't have the advantages of digital technology back in the 70s. Today, if one is an elected official, one is pretty much an open book. Secrets, personal or otherwise rarely remain buried."

"Thanks for that, Daniel." The Speaker appreciated that Daniel was prepared with his Cliff Notes version of how to implement the 25th Amendment, but he even more enjoyed, as did everyone else in the room, seeing Senator Lawrence Shepard squirm.

As the meeting broke up, Preston asked Senator Harwood if he could spare a moment. They walked together into the Speakers private office and closed the door. This room, paneled in elegant dark wood that shone in the afternoon light, also had a fireplace. Chester walked over to it and stretched his hands out in front of the fire, rubbing them together. "My old bones always seem to be cold these days. The fire feels nice."

"What do you think, Chester? Did that go as well as could be expected?"

Chester reluctantly turned away from the fire to respond. He found that the heat felt good to his backside. "Darn right it did. But with our overwhelming majorities in both Houses and Richter being one of us, did you expect anything otherwise?"

"Not at all. I don't think we'll be getting much more flak from our bayou friend, either."

"That was fun. Love to watch the ole rounder sweat. But I'm guessing you had something else you wanted to speak with me about."

"Right as always. Would you like to sit?" Preston pointed to the overstuffed leather chairs, cracked and worn with age, that he brought from the old family home in Charleston. "Let's move them a little closer to the fire."

Preston shifted them easily into place so that the old soul, whom he liked and admired, could enjoy the warmth. "What do you really think happened on the night of the 22nd? You were pretty circumspect at yesterday's Task Force meeting. I have the sense that you had more on your mind than not."

Chester placed both hands on the wide arms of the chair and eased himself slowly into the seat. "Was I that transparent?"

After the other man was comfortable, or as comfortable as an 89 year-old man can be, Preston answered. "Probably not to anyone else, but maybe us Southerners have a way about each other. May I offer you something to drink? Something warm, perhaps?"

"If by warm, you mean brandy, that would be very nice."

Preston jumped up and walked over to the bookshelves that lined the sides of the fireplace. He touched a door that popped open to reveal bottles and glasses of a variety of *medicinal* drinks. He found the brandy, poured two snifters to a proper amount for midday, and handed one to Chester. "Brandy it is."

Chester took a long draw on the amber liquid. His eyes closed for a moment in appreciation. "Thank you, son. Okay, then, if you don't mind humoring an old man, let me re-cap how I see things.

"There is still no concrete evidence, one way or the other, as to the identities of those involved. We could be dealing with domestic terrorists, or homegrown nutcases, or this might be the handiwork of some camel jockeys, like Hezbollah. But even if they are foreign born, they might have been in our country for years. We simply don't know.

"I'll tell you this. I was personally convinced that we had a lone gunman here, a Lee Harvey Oswald type. But when the news broke about Kate, well, there went that notion.

"Maybe I watch too much TV, but the old staples of 'means, method, opportunity and most importantly, motive' still apply. Look at you, Preston…"

"What do you mean, 'look at me'? Keep going, Chester. I can't wait to hear how you're going to get out of this one."

"Of course, just joshing, but on the domestic front you could be, how do they say it these days, 'a person of interest'? After all you've got a great motive. My God, come to think of it, you've got 'the mother of all motives'."

"For Christ's sake, Chester, that's not funny. Besides, as my wife likes to point out on an almost daily basis, I lack the one very basic element that contributes to motive – no damn desire!"

"I know that, Preston. Sorry. My little joke wasn't very funny."

"No shit. But what about the foreign side? Any new ideas?"

"There is some crazy stuff going on at our border with Mexico. But we don't want to jump to any conclusions. I'm still not buying the drug cartel angle. What would be in it for them? Why would you want to call down upon yourself the full wrath of the United States? Doesn't make sense. I suppose it could be some loose cannon in the Mexican Government wanting to make up for General Santa Anna, but that would redefine the meaning of a stretch."

Preston became agitated. "Chester, I was in the room with you yesterday and I felt sure that you were holding something back. I need to know. Have you heard something?"

The fire suddenly felt a little hot to Senator Harwood. He considered his options at this point. If he stepped off this ledge with Preston, he could never take it back. You can't unfire a gun. He did have a source in the White House. Maybe Preston had earned the truth to some degree. Chester stood and fiddled with a tiny book that he kept in his pocket and finally pulled it out.

"This is a copy of the Constitu…"

"I know what it is. You always have it with you."

"It helps me in times like these, Preston. Maybe I'm a little sensitive on the subject of secrets because of my home state. FDR kept too damn much from Truman, making it almost impossible for Harry to govern for his first six months after succeeding to the Presidency. My God, Truman didn't even know about the blasted Manhattan Project. Can you imagine?"

"But what does that have to do with us, Chester?"

"The President and her staff have already damn well concluded that it is not a domestic threat. They're going through the motions. They have some sort of source or information that is leading them to believe that Hezbollah is directly behind the plot. That's a hell of a specter, ain't it?"

"That can't be right. They would have shared that information with us yesterday, right?"

"Wrong. Until they have the source in their hands, they can't afford the risk of another leak. And they have a leak. Maybe more than one. How else would I have information that you didn't have? Furthermore, someone revealed to the press that the President was a target on that dark night.

Obviously they didn't want knowledge of an informant out until he, or she for that matter, is safely in custody."

"So, why are you sharing this with me?"

"I trust you and you are the next in line. You shouldn't be kept in the dark. In fact, you should get your ass on over to the White House and tell the President that she has to be more forthcoming with you. That you deserve more than hearing about things in the news. At the very least you ought to be having a daily security briefing."

"You're right, Chester. Thanks for the advice."

"Your backside is real exposed right now. Not only figuratively. Literally."

"Valerie keeps telling me the same thing."

Preston took a moment to process everything that he had heard. Then he rose, walked across to Chester's chair and held out his arm to give the older Senator a hand up from his seat. "Thanks for making a very difficult decision, Chester, about sharing information from your leak. Trust is a rare commodity in this city and I'm in your debt."

Harwood laughed. "Did I say that I knew anything about a leak? Me? Never."

CHAPTER 24

Monday, February 28
Bandera, Texas · Hill Country · Mid-Afternoon CST

"**H**oly shit." Deacon leaped off his front porch and ran across a wide field to the hub of activity taking place right next to his bullpen.

"Inca, you can't put anything this close to Mac. He will knock over the fence and make mincemeat of you and your equipment. You have to find another place to set up."

The Army Ranger, broad shouldered and thick necked, wasn't the kind of man to be scared by much of anything and he had ignored the bull. The bull was, however, taking a great interest in him. "Yes sir. I guess we haven't been around too many bulls. I thought that they were all sorta' like Ferdinand."

"Not damn hardly." Deacon knew from Roger that Ranger training was one of the most extensive available to the select few American soldiers who qualified for the Ranger Indoctrination Program. It took years to become Ranger qualified and still their training was never finished. However, despite the rigors of that training, from running full out for 12 miles with a 75-pound sack, to halo jumps, hostage rescue and wilderness survival, few had been made aware of the real danger a bull presented.

Inca was of Peruvian descent and looked like his Indian ancestors, thus the nickname. His skin was the color of smoke and his hair was the burnished black that appeared on the purest of indigenous people. He was famed for his ability to run over any kind of terrain, and run fast. The high Andes Mountains must still echo in his blood because altitudes had no effect on him, making him the perfect candidate for halo drops and rugged peaks. He had an otherworldly stillness within him and he looked solemnly at Deacon. He understood why they had unnerved this man and didn't want to make things worse.

Deacon removed his hat and rubbed his head. It felt like these people were taking over every inch of the ranch and they were driving him crazy, but he had to cooperate, up to a point. Mac was another story. They thought they were tough guys. Let Mac get a hold of them. Bulls could be some of the fiercest creatures on earth.

Deacon, Jr., known as Brother by family, friends, and associates, alike, came bounding out of the house at the sound of his father's voice. Deacon rarely raised his voice. He got people's attention by power of his personality, not by the volume of his words. Hearing him yell at the men out in the field was a real oddity.

"Hey, Pops. What's going on? Can I help?"

Deacon slapped his hat on his thigh to knock the dust off the brim. "You sure as hell can. Stay out here for me and protect these tough guys from Mac. They think he's Ferdinand for God's sake."

"Sure, Pops. Take it easy." Brother put his arm around his father's shoulders and led him out of hearing distance. "Look, they won't be here much longer. Are you feeling a little bit competitive with these guys? You know Green Beret to Ranger?"

"Oh, hell no. These are the country's finest. I know that. It's that…"

"…Your sandbox has been invaded?"

Deacon was embarrassed by the admission. His oldest son and he were connected by blood and proclivities and they could always see through each other. "Okay, okay. Leave an old man alone, wouldya'? These are the people I want across the border for us. I want them to get going."

"I'll stay until they leave, Pops. Butch has his hands full with running the ranch and keeping the livestock out of harm's way. He's off on his bike, managing the lower herd. The kids are with Maryanne and the law firm sort of runs on autopilot when I'm away. Glad I got here when I did."

Deacon pounded Brother on the back. "Me, too. Thanks, son. With your sister in Washington, it was starting to feel strange around here. Where is your other brother?"

"He's in the barn with Luigi and Bootsie, putting together their packs and provisions."

"Okay. Would you mind telling him that the conference call is in 20 minutes?"

"Yep. I'll go get him now."

Deacon stepped up onto the wide veranda of the white limestone house and sat in one of the many rockers placed around three sides of the house. He laughed to himself when he thought of the Governor's plane touching down yesterday right out on the landing strip across the field that would be nothing but wildflowers in a month or so. High on the Edwards Plateau, Aguila was covered with streams and hardwood bottom lands, and its rocky hills supported an amazing variety of shrubs and vines that sheltered and fed all kinds of critters. As far as Deacon was concerned, he had the best view in the Hill Country.

Governor Douglas had alighted, looking uncomfortable to be on a working ranch. He had never been invited to Aguila. Too bad they had to start now. That man was smarmy.

When he spied the press corps in waiting, the smile returned to his face. The guy was a hound for the camera. Roger handled him like a pro, leading him to the reporters for all the photo ops he could ever want, and then taking him out to Eagle Pass and Del Río to assess the situations there.

It was a perfect excuse to calm down Douglas. Kate had called and asked him to meet with Roger, as her representative. There was no love lost between Douglas and Kate, but when the President asks a favor, especially from one of her party members, you do it. And he liked feeling in the know. She assured him that the press would be there in droves and that their visit to the border towns would pacify the public in Texas. For her, it also had the added benefit of keeping the press away from the ranch after that first encounter when the plane landed.

The level of Douglas' cooperation surprised Roger. Usually the Governor could find any excuse to alter plans, but he let Roger take the lead in the conversations with the local mayors and police departments. In both border towns, they had long experienced the civil unrest on the other side of the border, but they had never seen anything like this. Their citizens were terrified, as were their Mexican cousins who lived a few hundred yards over the Rio Grande. Whatever was happening to the south was serious and increasingly mean. No one had been hurt on the north side yet, but the brutality on the south was escalating and pushing itself closer and closer to the border.

Tales of torture and mutilation were the stuff of daily reality. One panic-stricken mother shoved her way to the front of the rope where people were standing to catch a glimpse of the Governor. She thrust a picture of her 16 year-old son into Douglas' hand as he walked by greeting people. The boy's face was bloody and swollen and his arm was bound in heavy gauze and tape.

"This is my son. He went to visit his uncle who lives in Piedras Negras. He goes over most every weekend. This time, a gang of drunken..."

She paused in fear, daring not to utter the words 'Los Rojas', and quickly substituted the word 'soldiers', "found him playing in the street in front of his uncle's house and called him over. They asked where he lived. He told them and they grabbed him and threw him down to the pavement. They broke his jaw and his cheekbone and fractured two ribs when they kicked him. One of them told him to take this extra warning back to us and then they cut off two of his fingers. Cut them off. He is an innocent child. Why did they do that?"

Douglas was stunned into silence by her story. Roger even thought sincerely so. Douglas found his voice enough to ask, "Ma'am, where is your son now?"

"He is in the hospital."

"What about his hand?"

"My brother ran out of his house and saved my son from further torture. And he found the two fingers. The hand surgeon tried to stitch them back on. We don't know yet if it will work. It probably won't. There could be infection and the nerves might not regrow. But I'm afraid that my boy will never be the same. He won't talk or eat. You have to do something to stop this kind of thing from happening to another child."

The Governor turned to his entourage and instructed them to take him and the boy's mother to the hospital. "I cannot help with his physical healing but I can have a little prayer with him. Would that be okay?"

The mother, a short, stocky woman with hair pulled back into a modest bun, nodded solemnly and let Douglas lead her to the waiting car. When they got to the hospital, Douglas turned to the reporters and waved them back. "This is private. We don't need to traumatize the boy any further."

Roger thought, damn, Douglas is doing the right thing. When Douglas asked Roger if he would like to come along, Roger shook his head. "You do this for the boy, Governor. I'll wait here with the press."

Roger and Douglas did their best to reassure the people of the Rio Grande that the President was using every diplomatic means possible to deal with the Mexican situation. They repeated the President's promise that she would support the Governor in his efforts to stop the violence from bleeding into their towns and neighborhoods. Douglas became convinced that they were on the brink of an armed intervention, something both he and the President wanted to avoid.

They drove back to the ranch in preoccupied silence.

Before Douglas stepped back onto his plane at the end of the long day,

Madame President

he shook Roger's hand and with his left arm held Roger's right elbow, an old trick of LBJ's to keep someone from backing away. "Roger, this was more than a photo op for me. You saw and heard those people. This has become indefensible. We have to protect our citizens and the sanctity of our border. Does the President know that this is some deep shit we have here?"

"Yes, Governor, she does. And she will hear more about it from me after today. Thank you for arranging all of this. I'll be in touch."

The plane took off for Austin, and would be a 15 to 20 minute flight. Roger needed to call Kate before Douglas landed so he jogged back to the house. Fortunately, his call found her near a phone in the family quarters, where she was resting after the day of meetings and conversations. Kate was the first President since Obama to thoroughly reject the concept of a personal cell phone. Even if it meant 60 seconds between landlines, it was 60 seconds of pure bliss to her.

She was happy to report to Roger that Senator Richter said "yes" almost immediately and that they had enjoyed a productive discussion about how his nomination would unfold. He understood the need for expediency and would be ready to go on his end.

"But Roger, I know that you have things to tell me, too. How did our friend, Governor Douglas, conduct himself today?"

"Kate, he came through." Roger gave his mother the border town play-by-play.

She stopped him when he got to the mother and son. "My God, Roger. That's horrible. Would you please get me her phone number? I would like to speak with her myself."

Kate allowed herself a little pleasure amidst all of the pain of Roger's story. If the Governor could be an asset, that really was good news. "Well, honey, maybe there's hope for the old boy yet."

Roger jumped up to the veranda when he saw his father. The last 18 hours had gone by in a blur. "Hey, Pops. Thanks for sending Brother with the reminder about the conference call. Monday got here really fast didn't it? I think that we're all set up inside. You're coming, aren't you?"

"Sure, Roger. Let's not keep your mother waiting."

They walked into a house that had no pretensions. It was what it was – a home where four children had been reared and a thriving ranch business had been run. The furniture was old and solid and comfortably arranged around a carved limestone hearth and mantle. A surprisingly nice collection of art adorned the walls, but it was nothing new. Kate and Deacon had always loved art and bought it even when they were a struggling young couple with not much else but four small rooms in a tiny apartment. The collection included a little known French artist, Jean Paul Capron, and the beauty of his work struck everyone who saw it. Art, both the acquisition and study of it, was one of their delights, although they didn't take much stock in laying up earthly treasures.

The kitchen had been updated with top of the line appliances and marble counter tops, but even it had an air of being lived-in. The Viking stove was a present for Deacon, who was a student of authentic Tuscan cooking, thanks to a vacation in Siena a few years ago. One of his best friends owned an olive grove in a nearby Hill Country town that produced a damn fine olive oil, which was almost a miracle since the annual blue northers from Canada could drop the temperature in the Hill Country by 50 degrees in less than an hour. Many a winter, the trees had to be pruned almost to the ground, and his friend would start over. But somebody forgot to tell him that it couldn't be done with his trees exposed to such bitter wind and cold, so he had produced the only olive oil in the United States outside of California.

Out back, near the house, but placed so that it didn't intrude into sightlines, was a nerve center for the Secret Service and for the electronic accoutrements that grew in complexity with every succeeding presidency. Within milliseconds, Kate could be connected to any head of state in any country in the world, in addition to her military and civilian advisors.

She was on the phone, accompanied by Gabriel and Edgar, waiting for Roger, Deacon and Emilio, who had been in the house calling people who could help them. Emilio spoke first, "Good afternoon, Madame President."

"Hello to all of you. I am here with Gabriel and Edgar and we are eager to hear about how plans are progressing for OEN." The now truncated acronym for Operation Eagle's Nest.

"Hello, Madame President. I can fill you in."

"Hi, Roger. Deacon, are you there?"

"Sure am."

"Good. Go ahead, Roger."

"Luigi, Bootsie, and Inca – I mean, Sergeant Louis Tartaglia, and Corporals Thomas Boutsikaris and Paul Quintero – have been here since Saturday. They will enter Mexico ahead of Emilio, who is going to travel under an assumed identity supplied by the CIA."

Kate looked up at Gabe for confirmation and he responded by mouthing the words 'already taken care of'.

Emilio jumped in. "The three Rangers will trail me and two additional Rangers will be in place at Santa María del Oro when I arrive."

If you arrive Kate thought, but she kept the fear to herself.

"Emilio, Gabriel here. Please give us a few more details about your plan."

"Yes sir. All the team members speak perfect Spanish, with authentic, colloquial Mexican accents. In fact, they sound like me. I didn't know, however, how much Roger has been working on his Spanish. He still sounds like a gringo, but he's good."

Kate immediately chimed in. "Fortunately his accent won't be a factor. Is that understood?"

"Yes ma'am." Emilio looked at Roger and Deacon.

"We've already mentioned the five Rangers who are conducting the covert aspects of the mission. I've seen the way they work, Madame President, and they are top notch. We are coordinating this from the operations center here at the ranch with Special Ops at the Pentagon."

"Emilio, Homeland has some new and troubling intel that confirms the possibility of a coup in Mexico City. This needs to be factored in with your operational plans."

"We have considered that, Gabriel. But how do you think that might change our course of action?"

"We now know that Los Rojos is likely an integral part of the coup attempt. We can't predict how that will compromise your ability to move freely through Mexico. There are 50,000 or so uniformed thugs at the border. If they are part of some coup d'etat in the making, we don't know how it will complicate your lives…"

Edgar interrupted "…but we know it will. Sorry I jumped in, Gabe. But I need to add that Emilio will always be in radio range of the unit following him. Emilio, if I understand correctly, the three Rangers currently with you will cross the border separately and be your shadow until you arrive at Santa María del Oro?"

Roger added, "Correct, and as Emilio already mentioned, there will be two more Rangers already in place at de Franco's compound. They will provide us with eyes on the ground intel and additional backup, if necessary."

Kate let the word 'us' pass for now. "How will they be inserted?"

"A HALO drop."

Kate whistled. She knew something about this and that it was tantamount to a miracle that any one of them ever worked.

Edgar confirmed the President's response. "Yes, Ma'am. HALOs require precision and training, and not one second of inattention, but Rangers are not like mere mortals. Most Americans are not aware of their capabilities, and we keep it that way. I can assure you that Emilio will be in the best hands possible, as his shadows and those preceding him to Santa María."

Kate moved the conversation along. "Okay, then. Let's say that Emilio arrives intact to de Franco's, as do the five Rangers. How does this work from that point?"

After a long, unsettling pause, Emilio answered. "That's when I have to improvise, depending on whether or not my father is in the mood to cooperate…and in what kind of shape I find his so-called source."

"Emilio, if anyone can get your father's cooperation, it is you. Right now, he's our sole link to the bombing in Washington, and provides hope that our two countries won't be set on the road to war. But hey, no pressure."

Kate decided to be completely honest. "If there were any other option, this operation would never see the light of day. I can't stand the thought of putting you, or any of the others, in harm's way. So, keep your head about you and know that, whatever the outcome of this mission, you have my gratitude and that of the people of two countries. Even if they never know what you did, I know. Godspeed.

"Deacon, would you stay around for a minute? I'll call you back. And, Roger, don't spend any more time lying to your mother. We'll need to talk later today, too." Kate made a cut-off gesture to Edgar.

Edgar leaned back in his chair. He had been sitting ramrod straight for the entire conversation and was worn out. "Gentlemen, you have done an excellent job of preparing for a rapid fire mission with as little footprint as possible. Thanks for giving us the details. I don't have anything else to add at this point."

Roger, Emilio and Deacon sat in silence after the phone went dead. They had gotten the go-ahead from the President of the United States. This was no longer Cowboys and Indians. This was the real deal.

"Deacon, are we alone?"

"Well, honey, in a manner of speaking. There are too damn many people around here for me to feel exactly alone."

"I know, Deac. A little while longer and the ranch will be all yours again."

"Oh, hell, Kate. I'm sorry. I'll quit whining. Besides, I agreed to it in the first place."

"Deac, Roger thinks he's going with Emilio, doesn't he?"

"Yep."

"Can't you put a stop to this craziness? I need him in Washington."

"Kate, he's your son, too. He's made a good case for doing this along with Emilio. It's the only way we can be sure that de Franco doesn't pull a fast one. Roger's presence will be a clear indication to the bastard that you are serious and that he damned well better cooperate. I don't think that Emilio can pull that off without Roger. Roger lends all of this the full weight and authority of your office."

"Would you tell me if you had any real misgivings?"

Of course, Deac had misgivings. What parent wouldn't under the circumstances? But Roger had made a compelling case, and for Deac it sometimes came down to a man having to cowboy up. "Of course, I would, Katy. You're the President."

"But would you do it as Roger's father and my husband?"

"Always. Kate, I'll be there tomorrow and we'll get through this together. It's a good thing that I came back to the ranch. I can help iron out some of the wrinkles for these guys."

"You're the best ironer-outer I know, Deac. I miss you."

There was a tone in Kate's voice that worried Deacon. He didn't like the sound of the weariness there. "Okay, honey. Get some rest. I'll be there before you know it."

"I love you, Deac."

"I love you, honey."

Roger and Emilio, who had been waiting outside the door to give Deacon and Kate their privacy, saw Deacon emerge. He glanced at them, nodded and kept on walking toward the front door as he stuck his hat back on his head.

They went into the den and shut the door for Emilio to place a call.

"Martina! Hi. It's me, Emilio."

Martina chuckled. "Emilio, I know who you are for pity's sake. What's wrong with you?"

"Sorry, Marti. It's been a long day and I needed to hear your voice."

"What's wrong bro?"

"It's complicated and I can't really go into detail. But suffice it to say the President of the United States wants me to go see Father in Santa María."

"Does this have anything to do with Vice President Franklin's death?"

"Marti, I can't discuss it."

"Why Father? What's the old SOB done now?"

"Sorry, sis. Can't go into that either. But have you heard anything from him lately? How is he doing? Anything new you can tell me about?"

"No, nothing comes to mind, Emilio. I keep my distance. You know that. He did call a few days ago out of the blue, but he never got to any kind of point. Kept it general, acting like he cared about me. I don't buy it. But come to think of it, he sounded…well…softer or something. Why? Is he dying? Does he want to be a father now? That's a joke."

"He's not dying that I know of. I wanted to be prepared to see him."

"Emilio, you can never be prepared for that. Go and do whatever it is that you have to do."

"Thanks, Marti. Maybe I'll be able to talk to you more about this someday…"

Roger grabbed the phone out of Emilio's hand. "Hello, Martina. How the heck are you?"

Roger and Martina had history, something Roger had never entirely gotten over. Martina had married David, of course, when Roger decided to see the world and left her for too long, long enough to fall in love with someone else. For him, Martina would always be the one that got away. The sound of her voice made the little hairs on his neck stand out.

"Roger, is that you? Now this is getting weird. You and Emilio are in this together?"

"Well, I don't know that we're into anything, but we are both visiting the ranch."

"Okay, I won't try to figure this one out."

"Actually, Martina, I wanted to thank you if you helped Valerie get an advanced box of that new Valentine Pharmaceutical patch for my mother."

"You mean the SST?"

"Yes, that's it."

"Your mother has the SST? I didn't know that. It's not on the market yet."

"Oh. Well, thanks anyway. It seems to be doing the trick for Kate. And I'm glad. She has wanted to quit for years, even though she wouldn't admit it."

"Sure, Roger. Glad Valentine Pharmaceuticals could be of service. Give your mother my regards. She's the best President we've ever had. Please tell her so."

"Will do, Martina. Do you want to say anything else to Emilio?"

"No. Ask him to call me after he sees our father. That's never much fun. I want to know how it goes."

Martina hung the phone up, wishing she could see Roger in person. She closed her eyes and pictured him, but shook off the thought. Another thought wasn't as easy to tamp down. Her husband's daughter seldom did anyone a favor, much less Kate MacIntyre, whom she had never made any pretense of liking.

She wondered how Valerie had gotten her hands on an early package. All are tightly controlled, and the lots numbered. It wouldn't be a simple thing to grab a box off the production line or even from inventory. Recently, Martina had to tell one of her closest friends that she had to wait, like everyone else – with all the FDA regulations, it would be too complicated. But her friend wasn't the President.

Deacon walked to the stables where they kept their prized quarter horses. Best horseflesh on earth. Deacon breathed in the smell of horse and hay and it was like perfume to him. Out of one of the stalls, emerged a delicate sorrel head with a white blaze from eyes to nose. Dusty. She nickered softly at her visitor.

"Hey, there, Dusty girl. Miss me?" He rubbed her face and put his head on her neck. "I know. I'm not the one you miss. Kate will come see you soon. Til' then, how 'bout this apple?"

Dusty gently lifted the apple off of Deacon's outstretched hand and munched it greedily. He entered her stall and with a few practiced moves had her bridled and saddled and ready to go. She waited expectantly, her powerful chest muscles twitching.

Brother watched his father ride away from the barn in the distance. Deacon looked bent over and troubled. And his mother was up there in Washington with people trying to kill her. Brother never dreamed that his placid life on the ranch, growing up in the Bluebonnets and Indian Paintbrushes would turn into Shakespearean drama. At a little over 20,000 acres, Aguila wasn't huge by Texas standards, but it was big enough for a boy to ride and play in hidden meadows and forests. Maybe he would leave the law and help his dad with the ranch, after his mother had served her second term. No one should bear the weight of the world for as long as she has.

Deacon and Dusty rode together across the upper and lower fields, through a border forest of Texas Redbud, Honey Mesquite, Pecan and Chinquapin Oak, past his herds of Aberdeen Angus, dipping down to the Medina River that ran across a lower tree line of the ranch. He kept Dusty at a slow walk and then trot, wanting to savor the time on horseback. They approached the riverbank, overhung with Texas Madrone, Cypress and River Birch, blessed shade in the hot months and dappled shadows in the winter.

Dusty leaned over and drank her fill of the cold, fast moving water. Gin clear. And pure because it came from the aquifer and had a limestone bottom. Deacon thought of Kate and wished the world could see her as he knew her, atop this wonderful horse at a flat out gallop from barn to river, around barrels and back again. Woman and horse were as one. All grace and heat. When she raced like that, he couldn't tell where Kate ended and Dusty began.

Kate had raised Dusty from the time she was born breach from her beautiful mother, Daisy. Daisy survived but was too weak at first to fully mother the perfect little filly. Kate stepped in and Daisy trusted her enough to let her bottle feed the tiny newborn. For four weeks, Kate, mother and baby were inseparable, with Kate making a pallet for herself in the stall. Finally, Daisy recovered and took over the mothering duties, but never wanted Kate to be too far from her sight. That was fifteen years ago. Daisy never foaled again, but Kate and Daisy had Dusty. That was enough.

Deacon worried about Kate. He couldn't really protect her. He didn't kid himself about that. He was proud of her and glad she could serve their country in this way. But something had changed. This was different. This threat was so real. And that tone in her voice stuck with him, like she was bone tired, and didn't feel well and wouldn't come out and say it.

Deacon looked up at the house on the rise of hill in the distance. They could be happy there. No, they would be happy there. No force on the planet could keep Kate from coming home to him. Right?

CHAPTER 25

TUESDAY, MARCH 1
WASHINGTON, DC · 10:00 AM

Prisms of light spread through the ice on the cherry trees. A late snow, combined with freezing rain, had attacked the city, leaving spring in suspended animation.

As the convoy of black limousines paraded through Arlington National Cemetery, icicles, snapping and falling from the trees overhead, banged the roofs of the cars. It frayed the already jangled nerves of the President, her family, and the Secret Service agents because it sounded uncomfortably like gunfire.

The Secret Service argued against a formal funeral, preferring simple interment.

Kate mounted a protest. "The Vice President is," she corrected herself, "was my friend. There will be a State Funeral. He deserves, and will receive, no less from me. You and the Protocol Office figure it out."

They reached a compromise – they invited no foreign dignitaries and Vice President Franklin did not lie in state in the Capitol Rotunda. The funeral procession consisted of bulletproof cars, with no one walking behind the horse-drawn caisson.

In spite of security constraints, most of official Washington was already seated when the dignitaries arrived at the National Cathedral. Amelia, eyes hollow, still in shock, entered the church with her young children, followed by Kate and her family.

With Amelia's blessing, the Chief of Protocol planned the service. A string quartet from the National Symphony played Barber's "Adagio for Strings" and the lead cellist performed Bach's "Cello Suites, Numbers 1-6."

The soprano of the National Cathedral choir sang a perfect rendition of Amelia's favorite spiritual, "There is a Balm in Gilead." Then, before the final hymn of the day, in which the congregation joined in singing "Eternal Father, Strong to Save," Kate stood, smoothed her jacket, walked to the pulpit and delivered the eulogy.

She paused and took her time looking out to the congregation, and symbolically out to the citizens of her country.

"This man that we are returning to the earth today deserved to live a long and happy life. We can take comfort in knowing that his all-too-short life was rich with laughter, accomplishments, family, and friends. His wife and the children he loved will never entirely heal from this tragedy, but their pain will lessen because we promise them, here and now, that we will never forget Harris Franklin. We, his grieving countrymen, will carry his dreams forward. We will make very sure that he did not die in vain, that the enemies of our country who perpetrated this horrible act will be brought to justice, and that his family – and all of our families – will live in peace and prosperity again.

"Harris, my friend and partner, I promise you that as long as there is a United States of America, your memory will endure. You fought for your country as a naval aviator and you served in many other capacities for one so young. You have joined the pantheon of heroes who put country before self, sacrifice before selfishness, and honor before all. Rest in peace, my friend."

Kate returned to her seat next to Deacon, bowed her head, and let her mind wander. She massaged her left hand because of a little spasm in her fingers that wouldn't go away. She knew that she was exhausted, but sleep was elusive. Maybe it was the patch. Cigarettes might be the death of her yet, even the act of quitting the damn things.

The last eight days had been perilous for the country. Kate thought of the frantic calls between President Castillo and herself – the need for concrete proof of Hezbollah's involvement, mounting public pressure for retaliation, bold incursions into Texas, and a possible coup in the making. Both leaders tried to step in the way of a full-blown disaster, but peace was fragile and a dark void stared them in the face.

Kate felt Deacon's hand on her elbow, lifting her up. She heard the opening notes of the Navy Hymn, looked over at him without the hint of a smile. She was still furious about Roger's absence and no justification on Deacon's part made her feel better.

The small motorcade, comprising Amelia and her family in one limousine and Kate and Deacon in the other, drove as fast as possible to Arlington. Other dignitaries, the A-list of Washington, followed behind.

They stepped from their cars at the National Cemetery and lined up around the open grave. They prayed the Lord's Prayer. Valerie Sandermann moved in quickly as soon as the flag was folded and placed gently in Amelia's open hands. She eased next to the President and lowered her voice. "Kate, those were truly moving words about Harris."

"I will miss him."

Valerie forced out a tepid response. "Sad day for America. Such a young man."

Kate looked at her curiously. What was that tone? "Old enough to die in service to his country, Valerie. Now if you will excuse me, I need to pay my respects to Amelia and the children."

Valerie called after her, "Stay well, Madame President."

PART II

THE ARMY RANGER CREED

Recognizing that I volunteered as a Ranger, fully knowing the hazards of my chosen profession, I will always endeavor to uphold the prestige, honor and high esprit de corps of my Ranger Regiment

Acknowledging the fact that a Ranger is a more elite soldier who arrives at the cutting edge of battle by land, sea, or air, I accept the fact that as a Ranger my country expects me to move farther, faster and fight harder than any other soldier.

Never shall I fail my comrades. I will always keep myself mentally alert, physically strong and morally straight and I will shoulder more than my share of the task whatever it may be. One-hundred percent and then some.

Gallantly will I show the world that I am a specially selected and well-trained soldier. My courtesy to superior officers, neatness of dress and care of equipment shall set the example for others to follow.

Energetically will I meet the enemies of my country. I shall defeat them on the field of battle for I am better trained and will fight with all my might. Surrender is not a Ranger word. I will never leave a fallen comrade to fall into the hands of the enemy and under no circumstances will I embarrass my country.

Readily will I display the intestinal fortitude required to fight on to the Ranger objective and complete the mission though I be the lone survivor.

CHAPTER 1
Tuesday, March 1 · Mexico City
10:00 AM CST

For almost 24 hours, Jad Farrah had tried to rest. But even with 40 floors of the Presidente Hotel below him to muffle the sounds of the busy streets, he couldn't quite reset his internal clock. Funny, flying never used to affect his ability to sleep. Must be getting older he mused to himself. After all he was approaching thirty-three. The 'do not disturb' sign on his door didn't deter housekeeping from knocking twice already. Hospitality was a mandate in Mexico, much as it was in the Middle East. He pounded the pillow out of frustration and then closed his eyes to concentrate on the business at hand.

The Alitalia flight from Beirut had been long – 37 hours – with two layovers and Farrah's limbs were weak from lack of movement. His business class seat was adequate, but nothing was great after that many hours. He wanted to walk, or at least pace, but he disciplined himself to lie still. Rest was his ally now.

Farrah knew that, for others, Mexico City was one of the grand destinations, with its wide avenues and Chapultapec Gardens and colorful flowers, but it overwhelmed his senses. He found escape at this four-star hotel with its 700 plus rooms, 42 floors and international crowd, affording him the possibility of absolute anonymity, which was his greatest defense. After almost bumping into Abdel Salam on the flight, he needed privacy more than ever. Salam was in First Class but came back to Business for some reason – probably to chase a good-looking flight attendant. Farrah ducked his head and looked away and Salam seemed none the wiser.

After checking in under an assumed name the morning before, Farrah placed several calls to local contacts in an attempt to find Michel. So far he had come up empty handed, but he was a patient man and had other pressing concerns. Most important was acquiring the tools of his trade. Global terrorism had created a downside to Jad's profession. Flying with weapons, once a headache, was now almost impossible. Like any international businessman, he was forced to set up a network of suppliers in most of the major capitals of the world.

He scheduled a meeting for later that afternoon with an arms dealer, but all he could do for now was wait. He never trusted Hezbollah's Los Rojos contact, cartels were far too disorganized to suit Farrah, so he kept all of his transactions separate. He chose a little known Kuwaiti instead. The small man with the big guns had never let him down.

Hamad Montaya's Persian Rug store was tucked into a tall building on the Venida de las Palmas near the Paseo de la Reforma, an easy one and a half mile walk for Farrah from the Presidente. To stretch his legs, he walked through the Chapultapec Gardens and circled the Lago de Bosque. The day was cool and the air clear by Mexico City standards. Farrah's asthma usually acted up in sooty environments, and he was fine today. By the time he found the shop, his mood was much improved, luckily for the proprietor.

Farrah entered the store amid cases jammed with carved jade, brass platters, stained glass lamps, and real ivory. Hanging in back were the exquisite rugs for which he was known, along with passable reproductions of Louis XV desks and other wooden pieces. The wiry man with dark skin and a slightly crooked nose looked up from the counter and a momentary gleam came over his eyes.

"As-Salaam o Aleykum, my good friend." Montaya knew better than to call the visitor by any name, as his name changed with the seasons.

"Aleykum o As-Salaam, Hamad Montaya. You look well."

"Ahh, not so much so. My children will be the death of me. Their Mexican grandmother has ruined them and their Kuwaiti grandfather, may he be in paradise, would not have been so lenient. Perhaps they are confused."

Montaya saw the look of polite impatience in his visitor's face and, as was often the case, realized that he had talked far too much.

"But you did not come here on this fine Monday to learn of my troubles. I have not seen you in over a year. What brings you to my little business? A fine Persian rug, perhaps?" He noticed that Farrah's Spanish accent was decidedly French today. So, that was it this time?

Farrah handed him a list. Montaya nodded knowingly. He smiled and looked up when he saw a surface to air missile on the list and spoke in French. "You will be a busy man, it appears, monsieur. Some of these things will take me 24 hours, 36 tops, to acquire, except for the missile. That will take a day or two longer. Would you prefer Russian or American?"

"Russian, if you can get your hands on the latest IGLA 9K58 MANPAD. If not, the Raytheon FIM105 Stinger will do."

"But be assured, that will not present any problems."

Farrah answered in French. "That, my friend, is why I pray for your continued well being, and for your discretion."

Montaya understood immediately the intent of Farrah's response. "Is that all the business needs you have of me?"

Farrah nodded.

"In that case, will you join me in the back for a cup of coffee?"

"Not today, but perhaps when I return to retrieve my items."

"Do you wish to have the same model Jeep as last time?"

Jad paused for a moment. He hadn't specified a type of vehicle because he still wasn't sure of his ultimate destination. A jeep would suffice for most terrain. "Yes, thank you."

"I will drive it myself to your hotel. The Presidente, as usual? I will leave the keys and registration for you at the concierge desk."

"You are the soul of efficiency."

Yesterday morning proved to be less stressful than Abdel would have anticipated. He had missed his scheduled connecting flight to Sabinas, causing the Monday meeting with Guerrera and General Vilas to be delayed for, at least, a day. Consequently, with some unexpected time on his hands, he was in a chipper mood. He checked into the more luxurious and intimate Four Seasons hotel and after enjoying the morning buffet strolled to the Chapultapec Gardens.

Not that Beirut was without its pleasures. It still retained some of its reputation as the Paris of the Middle East. But it wasn't Mexico City and Abdel wasn't on a tight leash. He made the most of his one night in the city, visiting his favorite haunts and drinking without restraint. He had spent two years here and the city was like a second home. But his behavior in Mexico City had gotten him into trouble once before, so he kept himself from being completely debauched. Photos of his cavorting at the infamous La Toalla VIP Spa and Gym years ago placed him forever in El Escolar's service. Blackmail was such an ugly thing, so a repeat performance was out of the question, at least on this trip. He felt that he was close to snapping the leash and didn't want to ruin his chances.

While he still had his wits about him, he called de Franco to let him know that he had arrived. "I'm in Mexico City. Can we talk?"

"Briefly."

"I have acquired one more piece of information."

"Yes. What is that?"

"They have sent someone else to find Michel."

"By someone, do you mean a person who wishes to eliminate the threat that Michel presents?"

"I assume so."

"I thought that Michel was protected by the sheikh."

"Those days appear to be over."

"Ah, well then, not Michel's lucky day. I take it that this person has no idea where Michel is located?"

"No. But from what I overheard, he has good contacts here. It will only be a matter of time, I fear."

"I will be prepared."

"Good. Expect a call from me when I arrive in Sabinas tomorrow. As you already know, I'm meeting with Vilas and Guerrera in Michel's stead."

"Give Guerrera my deepest regards."

The way that de Franco said the word 'deepest' left no doubt in Abdel's mind that deepest was where de Franco wished the knife to be placed.

As Abdel was showering off the night's activities and preparing to leave Mexico City, Farrah finally fell asleep. Just as he entered a deep state of rest, he startled awake to the buzzing sound of his cell phone.

For several moments, he couldn't determine the source of the sound or then how to make it stop. Where am I? He shook his head and rubbed his eyes but the fog wouldn't lift. He put together that there was a lamp by his bed and he managed to turn it on and catch it before it fell over. He cleared his throat and cursed when he pushed the water glass to the floor, spilling all its contents.

"Yes." His voice sounded like he was chewing gravel.

"Who is speaking?"

"Who is calling?"

"Look at your caller ID, you piece of camel dung."

"Oh. Yes. Of course."

"Santa María del Oro."

CHAPTER 2
Tuesday, March 1 · Mexico City
10:00 AM CST

As soon as he returned to the grounds of Los Pinos, Vilas and his two top aides noticed the heightened security. Vilas laughed to himself. Does Castillo really think that some additional armed soldiers and gray-suited Secret Service agents will be his salvation? They wouldn't dare to stop the Supreme Commander of the Armed Forces. Vilas and his entourage barged into the President's office before one of the terrified secretaries could announce them.

The President jumped from his chair and, in that instant, his chief of staff hurled himself between Vilas and Castillo.

Vilas laughed a little too loudly. "Martin, I am not here to hurt the President. I am reporting, as ordered."

Martin did not relax his position and five soldiers also surrounded the President, weapons drawn but not pointed. "General, surely you remember the day that General Diaz walked into the old Presidential Palace, much as you have today, and murdered President Francisco Madero, one of the greatest presidents in all of Mexico's history. We will give our lives today to stop you from committing such an act of treachery."

"How dare you…"

"How dare you, General Vilas." Martin's face was dark with anger and determination.

Castillo made a calming gesture with his hands. "Gentlemen, gentlemen, it appears that we are all overreacting. Let's hear what the General has to say for himself."

Castillo pointed to a chair facing his desk and stood until Vilas was seated. His aides stood at the ready behind him. The President was not able to mask his fury.

Madame President

"General, something tells me that you were not on vacation. Where were you? Please tell me why you left your duties at a time like this."

"I was doing my duty, Mr. President. I was performing unannounced inspections of military installations on our border and I could not risk a leak of any kind. Please forgive my need for secrecy, but no one could know the details of my trip."

"Not even the person for whom you work?"

"Especially not you, Mr. President. You know there are security leaks among your own staff." Vilas shot Martin an accusatory look. "If the cartels got wind of my trip, our security in the capital would be compromised, and your very life would be in jeopardy."

"Bull shit."

"You do me an injustice. I was trying to serve the public good and the good of your office."

"Must I remind you that you work for me? We are a constitutional democracy. The military has been under civilian control for over eighty years. If you so much as step outside your office to take a piss, I need to know it. The Minister of Defense didn't know where you were. The Office of National Security didn't know where you were. It doesn't work this way."

Vilas kept his temper under control. The theater of this confrontation was simply going to buy him some much needed time. He wouldn't have to lick the boots of this fool for much longer. Vilas did not fail to notice that the President was wearing his formal sash, a symbol of power and authority in Mexico, as in most Latin American countries. *Did he know I was coming? Was there a leak on my end?* The sash was not to be taken lightly.

Castillo also needed time. He wasn't ready to put down a coup. He needed to amass much more support around the capital before confronting these traitors. He questioned whether or not to arrest the general. In a split second, he made his decision.

"General, I must take you at your word. There is mounting tension in the capital, as you well know, and the situation on the border with Texas has become untenable. I need you to perform your duties, now more than ever."

"Of course. I have always performed my duties."

"Are you returning to Military Headquarters at Zumpango?"

"I am."

The general stood and waited for Castillo to acknowledge him. Vilas' eyes darted around the room, taking in the big mahogany desk, the Mexican flag, the huge bookshelves, the lush gardens through the windows, the priceless art, the Presidential sash. For Vilas, they symbolized everything that was wrong with his beloved country – power in the hands of the weak, resources squandered by those in office, insulation from the real problems of the people, the show of power but no real moral authority.

Castillo looked at Vilas and thought of the irony of the situation. Both believed that they each had the best interests of Mexico in their hearts. Both were willing to fight – and give their lives – for what they believed. Both were willing to sign pacts with a variety of devils, some being the real enemies of Mexico. Castillo wondered…would de Franco do anything but take them all to hell? The die was cast. He would soon find out.

Vilas had no illusions about Guerrera. He knew that the man was a psychopath. But there were hard decisions to be made on the road to power. Guerrera was his. Lie down with devils, wake up with scorch marks. Vilas did not know of Castillo's connection to de Franco, but if he had, it would have come as a complete surprise to him because he thought Castillo was not capable of taking such a risk.

Castillo rose from his desk and appeared much taller than General Vilas remembered. This would be their last meeting before the battle would be joined. Man to man is how this encounter would end today. Who knew how it would end later. Neither man offered a hand to shake. They were long past such pleasantries. The General did snap a salute. Appearances were important. Castillo did not nod or smile. He stood impassively and watched the General and his aides turn and leave.

CHAPTER 3

Tuesday, March 1
Sabinas, Mexico · Afternoon CST

Abdel paced, as much as space allowed, in the tiny waiting room of the Sabinas airport. Where was Adán's man? The Aeropuerto Region Carboniferia was housed in a white stucco building about 30 feet square and could easily fit into Adán's kitchen. Abdel peered out the mud-streaked window and down a short sidewalk, lined with straggly, coned-shape junipers of its name, but no one appeared. Abdel hated to wait, especially today.

The airport was perfectly serviceable for Adán's small private jet that picked him up in Mexico City for the two-hour flight to the coal producing capital of Mexico. Hot and flat, Sabinas was well known by geologists, paleontologists, and adventurers, but it held no fascination for Abdel. He had a job to do and this suffocating waiting room was closing in on him.

The door swung open with a bang, and Abdel half expected to hear strains of "The Good, the Bad and the Ugly." Instead of a sweaty, scar-faced henchman, a small, impeccably dressed gentleman's gentleman appeared, backlit by the harsh sun. Abdel suppressed a smile. The man wordlessly picked up Abdel's small valise and motioned Abdel to follow him. They entered the dusty brown Land Rover and drove in complete silence. Abdel wondered if the man's dear boss had cut out his tongue.

The first five miles to Adán's retreat sped by on Highway 57, but the second five were almost entirely off-road. Abdel gave a silent thank-you that he didn't have any dentures that would have surely been bounced out in one of the thousands of ruts. Abdel smashed his head on the roof once and quickly fastened his seatbelt. He glanced up at the driver's face in the rearview mirror. He had a fiendish look, a mixture of joy and sadism. Was he aiming for the potholes, the deeper the better?

By the time the driver pulled up in the massive driveway in front of the house, his face had returned to its passive state. He opened Abdel's door and swept his hand toward the front door, still having spoken not a word. The door opened and Abdel stopped in his tracks, once again wondering who was on the other side.

"Mr. Salam, a pleasure. Please, come in."

Abdel shook the outstretched hand as he entered the grand hallway, the air sweet with a floral fragrance he couldn't quite place.

"It is a pleasure to finally meet you as well, Señor Guerrera."

Standing in the grand hallway at the base of a marble and gold gilded staircase, Guerrera looked like a genial host from the pages of Architectural Digest. "Now would you care for a quick libation to wash the desert out of your mouth before you freshen up for dinner?"

"Of course. And thank you for sending…well, I don't know his name as he never spoke to me…but thank you for sending him to pick me up."

Adán waved his hand dismissively. "Not at all. A mojito?"

It sounded more like an order than a request. Abdel nodded.

They stepped down into the sunken living room, and as if by magic, two mojitos appeared on a silver tray being carried by one of the most beautiful creatures he had ever seen – creamy skin, aquiline nose, hair swept back off his face – a twenty-five year old version of Adán. As they sat, Abdel thought he saw the man steal a look in his direction, but maybe not. The drink was refreshing and brisk, with a powerful taste of fresh mint.

"When can we expect the arrival of General Vilas?"

"I am afraid that you're going to have to wait another day."

"Another day? They why did you insist on my coming today? No offense, but the shorter time here the better."

"When your plane landed, did you not notice the bumpy landing?"

"That's putting it mildly. Of course I noticed. But what does that have to do with the General?"

"Nothing, if he doesn't mind putting his life at unnecessary risk. He is a brave soldier, after all."

"Risk his life? Come now, isn't that a bit of hyperbole?"

Adán sighed. "Wind shear's a bitch. Thanks to El Niño, weather patterns are changing by the minute. Take my word."

"Well, when should he be able to land?'

"We believe by tomorrow."

"Damn."

"In the meantime, I have some information that I think you will find interesting…"

Guerrera now had Abdel's full attention.

"A person you have been searching for has been found."

"Michel? Where?"

"Yes. My sources tell me that de Franco is holding him prisoner at his compound in Santa María del Oro. By all accounts, he is rotting in a cell in an ancient dungeon. De Franco is such an old fashioned sort. I have informed your people in Beirut of Michel's location."

"When did you tell them?"

"This morning."

Abdel looked at his watch. "I'll need to contact Beirut as soon as possible. Is there a secure phone line that I may use?"

"Indeed. You will find one in your room. But do you really want to wake the Sheikh in the middle of the night? If you wait a few hours, perhaps you can report that the weather has become more cooperative."

"Fine. Let's hope so. I wish that I didn't have to wait until tomorrow to see the General."

Adán turned his head toward Abdel and smiled a soft, inviting smile. "In the meantime, there is plenty to do here to content yourself." Adán rubbed a hand slowly over his own knee, picking off an imaginary piece of lint. Abdel did a double take. Was he being hit on by one of the world's most dangerous men? Did he actually lick his lips? This could be interesting.

He shook it off. Way too risky. One drug lord blackmailing him was quite enough. But if there ever were a situation where tact and diplomacy were called for, it was now.

"Adán, thank you. We cannot change the weather. I will be fine. But I think that another mojito would be nice after I freshen up."

"As you wish. I'll have Esteban bring it to your room."

Abdel wondered if Esteban were the beautiful or the silent man. Ah well. So many temptations, so little time.

After a meal of Kobi beef and too much wine, Abdel picked up the phone and took a moment to compose his words. He heard a ring on the other end, as though it were around the corner instead of 7,000 miles away. Next he heard the familiar voice of Talal, not the Sheikh.

"Why are you calling this early?"

"To wake you up, you fool."

"Go ahead."

"Did you get the information about Michel's location from my current host?"

"Yes."

"Do you believe it to be true?"

"Yes. Based upon our friend's source, we have no reason to doubt it."

His source? Had Adán told Talal the identity of the source in de Franco's camp, and not me? "Fine. I will return to the capital after my next meeting here, and will await further instructions."

"Correct."

Abdel had one more call to make. This one really did require complete privacy. He pulled out a device about the size of a memory stick, which acted as a scrambling device, and attached it to the back of the phone. He had no faith in his host's assurances of security. He dialed and was answered on the first ring.

"Yes."

"Do you know where I am?"

"Yes."

"He is aware of your guest."

"Are you certain?"

"Yes. He called him by name."

"How does he know?"

"Apparently, you are not the only one who deals in moles."

"Do you have a name?"

"Not yet."

"I need you here, along with that name, as soon as possible."

"That won't be easy."

"I don't give a shit about 'easy'. If you value your reputation, let alone your life, you'll find a way." Not softening a bit, de Franco added, "You've never let me down, don't start now."

CHAPTER 4

Wednesday, March 2
Eagle Pass/Piedras Negras · 9:00 AM CST

Capi Kessler, swiveling on his bar stool, appraised the appearance of the two men standing in front of him. "You look damn fine."

The smile on his face confirmed for Roger and Emilio, now Rick Beaudean and Billy Chesterbell, that they had indeed been transformed. Even their own mothers wouldn't recognize them now.

Yesterday afternoon was a different story. After checking into the Lucky 7 Motel they left for their prearranged meeting at the Kickapoo Lucky Eagle Casino. Six miles south of Eagle Pass and the border-crossing town of Piedras Negras, it afforded them a certain degree of anonymity by blending into crowds of over-buoyant gamblers, day and night.

They soon found their contact near the poker room at the far end of the gaming floor.

Capricorn Kessler was easy enough to spot when he wanted to be. And today he wanted to be. Wearing a Panama hat with a yellow band might seem a little obvious, but there was no time for secret handshakes or any other tools of the craft. With a full head of bright white hair and a beak nose, he looked like a heavy roller who had taken a wrong turn in Nevada and, instead of winding up in Vegas, had landed on the banks of the Rio Grande.

He walked toward them and casually struck up a conversation. "Can you believe that I would have to land in a casino that doesn't have craps? There is no justice."

That was the word Roger and Emilio were waiting for. Justice.

Capi lead them to a more secluded area of the casino, the Cazadores bar. After they were seated and had ordered their first round of longneck Lone Stars, Kessler introduced himself. He surely didn't look like a hardened CIA operative with almost thirty years of experience.

"Well, boys, what have you gotten yourselves into? Are you up to this? There are some badasses out there and you look ripe for the picking. No shame in letting the professionals handle this."

"But no likelihood of success, either."

"Okay, no offense, Roger. All I'm saying is this isn't going to be a cakewalk. An operation like this can get totally FUBAR'd in a nanosecond. Considering your high profile and the identity of Emilio's father, you could find yourselves in a shithole of trouble at the first misstep. After you leave here, I can't offer you much in the way of support. Hell, you are the President's son. I'm not looking for early retirement...or worse."

Capi drained his beer.

"Okay, Rangers. This marine isn't going to second guess the Prez. I've said my piece. Let's see what we can do to keep your sorry asses from getting' shot off."

"Thanks, Capi. By the way, what kind of name is Capricorn? An alias I assume?"

Emilio wanted to establish rapport with this man on whom their lives might depend.

"Well, if you call having hippies for parents an alias for something, then I guess so."

They gave him a curious look.

"Yeah. Okay, this is it. When my parents dropped out and went to a commune, they stuck me with Capricorn – you know the merry archer, or some such bullshit. They renamed my sister Sagittarius. My God, the crap she has taken for that all her life. At least I could make Capi out of my name. She finally settled on Terri."

Emilio shrugged. "That works."

"Well, I got the last laugh. I rebelled by joining the Marines out of high school and went to Vietnam. Isn't that a kicker? Then, when I was recruited by the CI-fuckin'-A in college, they practically went catatonic. Such an ass, I was. Good thing for me they were into that forgiveness thing. Flower power and the whole nine yards."

"Um, I know a little about rebellion. Had it all planned out. School on the continent majoring in 'Euro-trash' and then spending my allowance as fast as my father deposited it. Fortunately for me, I guess, my grandparents intervened. So it was Choate for boarding school, West Point for college, and then, as you know, the army. Later to Georgetown for law school."

"That accounts for your Anglo accent. But it must be confusing sometimes knowing where your loyalties lie. Mexico? America? The de Franco Cartel maybe?"

Emilio, never confused, started to stand and was balling his fist when Roger reached out and pulled his arm down. "I'm sure," looking at Capi, "that Mr. Kessler here wasn't insinuating anything. Were you Mr. Kessler?"

"No, no, of course not. And being half Mexican myself, I'm not one to judge. My mother was born less than 100 miles from here, in Sabinas."

"So that explains your accent." Emilio retorted now with a sincere grin on his face.

"Look Emilio, and this goes for you too, Roger, I don't mean to push any buttons, but you're going to have to take quite a bit of shit over the next few days and losing your temper over some dumbass remark, isn't going to cut it."

"Point taken. But since you've brought up the subject of my illustrious father, how much do you know about him?"

"Mostly by reputation. But we did have an indirect run-in a few years back."

"How so?"

"I was in charge of defoliating your father's poppy fields. It was a new program in cooperation with your government and we had made some progress. But then, your father was able to prove, so to speak, and the Department of Agriculture confirmed, that we were polluting rivers and water tables, and it was hurting legitimate farmers. Checkmate. We were stopped dead in our tracks. Your old man won. I think that happens a lot in Mexico."

"Yeah. I've learned never to underestimate the son-of-a bitch." Emilio admitted to himself that only his father could corrupt environmentalism to help facilitate the production of heroin.

"Well, let's not put all the blame on Mexico. After all, if it weren't for America's appetite for drugs...." Roger cut himself off not wanting to rehash that old debate.

"Capi, we hear tell that you're a magician when it comes to changing appearances. Is that true?"

"Damn straight. When I'm finished with you, your own dog won't even know your scent. One thing – if you ever try to do this again, God forbid, try to keep yourself from being photographed by every goddamn newspaper in the western hemisphere for the preceding 52 weeks. Fortunately, I've got some talent on this side of the border. I'll turn you over to them."

They stood and shook hands. Capi said something to them in rapid fire Spanish, with the perfect inflection for northeastern Mexico.

Emilio almost responded but caught himself. "Could you speak a little slower, my Spanish ain't quite that speedy."

Capi rubbed his hands together and smiled. "Boy, you learn quick."

As they faced Capi the next morning, all he could see were two bubbas with nary a trace of their former selves. Maybe the glint in their eyes would give them away, but only if you knew to look for it.

"Okay boys, lets get down to business. Outside in the parking lot is an old 1992 Ford F150 pick-up. We've done a little work on the engine so you shouldn't judge this book by its cover. She'll do…"

By the time Capi had walked them out to the truck, they were primed.

"Now remember y'all are on a hunting and fishing get-away from the little ladies. Ten days of glorious white tail bagging and bass catching. You've got your passports, hunting licenses and fishing permits. Gun licenses for two rifles and 40 rounds of ammo for each. $10,000 for each of you evenly divided into pesos and dollars. A week's supply of Drakes Cakes and Twinkies and two cases of some good ol' Mountain Dew. Beer you'll have to buy on the other side of the border. And speaking of that…"

"What no beer?" Rick playfully bemoaned.

"Then I want my ball back. I'm going home." Billy added.

"Don't think that because Piedras Negras is a relatively obscure crossing point, you have any time to spare. Once you're in Mexico, you're in Los Rojos country, and every gas station and roadside bodega will make note of your presence. Get yourselves onto Highway 57 and haul your sorry asses to Santa María."

CHAPTER 5

Wednesday, March 2
Sabinas, Mexico · Early Afternoon CST

Moments before General Vilas' plane landed early Wednesday afternoon, Guerrera learned that two Americans had been spotted on Highway 57, the road from Piedras Negras. There was very little that escaped Guerrera's attention, with his listening posts up and down the highway.

Apparently, these nondescript men stopped at a local bodega to deal with an engine overheating. Several bottles of Dos Equis later, they took off, but not until they engaged in a loud argument about their trip. One wanted to go straight to Santa María del Oro for the fishing and the other wanted to stop as originally planned for white tail hunting.

Though Guerrera assumed it was probably nothing, he was on heightened alert after his first meeting with Vilas. The General had suggested that an alternative American response were possible. Better to investigate, even if the two gringos were guilty of nothing other than trying to escape a dreary home life.

But where? After taking a moment to ponder the question he ordered the local police to set up a seemingly routine license checkpoint about 75 miles south of Monclava, where Highway 57 veered south and Highway 30 headed more westerly toward Santa María del Oro. If the men took Route 30, it could be an indication that they were trouble. Guerrera decided to be waiting for them as they descended out of the Sierra Madre Oriental Mountains, to make sure.

Guerrera also dispatched his silent driver to intercept the Americans at the roadblock. Guerrera knew that there were no parallel roads at this point along the route, so if the Americans were more than they appeared on the surface, he would have an extra surprise in store for them.

When the General finally strode through the massive doors of Adán's house on Wednesday, he was in a foul mood. The weather, the troops, the situation in the capital, the warring factions among the gangs all conspired to make his life as complicated as possible.

Abdel, on the other hand, was in a great mood. Turned out that Esteban, the man who brought him the second mojito, was, indeed, the delicious looking creature, not the scary mute. Life was good.

After making the formal introductions, Guerrera suggested they move to a more secure location within the compound. "Follow me, please, gentlemen."

Except for being windowless, the room looked innocent enough; however, it had as many state of the art security measures as the Situation Room in the White House. Money created such a space, and money was no object to Guerrera. In fact, Guerrera had instructed his designer to replicate the Situation Room as closely as possible. When it became apparent that most of the information concerning the structure and design of the room was classified and no amount of money would allow him to acquire the plans, Adán settled for a design based on whatever they could discern from public photos and old episodes of the TV series, "West Wing."

Vilas had seen the room several times before and the ego of the man never ceased to amaze him. Abdel, however, was quite impressed. Had he ever planned on returning to Beirut he might have taken a more serious look at the room for future reference.

They arranged themselves around a massive conference table, with hastily poured cups of coffee.

"Señor Salam, I know we have much to cover, but please remember we are pressed for time."

"General, I will try to be brief. There are several issues and choices you have before you, starting with the dismemberment of the de Franco Cartel…"

"Dismemberment? I like that word," Guerrera blurted out before he could control his emotions. "A thousand apologies. I didn't mean to interrupt."

"As I was saying, Hezbollah will cede the entire heroin franchise, both domestic and imported, to Los Rojos."

General Vilas looked quizzical. "Are you saying that your organization is getting out of the heroin trade in Mexico?"

"Not entirely. All we're saying is that once Señor Guerrera is able to produce all the Mexican heroin desired, and once we negotiate a consideration for trade in domestic heroin, we will cease exporting our heroin to Mexico."

Vilas tapped his feet. "Next?"

Madame President

"De Franco has vast holdings deposited in a number of banks around the world. Hezbollah will take control of those. You and Señor Guerrera can split de Franco's pharmaceutical business."

Good luck with that. You could probably draw and quarter de Franco and never get him to reveal where he stashes his drug money. "Let's not get ahead of ourselves. We'll determine the appropriate share of his assets later."

"Agreed. But remember, all is negotiable, General." In fact, a fifty-fifty split is what they wanted.

Guerrera asserted himself. "I appreciate being included in the conversation about heroin, but I have other interests. I highly doubt that de Franco would grant access to his bank accounts. However, his privately owned Banco del Republico is another matter entirely."

General Vilas focused more intently on Guerrera. *Did this man have mind reading equipment in this room as well?*

Horse-trading had begun and all three men were aware that, in the art of negotiations, whoever put the first offer on the table was often the loser.

Abdel broke the silence with a deal sweetener, one that would cost Hezbollah little, but would mean a great deal to the General. "We, Hezbollah that is, will use its considerable influence with its friends within the International Monetary Fund to achieve some relief, and perhaps even a complete restructuring, of Mexico's debt."

Vilas nodded.

They haggled for another two hours. Finally, Vilas, aware of the time, slammed his hand down on the table. "We should not be so damn certain that any of this dividing-up will take place. Don't forget that I have to be successful in Mexico City and I am a hell of a long way from being sure about that."

"Understood. Let me reassure you both that, despite the fact that this is a negotiation, we are not your enemy. The success of your revolution is our success."

Abdel looked the other two men firmly in the eye. "We have a common destiny. Please allow me to add that, for its generous support, Hezbollah will require ownership in, at least, one-third of all the American companies that operate in Mexico, once they are nationalized."

Vilas made no visible response.

When Abdel realized that this did not anger the General, he knew that they had miscalculated. *Damn. I told them we should have asked for more. He didn't actually blow my head off for that one.*

CHAPTER 6
Wednesday, March 2
Anse Des Flamand, St. Bart's · Noon AST
Atlantic Standard Time (11:00 AM EST)

Blood curdling screams and wild giggles. Those sounds, emanating from Beryl, always accompanied the approach and landing at the St. Jean Airport of St. Bart's.

The Cessna class puddle jumper from St. Maarten came in low between two mountain peaks. The pilot cut the engines, and the downdraft took the plane to the runway level and safe landing, without splashing in the Atlantic. Warning signs in English and French at the end of the runway cautioned people about low-flying planes.

The sensation was that of either a terrifying or delightful roller coaster ride, depending on the delicacy of one's stomach. Hyler always laughed, tapped the pilot on the shoulder, and asked if he could do it again. With a look, Beryl warned him not to push it. And the kids, now grown, egged on their father.

André, their housekeeper, met them at the airport. He was a graduate of the Cordon Bleu Cooking School and had taken an internship at one of the many local French restaurants in St Bart's. Unfortunately for him, the owner's son had decided on a cooking career, as well. So André was given two weeks salary and bid a fond adieu before he ever began. That would have been the end of André's St. Bart's story, but for Beryl and Hyler having had lunch at that same moment, as the boy walked out of the kitchen, fighting back tears. That was almost three years ago and André Moncrieffe never looked back.

In a matter of minutes, they pulled up to their tropical retreat down the road from the chic Hotel St. Barth Ile de France, overlooking Anse de Flamand, one of the most beautiful, white sand beaches in the world.

The villa had been a gift from a grateful congregation and staff, after twenty years of Hyler and Beryl's ministry. At first they would have no part of it, but they begrudgingly conceded to the Healing Light Board of Directors' request that they visit the property. It was love at first sight.

Hyler enjoyed the life that hard work and good fortune now afforded him and his family. Custom made suits and expensive watches were all part of the role of televangelist. But deep down, he was never really comfortable with his material success. Whenever he did have an uppity moment, Beryl was there to remind him that God had other plans in mind of a more spiritual nature.

"Hyler, pacing back and forth on the veranda isn't going to solve any problems. You haven't said more than two words since we got here. The children are all wondering what's wrong."

"Sorry, Beryl - I have a lot on my mind."

"Obviously. But since when do you hold back anything from me? And you're being very selfish."

"How so?"

"Well, here we are in what the good Lord must have had in mind when he created Paradise on Earth. The most beautiful skies and pristine water the color of aquamarines, all shared with our three wonderful children and our grandchild, and all you can do is walk around like you've got an anchor around your neck."

"Well, maybe I do."

"Hyler, you're a preacher. I don't normally have to say this to you, but maybe you need to pray to our heavenly Father and ask for guidance. If it's such a burden then he'll know what to do."

Hyler turned to the petite beauty who had agreed, for reasons he never fully fathomed, to marry him almost 35 years ago. "Beryl, that's why I married you. More common sense in your little pinky than I've got in my whole head."

And with that, Hyler got down on his knees and prayed for guidance. He asked to be led to a path of rectitude and to have the wisdom and strength and courage to do the right thing. Funny how those three elements of the serenity prayer always calmed him.

If what he suspected was true, how could he do anything but intervene. Was he crazy? Did he see what he thought he saw? Could anyone really have such evil intentions? He believed that evil existed, but this was too much. He must have imagined the whole thing.

As he was about to convince himself that it was nothing but his feverish imagination, his first grandchild, now almost three, ran over to him and asked, "Poppi, are you sick? Why are you on the ground?"

She pouted and tugged his arm. "Poppi, let's go build a sand castle."

In that moment of his granddaughter's pure innocence, Hyler realized that he had to face the truth that he had tried to deny, that something was terribly amiss and that he had to find the courage to do the right thing. God had indeed answered his prayer when he sent this angel skipping over to him to build a sand castle. How could he be worthy of calling himself her grandfather, if he refused to act on his suspicions and, perhaps, save someone's life?

But, oh my God, what if I'm wrong? These accusations, if misplaced could ruin me and nullify my life's work. Even if I'm right, who will believe it?

He rose and took the curly-headed youngster's hand. He knew what he had to do, but there was time for one sand castle before then.

CHAPTER 7

Wednesday, March 2
Washington DC · Afternoon EST

With the bang of his gavel, Senator Andrew Mutnick called the committee to order.

The elegant and ornate Caucus room in the Russell Senate Office Building was not Senator Mutnick's usual bailiwick, but because of the impromptu scheduling and importance of this particular hearing, it was the best choice available.

Its Beaux Arts style of architecture and stately ambience helped to enhance the work of the Senate's Committee on Rules and Administration. The room itself portrayed order and symmetry, with its Corinthian columns in soldierly array. Chaos did not have a home here. In this room, measuring 74 feet long and 54 feet wide, function followed form. Here was where rational thinking, studied legality and clear-headedness must prevail in the exercise of power. And power was on full display, with the eagle harkening back to its position at the throne of Zeus, as his personal messenger and immortal animal companion. The Founding Fathers chose, intentionally and well, the predominant symbol of their new country.

Rules and Administration was not one of the most sought after committee assignments, and Senator Mutnick of the great state of Rhode Island had achieved this surprising 15 minutes of fame by one quirk of history. He had been Governor of Rhode Island when its junior Senator had been forced to resign in a long ago forgotten scandal. Rather than naming another person as replacement, he named himself, usually not a long term career enhancement. But the people of Rhode Island forgave him this moment of hubris and faithfully re-elected him to the Senate for over 40 years.

Now, in what many had assumed to be a long and uneventful waning of his career, here he was bringing to order the first Senate Confirmation hearings for a new Vice President since 1975. Ironically, he sat on this very committee in this very room back on that auspicious occasion when they recommended Nelson Rockefeller, for confirmation by the full Senate, as President Gerry Ford's new Vice President.

"Order. We'll have order in the committee room. Order please. Will my fellow committee members take their seats? We have quite a busy schedule and need to get started." *Busy, indeed. How on earth do they think we can get to a confirmation vote in less than two weeks? What asshole came up with this schedule anyway?*

The aforementioned assholes were none other than the Speaker of the House, the Senate Pro Tem, Senate Majority and Minority leaders, House Majority and Minority leaders, with more than a little input from senior White House staffers. All Mutnick could do was wonder what the hell Preston and Harwood were thinking. At first, he objected to the aggressive schedule for confirmation but when the Majority Leader, Senator Cooper, had hinted that Judiciary was more than willing to take on the assignment – precedent be damned – Senator Andrew Mutnick of the great state of Rhode Island smiled and savored what he knew would be his finest moment in the political sun:

Wednesday, March 2 - Senate Confirmation hearings begin

Monday, March 7 - House Judiciary Committee hearings begin on nomination

Wednesday, March 9 - House Judiciary Committee votes on nomination and reports back to House

Thursday, March 10 - Senate Rules and Administration Committee votes and reports on nomination to full Senate

Friday, March 11 - House of Representatives votes on confirmation

Saturday, March 12 - Senate votes on confirmation

Initially Preston argued for the Senate to vote first since they would kick off the hearings. But Mutnick countered, with both Harwood and Cooper in agreement, that Richter was one of theirs. Consequently, they would need a little more time to look into his record, and they would like the courtesy of having the final vote. Either way, unless something unexpected came up, Preston would be off the hook in the "one heart beat away from the Presidency competition" in less than two weeks, which suited him fine.

"Ladies and Gentlemen, I'd like to open up this hearing on the confirmation of Senator David Martin Richter to be the next Vice President of the United States. But before we proceed, I think a moment of silence is called for to remember a truly great American hero, Senator, I mean Vice President, I mean the late Vice President," Mutnick fumphered, "Harris Franklin III of the great state of Connecticut."

Mutnick had not spent much time in the spotlight. He realized with horror that he would need a little practice to survive this experience.

The committee room became as quiet as a crypt, not a dry eye in the house, as everyone was suddenly reminded why they were there – the shocking events of not even ten days ago.

The gavel sounded again. Their work began.

CHAPTER 8
Wednesday, March 2
Bandera, Texas · Early Evening CST

Deacon adjusted and readjusted his seat on one of the Air Force's Presidential planes. But comfort was not to be his on this return flight to Bandera. His distaste for the Nation's Capital was at an all time high, so it was usually pleasant to journey back home and out of that quagmire, but he hated leaving Kate at a time like this. His gut told him that things were going to get worse, much worse, before they got better. He didn't have anything real on which to base that opinion, so he kept it to himself. At least Lucy would be a comfort to Kate while she was at the White House with her mother, but he knew it wasn't the same.

He also hated to leave at this particular moment because he and Kate had a knock down, drag out fight before she essentially ordered him to leave. "Dammit, Deac, this thing is already screwed up beyond all reason and you are the one person I can trust to do what is necessary to…"

"I know, honey, to get Roger home, and Emilio. But I should be here with you. You're in the middle of all this bullshit, and pick now to try to quit smoking? Kate, has anyone ever told you that you have seriously bad timing? I never thought I'd say this, but do you need a smoke?"

"No, I don't want a cigarette. The patch is working. And don't change the subject, Deacon. If you are not down there with your hands on this thing, I'm going to call off the mission."

"You can't do that, Kate. Operation Eagle's Nest is well underway. I'm sure that they've passed the point of no return."

"They can damn well return if I tell them to."

"Honey, I know you're upset about this, but they are grown, capable men. Let them do their jobs. I'll head back home and manage the situation from Aguila. Sit down. You're going to give yourself a stroke at this rate."

"It is not Roger's job. Remember? He has a job here in Washington, for God's sake."

Deacon knew better than to respond to Kate. He remained still and waited for her to sit next to him on the sofa in their living quarters. It had been a long day, and they both needed some calm before he left. Lucy was in the next room and he would give her the high sign when he headed out. It would be her turn in the cauldron. They sat together for thirty more minutes, having what their family always called a Quaker meeting. No need for words.

Within minutes of the plane landing, Deacon stood with Brother on the veranda in the waning light at the ranch. The air was warm and redolent with spring.

"What do you mean, Butch is gone?"

"Pops, he hightailed it out of here about two hours ago. Said he wasn't gonna' let his brother have all the fun. Total crazy words. I tried to talk him out of it, but there was no stopping him."

"What about the Secret Service? Why didn't they put the kibosh on it?"

"Are you kidding? He's always hopping on and off his bike to get around the ranch and half the time, they have no idea where he is. With over 20,000 acres to patrol, they and he have developed an understanding that he can go about his business and check in with them once a day."

"I had no idea."

"Pops, that's the point, and until now I never felt there was any reason to mention it. Sorry."

"All right, let's think this through logically. What are our options here?"

"Well, first off I alerted security as soon as I realized he was actually going through with this insanity. They've got three teams out looking for him, as we speak. But if he's already across the border, we've got a problem."

"No shit. That may be the mother of all understatements. We have no authority in Mexico, and we don't want to compromise Roger and Emilio's mission. Your mother is going to kill me."

"Us."

"Does he even know the plan? What does he think he can do?"

"He does know the plan, Pops. Somehow, he heard enough. He thinks that he can get ahead of them and be invisible on his bike. You know, he's a smart guy. He saw exactly what they were going to do and I bet he's already in the lead position. Ever since he finished at A&M and served his duty in the Marines, he's been hungry for adventure. He doesn't get enough thrills in these backwoods. We should have all seen this comin'."

"Goddammit."

Brother wasn't used to his father using profanity, ever. He heard it out of his mother's lips on rare occasions, but Pops never. For a moment, Deac's face went purplish red and Brother was afraid he might faint.

Deacon finally regained control of his breathing.

"Brother, if it is the last goddamn thing I do on planet Earth, I am going to get this goddamn family back together on this goddamn ranch and put you all under goddamn electronic monitoring."

Brother shook his head and suppressed a laugh as he kept his eyes down. His father, the calmest man he had ever known, had made up for years of watching the way he talked around his children.

CHAPTER 9

Thursday, March 3
Washington DC · Bistro Francais · Morning

The Senate Minority Leader was surprised when his aide informed him that Valerie Sandermann was on the line. He groaned. *That woman is nothing but trouble.*

"Why Valerie, what an unexpected pleasure. How can this little ol' Republican be of help to you today?"

"Cut the crap Lawrence. It's not how you can be of help to me. It's how I can be of help to you."

Shepard had been at this way too long to dismiss the Speaker's wife out of hand. Washington was a strange town and one learned to go with the flow.

"Mrs. Sandermann, do tell how you wish to help me."

"In person. Can you meet me for an early lunch today?"

Even though he was booked for lunch today and into the foreseeable future, Lawrence wouldn't miss this for the world. "I'd be deeply honored to have lunch with you. Let me know when and where."

Valerie knew the old fox thought he was playing her, but she played the game better than most. The information, or perhaps a better word, bombshell, she was about to drop on him would probably send his pacemaker into overdrive, maybe even more than an assignation with one of his bimbos.

Valerie chose Bistro Français, which she considered the perfect location, both for food and discretion. The butter yellow walls, lined with cheerful posters, and a perfectly trained wait staff, created an atmosphere of intimacy. It seemed the ideal spot to make her revelation, out of the way and, at lunch, with few of the Washington insiders that she hoped to avoid.

Georgetown's sidewalks were busy with shoppers and residents and she gave herself plenty of time to find a coveted parking place. She ducked in the restaurant a few minutes early and had her pick of tables. She found one in the corner and took the liberty of ordering herself an extra dry vodka martini. She needed to be relaxed to pull this off.

When Shepard arrived, Valerie motioned to him. He saw her martini and quickly ordered one of his own. "Anyone who orders a martini before noon is my kind of person." She tipped her head. He took a long sip of the drink and smiled at her. "So, I'm here, as requested. What's on your mind, Valerie?"

"I knew that you would be interested in something I've uncovered. Think of it as an early Christmas present."

"Why would you want to help me? I sit on the opposite – way opposite – side of the aisle from your husband. Does he know you're here?"

Shepard thought better of getting in dutch with the Speaker, Democrat or not.

"My husband rarely keeps up with my schedule. He has enough trouble with his own." She finished her first martini and signaled the waiter for another.

"I am here of my own accord. Take or leave what I have to tell you. But I think it's in the best interests of the country for you to know it. Let's say I'm a patriot." He would understand soon enough why she asked for the meeting.

"Sure. Let's say that."

"Okay, I have some information about Senator Richter, concerning his blind trust."

The mention of Richter's name made Shepard's interest soar.

"Why would I be interested in the man's blind trust?" Was this woman going to give him something he could actually use to make some mischief for his opponents? Is this why the president was rushing the confirmation – to keep something out of the public eye?

"Because his late wife's father was on the Board of Directors of Valentine Pharmaceuticals. Just because Richter has never made much money…"

Valerie made that sound like an indictment.

"…doesn't mean that he is not wealthy. He is the guardian of the trust for his children."

Shepard was beginning to believe that this was a colossal waste of time. "But there is nothing fishy about having a blind trust, Valerie."

"Of course not. But insider trading is damn fishy."

"Insider trading? Richter is guilty of that?"

"No, it's not quite that easy, Senator. Seems Richter's former father-in-law acquired much of the stock that's now in the trust through insider trading. He knew from information that he acquired at Board meetings when to buy, or occasionally sell, company stock. Over the years he became one of Valentine's largest outside shareholders. Richter is aware of how the stock was acquired, so he has a serious conflict of interest."

Shepard tried to keep a poker face. But Valerie was aware that she had gotten to him, even if she had no real proof that Richter knew anything about the stock.

And Shepard suddenly understood her motives. *She wants her husband to be Vice President and is trying to torpedo Richter's nomination. Damn.* Well, he would have to be sure to never underestimate this woman.

He didn't have anything against Richter personally, but it would feel damn good to give the opposition party's leadership a good twist in the wind, much as they had done to him the other day. He figured that nothing would come of an accusation aimed at Richter about insider trading. But he could keep things stirred up for a few weeks, with delays while the confirmation committees took a deeper look into Senator Richter's finances, and wouldn't that be fun? *Besides, who knows what real dirt we could find, if we were given enough time.*

CHAPTER 10

Thursday, March 3
Denver · Valentine Home · 11:00 AM MST

Martina put down the phone. *Now that has to be the strangest conversation I've ever had.*

She wished she could speak with David, but he would be next to impossible to reach. She paced the long living room in the house she loved. It appeared to grow out of the rock and brush of the Front Range, as though the mountain had extruded it millennia before. Built by David's father, the house was testimony to Valentine sensibilities. Elegant, but not one bit fussy, with spare furnishings and accessories, each room was a work of art, all guarded by the Rocky Mountains extending to the far horizon. The house derived its strength from its surroundings, rather than attempting to dominate nature.

As Martina was mulling over the first call from Hyler Ellison, the phone rang and caller ID indicated that it was Ellison again.

"Martina, please forgive this further intrusion. I'm afraid that I was rather oblique when I called a few minutes ago. Do you have time to let me take another stab at it?"

Martina was more puzzled than ever because Hyler was usually such a direct and forceful person. Today, he seemed old and at a loss for words. "Of course, Hyler."

"I alluded to the fact that I was concerned about something I overheard at last week's Board meeting. Let me ask you a question."

"Okay."

"Are you aware of any significant problems that occurred during the development of the SST patch?"

Martina thought for a moment. *What an odd thing to ask.* "Not really. Nothing beyond the usual fits and starts of research and development. Why do you ask?"

Madame President

"Because...David, Valerie and that scientist – what's his name – Jackson? – were talking after the meeting and said something to the effect that people had died during the early testing phase. But David said that it was for the greater good that they continued with their aggressive release schedule."

"That's ridiculous. It's absolutely not true. You misheard a conversation that, first of all, had nothing to do with you. You must have heard bits and pieces out of context. If something had been so wrong, I would have known and David…"

"Martina, I don't think I'm wrong."

"But you are."

"I heard what I heard. Let me continue and you decide if I'm overreacting. After the National Prayer Breakfast this past Sunday, I spent some time with the President in her private study. As I was leaving, she mentioned that she was appreciative of the Valentine SST patch. She said that she was one of our first customers. I was surprised since the release date is not for a couple of weeks, but she is the President of the United States."

Martina interrupted. "Okay, so what's the problem? Can't we do a favor for the President?" She thought back to her conversation with Roger when he thanked her for the SST.

"The problem is that she referred to the 'little red box'. I don't know if you've toured the plant since we started production, but the box is blue."

"Well for heaven's sake, Hyler. The prototype was in a red box. She probably has one of those. It couldn't possibly make a difference."

"Not unless there was a problem with the prototype, which takes me to that conversation I overheard."

Wait. What was that phrase that Hyler quoted David as saying? 'Greater good'? She had heard him say that a thousand times. Martina sat down as soon as she could find a chair. "Hyler, I have to go now. I'll get back in touch with you. Please don't speak with anyone else about this until we talk further. Thank you for calling…"

"But, Martina, we…"

"Not now, Hyler. I have to go." She unceremoniously hung up the phone and put her head in her hands. *What the hell? Roger brought up the patch on Monday and now Hyler?*

Two words tore though Martina's head, "Holy shit." Could Hyler be right? Was her stepdaughter capable of such an act? Roger indicated that Valerie had procured the patch in advance of its release. That's okay. But why would she get something in a red box, when the production boxes are blue? Security is tighter than a new facelift.

No. There was nothing deadly in the earlier versions. I would have known.

The room spun around Martina. If Valerie were a sociopath, could David be involved?

Martina made the decision not to march into David's office and make this absurd accusation against his daughter. But she had to do something to satisfy herself. Damn Hyler.

Panic stricken, she tried to think but had no clarity about how to proceed. As she pondered her predicament, an invitation sitting on the coffee table reminded her that she was attending tonight's grand opening of a new show by Denver artist, Frieda Harrison. She continued staring out at the mountains and suddenly the image of a man entered her head.

Peter Tate, the Assistant Vice President for Research and Development, would be there as one of the employee directors of the Valentine Endowment. David insisted that his leadership team be involved in the company's philanthropy. If she had the corporate flowchart correct, he was below Michel Hayek and Jackson Baines in R&D. She thought of Peter as a friend.

Some carefully crafted questions of Peter tonight would be a start.

CHAPTER 11

THURSDAY, MARCH 3
CROSSING MEXICO · LATE AFTERNOON

The jagged, gray Sierra Madre Oriental Mountains loomed behind them as the road descended into the flat valley ahead. They had driven 75 difficult, twisting miles from Monclova on Highway 30, and now enjoyed picking up speed on the way down. Very little green vegetation survived in the hardscrabble, desert mountains, but they had a parched beauty of their own. Still, it was good to see the straight highway laid out in front of them on the way to the small town of El Hundido. They could make good time.

"Damn, Roger. You nearly got our asses kicked back there at the gas station. Why do you always have to pick a fight?"

"I know, I know. I guess I don't get out enough. But I bet that you had as much fun as I did. Besides, with about 250 more miles to go, we can relax a little."

Emilio wasn't feeling quite so smug. "Let's hold off on the high fives until we're closer to Santa María del Oro. Probably nothing, but I could have sworn I saw one of those low-lifes flipping a cell phone as we were peeling out."

"I didn't see that." But he instantly regretted that he had brought unnecessary attention to them. "Well, let's hope it's nothing. Anyway, did I mention that you drive like a little ol' lady?"

"Old lady, my ass." With that Emilio gunned the accelerator, taking full advantage of the straight-a-way before them. Roger started to retell a story from their Ranger days that always cracked both of them up.

They stopped laughing at once when they saw a police roadblock with two cars about two miles ahead. "What the hell…"

Roger responded, "Yeah. Probably a routine traffic stop. What do you think?"

Emilio removed his foot from the gas pedal but the car didn't slow much since it was on a steep hillside. He tapped the brake lightly, so as not to make a sudden movement that would alert the police. They slowed enough to give themselves a few more seconds to make a decision.

"Dammit, Roger. Nothing routine about a roadblock in middle-of-nowhere Mexico. How far back are the Rangers?"

"I'm not sure. Let's give 'em a head's-up."

Roger dialed the SAT phone, with a burst of adrenalin that made his fingers shake.

"Luigi here."

"Luigi, we spotted a roadblock about two miles ahead, as we came out of the mountains. Which means we've probably been made. We've slowed, but haven't stopped. Didn't want to appear suspicious. Any advice?"

"One sec." Luigi communicated with his comrades by earpiece and microphone, and answered, "Keep slowing down as much as you can. Assume for now that it's a routine checkpoint and slip them a wad of dollars for their trouble. See if that works. If you sense there's more, stall them with your inability to understand Spanish 'til we get there. We're about five minutes behind and closing. These Yamahas are fast mothers."

Luigi had taken it up to almost 180 MPH on the straight-aways.

"Okay. Got it."

"Remember, as we come out of the mountains and spot you, I'll be on your right flank and Bootsie and Inca will be on your left. Play it cool."

The three Rangers throttled down and banked hard at the curves, taking them at about 100 mph. On the straight-aways, they got up to 160 mph. Luigi had been reassuring with Emilio, something he didn't entirely feel. A roadblock in these backwater mountains?

Luigi was the natural leader of the group, and it was through determination and hard work that he made it into the Rangers. He was of slight build, not quite 6-feet tall, with the blue eyes, sandy brown hair and creamy skin of an Italian poet. His superiors recognized early on that Luigi could fix anything – any engine or working machine or twisted stick found in the woods – and turn it into something usable. They also saw that people listened to him, with his quiet command presence. As he gunned the Yamaha R-1s, he realized that his Ranger days were limited, that he would return to civilian life with his wife and two sons soon enough. But not today.

Emilio and Roger slowed to a crawl and then stopped when one of the federales waved at them. Roger had already reached under the dashboard and snapped open the case for his compact, semi-automatic Smith and Wesson .45. Emilio decided to leave his hidden for the moment.

They grinned like happy tourists and morphed into Rick Beaudean and Billy Chesterbell. Emilio called out, forced joviality in his voice, "Hey fellas, how you boys today?"

He reached in his back pocket to retrieve his driver's license. The officer who was in charge walked over to Emilio's side, while the other two federales stayed close to Roger's window. When the officer saw Emilio lean over and pull something out of his pocket, he brought his sidearm up and aimed it at Emilio's head with his right hand, and with his left, gestured at him to stop moving.

Emilio complied instantly, but he stole a glance at Roger, whose weapon was tucked under his thighs. In decent English, the police officer said, "Put your hands on the steering wheel. Slowly, por favor."

Emilio finished pulling out his wallet and steadily brought it up. He handed it to the officer who was now standing by the window, his weapon still drawn but aimed at the ground. "Whoa there now. We don't want no trouble. We're lookin' for some good huntin' and some hot food and cold Dos Equis. Here's my ID. Take a look, why don't ya?"

The officer leaned down on the driver's side window and looked in the backseat and then at Roger. "What about you, Señor? Your ID please."

"Sure, man. What's up with the roadblock?"

The officer ignored him and pulled back out of the window. He waved another man over and said something to him out of the hearing of Roger and Emilio. But the officer seemed to have reached some conclusion.

"Get out of the car. Open the doors slowly and face your vehicle."

"Hang on, man. We ain't done nothin' wrong. We want to get on our way." Roger tried to sound like a guy who was inconvenienced, but who had nothing to fear. *What the hell gave us away?* He and Emilio nodded slightly. They knew what they had to do, if the police tried to drive them away. They could not get into another vehicle, under any circumstances, because at that moment, they would have lost control, and control was not an easy thing to get back. *It was the goddamned SAT phone. That was the only thing out of the ordinary and it was sitting on the back seat for the world to see.*

Before Roger opened his door, he tucked the gun under the seat, handle out for quick retrieval.

The officers pushed Roger and Emilio hard against the rear passenger sides of the truck, forced their legs apart and started a pat down. Roger pushed against his captor and twisted his head and neck, but the man was surprisingly strong. This was no lazy, out of shape local. He was the real deal. The man pushed Roger in the middle of his back and yelled at him in Spanish. Roger understood him perfectly, but said, "No comprendo Spanish. What's wrong with you, asshole?"

The man doubled his fist and hit Roger in the kidney. A blast of pain entered his back and traveled up his spine. He fought to stay upright.

Emilio yelled, "What the fuck? Man, you better stop this shit. We know people." *Yeah, and where the hell were they?*

The officers turned Roger and Emilio around and pulled their arms behind their backs, ready to place them in handcuffs. The man who held Roger lifted up his pistol and smacked him on the cheek. Roger grabbed his face. His hand filled up with blood. "Shit. You fucker. That's it, you sonofabitch."

The man, who was slightly taller than Roger, focused his cruel eyes on Roger's face and smiled. "Hay ningún ayuda para ti, comprende?"

He raised his hand for another well-placed blow to Roger's face, when his gun and two fingers flew away from the surprised officer. The sound of the gunshot ricocheted off the nearby cliffs, as the man fell to the ground screaming and writhing.

Roger pulled open the door and lifted his gun out. He spun and aimed it at the Captain. But the man had his weapon pressed against Emilio's temple. And in his eyes was the will to pull the trigger. Roger had a split second to decide whether or not Emilio could duck long enough for Roger to get off one shot, while the two other Mexican officers emerged from behind the second car and ran over.

In that instant, the Captain crumpled, a hole pouring out blood from the middle of his forehead. He was dead before he hit the ground. Emilio jerked away and yelled at Roger to get to the driver's side of the truck before the other officers started firing. Roger bent over and rolled on the ground in front of the truck, jumping up beside Emilio. They hadn't isolated the source of the shots, but they thought that the shooters were on higher ground behind them.

Suddenly, the Mexicans dropped their weapons and fell, nose first, to the ground. Roger and Emilio turned around and saw a beautiful sight – Luigi, Bootsie and Inca had fired up the Yamahas and two were pointing AK47s at the men on the ground as the motorcycles careened down the steep embankment beside the road. Inca held his sniper's rifle in his left hand. It had served him well, yet again.

Emilio leapt from behind the truck and quickly hogtied the arms and legs of the Mexican officers with nylon rope from his backpack. They made no protest, which surprised Emilio. Was that too easy?

Luigi dragged the Captain's lifeless body to the trunk of the first police car, and went to the ignition to find the keys. He popped the trunk and lifted up the corpse as though it were a rag doll and tossed him in. He slammed it shut.

The radio in the second car squawked. Luigi pushed receive and said "Sí."

Grainy and fuzzy, a voice asked, "Have you secured the Americans? We are landing..."

Luigi heard the whipping sound of the rotary blades of the helicopter, which had been flying in stealth mode. He dropped to the ground and half rolled and ran to Roger and Emilio, who had been joined by Inca and Bootsie behind the truck. "Get down. We've got company."

Faster than they could hit the ground, a bullet struck Inca's steel-toed boot, searing his toe but missing it by a centimeter, before burying itself in the dirt. Inca ignored the pain and fell on top of Roger while Bootsie covered Emilio. Luigi raised up and peered over the truck's hood. He saw the MH-75L Black Hawk land about 50 feet away in the packed gravel of the Chihuahuan desert.

"Holy shit. How did they get their hands on a DAP?"

The MH-75L Direct Action Penetrator was a super classified, specifically modified by Sikorsky, special ops bird. And as far as Roger knew, only a dozen or so were in service.

Roger looked at Luigi. "Do you know what that sucker is capable of? My God, Hellfire missiles, a 30 mm cannon, Hydra 70 rockets. Its M150D gatling gun is probably what took the bite out of Inca's boot."

Inca winced. "Ya' think?"

Luigi sat back on his haunches and delivered the bad news. "They've got us by a mile. There's nothing we can do at this point but stall for time. We can't win this one."

"Hell no. We didn't come this far to surrender to the mother fuckers, whoever they might be." Roger couldn't quit now. Too much was at stake.

"That's precisely what I'm saying. All we can do now is live to fight another day. And you damned well better do what I say. I've got my orders. Now, you stay down. I'll stand and see who we're dealing with."

Roger started to protest but Inca put an arm around his neck. He didn't choke him, but Roger couldn't make a sound.

Luigi stood as a voice called out over a microphone. "Stand up carefully. Leave your weapons on the ground and kick them out where I can see them."

Luigi saw paramilitary personnel, six in all, dressed in black with helmets and goggles, explode out of the side doors of the helicopter. They rushed to the opposite side of the truck and stood at attention, aiming their semi-automatic rifles at Luigi's head. He did not twitch.

The others stood and disposed of their weapons, as instructed. Naked. That's how Roger felt. The five Americans were silent.

A short figure finally emerged from the front of the helicopter. He jumped to the ground and headed for the truck. The pilot stayed in his seat, his Black Hawk's motors shivering with power.

Guerrera's mute driver was no longer voiceless. "Señor Beaudean, or perhaps I should say, Señor Dunham, please step forward and away from the truck. You and my employer have business to which to attend. That goes for you, as well, Señor de Franco."

Roger caught Emilio's eye, then Luigi. Luigi nodded. Roger knew what was going to happen next, unless he could think of something. The people who mattered to this man were himself and Emilio. Everyone else was expendable. Roger shook his head. He understood that the minute they left the group, the others were dead. And, as bad as being captured might be, for Emilio it would be far worse because he could be used against his father in unthinkable ways.

Roger realized that there was no use in denying who they were but he needed to stall for time.

"Because you already seem to know who I am, you must realize that interfering with the son of the President of the United States is probably not a great career enhancer."

"You make me laugh. If my career were an issue, you'd be - how do you Gringos say it? - 'my ace of spades'." Now move away from the truck, along with Señor de Franco. The head of one of your brave soldiers is in the sightline of one of my men. Come."

Roger placed his hand behind him and motioned for Emilio to remain there. He might be able to negotiate for all of their lives.

"I am coming out. Must I remind you that I am also the President's Chief of Staff? Do you really wish to bring down the wrath of the most powerful person in the world? I have found that negotiation is a far better tool for success than murder."

Madame President

"Please quit talking now, Señor Dunham. And please instruct Señor de Franco to come out with you."

"If you will let me call the President, I am sure that we can arrange terms to satisfy even the harshest employer. I have a SAT phone. I can reach her in a matter of seconds."

"Enough. I think that I must show you my intentions."

Guerrero's man spoke in rapid Spanish and one of the soldiers took aim. Roger screamed, "No. I'm moving. Stop."

The man raised his hand and the soldier lowered his weapon a fraction. Roger walked as slowly as he could, like a recalcitrant child approaching an angry father. When he was fully exposed, without any cover from the Ford F-150, he slowed even more, trying to give himself time to think. There was a booming clock ticking in his head, counting down the seconds before his friends were executed.

Across his shoulder, he felt the stinging whistle of...what? A bullet? What the...? The face of the former mute exploded in a blur of blood and bone. The man's body collapsed, practically headless. Roger dove and crawled under the truck behind him.

The scene played out before him like a medieval joust, but with far more deadly weapons. He heard the rapid report of AK 47s, a sniper rifle, and ...the full-throated rumble of a motorcycle? From where?

Luigi called out, "Stay down, Roger. Bootsie, move in front and cover me while I go left and get to the first police car. Inca, stay with Emilio."

The motorcycle driver stopped and spun around, kicking up debris and gravel along the shoulder of the road. He balanced the bike with his right leg as the rear wheel skidded and downshifted as soon as the Yamaha righted itself. Best turn in the business. He lurched forward, firing his Walther PPK as he headed toward the police cars.

Inca, still shielded by the truck, stood and took down two soldiers, killing one and wounding the other as they backed up to the helicopter. Bootsie fired round after round to cover Luigi as he crawled to the second police car. One more soldier went down.

Bootsie, the tall, slim son of a Greek fisherman whom he had not seen in years, was born to be a Ranger. His stealth, along with his pinpoint accuracy with any kind of weapon, made him an asset in almost every situation. His black eyes were usually hidden under thick eyebrows, and he rarely spoke before spoken to. His economy of words earned him another nickname, Lippy, from some of his buddies. A loner, with few friends, he knew that the Rangers were his true family, so he would damn well protect them with whatever it took.

Three soldiers made it to the relative safety of the helicopter and the pilot revved the motors. The blades whirred, turning faster and faster. It would assume air speed in seconds. Luigi stood, aimed, and hit the side of the pilot's head, who slumped forward in his seat, his dead body pulling against the seat belt. The blades slowed. The engines stopped.

Luigi motioned for Bootsie and Inca to come forward and the motorcycle careened in from the right. Luigi turned and faced the driver, holding his pistol shoulder high. The driver slammed on the brakes and skidded to a stop. He dropped his weapon and held up his arms. Luigi ran toward him, and the driver unsnapped his helmet. His face was covered with a protective ski mask. Luigi gestured up and down with his gun for the driver to remove his mask.

All hell broke loose again. The sound of horns, gunshots, and motors came at them from Luigi's left. Two black SUVs slid to a stop and five soldiers poured out of each vehicle, armed to the teeth. Rocket launchers, Uzis, grenades, sidearms, AK47s, and flame throwers. Luigi didn't know whether to laugh or cry. And he thought he had regained control.

One of the soldiers ran up and Luigi trained his gun on him. "Sir. Do not shoot. Señor de Franco sent us to help you. But it appears that we got here too late. Lucky for you, the motorcycle could make better time."

Emilio yelled, "My father sent you? How did he know?"

The motorcycle driver finished pulling off his mask. He answered, "Because I told him."

Roger gaped at his little brother. "Butch?"

CHAPTER 12

Friday, March 4
Herzliya, Israel · 10:00 AM Israeli Time · 4:00 AM EST

General Stern waited for the secure line at the home of Gabriel Sanchez to ring through. It was 10:00 AM, Israel time and six hours earlier in Washington, DC. Stern knew that he would be waking up his American counterpart in the war on terrorism, but that could not be helped. He had waited as long as he dared to deliver this vital piece of information to the Director of Homeland Security.

On the northern coastal edge of Tel Aviv, Herzliya was home to the headquarters of Mossad, where over 1,200 people worked twenty-four hours a day, even on the Jewish Sabbath, ensuring the fragile safety of the Jewish State of Israel.

A Sabra, Stern's family had lived in Israel since before the Balfour Declaration of 1917, which promised that the British government would back the establishment of a Jewish homeland in Palestine, in order to win the support of the Jewish community in England and throughout the Commonwealth. Immediately after the end of WWI, England began tacitly, but eventually overtly, backing out of the deal because of the discovery of oil on the Arabian Peninsula. The British Foreign Office also happened to be rabidly anti-Semitic. Lord Balfour had to sweat blood to get the resolution passed, and it had few other supporters. Even Sir Winston Churchill, long a Zionist supporter, had to acquiesce to the prevailing winds of change. Oil and the control of oil pipelines checkmated any Jewish aspirations.

The Sabras, those early Zionists, believed that they and the Arabs would live in harmony and would farm the land and create a secular democratic society that would be the envy of the world. As Stern gazed out his window on the Sidna Ali Mosque in the long depopulated Arab village of Al-Haram, he knew the dream had failed. Try as he might, Stern could never quite overcome his generation's genetic suspicion of everything English. He found it especially ironic that it was an English contact who had delivered the piece of information that he was about to present to Sanchez.

Gabriel's voice, still raspy from a deep slumber, became instantly alert when he recognized the caller on his secure private line. "General Stern?"

"Yes, Gabriel."

"Give me a moment." Gabriel slipped out of bed and went to his study off the bedroom. His wife, used to middle of the night calls, did not stir. "Yes, Yitzak, I am ready."

"Forgive me for the hour, but I knew that you would want to have this information."

"Of course."

"Does the name Abdel Salam mean anything to you?"

Gabriel paused and worked his way through the name bank in his brain. Nothing. "No, Yitzak. Should it?"

"As you know, we have long believed that there might be a double agent working inside the ISRO. But we didn't know who was pulling his strings. Now, thanks to our British, um, friends at MI-16 and some superior spy craft on their part, we know the name of the person…"

"This Abdel Salam?"

"…yes, and to whom he is delivering inside information about Hezbollah. Here's where it becomes really interesting."

"I can only imagine."

"The organization for whom he works is a Mexican drug cartel run by one Federico de Franco."

"Oh shit."

"I thought you might appreciate the connection. And it gets even better. His position in the ISRO is second to Talal El-Hussen, Nasrallah's right hand man."

"Yitzak, you're telling me that de Franco has infiltrated that deeply into the Hezbollah infrastructure? My God, we've all been trying to do that, without success, for years. Of course, you realize how valuable an asset we now have. If this is true, this intelligence could lead us to verify de Franco's claims that he has been set up."

"What are you talking about?"

"Oh. Well, okay. Here it is. De Franco, through his son, told us that

Madame President

Hezbollah was behind the assassination of our Vice President and the attempted assassination of our President. A fact, I'll assume, you already know. We couldn't verify it through any of our usual sources. We thought that some of the evidence pointed to de Franco and that he was simply trying to shift the blame away from himself."

"But it doesn't make any sense that de Franco would be involved in the assassination. Why in hell would he want to bring down the wrath of the United States government? That doesn't help his business interests. First, last and always, he is a wily businessman."

"Right. We couldn't figure it out either. But the evidence kept leading us to his door and we had to follow the evidence. If Abdel Salam is who you say he is, he might be able to provide us with the critical intelligence we've been struggling to find."

Stern leaned back in his desk chair and closed his eyes. "I thought he might be important."

"You are a wise man and a friend. Any idea where Salam is right now?"

"Not right this second, but one of our agents spotted him in Mexico City yesterday."

"Can you send me a description? Photos? Anything you have on his background."

"Of course. It's probably already on Homeland computers."

"One last question. Have you gained any insight as to why he would be working for de Franco? What's in it for him?"

"Who knows what goes on in the secret heart of men…but perhaps you can ask de Franco directly when your people in Mexico arrive at his doorstep in Santa María del Oro."

Mossad already knew about that? Couldn't be a lucky guess or a fishing expedition. He had too much detail. "I hope that one day we can share more about our search for the assassin or assassins, but for now what I can say is thank you. You have helped us more than you know. And I'll never forget it."

Precisely the words Stern wanted to hear. As his father admonished him years ago, never owe anybody a favor. Be the one that everyone owes. Eventually that adds up to real power.

CHAPTER 13
Friday, March 4
Santa Maria del Oro • Early Morning

The helicopter landed on an unexpected grassy meadow in front of Casa del Pescadoro. Emilio, Roger, the three Rangers, Butch and three of de Franco's men had commandeered the Black Hawk, patched a fuel tank leak and jury-rigged a repair of the bloody windshield making the bird serviceable enough to ferry them safely to de Franco's stronghold. He was expecting them.

He stepped onto the field and walked through a formal garden of boxwood and colorful perennials, accompanied by the ubiquitous Lorenzo Muñoz, his chief of staff. De Franco waited until the wind died down from the blades and came forward to greet them, especially Emilio. He hadn't seen his son since Martina's wedding five years ago. Despite Emilio's thoughts to the contrary, de Franco loved his son to the point of pain. But the time to express those feelings had long since passed.

Now, he lived in an armed encampment on Lake Lazaro Cárdenas, not quite the casual summer retreat that his grandfather had created, but probably still the best bass fishing in the world. The House of the Fisherman was his grandfather's place of perfect peace on the western tip of the lake, about 25 miles southwest of Santa María del Oro in the foothills of the Sierra Madres. He built it to escape the oppressive crowds in Mexico City and to enjoy its cool nights, even in mid-summer. It rarely rose above 70 degrees Fahrenheit during the day, and in the winter it was still temperate. Obscure to the world, but easily accessible by small plane or helicopter.

It was the center of drug operations for de Franco's empire.

Emilio stepped out first and greeted his father with a stiff handshake. With Lorenzo, however, he offered a hug. "Tío Lorenzo, it's been too long."

Madame President

"But now you're here safe and sound and you and Señor Dunham have much to discuss with your father."

De Franco understood the warm relationship between his son and Lorenzo. The jealousy he felt was about his own inability to express affection to his children. *I've got my own father to thank for that.*

As they ducked and moved away from the still whirling blades, Emilio introduced his companions to them. When he got to Butch, he stopped and looked at de Franco. "I believe that you two have already met?"

De Franco extended his hand to Butch. "Yes, and I am much relieved that he was successful in his mission to bring you help. I fear, however, that his mother may not share our enthusiasm for his courage."

Butch shrugged his shoulders. "That's the understatement of the year. Let's hope she never finds out."

Roger laughed. "Not a chance in hell, baby brother. But, we have more urgent concerns at the moment."

"Yes, Roger, we do. But I know that you are hungry. May we have breakfast before we get down to business? It is all prepared and we can talk while you eat."

The men waited for Roger to give the go ahead, and when he did, they bolted to the door. The one certainty in life for a Ranger was that firefights are the ultimate appetite builders. They were starving. Halfway there, Butch stopped and looked back at Roger, "C'mon on, bro. You need to eat, too."

"I'll be there in a few minutes. I'd like for you to go with the men, keep them company." Butch figured that was code for 'remain alert'. He nodded. Lorenzo caught up to them and showed Butch and the Rangers into the dining room, where a feast was set. Roger and Emilio hung back with de Franco. Roger purposefully excluded Butch from his conversation with de Franco because Butch had exposed himself to enough danger, as it was.

"I know that you are impatient to meet with my, how should I put it, the source of all my information. He is still reluctant to talk much, but I think that you will hear from him what you seek. You should also know that I have convinced President Castillo of the importance of meeting with my source, and with both of you, as well. Assuming he can escape from the capital, he will arrive here mid-day tomorrow. I suspect that Kate, the President that is, will need more than my say-so for proof about Hezbollah's involvement in this whole affair."

"Does this 'resource' have a name?"

"His name is Michel Hayek and he is expecting you both."

Emilio experienced a flash of déjà vu. There was something strangely familiar about the name 'Michel Hayek'. He couldn't place it. As he was about to mention something, Roger's secure cell phone beeped.

Roger had forgotten about having it, since reception had been spotty or nonexistent in the mountains. He glanced at the caller ID. It was Gabriel. "I need to take this. Please excuse me."

They watched as Roger spoke with his caller. His face became animated, then frustrated. He snapped the phone shut and regained his composure before returning to the others. He caught Emilio's eye and shook his head slightly so that Emilio wouldn't ask him about the call.

Roger hurried through breakfast and Emilio could barely sit. Roger's appetite had been stifled by Gabriel's call and he was impatient to meet Hayek. Finally de Franco led him and Emilio to an upstairs bedroom, while the rest of the group stayed at the table.

The door opened onto a sunlit room painted in soft yellow. A physician ministered to the figure lying on the bed, taking his blood pressure and changing facial bandages. The armed guards stepped aside and de Franco asked them to remain nearby in the hallway. The physician looked up to see de Franco and quickly packed his bag and scurried by without a word.

De Franco stopped the doctor and asked, "How is the patient today?"

"He has made remarkable progress over 14 days. He no longer needs pain meds and apparently has excellent powers of recuperation."

"Thank you, doctor. You may go."

The door closed.

Roger and Emilio moved next to the bed and pulled up chairs on either side. De Franco remained standing. Michel's face was a mass of greenish-blue bruises, with the left cheekbone especially swollen and the eye partially able to open. The right arm was in a cast. He lay still as much as possible, wincing in pain when he shifted his weight. With his one good eye, he looked at his visitors.

"Roger Dunham and Emilio de Franco? Yes. I see it is you. You are here to confirm what I told my host, I imagine." Mouth lacerations made his words garbled.

Roger took the lead. "Yes. And I am sorry what it cost you for us to have this information. I wish that we could have been in charge of your interrogation." In truth, with Kate's life at risk, Roger wasn't at all sure how politically correct he felt about torture.

Madame President

"Why? Are you not familiar with Abu Graihb? I am. Torture is torture, Mr. Dunham."

"I would like to believe that we have learned from that mistake. But, we are not here to debate philosophical beliefs about information retrieval."

Emilio turned to glare at his father. In that dark, rancid place at the bottom of the stairs, that man became someone else. The family's Mr. Hyde. Emilio wondered, was this a gene that could be triggered in the son? He turned back to Michel.

"Mr. Hayek, while I don't approve of my father's methods, please don't expect any apologies from me. Because of your actions, the Vice President of the United States was assassinated and the President almost killed. And now we have the makings of a full blown coup d'etat in Mexico."

Michel nodded. He was aware of some vague connection to this man, de Franco's son. He couldn't connect the dots. But he was ready to speak. He had nothing left to lose. De Franco had convinced Michel that the man who raised him as his own son had sent a contract killer to Mexico to eliminate him.

He started. "My adopted father is Sheik Hassan Nasrallah. I have always believed his cause to be righteous. I have done small things for him through the years, mostly acting as a courier. Because of my job with Valentine Pharmaceuticals, I have excellent cover."

And in that moment, both Emilio and Michel connected the dots.

Emilio spoke first. "You work for Valentine Pharmaceuticals?"

"You're Martina's twin brother?"

"I don't believe in coincidences. How is Valentine connected to all of this?"

"To the best of my knowledge there is no connection. But let me tell the rest of my story and you decide."

For about an hour, Michel shared, this time not under duress, all that he had revealed to Federico, even adding a few more pertinent facts that the master torturer hadn't elicited - specifically about the Arab Student Alliance at Georgetown where he had handed over the IED components before his lecture. On one point Michel remained adamant. He never knew the intended targets.

Roger immediately took note of the ASA involvement.

But one piece of Michel's tale wasn't adding up, in Roger's way of thinking.

If it were true that Michel didn't know who the targets were in

Washington, how was Federico able to warn Emilio about the assassination attempt before it occurred?

Then it hit Roger that de Franco had, as Gabriel reported to him, a second, higher-up source in Hezbollah, one of which Michel was not aware. This source must have exposed Michel to de Franco in the first place and probably had firsthand knowledge of Hezbollah's entire involvement in this whole sordid mess. *But why hadn't Federico mentioned a second source? Why was he holding back? Could it be he was playing both ends against the middle?*

No longer pussyfooting around, Roger turned to Federico with a look of consternation in his eyes and shouted. "Who the fuck is Abdel Salam and why haven't you mentioned him before?"

CHAPTER 14

Friday, March 4
Washington DC · Late Afternoon

Kate threw down the newspaper and said to no one in particular. "What are these people thinking?"

"Ma'am, did you call me?" Rose stuck her head into the Oval Office.

"No, Rose. I can't believe the reporters at the Washington Post would go with a bogus story like this about Senator Richter. The sons…uh, jerks…ought to know better. Where is their verification? Rose, would you get Sy on the phone for me."

"No need, Madame President." Sy Lippman, the Press Secretary, slid around Rose and walked into the office. "I've been in touch with my sources at the Post. We need to get on top of this if we want to make the evening news."

"Rose, thank you again. Would you call Secretary Sanchez for me and re-confirm our dinner?"

"Of course, Madame President."

Kate sighed but managed a wan smile for Rose. Kate would be glad for her friends and colleagues to call her Kate again. Plain Kate. But there was no time for self pity today.

"Sy, where the hell did this come from? Could this hurt Richter's nomination?"

"Not sure on either count. I'm using every source in my contact file. You know it didn't start with the Post, Madame President. The Drudge Report ran the first tease headline last night, 'Does Senator Richter have a conflict of interest?' Not even a link to click through —the barest scent of something in the air."

"Yes, and come it did. Seems like the floodgates opened up all the way to the Post, after that moronic reference on Fox News." Kate's voice took on a mocking, singsong tone. "'Who is Senator Richter?' Who the hell do they think he is? And all they had were the usual unnamed sources and attributions. It's smoke and mirrors, Sy."

"Oh, but do they ever pull the strings on the blogosphere. It's all anyone can find on the internet right now."

"But, Sy, dammit, they know absolutely nothing. We've got to keep this nomination on track."

Lippman held up his hands in a placating gesture. "I know. I know. Let's start at the beginning and try to determine what we're really dealing with."

Kate nodded slightly.

"Okay. Here's the gist of the story as being reported by major news outlets. A member of Richter's family had been involved in some sort of insider trading of unnamed stock and David Richter had direct knowledge of this. The sources maintain that the still unnamed company would be directly affected by new policies soon to be announced by the administration."

Kate appreciated Lippman's ability to distill all the endless verbiage into a few sentences. "Okay. I know you have a question. I'm sure others will ask it too. Should I insist on the aggressive confirmation timetable in light of this brouhaha? Well, let me assure you that the answer is hell yes. Hell yes, Sy. We can't be deterred from doing the right thing because of foolish and wicked gossips. We need to get with Ford and Georgeanne immediately and craft our response. Let's retake the high ground on this.

"Sy, we have to face this story head on. Things like this are insidious. They start out like the tiniest beep of a smoke detector with a dying battery. Hardly perceptible. Small enough to doubt your own ears. Then it takes over and that pesky drone is all you can hear. It drowns out every other sound. Remember "The Telltale Heart"? That's what we have here. The hum overtakes sanity. And we cannot let this vain noise ruin a good man and a potentially invaluable Vice President of this country."

Rose appeared at the door. "Madame President, Mr. Lowery and Ms. Wright are here."

"Thanks, Rose, show them in. Oh, did you hear back from Secretary Sanchez yet?"

"Yes ma'am. He'll be joining you at the White House for an early dinner."

"Rose, one more thing. We need to get Senator Richter on a conference call, right away. Okay gentlemen and lady, what do we know? Not what we speculate. What we know."

Madame President

"Madame President," Ford had some ideas about how to proceed, "we don't know much. Senator Richter can confirm how he has handled his financial affairs since he was elected to office. Let's start there."

"Certainly. But I smell a rat. A big, ugly hairy rat. And it embarrasses me to have to drag the senator through another unofficial vetting session. I am absolutely certain that he is guilty of nothing other than responding to my request that he serve his country and this is the thanks he gets."

Kate looked up and saw Rose, yet again, at the door. "Rose? What is it?"

"I'm sorry to interrupt another time, but I thought you should know that Senator Richter's aide, Jeffery Townsend, called to say that the Senator would like to see you, if at all possible. What should I tell him?"

Kate looked at the others in the room and they all nodded. "Please tell him to come right over."

"Yes, ma'am."

Kate laughed. "I guess it's better to talk about a person in front of his front, rather than behind his back."

The door opened again and Richter strode in.

Kate was astonished to see him after less than a minute had passed. "Did you teleport yourself, David?"

"No, Madame President. I thought I would start walking over and then have Jeffery give you a call. If you had not been available, I would still have gotten in a good walk while anonymity permits. I know that an entourage will soon be a way of life for me. I guess that I could have called you, but I find I talk better in person."

Richter knew that he was going to miss his strolls along the Mall, people-watching and picking up a random Frisbee game. People were friendlier on the Mall than any place else in D.C. It was like they felt free, literally and figuratively, in the shadow of democracy's most vivid symbols – the Washington Monument, the Capitol and the Memorials. Then any stolen moments he could spend in the Hirshhorn sculpture garden cleared his mind and lifted his spirits. He and his wife had called it their own special place in Washington.

Kate rose and walked over to David Richter, genuinely happy to see him. "David, thank you for doing this. I prefer in-person myself. Can you use a cup of coffee? Grab a mug and pour yourself some from the cart there, and sit with us."

Richter admired the mug with the Presidential seal and laughed to himself. What the hell had he gotten himself into?

He turned back to the group. "Okay, why don't I tell you everything I've discovered over the last 24 hours about my own life. Then let's figure out together if I should step aside."

Well, thought Kate, he doesn't beat around the bush, does he?

"It's actually pretty simple. I had a blind trust set up when I was elected to Congress over ten years ago. As you know, my wife's family was quite wealthy and I came into the marriage with means, albeit modest by comparison, of my own. We combined all of our assets and placed them in a blind trust. The twins were babies and my wife was busy raising them, so I turned everything over to my father-in-law who was a shrewd businessman and someone in whom I had complete faith. Because of the nature of the trust, I had no knowledge of any stock transactions, only that it yielded enough to help my family live comfortably. When my father-in-law died, I turned the trust over to a new manager from my home state. And that's about it. We should probe a little further to see if my father-in-law had any kind of shadowy dealings, but I can't imagine such a thing."

"Well, David, where do you think this allegation is coming from? It makes no sense."

"Madame President, all I can say is to keep it simple. Who has the most to gain from my withdrawing my name from nomination? Seems like we should start there."

The people sitting in a circle with the President erupted, all speaking at once. Each had an idea about who would want to hurt the President in this way.

Kate sat back and let them talk. Did she know David Richter well enough to believe everything he said? No, not exactly. Was he holding back? Maybe. But she felt in her bones that this was a hatchet job.

Maybe there would be an opportunity here to finally draw the line on "gotcha politics," and the absurdity of the blogosphere. The politics of hate had been festering since even before Obama's Presidency. Where were the days of verification by two reliable sources before a paper ran a story? The web had no such rules. Where was journalism 101 – the who/what/where/when/why of a story before it was ever reported to the public? Enough was enough. Good men and women of both parties – conservatives and liberals – had careers ruined by this garbage.

"Listen up."

The room became silent.

"Folks, the list is too long for us to be sure of the source of this lie, and whether or not this is a carefully crafted set-up or simply mischief-making.

However, I'm going to put a lid on this kind of smarmy gossip if it's the last lid I slam down on anything."

Lippman shared her passion on this subject. "We can help with that, starting now. We should call a press conference for this afternoon before the story gets legs during the weekend."

Georgeanne answered, "Maybe we should hold off on that. Let's do a little more background research and formulate a response for the Sunday morning talk shows. Then we can hold a press conference on Monday morning with more of the facts in hand."

Lippman saw the merit in that. "That's probably a good idea. We can develop our counter attack over the next 24 hours. We may even decide that the President should address the nation on Monday evening, if the thing gets big enough."

Kate made her decision. "Oh, things will get big enough, of that you can be assured. But maybe we can give them enough rope to hang themselves before we counterattack. We'll do whatever damage control is necessary. Generally, I believe that less is more, but I'll address whomever I need to, under whatever circumstances work best. Let's find out everything we can between now and then."

Ford Lowery thought about the political landscape in Congress. "We need to ask Preston and Chester to keep a lid on this. Capitol Hill has to hold its collective tongue, if at all possible. I'll place the calls right away."

He turned to Richter. "Senator, how do you feel about not addressing it for now? Let us do our jobs in finding the best approach. Can you live with that?"

"Sure. I have no interest in speaking about it. As far as I'm concerned, the reporters aren't doing their jobs and I'm not going to reinforce their bad behavior. I believe in the First Amendment as much as the next guy. Freedom of Speech is the cornerstone of the Republic..."

"But this is like yelling "Fire" in a crowded theater, isn't it?" Kate liked this man from North Dakota better and better. She saw that they thought alike in many ways. "And that still violates the spirit and letter of the Constitution. I, for one, am going to make that point loud and clear before this is done."

CHAPTER 15

SATURDAY, MARCH 5
ST. BARTS AND DENVER • EARLY MORNING

"No, Hyler, I wasn't able to find any definitive information about the patch from Peter. He's in R&D so he would have known of a crisis of the kind you are contemplating. One thing, though," Martina hesitated to even mention it, "Peter did remember that it was kind of odd in the way Jackson took over the project when Michel went abroad."

"Odd, how so?"

"Well, according to Peter, right after Michel left, David ventured down to R&D and had a heated conversation with Jackson about something. Peter never knew what, but right after that, he was reassigned to work on some new ED pill or some such thing. Peter said that since it was the beginning of the testing phase on SST, and since he prefers more hands on research, he didn't give it much of a thought at the time."

Martina gripped the phone. She tried to prepare herself for this conversation with Hyler but the magnitude of the betrayal on the part of her husband was beyond her ability to imagine. But Hyler seemed more and more convinced of trouble and wouldn't be deflected.

"Martina, I know this is hard for you, but we cannot be sure, especially in light of what Peter did or did not reveal, that my suspicions are wrong." Hyler looked out at the blue, blue Caribbean and momentarily questioned his sanity. Every instinct he had honed over the years told him that something was terribly awry and that it involved the President. "Did Peter say nothing else of note? Anything, even small, might have significance."

"Like I said, he told me that the patch had few, if any side effects, even when the wearer didn't complete the full fourteen-day course. The other unusual occurrence he discovered was that all the passwords and access codes to the SST project were changed right after he left the project."

"If he were off the project, how did he know about the changes?"

Madame President

"Again, Peter indicated that it puzzled him that they changed the codes and he wasn't on the circulation list for access. He became aware of the change when he tried to access some information that he thought might be useful for his new assignment. He e-mailed Baines and got the information he was seeking, so he put it out of his mind.

"Hyler, I have to tell you we may be pushing people here, good people, and I'm not sure that we have anything to justify the kind of questions I asked Peter. Frankly, he looked at me as if I'd lost my mind."

"Better your mind than someone's life."

Martina gave a brittle laugh. "Conspiracies everywhere, Hyler? Aren't we being a little melodramatic? I think that this has gone far enough. I do not want to disturb David at the global conference in Shanghai. He needs to concentrate on events there, not be distracted by me."

"No. Stop for a second. You have got to talk about this with David. He probably knows nothing, but he could put the pieces together better than you or I."

Martina had thought to mention something to David before he left for China, but now he wouldn't be back until Thursday or Friday. That might be, if Hyler isn't totally paranoid, too late. She hated the idea of having a conversation like this with David on the phone, but now had little choice. "Okay, okay. I'll call David. I'll call you back when I know something."

"Please do, Martina. One last thing. I really am sorry for having dragged you into this and I pray to God that I'm wrong. In the meanwhile, I am going to return to Washington. I told the President that I would be a support to her during this difficult time, and I intend to keep my word."

Martina flopped down on the couch and gathered her thoughts for the call to David. He loved her. He would forgive her for this craziness, wouldn't he?

He picked up on the second ring, even though it was late in Shanghai. "Marti, what a nice surprise. I thought you were going to some kind of leadership retreat in the mountains. Is everything okay?"

"I canceled the trip, David. I'm fine, but I have to speak with you about something important that Hyler Ellison brought to my attention."

"What does that old goat have on his mind?"

"David, he is a trained observer of people, and he has some troubling suspicions that you should know. I couldn't keep it from you any longer."

David subconsciously straightened his tie and patted down his hair, old nervous habits. This sounded serious. "Go ahead."

Martina explained what Hyler had overheard or thought he overheard at the board meeting. She was about to mention Hyler's other suspicions about Kate and the possible prototype patch box, but before she could get in another word, David lost his cool.

"That old fart, what is he insinuating? Does he really think we'd keep something like that under wraps? I should have never re-appointed him to the board. What was I thinking?"

"David, if it's nothing, why are you getting yourself so worked up?"

"Because, if someone hears something out of context and mentions it to someone else, which is quite obviously what happened here, that's how rumors start to fly. And before you know it, all hell breaks loose. Do you realize what an insinuation like this could do to our stock price, let alone the harm it would do to the health of the nation, the world for that matter? Martina, the patch works and works well without any appreciable side effects. Is he crazy? If he had any doubts or suspicions about what he thinks he overheard, why didn't he come to me directly instead of to my wife?"

Martina had to admit there was some merit in David's question. And considering how a rumor in Washington was already threatening to sink the new Vice President before his confirmation hearings were concluded… well, she got David's point. Baseless rumors can cause great harm.

But was what Hyler said baseless?

"David, I totally agree. Rumors will be the death of us all. What can I do to help shut this down before Hyler says something to someone else, and this really blows up in our faces?"

"Martina, I've got another call coming in I must take. Give me a sec. I'll be right back."

Martina was almost convinced of her husband's sincerity. Yet his total loss of cool was out of character. She needed to push the envelope a smidge more before she was totally assuaged.

David came back on the line. Martina picked up her train of thought. "David, there is one other thing. Hyler mentioned a meeting he had last Sunday with the President and that he discovered that she was on the patch."

"Well, good for her. But you wonder how she got her hands on the SST ahead of the rest of the…silly me, she is the most powerful person on the planet."

"Yes, David, she is. So can you think of any reason that the patch might do her harm?"

Well, there it was, the cat was out of the bag. "Martina, what the fuck are you implying? Have you actually let Hyler's obvious craziness infect you?"

Nothing was obvious to Martina. That wasn't an answer from David, only a deflection.

"David, I'm serious."

"Okay, then why would you ask such an absurd question in the first place? So the President has connections and manages to use them to secure an advance stash off the assembly line. Hell, she's got the whole Department of Homeland Security at her beck and call. How did we go all the way from your initial concern about the problems with the patch that Hyler purports to have overheard to a threat to the President?"

"Because she referred to the 'Red Box'. And, if I'm not wrong, the packaging is blue."

David's anger boiled over. "Martina, why do I get the sense that you may believe this terrible accusation? How could you?"

"David, all I did was ask a question and you still haven't given me a straight answer. Is there a problem and could the President possibly be in danger?"

He clicked off without so much as a goodbye, let alone any resolution to her nagging suspicions. Martina held the phone to her ear, not believing that he was gone. She placed the phone by her side and sat still, feeling like the loneliest person on the planet.

CHAPTER 16

Saturday, March 5
Santa Maria del Oro • Mid-Afternoon

The mere mention of Abdel Salam's name changed the barometric pressure in the room.

Federico, the master of emotional control, turned towards Roger and smiled. "Fascinating."

Michel on the other hand, turned sickly pale. *No it couldn't be the same Abdel Salam. It must be a coincidence.* But too much didn't add up. How did de Franco know about Michel's return to Mexico City from Washington? How did he know about the IED's? And how did he know Talal El-Hussen?

Sometimes the truth is so obvious as to be completely unbelievable. But Abdel a traitor? It made perfect sense in terms of the intelligence de Franco was receiving about Hezbollah's drug activities. Still, Abdel had always been one of his father's most loyal supporters. My God, he was the number two person at the ISRO. What possible motive could he have to betray the sheikh? No. None of this made any sense. It must be someone else. Then, again, there had been some rumors about Abdel. Could they have led to blackmail?

As Michel was coming to grips with this conundrum, a familiar face appeared at the doorway into his room.

De Franco was the first to acknowledge this new presence. "Abdel, my friend, I knew you wouldn't let me down. See? All that complaining about traveling from Sabinas, and here you are, none the worse for wear."

"Easy for you to say. You didn't have to dodge Guerrera's pigs, crawl on your belly through a minefield, eat enough sand to choke a horse, and… well…let me say that the bullet that grazed me will make sitting a chore for the next few weeks."

"I am truly sorry my comrade, but now you are here, in time."

Roger turned to the tall man with the dark Mediterranean good looks, and immediately recognized the face from the file Gabriel had forwarded to him. Abdel Salam in person.

Michel, filled with rage, tried to get up from his bed but was still a bit too weak to support his own weight and fell back down in a spasm of coughing. But there could be no mistaking his animosity towards Abdel – the hatred and sense of betrayal were palpable.

Roger and Emilio looked from de Franco to Salam to Hayek and waited for de Franco to make some kind of move. He finally introduced Roger and Emilio to Salam, ignoring Michel for the moment, at which point they attempted awkward handshakes.

Michel interrupted. "Isn't this a pleasant scene? I'm crippled at the hands of the genial host and you all shake hands like we're at a tea party. Get the hell out of here."

"I understand your grievances with me, Michel, but I think you might want to listen to what Abdel has to say concerning Hezbollah's role in all of this…."

"I don't give a shit what this traitorous pig has to say. He is a disgrace to his God and nothing he vomits out will alter my belief in the cause and in my father."

"Well then, my little mouse, what possible harm can come from listening? Besides, my other two guests have come a long way to hear what both of you have to say. I think once you have focused on Abdel Salam's entire story, especially the parts that concern your family, you may have a change of heart."

"What about my family?"

"In due time, Michel, in due time."

De Franco motioned for everyone to take a seat in the large room, close enough to Michel's bed for him to hear easily. "Let me begin before Mr. Salam joins in. What I have to say might seem a bit self-serving – mostly second hand information and speculation. You've all read the intelligence reports of my interrogation of Michel, but even that might be suspect considering the means that were used to illicit Mr. Hayek's cooperation. And I make no apologies for my methods, but I do wish I had been left with another alternative. Time was short and, Michel, you're all we had."

Not expecting any sign of forgiveness on the part of Michel, de Franco continued. "I think it best that we hear Abdel's story from the beginning. Michel can confirm the parts that he knew, and Roger will probably have a few of the missing pieces from his intelligence services. Abdel has some information for Michel's ears alone, but we can save that for the end.

"Let's keep in mind before Abdel begins that our time is short. President Castillo will be here in about two hours. I hope by then that all of us will be in agreement about the details of Hezbollah's plot. I think it is important for both our countries to know the reality of the past two weeks – and the threats we both still face."

With that, de Franco found a chair and all eyes fell upon Abdel.

For Abdel, the next hour was the most public display of honesty he had ever endured. He held back nothing, from the initial planning sessions with Talal and the Sheikh, to the help and possible blame, if necessary, of the Iranians. He indicated that Hezbollah had decided that de Franco was a threat to their drug operations in Mexico, but that they couldn't get to him directly. The strategy emerged to attack America's President and Vice President. This served as a pretext to have the United States retaliate against de Franco, creating a new alliance among Vilas, Guerrera, and Hezbollah to take over the rule of Mexico.

As Abdel's story continued to unfold, Roger and Emilio peppered him with questions, with an occasional clarification by de Franco. Michel remained strangely silent. His demeanor towards Abdel had not changed one iota. He stared at him as though he were lower than a pimple on a protozoa's ass. *My God how could you be such a turncoat?*

By the time Abdel was done speaking, Roger, Emilio, and de Franco had no doubt about the veracity of his words. A detail here and a partial fact there might be tweaked, but it had the ring of truth. It was a master plan, strategic in every element, one in which Hezbollah's risk/reward ratio was extraordinary.

Emilio spoke first. "My God, what audacity on the part of Hezbollah. The bastards treat Mexico like it's chattel. Do they really believe that the Mexican people would stand for this? Vilas would be Hezbollah's puppet and Mexico would once again be under the thumb of foreign oppression."

Roger was furious enough to want to hit something or someone. Kate was the one in Hezbollah's bull's eye. "There's never any justification for political assassination, but to use it as a ploy to put the blame on someone else in order to gain an economic or political advantage in another country is beyond disgusting. And you say the words as though you are describing a cricket match." Roger rose on shaky legs and stood in front of Abdel.

Abdel ducked his head and shoved his chair back. There was no mistaking the threat.

De Franco appreciated the elegant chess-like strategy on the part of Hezbollah. "This is the classic King's Gambit. Sheikh Nasrallah sees himself as a grand master. Unfortunately for him, but most opportune for us, we seem to have achieved a sort of chess miracle. We have turned Abdel, our black bishop, into a white queen.

"Enough of my chess metaphors." De Franco stood and motioned to Roger and Emilio, "I think it might be time to give Abdel and Michel a few moments together. I'll remain close by, in case. They have much to discuss, which might give Mr. Hayek a far different perspective on life."

Before leaving, Roger decided to ask something of the 5000-pound gorilla in the room. It was the question that had been on all minds, except de Franco's. "Abdel, why?"

"Because he is a treacherous pig." Michel attempted to shout, but emotion constricted his throat and it came out a hoarse croak.

"It's a little more complicated than that, Michel. Señor de Franco left me with no choice but to cooperate with him."

"Bullshit. Everyone has a choice."

Federico stepped back into the room and looked long and hard at Abdel. "Señor Salam is right. It was my doing that turned him. It's not my place to offer any additional information, since none of it would be relevant to the situation at hand. I will say that certain facts came into my possession that left Abdel in an untenable position and I took full advantage of that. Now enough said, unless you want to add something, Abdel?"

"I'm fine. If I could have a few moments with Michel? That's all."

Roger and Emilio returned to the dining room with its never-ending assortment of food. They filled their plates and ate hungrily at the table. Most of their Ranger buddies were out in the courtyard kicking a soccer ball to pass the time. Butch had remained inside and was relieved to see them. He pulled up a chair next to his brother.

"So did de Franco's source reveal all? And can we blow this taco stand now? The sooner I'm back in the States, the sooner I can start preparing my defense for mom."

Roger shot his kid brother one of those easy-to-read grins. "Good luck with that…I'm not sure Moses could save your sorry, albeit well-meaning, ass."

"Well, Emilio, you'll plead my case for me with mom, won't you? After all, you went to Georgetown and studied international law. If this isn't a matter of international law I don't know what is."

Roger interjected, "Bro, I'm afraid you're going to have to handle this on your own. We'll, of course, mention some minor things like you saving our lives, but how much that will get you in a sentence reduction is not clear. Remember the President is a firm believer in capital punishment, especially when it comes to this family."

"Very funny, ha ha. Tell me you learned enough from the guys upstairs to have this all be worthwhile, anyway."

"I think so. And we'll deal with mom after we get all our facts lined up and are heading back home."

As Emilio was going to offer another solution to Butch's seemingly insurmountable problem, de Franco and Abdel walked into the dining room with countenances that were impossible to read.

Roger looked up at de Franco. "That bad? Were you able to learn anything else from Michel that might be of use?"

"Actually it's what Michel learned from Abdel here that seems to have won Michel's cooperation."

Emilio looked back and forth between his father and this strange Arab man. "What could Michel have possibly learned from Abdel that would make any difference to him, let alone be relevant to us?"

Federico contemplated Abdel. "Why don't you share with my son and Roger what you told Michel? I think it important that we understand everyone's motives. They need to hear the justification and credibility of Michel's sudden change in alliance in your own words."

Abdel remained standing while he told the Machiavellian story that he had overheard weeks before in Beirut, beginning with the discussion between the Sheikh and Talal of Michel Hayek's father being an Israeli spy. He spared no detail in what he had overheard – that the village where Michel and his family lived was bombed by the Israelis, in a raid that was a setup by Hezbollah. Everyone in Michel's family, his mother, his father, his baby sister, were all killed.

He told them the supreme irony of Nada Nasrallah finding Michel in a Red Crescent first aid camp and ultimately adopting him. Abdel didn't know whether Nada knew the true story behind the death of Michel's family.

De Franco placed his hands on the table, palms up. "So, gentlemen, you see we have turned a black knight into a white knight, and the weapon I used was the truth."

Emilio felt a moment of doubt about his father, but quickly buried it away under the oppression of his father's reputation. "This must be an original experience for you, father – being on the good side of the law."

Federico took the rebuke in stride, as well deserved. "Emilio, I don't expect any real salvation in this world or the next. But I'm going to give it my all to fix as much of this mess as God will allow."

Roger recapped what they now knew to be fact and what they would be able to share with President Castillo. He made a quick decision not to call Kate right then with what he had, but to wait until after the Castillo meeting. He could buy his kid brother a few more hours of peace and, perhaps, learn more from the Mexican President.

In hindsight it was a decision that would cost them all dearly.

They walked outside and saw the compound in the full throes of a lockdown. Workers scurried to remove as much equipment as they could get into carts. Paper shredders hummed at capacity and men tossed sensitive computer equipment into compactors.

"Father, it looks like you are expecting company. And I don't just mean the President."

Tío Lorenzo added, "If you mean by company about 40,000 soldiers of the Los Rojos cartel, you'd be quite correct."

"Not to worry, my son. We were forewarned of our visitors' arrival, and your old man still has a few tricks up his sleeve..."

De Franco was about to add something when they heard the roar of a helicopter heading in from the southeast. De Franco glanced at his pocket watch and smiled to himself. "If nothing else can be said about the President of Mexico, his timing is impeccable."

It was exactly 2 PM when President Castillo's helicopter landed at Casa del Pescadoro, accompanied by the sound of distant gunfire.

Castillo deplaned rapidly, not sure whether he was dodging the blades or a stray bullet. The noise was deafening.

De Franco surged forward and caught Castillo by the arm. "Come quickly, my friend. Time is short and we have much to discuss." The entire greeting party sprinted for cover at the house, with snipers now placed every five feet along the courtyard wall perimeter. They shouted at each other as they ran.

"Armando, I must apologize for this reception. I didn't expect Guerrera's advance forces to be here for another 24 hours."

"Will that affect our plans in any way?"

"No, not at all. It's confirmation that they've taken the bait. But we will have to move more rapidly now."

While the Rangers joined de Franco's men outside, assisting in strengthening the perimeter defenses, Luigi slipped away to meet up with two other Rangers who had been imbedded into the area prior to the mission's start.

"So how bad is it guys?"

"Pretty bad," Dominick offered. "If we don't get our birds in the air in the next hour or so, I'm afraid we may be here for an extended stay."

"How extended?"

"From the looks of it, Los Rojos is amassing in full force about 20 clicks from the hacienda. President Castillo's helicopter will be lucky to lift off. I'm afraid we may need a ground extraction for our guys, and that could be kind of dicey.'

Andy, the other Ranger, offered one other piece of intel. "De Franco's forces have been slipping away towards the capital, I think. Once Guerrera realizes that, he may start moving his forces south…making it safer for a bird to leave."

Luigi crossed himself. "We can hope."

"One other thing. Remember the warning about a possible sniper in the vicinity."

"Well, Dominick discovered a pretty good vantage point in the high crest overlooking the villa. If I were hunting, it's where I'd set up shop."

"Okay guys, keep a watch on that hillside for any signs of movement. We can't afford to lose any of our charges. For the moment, no one knows of your presence. Let's keep it that way for as long as possible. Rangers Lead The Way."

Andy and Dom responded in unison, "RLTW."

President Castillo and the others had already gathered in the hacienda's main room and scraped chairs over the wood floor to form a makeshift circle.

"If anyone is thirsty or hungry, please avail yourselves of what we have placed in the dining room. We have no time for niceties. Now, let me introduce you to…well, you know my son Emilio."

"Of course. He is our number two man at the UN and I appointed him personally." They started to shake hands but Castillo drew him into a hug.

"I also have the pleasure of presenting two of the sons of the President of the United States…"

"Two?"

"Oh, did I not mention that Señor Butch MacIntyre joined Roger and Emilio on their little joy ride through Los Rojos country?"

"Aye de mi. Kate, the President, she knows this?"

"Not as yet, but that will be Roger's next call."

"Mister Dunham, it is a pleasure. On behalf of the Republic of Mexico and its people, I must express how grateful we are at the risks you've taken in coming and for the information you have uncovered."

While they sat in the sunken living room, they heard another round of gunshots, louder and closer. De Franco insisted that they take the time for a dose of hard liquor that would calm their nerves for the discussion ahead.

As de Franco passed around shot glasses, Roger and Emilio looked up and stared, speechless, at a sight they never thought to behold. Abdel Salam walked slowly down the long staircase, his arm around Michel Hayek, assisting him into the living room. Arch enemies hours ago, they now acted like long lost brothers.

"Well, I'll be damned." Roger jumped up to give Salam a hand. "I never thought I'd see you two cooperating. Emilio, would you move the coffee table to give Michel some more room."

Both Abdel and Michel saw President Castillo at the same time. Michel strained under the effort of walking, but Abdel managed to stammer, "a pleasure, even under these circumstances, to meet you, Mr. President."

Castillo crossed the room to offer his hand to both men. "No, it is my honor to, at last, meet the two men who may have it in their power to help save the Republic of Mexico. I realize that you both have traveled different, and looking at Michel, difficult paths, but all I ask is that you share with me as much of the truth as you know it to be."

De Franco suggested that Abdel tell his story from the beginning and that Michel add, subtract and verify, wherever appropriate. He also suggested, in the interest of time, that they allow President Castillo to ask all the questions and hold off asking any of their own until the end of the narrative.

De Franco, Emilio and Roger knew most of the information, but President Castillo was stunned to learn the extent of the duplicity and betrayal on the part of Vilas and Guerrera. Castillo felt the underpinnings of his world give way.

By the time Abdel and Michel came to the end of their stories, every face in the room was set in stone. President Castillo was the first to react.

And his reaction was an explosion of words. He hit the open palm of one hand with the fist of the other as he stormed throughout the room. "I must get back to the capital at once. This isn't mere treachery, its treason.

Hezbollah?! How dare that bastard look me straight in the face and claim he was only looking out for Mexico's best interests? How dare he? By the time I'm done with Vilas, he'll be begging for a firing squad. That is, if there's enough skin left on him for a bullet to find. And as for that Guerrero piece of shit, I'll leave it to you, Federico, to settle that score. Now, I must return to Mexico City."

Castillo paused to catch his breath. "Roger, I'm counting on you to confirm these facts to your President. Please inform her I'll be in touch with her when I know more about the situation in the capital."

"She's my next phone call, Mr. President."

"Federico, how are our other plans proceeding?"

Emilio snapped his head around, toward his father, "What other plans?"

De Franco looked at Castillo as if seeking a nod to reveal something else. Castillo confirmed with a flick of his eyelids and de Franco continued.

"President Castillo and I entered into an arrangement to undermine the alliance between General Vilas and Los Rojos."

Emilio stared at the president. "You would get into bed with this man? Knowing all that you know about him, his business, his disregard for human life, for decency? How could you?"

"Emilio, let's not talk as though your father isn't sitting directly across from you. Hear me out and then you decide on the merits of my decision. Your father approached me several weeks ago, actually before all of these evil forces aligned against me. He started a dialogue with me on the Republic of Mexico, all its strengths and all its weaknesses. And by the time he was done, he had admitted to me that he was responsible for much of what was wrong with our country."

"Because he is."

"Yes, at one time, those were my sentiments. But actions do speak louder than words. Over the past few weeks, your father trusted me enough to share his inside contact in Hezbollah," nodding to Abdel, "with me. As to your father's motives, I think that is between him and his God. Perhaps, one day, you will be able to forgive him his previous life, as have I."

De Franco never raised his head during the president's description of him.

"Anyway, once Abdel alerted us to General Vilas' duplicity, your father and I devised a strategy to counteract the general. As you must realize by now, the fate of Mexico rests in two capitals…Washington, where they are deciding, as we speak, whether to bomb us to smithereens for the assassination of Vice President Harris…and Mexico City, where the allegiance of the armed forces is still up for grabs. Perhaps, Federico, you would like to share what we have planned?"

All eyes in the room turned to de Franco, none more curious than Emilio, who rose to stretch his legs. He stood in the far corner of the room. He needed physical distance from his father. Roger looked around and found him. He started to join Emilio but Emilio shook his head. Roger understood. Emilio's position in all this was precarious, at best. At worst? Probably the end of Emilio's diplomatic career.

Roger also noted the steadier sound of gunfire.

"Of course, Mr. President. The first and most important part of our plan was to get irrevocable proof of Hezbollah's plot…in all its elements, from framing me for the assassinations, to assisting Los Rojos and General Vilas in a military coup. Nationalizing American assets in Mexico and increasing production of domestic grown heroin were the, how do you say it, the icing on the cake. There is much more, but time does not allow us to get to the mundane details. But be assured that if their plan succeeds, no part of the Mexico that we love would be recognizable."

Emilio stepped closer to his father and looked him in the eye. *Can I really trust what you are saying? Could you really have experienced such an epiphany, such a change of heart? Is that even possible?*

As if reading his son's heart, Federico grabbed the boy with both his arms and gave him the first hug he could remember giving his son.

"Father, can it be true? You did this for Mexico, not out of self interest?"

"Forgive an old man for having taken so long to see what really is important. Yes, it is true."

President Castillo took this momentary lull to lead Roger into the small study next to the great room. He needed to speak with the young man privately about President MacIntyre. As he shut the door behind them, both of their cell phones rang.

"Who is speaking?" Castillo bellowed into the phone. It was a bad connection and he could hardly understand every third word.

Roger listened to his phone going through the clicks of security filters, and soon heard the voices of Kate, Gabriel and Edgar. They were sitting at the table in the Situation Room.

"Yes, Madame President, I can now report with 100 percent certainty that this all was a Hezbollah plot, one intended to implicate de Franco. They conspired to manipulate us into retaliating against de Franco. This would leave the other cartels, especially Guerrera's Los Rojos, in conjunction with General Vilas and his forces, to mount a coup against the legitimate government of Mexico…"

Across the room President Castillo was deep in conversation. "That cannot be. Are you sure? Who would do such a thing? Those animals."

Castillo held the phone down and away from his face. He was ashen and felt faint. Roger noticed that Castillo had dropped his phone and was swaying "Mr. President. What is it? What has happened?"

Castillo swallowed hard. His Adam's apple bobbed up and down as he struggled for words. "Roger. It's Martín. I…"

"What. What happened to Martin?" Roger saw a wet bar across the room and filled a glass with bourbon. He handed it to Castillo and pushed him gently down into a chair. Castillo drank too quickly and began coughing and choking. Saliva ran down his chin. "Catch your breath. Now, try again. What has happened?"

Roger slapped his cell phone to his ear and told his mother to hold on for a few more minutes. She heard the urgency in his voice. "We'll stay on the line, Roger."

The color returned to Castillo's face and he spoke slowly. "Roger, the animals attacked the Presidential Palace. Our seat of government. They took Martín's life. They put a bullet between his eyes. How could they do such a thing? In my office? The guards found his body on my desk. Martín was an honorable man. And my friend. One of my closest confidantes."

Castillo stopped and began rocking back and forth in the desk chair. He pulled at his hair. Roger looked at him, helpless and paralyzed. What the hell was happening?

Castillo jumped out of the chair, accidentally knocking Roger back into the bookshelf. "I can't sit here. I must go back to the capital. Now. Right now."

"But President Castillo, there can be no safety for you there. Let us assess the situation and get you some firsthand reports."

Castillo's face was contorted with rage. "No. By all the saints, I will go back to the palace and meet these bastards face-to-face. They have brought the fight to me, and I will cut them into bloody pieces."

The President picked his phone up off the floor and barked into it. "Get me CISEN Director Marcos on the phone right now. If you can't reach him, find his assistant, Antonio Pasqual."

Juan Marcos, the Director of the National Security and Investigation

Center, clicked on. "Juan, you've heard the news about Martín? What the fuck is going on there? I am returning to the capital within the hour."

Castillo listened and shook his head. "No. No. I don't give a damn for my own safety. I want the pigs responsible for this despicable act, and I want them now. Look, I don't care who you have to question or arrest, I'm still the President of Mexico and this is a direct order."

"I understand, Mr. President. We've already made several arrests and, as you thought, this has the hand of General Vilas behind it. I suggest you land directly at Los Pinos, where I can guarantee your security…for now. I've also arranged a meeting with the Minister of Defense and several other loyal officers of the three armed services. But Mr. President, if you are determined to come back here, you need to move as fast as possible. I'm not sure how much longer I can hold things together."

Roger knew from what he had heard of the conversation that Castillo would not be deterred. He was about to speak again to his mother, when he caught the next words of Mexico's President. "I'm going to need one additional favor from you, Marcos, that might sound strange. But I believe that it may be our country's best hope."

"Yes, Mr. President."

"I'm going to need for you to arrange free and unfettered access into the Capital district for the soldiers of the Escolar Cartel.

"Marcos? Are you there?"

"Yes, Mr. President. But I do not believe my ears. Do you realize what you are asking? You would be turning our capital city over to a drug cartel. I doubt that the military staff would obey such an order."

"Marcos, we have no time for polite discussion. Sometimes you have to fight the devil with a devil of your own. Why do you think that I traveled to Santa María del Oro in the first place? For the fishing? Federico de Franco is a bad man, but sometimes even bad men do good things. He is a Mexican at heart. He has proven that to me. And that is more than I can say for scum like Vilas and Guerrera."

With unmistakable hesitancy in his voice Marcos responded. "It will be as you wish Mr. President. I pray that you are right."

Roger, still listening to Castillo's conversation, realized that he needed to give the man his full attention. He spoke hurriedly into his phone, "Something big is going on in Mexico City. Let me speak with President Castillo before he leaves. I'll call you right back."

Kate's voice was firm. "Roger, I understand the urgency of your situation but you must appreciate the pressure we're feeling here in DC. Call back as soon as you can."

With that she clicked off. "Well Gentlemen now we wait."

Roger caught Castillo at the door of the study. The President kept walking and turned to face all the men assembled in the great room. "Señors, I'm not sure how the next few days will play out. I know that many great men have found themselves in the same position I find myself in now. I am not a fool. I know that the results have not always been favorable. I pray to God that we are in time, that the government of the United States will assist us in all ways possible, that Señor de Franco and his family will be honored as patriots when they write this next chapter in Mexican history, and that the efforts of Roger and Butch will not have been in vain."

With the now constant barrage of gunfire coming from the east and uncomfortably close, the President turned to leave. He looked back. "I return to the Capital and God knows what. But I leave here knowing that you were true to my country and to me. That makes me a fortunate man. Pray for me and pray for Mexico. Gracias."

CHAPTER 17

Saturday, March 5
Washington DC · Late Afternoon

Gabriel and Edgar waited at the conference table in the Situation Room while the President paced from corner to corner of the large space. When she disconnected the speakerphone, they looked at her expectantly.

"It seems I may be the last person in this government to have learned that I have not one, but two sons, in Mexico – Santa María del Oro, to be exact?"

"Yes, ma'am."

"At the moment a mother's wounded pride will have to be subordinated to the real problems at hand. They are both grown men and, in spite of my personal reservations, are serving the nation."

Kate was actually furious at her orders being ignored, but did not want to reveal that.

"Roger informed me that he has acquired unequivocal intelligence that Hezbollah killed Vice President Franklin and made the attempt on my life. I don't have to tell you that this cannot go unanswered."

"No, ma'am."

"But there are complications that will prevent us from moving too overtly."

And with that, Kate retold Gabriel and Edgar, as well as Barbara Lowery, her Secretary of State who had entered the room, the entire story of Guerrera, de Franco, Vilas, Castillo, and Hezbollah.

"Roger knows that he and Butch must be extracted immediately from Mexico. Emilio is resisting – he is insistent that he will join his father in Mexico City to support President Castillo. I can't argue with that, much as I wish I could. However, Edgar, I am relying on you to coordinate getting those boys of mine back to Texas."

Edgar looked at the President and her eyes left no room for doubt

– this was his primary job at the moment, and perhaps the most important of his life. "Yes, ma'am. I need to make some calls. The Joint Chiefs are working on an extraction plan as we speak, and I'll get you an immediate update." Edgar sent an aide scurrying.

"Gabriel, I need you to deal with your counterparts in Mexico City and give President Castillo as much support as possible. Our Embassy should be informed right now. Is Mickey, Ambassador Sanchez on location?"

Gabriel nodded.

"Then, start with your brother. I know that there is a line that we can't cross. But I'm not sure where that is currently. We have enough CIA agents on the border to fill a C130. Should we shift them to Mexico City to give us eyes and ears on the ground?"

Gabriel nodded, again.

"I'll call President Castillo as soon as we're done here. We'll see where he wants us to draw the line. Materiel, armed forces, weapons, high cover from the air? I'll pin him down. Edgar, you will have to coordinate with the Joint Chiefs on this, as well. Gabe, you get with all the spooks – CIA, NSA, DIA – you know who they are. We need every shoulder to the wheel."

"Madame President, we can also offer Castillo satellite imagery. I doubt that the insurgents have such capability."

"How long will it take to reposition the Keyhole-class satellite?"

"Maybe 6-12 hours. With it in place, we should be able to read every candy wrapper on the streets of Mexico City."

"Then you'd better start."

Gabriel got up so quickly that he tripped on the legs of the table. He righted himself and jogged to the door. He stopped. He wanted to say something of comfort to the President. "Madame President…Kate…we're good at this. We'll make a difference."

A wistful smile played across her face. "Thanks, Gabe. One more thing before you leave. Where do we stand on the raid at Georgetown of the Arab Student Alliance?"

"We've acquired credible proof from de Franco that Hezbollah supplied the six or so students with the IED's that killed Vice President Franklin and that could have killed you."

"When will you put them under arrest?"

"Not yet. They are radicalized and are well trained in resisting interrogation. A deadly combination. We need ironclad proof before we bring them in. They are under 24-hour surveillance and can't flush a toilet without our knowing about it."

"Gabriel, we have to be purer than Calpurnia in the way we handle their questioning. Since we already have independent confirmation of their involvement that would stand up in a court of law, we don't need to take draconian measures. Do you follow me? They will break sooner than later once they are in our custody. The assassination, or even attempted assassination, of a federal official is a capital offense, and believe you me they will be made aware of that. I suspect that thought alone will elicit cooperation. While I'd like to see the sons of bitches hang from Times Square, it's really their handlers we're after, isn't it?"

Gabriel still stood by the door, holding on to the handle, like a greyhound at post. "Yes, we need to make an example of their handlers. The torture and execution of misguided students will ultimately serve no purpose."

"Gabe, I know you agree with me about interrogation techniques. I had to say it out loud, more for me than you."

"Yes, ma'am." He stepped outside the room, barking orders into his cell phone.

Kate and Barbara were alone for the moment. "Barbara, you have a special role in this."

"Let me guess. You want me at the U.N.?"

"You bet. You need to request an emergency session of the Security Council. How long will that take?"

"Historically, at least 12 hours."

"Okay, it's now 5:18 PM, Saturday. Why don't we shoot for 1:00 PM Sunday?"

"Yes, ma'am. How do you want me to frame the request?" Barbara knew that they had to parse every word.

"The governments of the United States of America and the Republic of Mexico have irrefutable proof of the involvement of Hezbollah in the attempted overthrow of the duly elected government of Mexico."

Barbara whistled. She had heard parts of the conversation leading up to this. "Irrefutable proof? Really?"

"Yes. Really. In addition, we have substantial proof that General Vilas, head of the Armed Forces of Mexico, Adán Guerrera and the Los Rojos cartel are working with Hezbollah as part of this plot."

"Brilliant. We undercut Hezbollah and Vilas, and no one will speak up for them. Not that weasel Ambassador from Mexico. He won't stick out his scrawny neck. As to Hezbollah, they do have one or two delegates as part of the Lebanese delegation to the UN."

"I wouldn't worry about that. I've already spoken with President Suleiman of Lebanon and informed him that both of those delegates are declared persona non grata and will be escorted out of the country in the morning."

"You do think of everything. And I imagine that the Iranian Ambassador is going to suddenly turn into a Persian sphinx – no defense of Hezbollah will be issuing forth from his lips."

Edgar walked back into the room. "Iranian sphinx? Sounds interesting."

"Yes, Edgar. And the old Chinese curse, may you live in interesting times, seems to apply."

"Indeed, Madame President. Barbara, you were talking about our position in the U.N. Do you think we're on safe ground there? We've never been the most popular kid on that block."

"In light of Hezbollah's alignment with a well-known and feared drug cartel in Mexico, no one can afford to openly come to their defense. And frankly, I don't give a rat's ass who supports them in private. That's of no consequence to us. Edgar, Madame President, if there is nothing else, let me return to the State Department to organize a few details. Then, I'll be on a plane to New York."

"That's it. You corner Hezbollah at the U.N. Others will corner them in Mexico and Lebanon. Don't be the first one to show your six gun, Barbara, but keep your powder dry. By the time you reach New York, we'll have you a fully detailed situation report."

Barbara grabbed her briefcase. She was glad that she had chosen to wear practical, flat shoes today. Looked like she would be running for the next 24 hours. Before the door closed, they could hear her voice echoing in the hallway as she placed her first calls.

Kate turned to her Secretary of Defense. "Edgar, we need to buy President Castillo as much time as possible. What do you have at the Pentagon in your bag of tricks, short of dropping paratroopers into Mexico City? We've got to do something. Maybe interrupt communications?"

"There is one thing, Madame President. We've been working on a new technology. We can give the President a secure communications system, while, at the same time, we can knock out the general system across the country. This should give us 18 to 24 hours before the insurgents recover any means of sharing information."

"Sounds promising."

"I've already spoken with Gabriel, and as soon as you get President

Castillo to sign off on the communications disruption, we can implement it."

"Powerful little thing, eh?"

"Yes, ma'am. He can take over the Internet, broadcasting, Twitter, and radio. We can usurp pretty much every form of communication for the government's benefit."

"Mercy. Okay. I'll get President Castillo's go-ahead. I also need to inform him about the two Carrier Strike Groups that will be closing in on the coast of Veracruz sometime tomorrow evening. I'm certain that he will approve. But even though I don't need his permission, I shouldn't let it be a surprise to him."

"Now, what have you accomplished with the extraction of Roger and Butch?"

"We're still working on it. The ground fire has made it impossible for a safe landing at Santa María del Oro."

"Roger told me about the situation there. How long can they hold off this armed cartel mob?"

"As long as they need to."

Kate recognized that she was not going to get the information for a few more hours.

"Okay, Edgar. Thank you. You'll give me hourly updates, right? I'm going back to the Oval Office now. And you're going back to the Pentagon?"

"Yes, ma'am."

She stood and Edgar jumped up. They shook hands. There was nothing left to say for now.

Ezra Jefferson was standing by for the President and walked one step behind her on the way to the West Wing. They took the elevator up to the first floor. He could tell that she was tired, but it was more than that. She looked pale, she had dark circles under her eyes, and her face was drawn, which was unusual. She always managed to look well rested, even when that couldn't have been further from the truth. Her shoulders drooped slightly, too. Normally, she had excellent posture and sat and stood with her shoulders squared. But not this afternoon.

They reached the Oval Office without exchanging a word. Ezra left to stand his post on the other side of her door when her words stopped him. "Ezra, could you stay a moment?"

"Yes, ma'am."

"How are your children? Is Davis still working at the National Arboretum?"

"Why, yes, ma'am. He is happy there with his orchids and succulents."

"And Annie? Wasn't she recently made a lieutenant? Is she still in San Diego?"

"Yes, ma'am. She is hoping that she really will be able to serve as an officer on a submarine. It looks possible."

"I hope so, Ezra. We still have a few hoops to jump through on that."

Ezra smiled at his President, wondering when she would get to the real point.

"I know that you enjoy and support your two children."

"I try to do that. Not always easy."

"That's an understatement." Kate's voice cracked and she squeezed her eyes to keep the tears at bay. She hated to cry. "My boys have put themselves in some danger…for me. I don't know whether to thank them or kick them from here to San Antonio. They…"

Ezra waited. But he moved slightly closer to her.

Kate coughed. "I'm sorry, Ezra. They are grown men. But they disobeyed me. I don't know whether they disobeyed the President or their mother."

"No, Ma'am. But…"

"But what, Ezra?"

"Not my place to say, Madame President."

"Please do. I need a friend who will be honest with me."

"Madame President, your sons are fine men. They saw a job to do and they did it. They are patriots. You are the President, but when families are called on to make sacrifices, you are not immune. TR lost two sons to war and FDR had to send his four sons to war during WWII."

"And my sons went to Mexico to protect this country, and in so doing, protected me. You make such good sense, Ezra. Thank you."

Kate smoothed her hair and rubbed her temples. She attempted a reassuring smile at Ezra, but fell short. "I'm fine now. And I have to make many calls before this night is over. I'd better get with it."

"Yes, ma'am. I'll be right outside the door until you leave again. And I'll be with you then."

"Thank you, my friend."

Ezra quietly left the room, but remembered that he needed to ask about

Madame President

her dinner schedule and pushed the door back open. He shut it without disturbing her when he saw her sitting behind her desk, facing out the window to the Rose Garden, shoulders slumped with fatigue.

Moments later, Kate was on the phone to Rose, asking her to place a call to President Castillo in Mexico City and then to set up a late supper meeting with Ford, Georgeanne, and Sy to discuss tomorrow morning's talk shows.

Washington was a demanding city and presidents were allowed only the briefest of moments for reflection. *Well, Kate, ol' girl, no rest for the weary.*

CHAPTER 18
Sunday, March 6
Denver · Noon

Frost hung in the air outside the windows and Martina couldn't see much past her back yard. She tried to watch a golf tournament on TV and then a movie, but nothing could hold her attention. She and David hadn't spoken again since their previous conversation ended so badly, and Martina felt like a prisoner of time. Everything moved in slow motion.

The doorbell startled Martina out of her misery. "Peter, what a surprise. Make a wrong turn? Kidding. Boy, I'm glad to see you." *I think.* "If you had called first, I could have rounded up some lunch for us."

"Martina, I didn't come here to eat. I came here to talk. The implications of your questions last Wednesday evening have been gnawing at me all week. And I can imagine your anxiety level is off the charts."

There was a moment of hesitation on Martina's part as she realized any additional conversation with Peter would set her on an irreversible path with no certain outcome.

"Well, don't stand there. Come in. I've made a fire in the den and we can sit and warm our bones. It's raw out today, even for the Rockies."

Peter got right to the point. "Martina, I have a friend at the FDA. I trust him enough to bring him in on this and let him make some discreet inquiries as to what the FDA knew about the SST drug trials and when."

Martina was taken aback at the thought of opening the company up to the FDA. "My God, Peter, couldn't that cause a devastating blowback onto the company, even if they don't find anything…and come to think of it, you could find yourself in the middle of a hornets' nest. Nobody likes a whistleblower."

"Yeah, and I imagine it wouldn't do much for your relationship with David."

"My relationship with David? Who knows where we will wind up after my attempt to talk to him. I'll deal with that later."

"We have to do something, don't we? I even tried using some backdoor passwords to access the data, but they've turned the security into a Manhattan Project. Attempting to open the program has already gotten me into hot water with Baines. I have three emails from him already, warning me to back away or else. I can't think of another way to get answers, other than letting me talk to my friend at the FDA."

Martina stood abruptly. "Let's walk. I'll grab my coat. I need fresh air."

They hiked through the wooded acres and talked over every angle, but no other workable ideas surfaced. Finally, shivering and damp, Martina agreed to let Peter make the call. They stood at the door of Martina's striking house, realizing that this might change everything for both of them, but seeing no way around it.

"You'll call as soon as you know anything, right?"

"Of course, Martina. And if you should learn anything else from David..."

"You'll be the first on my call list."

"Fair enough. In the meantime, try to get some rest."

"Right. Easier said than done. Peter, I really am sorry to have drawn you into this, but you were the one person I could trust."

Peter leaned over and kissed her on the cheek. "We'll talk soon."

Martina had more calls to make, but she first tarried in the kitchen to make herself some hot chocolate for warmth.

She dialed from memory and the person on the other end of the line answered after one ring. "Hello Hyler. Can you talk?"

"Yes. I'm back in D.C. It took some coaxing, but I was able to convince Beryl and the kids to finish out the rest of their vacation. I decided I needed to be close at hand, if the President needed me."

"Well, I need you. I think the time has come to ratchet this up a few notches and since we're sitting on the deck of the Titanic together, I thought it fair that we make collective decisions from now on."

Martina updated Hyler on her conversation with Peter and suggested that it was time to inform Roger about their suspicions. Hyler was guarded at first and proposed that they wait to see what Peter turned up from the FDA. But before Martina could respond, he cut himself off. "Oh heck, if we don't inform Roger sooner rather than later and our suspicions turn out to be correct, we'll never forgive ourselves. Do you have any way of reaching him while they are on mission?"

"I'm not sure, but since he's with my brother and my father, I should be able to get through to Santa Maria del Oro."

Now it was Hyler's turn to be flabbergasted. "Mexico? Federico de Franco? Roger? What the blue blazes is going on here?"

"Hyler, you're going to have to trust me on this. I've probably said too much already. Let me try to reach Roger, and if I do, I'll conference you in on the call. It may take a couple of hours until I get through, so please keep your cell close at hand."

As Martina was about to hang up, her other line rang, the one David used. "Hyler, I've got to go. David is calling me from Shanghai."

"Well, good luck with that. My advice? Say as little as possible. And for God's sake, don't mention Peter."

Martina figured that Hyler had to know that she was smarter than that. But the stress was getting to all of them. So rather than be defensive, she signed off. "Wish me well, and we'll speak again shortly."

She picked up the phone and waited a moment longer to answer. "David, it's late there. You should be in bed. But I'm glad you called."

She hoped the tone in his voice would give her an indication of his state of mind. His voice was slurry, a bad sign.

"I thought I'd better check to see what other conspiracy theories you have hatched against members of my family. How about my ex-wife? After all, she's not a very nice person; maybe she has it in for someone."

"Oh, David. I know that you are hurt. But I really did think that I should tell you about my…misgivings."

"Tell me, yes. I can't figure out why you had them in the first place."

"Okay, David. Let's talk later. I don't have it in me to fight now. Get some sleep."

She pulled the phone away from her ear to hang up, but heard David yelling into the line.

"Wait. Don't hang up, Marti. I'm sorry. I actually called to tell you that I am going to do some quiet investigating of this. In my heart, I know it's a wild goose chase, but the answers I find should allay your fears. Do you trust me enough to handle this?"

"Of course, I trust you. That's why I thought we could talk about anything. Would you mind telling me who you are going to question?"

Martina could hear the hesitation in his voice. She chewed on her thumbnail while she waited, a habit from her childhood.

"I am going to ask Peter Tate to audit the patch inventory, even the prototypes. He has to do it on the QT or all hell will break loose for no damn reason. I guess he can do that. You know him. What do you think?"

Martina heard Hyler's voice in her head. Bastard guessed right about David's intuition. Baines must have made sure that David knew of Peter's attempts to get into the SST computer files. *Dropping Peter's name out of the blue was a fishing expedition.* "I think he'll be discreet. He's the right one to look around on your behalf."

Now, it was David's turn to hear that Martina was holding something back.

"What is it, Marti? I can tell that you have something else to say to me."

"It's that…that we don't have a lot of time. You can't move too slowly on this, David. Please make your call to Peter right away."

"Is that all?"

"Yes. What else could there be?"

"I don't know, Marti. It feels like all the rules have changed between us."

"No, David. We're separated by so many miles and I need you to get back here and be absolutely certain that we've done all we can do…to make this right."

"But, Marti, there may not be anything to make right."

"Of course. This may all be my wild imaginings. I pray that's the case. If it is, I hope you can forgive my suspicions."

David was flooded with relief. She sounded sincere. "Sure, babe. I'm trying to get out of here a day or two early. I'll let you know if I uncover any red flags."

"Thanks, David."

"Love you, Marti."

"Love you back."

Martina set her cell phone down on the coffee table and wondered why those last words sounded so sad.

David had reasons of his own to feel sad. He had not told Martina the entire truth. He had already asked Jackson Baines if there were anyone who could get his hands on the initial testing data about the patch. Baines immediately thought of Peter Tate.

According to Baines, Michel Hayek was the real threat and he was still on his annual sabbatical in Beirut. But Tate, even with a fraction of Michel's expertise, might be a problem. Jackson had revamped the entire security system protecting the SST project. Passwords changed on a random basis and firewalls and encryption programs were further enhanced. Still Peter had already made three attempts to access the program. And while he had good reasons for the information he was seeking, Baines, who lived by the "trust no one" motto, was already suspicious.

It was time for David to quit feeling sorry for himself and take control of his company. Why he ever thought that the company could become a democracy was ludicrous. He hoped that Martina wouldn't be collateral damage, but so be it. Her doubt of Valerie might be her undoing.

CHAPTER 19

Sunday, March 6
Santa Maria del Oro · Late Afternoon

"**D**uck!"

Roger, Emilio, Butch and de Franco bolted under the dining room table, while shards of glass and wood pelted the room. Some kind of projectile had hit its mark on the lead glass windows of the hacienda. But it was one missile, this time. More would come as the Los Rojos army advanced on Casa de Pescadero.

Federico, up first, called out, "You okay, Emilio? Roger? Butch?" They nodded and dusted the razor-edged glass off their slacks and shirts. De Franco was about to send one of the men upstairs to check on Michel when Abdel called down that they were fine.

They picked up the conversation where it left off, once de Franco touched base with Lorenzo about the current disposition of his men and a damage assessment of the compound. There were about 100 soldiers remaining on the property, with the domestic and farm workers having been shuttled back to the nearby village of Trés Vados. Most of de Franco's staff were from the village originally and had family there. He had to strongly insist that they leave, to which most readily agreed. For some, however, this was their home and no amount of cajolery would get them to abandon Casa de Pescadoro.

The old house and grounds did not look like a typical cartel compound. To an outsider or even from an aerial view, it would appear much like it did when his grandfather built the fishing lodge.

The hacienda, stables, barn, servants' quarters, pool cabana, boathouse and a dock on the shore of Lake Lazaro Cardenas were unchanged. The visible indication that it was the 21st century was the floating helipad and the custom fitted de Havilland DHC-3 seaplane with STOL capability and seating for 11, next to the dock. Everything else that supported his drug empire had been built underground, with a system of elaborate tunnels connecting all the buildings.

The communications bunker was Lorenzo's first stop. It was state-of-the-art, with a satellite dish cleverly hidden in nearby rocky crags, and so well camouflaged that the casual observer would never spot it. The cell tower grew up in the woods a few miles from the main house, and unlike the bizarrely undisguised cell towers in the States, it actually did look like a real tree, one of the massive Douglas Firs in the Occidental pine-oak forests of the Sierra Madre Mountains. De Franco had been a leader of the reforestation program in these mountains, a felonious, drug dealing, environmental, local hero.

It was a happy little bonus that the beautiful, dense forests did a thorough job of hiding cannabis and poppy plants.

When Lorenzo reported back that there was minor damage and no casualties, other than some very spooked horses, De Franco poured them all a double shot of brandy to calm their nerves, and Butch passed around the glasses. *The bastards did not shatter the liquor cabinet, thank God.*

Federico left the actual coordination of the compound defenses to Lorenzo, while he took on the more complicated task of managing the 1000 or so men beyond the compound's perimeter. He did have some concern about the status of the communications bunker and stables. In order for his plans to succeed, his contact with the outside world, especially Los Pinos and The White House, was critical.

As if reading his padrone's mind, Lorenzo reemphasized, "The communications bunker is in order and as I already said, except for some skittishness on the part of the horses, the stable is calm. The rest of the men have been deployed as lookouts and snipers."

De Franco was no novice in the art of guerilla warfare. Beyond the five-acres, the men he commanded would attack and fade back, appearing as if by magic in another location, making the opponent believe that there were many more men present. They hid in rocky outcroppings and the dark forest, with a main purpose of convincing Guerrera that de Franco's forces were largely concentrated in the vicinity of the lake.

Fortunately for Federico, Guerrera had decided to coordinate this part of Los Rojos' operation from Sabinas, leaving the field command of his army to his chief lieutenant, Manuel Garza. Garza, a former colonel in the Mexican Army was competent, but had little imagination. A flaw that would prove fatal.

"Perhaps it is time I explain in more detail what exactly I have planned for our friend, Señor Guerrera. Please, let's sit for a moment while we have some quiet." De Franco pointed to the living room. "As you know I have aligned myself with President Castillo and Mexico. As part of the agreement, I have deployed men to the outskirts of Mexico City. That began last night."

"But, Father, how could you accomplish that with any degree of secrecy? My God, aren't we talking about 20,000 men?"

De Franco answered the question directly but noted that Emilio had used the word 'Father' for the first time since he was a small boy. De Franco inwardly smiled.

"Thirty thousand, to be more precise. And they are highly disciplined and heavily armed. I think you would say that they are ready for a good fight." In his voice was a hint of pride. In order to continue his explanation of the strategy he and President Castillo had devised, he needed to share a little more background of the organization of his forces. He had parted ways with the other cartels in the management of his army and was always low key in his activities. Yes, violent and cruel when necessary, but good to his soldiers and their families.

He realized that, rather than support a standing army of unruly army deserters and lowlifes, it would make more sense to shape his forces on the Israeli model of having a huge, well-trained reserve that could be called up on 12 hours notice. And he would keep a small force of protectors and enforcers for his day-to-day business operations.

Over the years he was able to refine and develop this system and achieve unheard of loyalty from his men. He hired Israeli ex-military to train them, instilling in them determination and confidence. He created a social network of healthcare and schools that the government didn't provide to the peasants, and in return he gained their trust. One good doctor supplying medical care was worth 1000 times more than the intimidation of lobbing off a few dozen heads into a town square. Ironically, Hezbollah employed this method of social services throughout Lebanon with great success.

And de Franco maintained good relations with the regular Mexican army, never picking a fight with them unless totally necessary.

"I called up my reserves as soon as the President left yesterday. They have pre-designated staging areas where we stationed covered transport trucks to move them toward the capital."

Roger, now totally engrossed in the operational details of de Franco's plan, asked, "How far is Mexico City from here?"

"Oh, about 700 miles. So, it will be late Monday at the earliest before the troops will be in enough force at the outskirts of the capital to be of any use to Castillo."

"I don't understand how you can do this without Los Rojos becoming aware of it." Roger was always the strategist.

"That's where the conversation I had with your mother comes into play."

De Franco remembered the tone of Kate's voice when she asked about her sons. She volunteered to give him real-time satellite imagery of Los Rojos' troop movement (a strategic advantage that Guerrera did not possess), and he promised to get the sons out of harm's way. At one time, such a promise would have meant little to de Franco, but this was one promise that he intended to keep. His word would mean something before he died.

Emilio, who had been uncharacteristically silent, said, "I have always found the President to be a generous person, but real-time satellite imagery is above and beyond. There must have been a battle royal between Edgar and Gabriel over that bit of intelligence sharing."

De Franco laughed. "Decorum prevents me from telling you all that I know."

Roger returned to strategy. "I see. So, the imagery gives you the placement of Los Rojos troops, allowing you to gather your numbers along the way, while avoiding detection?"

"That's the plan. I have received word that the last of our trucks has passed the intersection of Highways 30 East and 57 South and are on route to the Capital. I suspect that we, as you Americans say, were in the knick of time, since the advanced guard of Guerrera's main army has now been spotted east of Monclava.

"We are well underway. If the plan holds, we'll be close to Mexico City before Los Rojos becomes aware of it…and then it's too late."

"But Father, with you and Lorenzo here, who is going to coordinate their movements once they reach the capital? This could be chaos. Seeing armies march into Mexico City is nothing new to our country. But this is a coup, not a revolution."

"That's why I have agreed to place my men under the supervision of Juan Marcos, Castillo's Director of National Security."

Roger whistled. "I bet that's a first."

"I hope that Adán Guerrera sees it that way, as well. My entire strategy is predicated upon both General Vilas and Guerrera underestimating what President Castillo and I are willing to do to preserve the Republic of Mexico.

"I doubt either of them could conceive of our having formed an alliance, let alone my putting my troops under the government command. But perhaps the greatest underestimation of all for them is that a drug cartel leader might actually prove to be a patriot."

Emilio winced at that last reference but continued his questioning, "Will they be able to obey him and not you?"

"Of course, Emilio. By obeying him they do obey me. They understand that. Do not forget that these men are trained to follow orders. And by the time that might be a problem, I will have arrived in the capital."

Emilio wasn't as confident as his father about the behavior of so many armed men without his father's or Lorenzo's direct leadership. But while questioning this decision, they heard the whine of the mortar. It hit its mark at the lake, exploding the seaplane and smashing the helipad into dust. Before the seaplane sank, the fuel tanks erupted and two-story tall flames engulfed the docks. The entire hacienda trembled on its foundation from the ensuing shockwave.

De Franco, always the epitome of self-control, leapt up and screamed a long stream of obscenities. This changed everything. How could he get to the Capital without the seaplane? One impossibly lucky hit from an untrained shooter, and de Franco's promise to Kate was in ruins.

Luigi and Bootsie ran into the house, calling out names. Inca stayed at the front door, weapon up and standing at attention. Lorenzo went down to check on the communications bunker, which was now more critical than ever.

Roger shouted out to let them know his location, which brought Luigi and Bootsie screaming into the room for everyone to hit the floor. The Rangers looked out all the windows and listened for further incursions, but it was quiet.

Luigi told them that they could stand back up. "I'm sorry, but that was too close for comfort. It's time for you to evacuate. What's that going to take now, Mr. de Franco? The seaplane has been blown to hell. Any ideas?"

De Franco's cell phone made a shrill sound. Simultaneously, rings came forth from the phones in Roger and Emilio's pockets.

De Franco answered his first. "Hello, Mr. President. I was going to call you…"

His phone went dead.

Kate had finally gotten through to Roger and was asking about the status of the evacuation. The last words she heard were 'they've blown up the seaplane' when she lost the signal. Roger shook his phone, to no avail. The status bar read "No Service."

And Emilio, glancing up from his phone said, "That was Martina. She has some kind of urgent reason to reach you, Roger. But she didn't finish. We were cut off."

Luigi looked at Bootsie. "Try your SAT phone."

Bootsie did as he was told. Every eye in the room was on him. He turned to Luigi. "Nada. Zip. Zilch."

They were no longer a part of the outside world.

CHAPTER 20

Monday, March 7
Washington, DC · Morning

The waving hands suddenly looked like a sea of angry snakes to Sy, atop the shouting reporters in the press briefing room. He didn't know whether to keep letting them ask questions or to make them slither away. Sighing inwardly, he pointed to another red-faced correspondent "Yes, Bob?"

"When is the President going to make a statement about her Vice Presidential nominee? Will we get to hear from Senator Richter, as well?"

"I've already answered that Bob, every which way but Sunday, so if you don't have something new to add…"

Sy was about to call the press conference to a close. They were circling back to the same questions now, not listening to his previous ten answers on the topic. It was up to the President to speak her mind on Senator Richter's nomination, no one else. All Sy could do was to keep them at bay by asserting her continued faith in her nominee. But he had silently given himself a new title, snake handler. He hadn't been able to achieve snake charmer status.

"Ladies and gentlemen, that's all I have for today. The President stands by her nominee and there are no new reports as to the American response in Mexico. Thank y.."

Sy jumped when all assembled rose without warning, books and cell phones thumping to the floor. He looked around and saw Kate striding into the room, her mouth set in a serious and purposeful line.

Sy cleared his throat. "Ladies and gentlemen, the President of the United States."

"Thank you, Sy. I'll take it from here." She turned to the reporters and made a downward motion with her hands. "Please sit."

Sy stepped away from the podium, standing back and to Kate's right.

She waited a respectful moment for the reporters to retrieve their writing utensils.

"I will not entertain questions today, but I do have a statement. I have been President for over four years now. I am used to the machinations of politics. Healthy partisan debate is good for the country and I do not shy away from it. However, I will shy away from allowing you to be misled by purposeful lies and distortions on the part of those who would hurt our country. This is a vicious rumor campaign about my nominee for Vice President. I do not know yet who is behind this attempt to derail the process, but – and you have my word on this – I will find out, to shine the light of reason on a dark corner of deceit.

"Senator Richter's dealings - personal, political and financial – are above reproach. Simply put, his finances were placed in a blind trust upon his first run for Congress, and have been managed at arm's length ever since. It's that simple. I wasn't going to glorify this silliness with a response until one of the so-called networks took it upon itself to determine that this is news without doing one whit of research. Any simpleton could have discovered Senator Richter's handling of his finances and this rumor could have died the undignified death it deserved. It's in the public record, for Pete's sake. Look it up, people."

A murmur passed through the room. It was a rebuke they apparently deserved, but FOX was putting all the legitimate reporters who worked the White House beat in peril, especially when the network claimed "high level sources" in breaking the Richter story. Most reporters realized that they had enough issues of real importance to keep them writing for the rest of their careers, but they were constantly distracted by trash.

"This is a time when our country needs the kind of faithful leadership that Senator Richter can provide. Characteristics like integrity, devotion, and intelligence come as naturally to him as breathing. He is precisely the person we need during this time of national tragedy and loss, and with the profound unrest in many other parts of the world.

"Which leads me to the situation on our border with Mexico. Mexico is our ally, our partner, and any assault on the people and government of that country is an assault on us. To those who would undermine that country and bring civil disobedience to our border and to the highest levels of Mexican authority, I want to tell you…"

Kate looked directly at the camera.

"that the full faith and backing of the United States of America is at work in this hemisphere. Need I remind you that, while the policy is almost 200 years old, the Monroe Doctrine is as viable today as it was in 1823? Let there be no doubt. We will not allow the incursion of violence into our country, and we will not stand silently by while harm is done to our brothers and sisters on the North American continent. I will have more to say on this topic later, but we are vigilantly watching as events unfold and we have developed a response that will protect American interests, as well as those of the legitimate government in Mexico. To those foreign interests who are neck deep in this, this is our hemisphere. Stand down. Or we will stand you down."

"This is not a time for shrinking violets. It is also not a time for unmeasured action. So, measured we will be, but never afraid or reluctant to defend our allies and ourselves when that is what remains for us to do. Thank you. God Bless America."

No one moved. Kate held the camera with her eyes for a few more seconds, then turned and walked straight and tall down the steps from the podium and out of the room.

The press corps stood as quickly as they could. One wizened reporter turned to his colleague and whispered, "That's a hell of a broad. And now they've made her mad. The bombshell she dropped will completely move the story away from Senator Richter. The next few days could be interesting." He shook his head and laughed, while he packed up his netbook. He had a story to write. A real story.

The foreign interest angle was news, but who the hell was she referring to? He grabbed his cell to call his office before the door had closed behind Kate. Every other reporter in the room did the same thing. This was hot and they were in the dark. But not for long, dammit.

A few miles away in Georgetown, Valerie looked at the teacup in her hand and back at the flat screen television on her sun porch wall. The tea tasted bitter in her mouth. Hatred etched itself in deep lines on her face. She raised her arm and hurled the cup against the porch's brick wall. It fell onto the floor, smashed in a hundred pieces, much as her heart felt. Broken in a hundred pieces.

The fools. Don't they see what she's doing? Manipulating the media, plain and simple. And why hasn't Senator Shepard gone to the mikes to rebut the President. Where's the minority Party when you need them? They're all a bunch of wimps. Men.

Well, they've got their timeline and I've got mine. And with any degree of luck it will be Preston on the TV monitor come the weekend.

In her private study, Kate sat in her favorite chair, surrounded by her most trusted friends. Barbara had begged off. After the reference to 'foreign powers' she needed to get back to State, ASAP. Hezbollah's involvement had been a tightly guarded secret, but soon some inquisitive reporter would land on the truth. Off-the-record comments that State was famous for would work for only so long.

"Madame President, you galvanized the country today. Thank you." Kate smiled at him.

"It's nice to be seen through the eyes of friendship, Ford. Thank you."

"I agree, Madame President. You have set the course for the nomination process and for our response to the situation in Mexico. I'm not quite sure how you did it. But I bet that we move to the final phase of Richter's approval without so much as the blink of an eye now. Congratulations."

"Congratulations are not in order yet, Gabriel. But thanks. I take it that we have heard nothing from Santa María del Oro. Until we know what has happened on the ground there, there's not much comfort for me in any of this."

"I know. But we'll have our forces there within the hour. Now we need to move on to the Situation Room and review the latest updates on events in Mexico City."

"That's fine. But I'd like to know the second we have more information from de Franco's compound."

Kate rose slowly and stretched her neck. She couldn't shake the headache that started in her shoulders and worked its way up. She was as tired as she could ever remember, but that probably shouldn't be too surprising. She missed Deacon and had two sons who had disappeared into the forbidden mountains of Mexico, where a full-blown insurgency was fomenting.

She managed a weak smile. "Come along, gentlemen. We have a coup d'etat to stop."

CHAPTER 21

Monday, March 7
Santa Maria del Oro • Early Morning

The sun had not yet risen over the peaks of the Sierra Madres. Luigi, Bootsie, and Inca huddled together with de Franco and Lorenzo over a topographical model of the surrounding terrain within a 10-mile radius of the compound. Dominick and Andy, the advanced Ranger team, had, also, joined them. De Franco had it updated weekly, with minute details in place, from rock formations to individual trees. The air in the communications bunker was chilled and damp, but they did not feel it. They were deep in the discussion of their mission. All else meant nothing.

"I have been told that Guerrera considers me to be old fashioned. But I would rather have this room and this model than his vainful replica of the White House Situation Room. His hubris will be his downfall."

Luigi stabbed the model in two locations with his Ek F-S MkII commando knife with its 6.6 inch blade made of high carbon surgical steel: one gash mark lay east across the lake and up a steep, forested cliff, about two miles by foot; the other was west between the compound and Trés Vados, about three miles. He pulled the knife out by its walnut grip and put it back in the sheath on his belt. "With our walkie-talkies, we've been able to triangulate the jamming devices to approximately these two locations. Low tech and not precise, but we're pretty sure where that bastard Guerrera placed them."

Inaccessible and well protected. "Fortunately for us, we can hoof it there and back in a matter of hours. If we leave now we should be back right after sunrise. Questions?"

Inca nodded. "Aren't we compromising our main objective if we leave the compound? Doesn't the protection of Emilio, Roger and Butch come first?"

Luigi considered this but pressed on with his initial plan, watching de

Franco. "Señor de Franco has about 100 well-trained men." To a Ranger, no one else is really well trained, but he gave de Franco's soldiers some credit. "And there doesn't seem to be any indication that Guerrera's men are in full force yet. Yes, they can lob a few mortar shells at the compound, but I don't think they can mount a full scale assault…yet." *Lets hope not anyway.*

Luigi continued, "Besides, Bootsie you'll be staying here to coordinate ops and get us uplinked as soon as we knock out the goddamn jammers. If you run into any problems, fire a signal flare and we'll come a-runnin."

Bootsie laughed, tilting back his big, blond head, "Sure boss. Let's not forget that Roger and Emilio were Rangers, so between them and Señor de Franco's men, I think we'll be fine. Go on and have your picnic. Just don't linger."

"Sir," Luigi, turning to Lorenzo, chose his words carefully, "we Rangers believe that we should plan for the worst and hope for the best. We may need to do a helicopter extraction off site. Any suggestions?"

Lorenzo studied the map for a moment and pointed to a relatively flat patch of ground about eight trail miles north of Trés Vados. "Difficult to get to by foot, but definitely do-able." Looking across the table to de Franco he added, "Do you agree?"

De Franco scanned the topography and nodded. "Yes. Difficult but do-able. Let's hope it won't come to that and that we can call in a landing on the grounds here."

"Again, this is worst case, but if we are breached, the shelling will make it impossible for a helicopter to land. I'm trying to protect our options."

"Ah, yes. Of course."

Dominick tapped on his watch and stood. "Let's do this thing before the others wake up and protest. It won't be long before they sense that something is going on."

Luigi looked at de Franco.

"Dominick is right. We are locked and loaded and have to get started. Roger, Butch and Emilio are in your hands. Anything else you need from us?"

"No."

"Okay, Inca and Andy. You've been quiet. Any questions?" Luigi knew full well that Inca would not say a word, but wanted to pull both of them in, a tacit way of putting a claim on them for 100 percent of their resolve.

Andy simply said, "R-L-T-W."

Inca echoed Andy.

De Franco looked at them questioningly. Luigi decided to bring him into their circle. "It means 'Rangers Lead the Way,' sir."

"From what I can tell, I wouldn't argue with that. Emilio never told me of those words before. Thank you." Lorenzo turned away and half smiled to himself, *not to his padre but many times to his Tío.*

"Thank you, sir. You and Bootsie have to realize that we don't know how many men we will encounter between here and the jamming stations. Once communications have been re-established, don't wait for us if you have to pull back to the extraction site. Remember, Guerrera will have the same communications uplinks and will soon know about where the helo will pick you up. I repeat. DO NOT wait for us. Get the hell out, if you have to. Bootsie, you're in charge. Don't take any crap from anyone. You understand?"

"Yessir."

"No other questions? Then let's haul ass. Guerrera is determined to let loose the dogs of war. We must be ready to accommodate him."

Luigi held up the forefinger of his right hand and twirled it twice.

Like a wisp of wind, they were gone.

Leaves rustled to reveal an old wooden platform used as a hunting blind, where now stood a black-clad figure. He bent over and lifted up the large sniper rifle, setting it into place on the warped railing. The AIAW (Accuracy International Arctic Warfare) number L115A1 series was the long-range weapon of choice for the British Army whose influence was still felt all across the Middle East. Its free-floating, stainless steel barrel could be changed in minutes. More essentially, Jad worked alone and this rifle allowed him to carry out most repairs in the field with wrenches and a screwdriver.

Jad looked up and gauged the wind. The air bit into his exposed fingers. He jammed them into his pocket, needing to protect their suppleness. Stiff fingers on a trigger for a target over half a mile away could spell disaster.

He retrieved his small telescope and peered into the lightening gloom. He could make out the rooflines of the compound, and found the front door. When dawn broke, he would be ready and would easily see Michel whenever he showed himself. If his calculations were correct after studying the movement of Guerrera's men, everyone left at de Franco's would be forced to escape. So Michel would have to come out of his hidey-hole. And that meant he could be dispatched and Jad could get back to warm Mediterranean breezes and out of this barren, wind-swept pile of rocks.

Being an assassin meant that he had learned patience long ago. He sat Buddha style on the cold platform and slowed his breathing with meditation. He could wait and he repeated his mantra, smiling. "Jackal." When the moment came, he would separate Michel's head from his body. Just like that.

Adán Guerrera felt a humming in his brain. It began as a small sound, below his conscious awareness. Now it sounded like a blitzkrieg in his ears. It maddened him. He had the compulsion to break something or someone. Fortunately for the servants at the Sabinas hacienda, they were conveniently occupied in other parts of the house. They knew the signs. Their master was a vicious sadist on his best days. When he was like this, he had rot in his soul.

Guerrera lifted an exquisite Chihuly vase with colors of the ocean and he hurled it across the room where it crashed against the stone fireplace. "Damn de Franco and damn Vilas," he said to no one in particular. The General had just informed him that they had made a mistake in committing their troops to take de Franco's compound at Santa María del Oro. Apparently, de Franco had all along wanted to draw Guerrera's men away from the Capital.

"Bastards." Again, Guerrera spoke to the walls. He felt in a fever. How could he order his men to disengage the pursuit of de Franco's compound when he couldn't communicate with the head of his ground forces? The jamming equipment he used to cut off de Franco from the world had the unintended consequence of cutting off Guerrera from his own men and from Manuel Garza in particular.

If he could break through to Manuel, there might be time for him to halt the fight at Santa María del Oro and outflank de Franco's army before they reached Mexico City.

I must think of something before Vilas realizes the jamming devices have prevented me from giving his order. If de Franco eludes the snare around his compound and escapes to the capital with enough men to change the balance of fighting power, well…that must not happen.

Guerrera picked up another vase from his collection. But as gruffly as he had picked up the previous vase, this one he gently placed back in its display case. An idea had gelled. *I'm sure Vilas would have some pithy Sun Tzu piece of advice right now. At least I don't have to listen to the bastard this time.*

CHAPTER 22

Monday, March 7
Washington DC/Mexico City · Mid-morning

Kate wandered through the Rose Garden, still beautiful even without the blossoms. Her thoughts turned to family, some of whom were god-knows-where, if they were alive at all. Communications with Santa María del Oro were still down. At least, she knew that Deacon and Brother were safe in Texas and Lucy was in Washington to hold her mother's hand, quite a role reversal. She smiled.

Well, I ran for this damn job. Twice. Can't complain when it gets hard.

She turned and sat, waiting for the secure line to be established for President Castillo. It beeped. "Hello, Armando. I know that you are in the middle of a terrible situation so we can be brief. Please let me know the lay of the land today."

Kate could hear the weariness in his voice. "All hell is breaking loose. I don't know any other way to describe it. Things in the Capital are unraveling by the second. Troops loyal to Vilas are setting up roadblocks around the city, effectively isolating us. Two of the three major television stations are occupied and I fear that we will soon lose the ability to communicate country-wide."

"Remember, Armando, that we can help with the communications angle. Just say the word."

"Yes, Madame President, I remember and I would be deeply grateful if you could make that happen as soon as possible."

"Of course. Please hold for a moment."

Kate loped to the French door into the Oval Office and told the waiting Edgar to pull the trigger on the communications interference that he had described earlier. "I should remind you that we will lose communications with our Embassy in Mexico, as well. It will take us several hours before we can re-establish contact with them."

"Ambassador Sanchez and Barbara at State are well aware of this possibility and have made contingency plans. The CIA has also been helpful." She raised her left eyebrow in a mock conspiratorial gesture.

Edgar nodded, opened his cell phone and began the process. He looked back up and Kate was walking back to the Rose Garden. He ran to the door and said, "Please tell President Castillo that this should take about 30 minutes. Get everything said that is important to you. Quickly."

"Got it. Thanks."

She sat back down on the bench. "Please forgive me for keeping you waiting, Armando, but I had to speak with my Secretary of Defense to give him the go-ahead on the communications blockade. He said that we should talk fast."

Castillo said something that sounded like "Díos Mío." Then louder, "Thank you, Kate."

"Have you had any word from de Franco?"

"Not since I met with him on Saturday."

"Have his men arrived to help you in Mexico City?"

"My understanding from satellite data that you shared with us is that they are on the way. The first wave from Santa María del Oro should arrive by tonight."

"Who controls the airport?"

"We do. We've managed to hold off the attacks so far. But without de Franco's reinforcements, we will lose it by tomorrow."

"Do you have any sense of the level of support that Vilas has with the Mexican army?"

Castillo weighed his words carefully. "Much of the Mexican army is standing down, not taking sides, because they don't want to move against the government that they have sworn to support. They know that their general is staging a coup d'etat but most of the enlisted men don't support him outright. If reinforcements arrive in time, the enlisted men will see that my government is going to survive and will stick with me. They want to be on the winning side."

"I believe that Ambassador Sanchez has issued orders for all Americans to stay inside. Do you think that's adequate for now?"

"Yes, because regardless of the outcome, Vilas isn't foolish enough to bring your wrath down on his head. He will go out of his way to make sure that American citizens are protected."

"That's what we had assumed, but it's good to hear it from you. Now, Armando, for another difficult issue. Our carriers will soon be in place in the waters off of Veracruz. I am told that our Marines can be in the capital city within two hours of being ordered to do so. I realize that neither of us would wish for this solution, but we stand ready."

"Thank you, Kate. It all hinges on de Franco and his men. I need another few hours to see when and how many arrive. I am certain that you have mounting pressure to deploy those Marines, but it is not time yet."

"I understand. I hope that you understand that the decision may become necessary if we hear of American lives being at stake, or worse, being lost. At that point, I might have to move without your permission."

"Let us both pray that it doesn't come to that. The long lasting effect of American soldiers on Mexican soil would not be a pretty one for either of us."

"Of course. But things will tend to move fast on the ground, once the tipping point has been reached." Kate had made it a point to learn military history. "Don't delay and make it too late for the Marines to be of help to your government."

"It is such a paradox, isn't it? Marines coming to save my government might be the kiss of death to my government."

"And the other paradox is that the most dangerous cartel boss in Mexico is potentially going to be a hero to your country. Life is strange."

"De Franco as the next Pancho Villa? Perhaps."

Kate snapped the phone shut after they promised to stay in communication as much as possible. She paced through the rows of roses. Castillo has to know that she will be damned to wait to deploy the Marines until after Americans are shot at, doesn't he?

Then her thoughts jerked her back to Roger and Butch. Where on earth were those boys?

In his command post, northeast of the capital, at Zumpango, Vilas did a slow burn. He sensed that Guerrera was losing his wits but he couldn't be sure. And then there was the matter of President Castillo actually cutting a deal for aid from a man like de Franco. Could that be? Vilas stopped and laughed out loud. Who am I to talk about cutting deals with the devil? Let's hope that my devil is the more capable of the two.

"General? May I interrupt?"

Vilas waved in his aide. "Yes?"

"The airport is still not under our control, but two television stations have been locked down."

"Good. How soon before I can be on the air and broadcasting?"

"Within the hour. If you intend to do that we should leave for the capital right now."

"Fine. But back to the airport. When should we expect to control it?"

"Of that, I am not certain. We are running short of manpower because there has been more resistance than we anticipated."

Vilas called the man over to a large wall map. "Look here." Vilas pointed to Benito Juarez International Airport. "Those troops are waiting to see who will land on top. When we have the airport and start broadcasting, we will have the advantage. We must redouble our efforts to seize Benito Juarez."

"Yes sir. When will you be ready to leave for the city? I will bring the car."

"In about five minutes. I must first call Guerrera. We need to know when his forces will arrive."

"As you wish."

The General punched in the numbers for Guerrera. Was his devil a match for de Franco? We shall see. The phone rang on the other end. Vilas thought through his remarks. He had to handle Guerrera carefully, to keep him on the string. When this was over and done with, he would personally take great pleasure in putting a bullet in that man's brain. But not yet. Patience.

Vilas heard Guerrera's exasperated voice. "Yes, General Vilas. What do you wish of me now?"

"To be sure that…" The line went dead. Vilas dialed again. Nothing. Damn cell.

He picked up the phone on his desk to try a landline. But there was no dial tone. He looked up at the three television monitors in his office, and noticed that the screens were filled with static. What the hell?

On a tree-lined street in Georgetown, ten black-clothed members of the city's elite S.W.A.T. team crept beneath a first floor window to the back door of a rundown duplex. Venetian blinds hung askew in the windows, revealing five young men gathered around a small television set. They cheered for the Lebanese National soccer team.

The officers took that moment to line up by the back door with a battering ram in place. They did not politely announce themselves but smashed in the thin door and poured into the tiny apartment, guns drawn, screaming at the students to lie down on the floor with their hands behind their backs.

One of the students yelled, "We have rights. What are you doing here? Stop."

A burly officer kicked the feet out from under the noisy one and he tumbled to the floor, stunned and bruised. The student chose to remain still but started to say something else. The officer stood over him, straddling the man's body and pointing a Glock straight down at the base of the his skull. "Shut your ugly face. Keep your head down or I will blow it off."

The officer turned to the back door and waved his hand, indicating that the suspects were all subdued and under their control. A tall man with salt and pepper hair, dressed in a sleek, black suit stepped into the room. He slowly surveyed the dingy place, noting a poster here and there, but nothing more for decoration or warmth. It smelled like stale Turkish tobacco.

The man stopped underneath a banner, attached to the wall with thumbtacks. He studied it. It had geometric lines and stars in gold and red. Three words seemed important to the man because he tapped them with his forefinger. Since he was fluent in Arabic, he read aloud to them in that language. "Arab Student Alliance."

He continued in what he assumed was their native tongue. "Gentlemen, even though the Patriot Act does not require me to do so, I am going to tell you why I am here. You are under arrest for the murder of the Vice President of the United States of America and for the attempted assassination of the President of the United States. On a day when I felt like it, I might ask if you understand the charges that I have stated. However, today, I don't give a flying fuck what you understand."

He spoke to the head of the S.W.A.T. team. "Get them up and out of here. They are mine now."

CHAPTER 23

Monday, March 7
Santa Maria del Oro · Mid-Morning

Brambles tore at Luigi's clothes and scratched his face. He brushed the thorns away from his eyes, stayed in his low crouch, and kept running, catching a glimpse of Inca's back up ahead by fifty yards. Damn that man was fast. They had been at it for almost two hours, but he showed no sign of slowing. The sun was low in the sky, casting muted gray shadows on the dry forest floor, making it hard to determine distance in the haze.

Luigi pressed the walkie-talkie. "Inca, hold up. Map check, over."

Static changed to Inca's voice. "Roger that. Coming up to a small rise in the terrain. Will wait for you there. Over."

Luigi kept his steady pace and caught up to Inca. The light improved by the minute. He pulled out his waterproof maps in their plastic covers and spread them on a flat rock. Inca had his flashlight ready. They studied the marked trails and peered around them. At this higher elevation the trees had thinned and the forest floor became gravel chunks, some with razor sharp edges. Footing was treacherous. Luigi knew that they would have to slow. They could not afford injuries. There were not enough of them. Each man was indispensable.

"Inca, the nest they put in for the jamming device is no more than a half mile from here. We need to circle and approach from the opposite side in order to take the position by surprise."

"According to the map, they have the high ground. C'mon, Luigi. The shadows are still with us. We need to beat the light. We'll reconnoiter, count the fuckers, and take them out."

"No noise, Inca. Up close and personal, like we planned."

"Roger that. Let's go."

Inca blasted off the slippery rocks and Luigi folded his maps on the fly. Within minutes, they circled the device, finding it right where they had anticipated. They saw four men. Luigi pointed at the two in the forward position near the five by five foot wooden platform. The device itself was a harmless looking, misshapen metal contraption expanded from what appeared like an open metal briefcase that emitted a low beeping sound. The guards were half asleep after a long, cold night and heard nothing.

The first one on the east side of the platform felt a momentary surprise before blood oozed from the clean nick in his neck. Luigi quickly realized that this man was no match for him. He turned the man around and looked at him in the eye, the question unspoken. The man nodded and let his body go slack in surrender. Luigi knew that with a flick of his wrist that muscle and tendon could drop down onto the man's chest, along with gushing blood. But Luigi, now behind the man he had spared, set him down. He pressed a piece of cloth in his mouth and secured it with a fast strip of tape. Next, he pulled the man's arms and legs behind his back and hog-tied them with plastic wire, like a cowboy tying down a calf, racing the clock. The man turned his head and looked at Luigi in gratitude, knowing how close he had come to a lonely death on this mountain.

Luigi kept his mind on the task at hand, but allowed himself a moment of surprise and relief that these men guarding the device were young and untrained. *You'd think Guerrera would have deployed his best soldiers to protect such a valuable asset. Well, no time to ponder and no honor in killing these boys.* One of the distinguishing moral guides to a Ranger was that life was precious. They were not mindless assassins. They were soldiers. Honor guided their every move. If it didn't, they washed out. Luigi wiped the blade on his sleeve and held it in his right hand as he slithered along the rock.

On the west side of the structure, Inca found his man and grabbed his head in one hand and his neck in the other. All it would take is one smooth and unhurried motion; he could twist his hands in either direction and the neck would snap like a dry twig. Instead, he secured the boy with restraints and gag in an economy of movement.

Now, where was the man who should be on the other corner of the small platform? Inca felt a surge of adrenalin. Where the hell was he?

Suddenly, a man emerged from the sparse ring of trees, zipped his pants and arranged his boxer shorts. Inca dropped to the ground and held his breath. The man called out in Spanish, "Pedro, where are you? Come out, man. Our orders were to leave one at a time to take a piss. Pedro?"

The man's instincts kicked in. He looked up over the platform, in full alarm. His breath came in ragged jerks. "Esteban? Pancho?"

Pancho answered. "I'm here. Haven't seen Esteban for a few minutes. Hang on. Let me look."

At that moment, Luigi hurled himself against Pancho. He put his hand over the terrified man's mouth and slung him down. Luigi didn't see any reason for killing him but wrapped the plastic cord around arms and legs. Luigi knew that the man, Pancho, would not budge until he was rescued.

Inca slid behind the fourth man. "Don't move."

The fourth man's hands shot up, involuntarily. He felt the knife against his kidney.

"What's your name, mother fucker?"

The man gulped for air. "Felipe."

"Keep your fucking mouth shut, Felipe. Try to stay alive." Felipe, young but no fool, recognized the hopelessness of his situation and would be compliant. Luigi pushed him to the ground and with one swift sweep of his hands, restrained and gagged him, much as he had handled the others.

Luigi called Inca over and they walked around the device. "Let's be quick about this. How 'bout the direct approach? Grab that rock." Luigi found a rock for himself and both men raised their arms and pounded the stones into the device until the beeping stopped and the twisted metal was a pile of tiny shards.

Just then Luigi's walkie-talkie squawked. It was Andy and Dominick reporting in. "We knocked the sucker out and are heading back to the compound."

"Any complications?" Luigi didn't need any additional surprises this morning.

"Not a one."

"Copy that. High-tail it back to the compound. I'm going to assume Bootsie is back on the air and our evac plans are now moving rapidly."

"Wilco. Over and out."

"Okay, Inca. How fast can we get back to the compound?"

"Mostly downhill. One hour. Tops. Can you keep up with me, old man?"

"Watch and learn, asshole. Keep your eyes open. We didn't pass anyone along the way, but the troops will soon be aware that somethin's happened up here."

Inca stopped and looked back at the four Mexican boys who were not ready for primetime. They might get to see their mommas tonight. Not bad.

Madame President

When Inca looked back up the faint trail, Luigi had a head start. No problem. Running was what he was put on this earth to do. It calmed his mind and steadied him.

Rearing and bucking, the horses were a danger to themselves and anyone who approached them. Their hooves battered the stalls, splintering the wood and putting them at risk of shattered fetlocks and knees. But de Franco moved slowly down the center aisle of the stable and spoke to them by name in low, calm tones. Their ears turned in his direction like antennas. The master's voice was all they needed to distract them from the now constant and closer shelling.

De Franco gathered bridles and saddles for the ten quarter horses that remained at the compound. The other 20 in the Pescadero herd had already been ridden to the safety of Trés Vados. With help from several of his men, along with Lorenzo, Bootsie, Roger, Emilio and Butch, de Franco oversaw the preparations for the ride. He gave a silent prayer of thanks for the native intelligence of this breed. The quarter horse had the gifts of bursts of speed, coupled with endurance and an easygoing nature. It took this kind of intense noise and fear to get a quarter horse spooked, a good early warning system. If these horses were nervous, it left no doubt that it was time to leave. They would take all ten horses. Not one would be left to suffer without his herd.

Michel stayed in the house, resting in the downstairs library until the last possible moment before they had to mount up. Bootsie worried that Michel wouldn't be able to sit in the saddle but they would not cross that bridge for a few more minutes. The house and grounds were almost deserted because de Franco had sent most of his staff on to Mexico City. Bootsie pushed the remainder of them to get moving, and fast.

Lorenzo touched de Franco's shoulder. "Federico, I will help Michel prepare for the ride. Do you need anything else from the house?"

De Franco thought about all the beautiful things he would probably never see again. They would be destroyed before he could return. He wished he could take some family portraits and photographs, but no. They could take the clothes on their backs and some water and food. He kept the sadness from overwhelming him with a shrug of his shoulders. Looking up from over the ample rump of his favorite horse, Tornado, he simply said, "Thank you, Lorenzo. The house can be rebuilt. But not so easy for broken bodies. Please retrieve Michel. We will ride and not look back."

Emilio looked at his father from the other side of the next stall and smiled at him, a genuine, heartfelt smile. "We'll be back here, father. It will once again be the home of our family."

De Franco's spirits lifted. Even if he had to lose everything in order to keep his son, then so be it. He called out to Lorenzo's retreating form, "Thank you, Lorenzo. No man ever had a finer friend than you."

Lorenzo raised his right hand and turned. "It is good to ride with you, once again. Let us show these boys that we are not so old, that we can win this horse race to the helicopter. What shall we wager?" The sound of his hearty laughter could be heard all the way to the house.

Lorenzo found Michel on the couch where he had left him, and he groaned inwardly at the difficulty Michel would pose on horseback. Lorenzo figured that he and Federico were the best riders and could take turns holding the reins of Michel's mount. It was tricky when going at full gallop, but manageable. The best horse for Michel would be the sturdy and pliable mare, Bella, who would help them tend to the still-broken man.

"Michel, it is time for us to leave. I don't know how much time we have before all of the perimeters will be breached. We must ride to safety. I will help you. We pledged to get you out of here alive, and that we will do. Please stand up."

Michel looked at the handsome older man, with his wavy auburn hair streaked with white and his clear gray eyes. All he could muster was a nod at Lorenzo and then he pulled himself to a sitting position. Such a strange place. It had been wonderful and terrible, not in that order, of course, and had become a paradoxical kind of refuge.

Michel bent over and reached for his shoes. He was fully dressed otherwise. Lorenzo leaned in and grabbed them. He knelt and placed Michel's feet in the sturdy leather walking shoes.

"Thank you, Lorenzo. I don't know how it could be so, but I actually believe that you will get me out of here."

"Yes. Of course, Michel. We have enough regret about you to last two lifetimes. We do not need more shame heaped on our poor heads. I hope that you can, one day, forgive what occurred here."

Michel thought that over. Probably not. But he allowed Lorenzo to help lift him off the couch and he took the older man's arm as he limped to the door and began to push it open. They both stopped at the same instant as if held back by an invisible wall. They looked back into the room.

"I will try, Lorenzo."

Lorenzo pressed against the door with his free hand.

A half-mile away, Jad Farrah sat perched on a massive stone outcropping, his rifle's telescope trained at the door of de Franco's house. Minutes earlier, he had spotted Abdel leaving the house through a side entrance, looking in all directions and bent low to avoid detection. *What the hell is that piece of camel dung doing here?*

No time to ponder. He returned his concentration to the door. Michel and company couldn't afford the luxury of any more waiting time. If they didn't leave now, the incoming soldiers would take care of the job for him. That wouldn't be right. Michel was his.

In his rifle sights, he saw the wide wooden door move a couple of inches.

Andy and Dominick had been running, kicking up dust and rocks, for an hour. Their arms and legs were pulsing with the adrenaline that came from the successful elimination of the jamming device. The run back to the compound felt like a jog in the park, compared with their Ranger training outside of Fort Benning, Georgia. And because they completed training in the same class and had been deployed together for over five years, they knew each other better than they knew their own brothers and sisters.

So, when Andy held up his right arm with his hand in a fist, Dom saw it and pulled up without question and without making a sound. He followed Andy's lead and dropped in low behind a boulder. Andy pointed to a sharp right bend in the path. A stand of trees encircled an outcropping of rock. Then Andy motioned Dom to look up from there. He saw the man poised behind the L115A1 sniper rifle, saw the finger on the trigger, saw the man slow his breathing to steady his shot. His aim was in the direction of the compound. But who was his target?

Without one wasted motion, one twitch or blink, Dom pulled his M9 Beretta out of his holster and rose, as though a marble statue found a way to stand without having flesh and bone. He planted his feet. He knew that he had one shot, that the killer ahead was within a split second of finding his target. The boulder that provided Dom's hiding place impeded his line of sight and he couldn't risk stepping out for a better shot. This position would have to do.

Jad saw the door move and then open. He held his breath. His pulsebeat slowed even more. Out walked the target with an older man. Between the next two beats of his heart, Jad knew the time was now. He waited. One beat.

Dom's eyes did not waver. He pulled the trigger.

Jad felt the scorching burn in his left arm just before he pulled his own trigger. It jostled his right arm enough that his shot was a fraction out of line. He screamed, the sound of a wounded animal, and whirled around before knowing who or what his bullet had found down below.

Lorenzo spun and fell back from the impact of the high velocity bullet. He looked surprised when he caught Michel's eye. He put his hand up to the base of his neck and it was covered with blood. What was this?

Michel yelled for help and managed to hold on to Lorenzo so that he wouldn't fall hard. Men came running from the stable and saw that Lorenzo and Michel were on the ground. De Franco slumped to the ground next to Lorenzo and listened for his breathing. He was still alive.

Michel's voice trembled. "What happened? We were walking out of the house and then we were on the ground. How is Lorenzo? Do something."

Through a film of blood and narrowing vision, Lorenzo saw de Franco. He inched his hand toward him and tried to smile. "Looks like you're going to have to get these people out of here without me."

De Franco rocked back and forth on the hard ground. "Don't talk. You'll be fine. We'll get a doctor and put you back, good as new."

"No lies, Federico. There's not much time. Make this right with Emilio. He's a good boy. Fight Guerrera."

"Don't talk, Lorenzo. We'll patch you up."

Lorenzo looked at his friend. Then the light left his eyes.

Dom fired again, but missed. Andy pulled his gun, a motion that caught Jad's eye. He found Andy and blasted away with the sniper rifle.

Dom saw a hole explode in Andy's chest and deep red blood poured out. Miraculously, Andy moved; he was still alive. Dom fell over him, facing out, to protect him from another shot. He looked up and raised his gun. He would make a stand here. By God, he might die, but not before he took out the assassin.

Jad rolled off the boulder and took cover. He peered between a slit in the rocks. One man was wounded but there was the other to deal with, the one who was lying on top of his comrade. Jad pulled his spare gun out of its vest holster, checked to be sure it was loaded, and fired in the direction of the men.

Jad made a rapid mental calculation. The one could still get a shot off. He could start running now, leave his gear here and beat that one man down the mountain to safety. Why stay and die?

Jad crawled and fell away from the high ground while Dom kept his arm raised and his aim sure. He heard the scrabbling, slipping sounds that Jad made as he ran down the trail that careened to the valley. Dom stood and chased the sound but knew he could never catch him now.

He returned to the side of his friend and sat with his back against the boulder. He cradled Andy's head in his arms and pressed cloth into the wound. He could slow the bleeding but not stop it. Every time Andy's heart beat, blood spurted. Dom figured that this whole encounter had lasted less than one minute and Andy was going to die. How could life change that fast? What the hell was he going to say to his friend's parents and his wife with a baby on the way?

Andy stirred. In a whisper, "Dom. Dom. I need to tell you a couple of things. First, call this into Bootsie and Luigi. The walkie-talkie is in my front vest inside pocket. Get on the horn and tell Luigi what happened. Now."

Dom fumbled around and found the vest pocket. He pushed in the talk switch, "Luigi, over. Over."

Luigi answered, "Dom. What the hell is happening man? Bootsie called in..."

"Luigi, listen to me. Andy was shot by this bastard we stumbled on between us and the compound. Andy...it's bad, Luigi. Real bad."

"Dom, what is it? You mean he's not gonna' make it?"

"No, Luigi. Gotta' go. Oh yea, I wounded the dick head before he got his shot off. I'll get back to you in a couple of minutes. I've got to check on Andy."

"Wait, Dom. Just stick with Andy. We've got to get these people evacuated. We'll come back for you after we get them to safety. Got that? Stay put. What are your coordinates? Over."

"Jesus, Luigi, I don't know."

"We are at 25°40'58.67" N and 105°12'38.99" W, Dom."

How could Andy's brain still be functioning?

"Luigi, over. Andy says that we are at 25°40'58.67" N and 105°12'38.99" W. You know how he always keeps up with that shit. Oh man." A sob caught in Dom's throat. This couldn't be happening.

"I copy, Dom. You'll be safe there. All the action is down here now. Tell Andy to hang on, over.

"Hurry man."

Andy groaned. "Dom. Listen to me. Tell Deb that you'll help her with the baby. I appoint you. Say you will."

"Yea, okay. I'll figure it out. You know I'm no good with kids."

Andy tried to smile. "Okay, figure it out. Tell her…tell her that I thought of her last."

"Quiet, Andy. You always did talk too much. They'll be here for us in a few minutes. Just be still. Come on, Andy."

Dom looked up at the brightening sky. It was clear, icy blue. He looked back down at Andy, who was now still. He rested his forehead on the top of Andy's head. "Go with God, Andy. I'll watch out for us now."

Dom leaned back against the rock and focused his eyes on the trail. He kept his left hand on the hole in Andy's chest and held his gun at the ready in his right. *I will never leave a fallen comrade to fall into the hands of the enemy.* "I'll take care of things here."

Roger and Butch ran to the porch and assumed a protective stance, guns held at the end of outstretched arms in the direction of the shot.

Emilio came up beside his father and put his hands on his shoulders. He looked at his Tío Lorenzo whose unseeing eyes were still open. Emilio bent down and gently closed the lids. "Father, we must leave. We can hear the troops approaching. Tío is gone."

"But…but what happened? Who shot him? Why?"

"We don't know that now. We will find out later and I will kill him with my own bare hands. But now we must leave."

De Franco bent down and kissed Lorenzo on the forehead. "Farewell, old friend. Perhaps, we will be meeting again soon."

Bootsie and Emilio half carried and half dragged Michel to the stables. They loaded him on the mare and tied his hands to the saddle horn. De Franco, mounting his own horse, began to assert some control. "I would like for Emilio to lead us out of here. He knows the way. Emilio, take the trail that's about fifty yards off the road. We'll circle Trés Vados and find the evacuation site to the northeast about three more miles. That is the most secluded route. It should take us about two hours, at most."

Bootsie held it together, not allowing himself to think of his two men left on the mountain. First things first. The helicopter then his men. He pointed at the last stall. "Emilio, I have secured two horses for Luigi and Inca. They will be right behind us and will probably catch up since we will be slowed by Michel."

Emilio was puzzled. "But what about the other two Rangers. Wasn't it Andy and Dominick? Won't they need horses?"

Bootsie shook his head sharply no. Emilio asked no further questions but looked at Roger for confirmation. Roger nodded.

Emilio gave his order firmly and quietly. "Okay then, I will take the lead. Butch, you're good on a horse. Can you guide Michel's horse and keep you both at a gallop?"

"Yep."

"Roger, you bring up the rear. Father, you're behind me. Diego, Pepe, you're behind my father. Is that all the horses? No, there's Rosa. Who should be riding her?"

Butch figured it out immediately. "Where the hell is Abdel? I haven't seen him since we left the house."

Roger yelled, "Dammit. That weasel. I bet he left on his own. I have to find him." Roger wanted to take Abdel with him as confirmation of the conspiracy to frame de Franco.

De Franco intervened. "Roger, there is no time. Abdel served his purpose. We got what we needed from him."

Roger wasn't sure about that, but he let it go.

"All right. We will stay in single file as much as possible. But we must ride in close formation. Stay alert. Keep up."

Emilio raised his right hand and twirled it twice. The horses had been dancing with nerves, and exploded from the stable yard. Since everyone was a decent rider, they soon formed a single line of horse and man, galloping flat out, leaving Casa de Pescadero behind, as though it were a mirage, never real.

CHAPTER 24
Tuesday, March 8
Northern Mexico/Bandera, Texas • Morning

The blades, coupled with the roaring engines of the Sikorsky UH-60 Black Hawk, made too much noise for the passengers to speak easily, even with their headphones. So they mostly didn't try, preferring to ride consumed by their own thoughts.

Roger took another head count, out of nervousness and fatigue. Butch, thank God, Bootsie, Michel, the pilot, and two other Rangers sent as reinforcements. They had narrowly escaped, thanks to de Franco having some of the best horses in the world. The two minutes head start had given them just enough time to reach the evac site. Roger could still see the rage on the face of that maniac Garza as the birds lifted off and out of range.

De Franco's men spirited the horses out of harm's way and disappeared into the forest. Roger remembered the line of the now bare horses evaporating into the dark green rim of trees.

Roger had questioned Emilio's decision to go to Mexico City with de Franco. Then he felt selfish. With Lorenzo dead, Emilio probably thought he needed to support his father and President Castillo. And why the hell send in a sniper just to take out Lorenzo? Sure, taking out de Franco's second in command would be a plum in Guerrera's basket, but a sniper in the middle of an attack? Makes no sense.

Roger's thoughts turned to Luigi and Inca. They had gone back for Dom and Andy and he prayed that they made it to them before anyone else.

Worst of all was the loss of a Ranger, and on his watch. *Dammit it all to hell.* He suddenly felt queasy and realized to his horror that he was going to be sick.

Before he could reach for the airsickness bag, his cell phone buzzed insistently. He hadn't felt that vibration for days because of the communications

240

breakdown. No contact with the outside world for over 24 hours. He pulled it out of his front pocket. "Yes. Speak up. I can barely hear you."

He heard a familiar voice, but it was out of context and the connection was bad. He couldn't make it out.

"I'm sorry, who am I talking to?"

Martina yelled, "Roger. Roger, it's me, Martina. Thank God I've reached you."

"Martina? Why are you calling me?"

"Because I have some urgent news that can't wait and Emilio told me that you all had separated and I should call you on your private cell. What is all that noise?"

"The sweet sound of a Blackhawk's blades. Okay, you've reached me. Can't this wait until I'm back at Aguila?"

"No. Roger, before I say any more, I'm going to conference in Hyler Ellison."

"Hyler Ellison? The televangelist? You've got to be kidding."

"This is serious and it concerns your mother, I mean, the President, and I need Hyler to verify what I'm about to tell you."

The tone in Martina's voice, coupled with the strange circumstances, shook Roger out of his lethargy. The adrenalin kicked in again and the fatigue vanished, as did the nausea.

"Go ahead."

Fifteen minutes later, what little color that had returned to his face, once again disappeared. He cradled his head in his hands, mashed his forehead, and tried to marshal his thoughts. Michel had watched Roger during the conversation and gathered that something huge had just happened but knew that it was not his place to question Roger.

For his part, Roger had not wanted to sit next to the man who brought explosives into America, even if Michel didn't know the targets of the bombs. Michel was still completely responsible for the consequences of his actions. He crossed the border with terrorist weapons. And by all that was holy, he would pay for the death of the Vice President.

In a moment of stunning clarity, having processed what Martina just told him about the quit smoking patch that his mother was wearing, Roger snapped his head up and looked at Michel. "You son-of-a-bitch. You tried to blow up my mother, now you're trying to poison her. De Franco should have finished what he started with you." With blood in his eyes, Roger threw himself on Michel and placed him in a guillotine hold. With any luck, the bastard would be dead in two minutes. Tops.

Fortunately for Michel, Bootsie's reactions were faster than the effects of the chokehold. He leapt across the chopper and with his strong arms, encircled Roger's chest and yanked him off of Michel. "What's wrong with you man? Our orders are to get him back stateside for questioning."

Michel sat back up, sputtering and coughing. He rubbed his neck. Roger was stronger than he looked.

"This bastard tried to kill my mother with a bomb, and when that didn't work, he decided to poison her."

Bootsie looked back and forth between the two men, then fixed his gaze on Michel. "What the hell is he talking about? Better talk fast, mother fucker. Or I'm gonna' let him have you."

Michel choked out, "I don't know. He took a phone call and then went berserk. I'm not trying to poison his mother." Michel moved down the bench as far as his straps would let him. "Keep him away from me."

"Listen, you sniveling little worm, it cannot be a coincidence that some kind of patch designed by Valentine Pharmaceuticals to help people quit smoking is now on my mother and probably delivering poison into her system. You're the only person connected to both events."

Michel screamed. "But I'm not. I don't know what you're talking about."

"Weren't you the lead scientist on the – what's it called – the SST patch?"

"Yes, but what has that got to do with poisoning your mother?"

"Weren't there some bad side effects before you got it right? I mean side effects like death."

"How would I know? I left on sabbatical months before the first test results came in. If there was a problem with the patch, no one shared that information with me."

"So you want us to believe that you've had no contact with Valentine Pharmaceuticals in almost a year?"

"I don't care what you do or don't believe. I was in Beirut teaching before the first test trials began. You can check with both Valentine Pharmaceuticals and with the University in Beirut."

Roger was now a little less sure of himself. "You had damn well better believe we'll check."

Roger made the calculated decision to probe further with Michel, knowing that he couldn't entirely trust the answers. "Okay, maybe you could help me understand how something like this is even possible? The patch has FDA approval, right? Is it possible a prototype could have had deadly consequences and the Government wasn't made aware of it?"

"You bet. Let me try to get this straight. You're implying that somehow the President got an early box of the fatally flawed SST and that the patch may be poisoning her?"

"Not implying, saying." *Asshole.*

Michel held up his hand to stop Roger from asking another question. "Give me a moment to try to make some sense out of this."

By the time they had landed at the ranch, Michel had postulated a theory that just might make sense out of what Martina had told Roger. He kept it to himself. It could be his bargaining tool out of this mess.

CHAPTER 25
Tuesday, March 8
Beirut • Early Afternoon

Nasrallah nodded into the phone as he gazed around the cramped ISRO office. Talal, standing because the Sheikh had usurped his desk, waited expectantly.

"I know, but you never mentioned US Army Rangers. What in the name of all the prophets are they doing with de Franco?"

"Listen you dog I don't give a shit who your mother fucks. If Michel is still alive, you have failed me."

"Eminence, please understand I had the perfect shot but a Ranger came out of nowhere and winged me at the moment I pulled the trigger. I know I hit someone, all I'm saying is that the trajectory may have changed slightly and I turned before I could confirm the hit."

"Not good enough. We must assume that the Rangers were there for one reason. The fuckin' Americans got to Michel before we did."

"But Eminence, even if by the curse of Allah I missed, and he is now in their hands, all he can confirm is what they already know."

"I don't pay you to speculate on such matters. Did you see anything else of interest?"

"Two US Army helicopters taking off. One heading due east and one heading south."

The spittle was now noticeable on the Sheikh's beard. Talal tried to move closer to the Sheikh, fearing that he might be having a seizure of some sort. But Nasrallah just waved him off and continued speaking into the cell phone, but not before he switched it to speaker so Talal could hear.

"Do you have any thoughts on where they might be heading?"

Jad laughed to himself after the reprimand about speculating. "Eminence, based upon what I have been privy to in terms of our strategy in Mexico, I would assume that de Franco is heading for the capital. As for the other bird, who is in it and where it is headed, I'd guess it's the Americans. And probably, if he is still alive, Michel."

"Perhaps you are right. Michel will be of limited use to the American pigs. I still want him eliminated, but there is time for that once the Americans realize how little he knows. Hold while I speak with Talal."

Talal, who was looking down at a flyer, felt Nasrallah's eyes boring a hole in his head. He visibly shrank back into a chair and waited for the onslaught.

"This is all your doing, Talal. This was your strategy, starting with the cartels and then the assassination to keep the Americans distracted."

"But Eminence, don't forget that we set this up in such a way that it would appear to be the Iranians who were behind it. And the students who were arrested will confirm Tehran's involvement."

"The Americans may be gullible but they are not stupid. They have other sources and will get to the truth."

Taking Jad off hold the Sheikh continued to think aloud. "Do you have any thoughts on what the Americans will do with Michel, assuming they have him, once they are done interrogating him?"

"If it were we who held him, I'd say cut him into a thousand pieces and scatter his flesh for the crows to eat. But Americans are different and, as you say, Michel will be of limited help to them in terms of the assassination plot.

"Oh before I forget, your Eminence, there was one other curious thing I spied at the compound."

"Yes?"

"Abdel Salam."

Nasrallah's eyes narrowed to cobra slits. His face became mottled with dark purple blotches. "Say that again."

"Abdel Salam."

"Are you certain?"

"Yes. I saw him escaping the compound as they were coming under attack from Guerrera's forces."

This time Talal ignored the Sheikh's hand gesture to stay put and leapt to Nasrallah's side.

Nasrallah attempted to gain control of his trembling body, to no avail. He pushed some papers aside and leaned on the messy desk, with Talal's help. Nasrallah, now gasping for air, spoke into the phone. "I understand. This changes everything. Again I must ask you to hold."

"Talal, you realize the implications of what Jad has said?"

"If Abdel was a mole, and if he somehow learned the truth about the demise of Michel's family, we are dead men. But Jad must be mistaken about seeing Abdel. Besides, there is no way Abdel could have learned about all that."

"Usually, Jad is not a man who makes mistakes. We have to assume that it is true, that Abdel is a rat in our midst, gnawing on our insides."

"Even if that is so, how would Abdel know anything so personal about you? He was never privy to that kind of information."

"Privy...no. But there are other ways to know things. It is time to search the office, and my house, for bugs. I told you that Abdel was an abhorrence to God."

"We sweep the offices every week. It's not possible...."

"Don't tell me what is and what is not possible. Check again and, for your sake, I hope you find none. If Michel has discovered the truth from Abdel, he will write chapter and verse about us for our enemy...and then, he will come after us. I do not underestimate the man who once considered me his father. Neither should you."

"I do not, your Eminence."

Talal waited for a response, but Nasrallah's eyes were closed and he rocked back and forth on the edge of the desk. "All of our plans, Talal...all of our plans to control Mexico and use it as a gateway to further corrupt and ultimately destroy America...all of it could be gone. Now it all may come down to a traitorous General and a psychopath drug lord and the next few hours in Mexico City.

"How could it have come to this?" His lips pulled tightly against his teeth, biting his upper lip until he drew blood.

As Talal backed out of his own office, Nasrallah shouted to him, "Talal, Abdel is your creation and your problem to deal with. Do you understand?"

"Yes, your Eminence. But back to Michel, surely the Americans would not let a man continue to live who had assisted in the assassination of their Vice President."

Picking up the phone once the door was closed, the Sheikh hit the speak button. "Jad, are you still there?"

"Yes, Eminence."

"Talal thinks the Americans will take care of our Michel problem. I'm not so naive. The Americans have a long track record of expediency and little conscience when it comes to these matters. Look at how quickly they recruited former Nazis, Stassi members, and even KGB agents."

"But your Eminence, do you think public opinion in America would allow such a choice in this instance? Michel participated in the assassination, even though he did not know the purpose of the explosives."

"What I think is of no importance. But what I know is that war is strategic and not moral. If Michel can be of help to them, especially in their quest to get to me, then they will do so without compunction." *And I'm not about to share with you the leverage Abdel might have to help turn Michel against us.* "Yes, I understand that Michel's involvement in this affair was tertiary at best, but if you really did see Abdel coming out of the compound and if Abdel had time to speak with Michel alone, Michel might become a very valuable asset to the Americans."

"Eminence, it is not my place to question your reasoning. What do you wish of me?"

"It's time for us to be one step ahead of those accursed infidels. Figure out where the Americans will take Michel and be there to greet him."

"As you wish, Eminence."

"Oh, one last thing. Once you've dealt with Michel, there is one additional assignment that requires your unique expertise."

The sweat poured down Nasrallah's face as he contemplated the past few days. He opened and closed his fist and slammed it against his other hand, in a hypnotic rhythm that became faster and faster. Suddenly, he stopped and tore through the papers on Talal's desk. He saw his worry beads and grabbed them, like a drowning man grasping for a life preserver in a storm.

He rolled them in his hand and began rocking again. He emitted a low guttural sound and palmed the beads harder and harder. They snapped off of the leather thong that held them together, scattering and bouncing across the floor like so many broken dreams.

CHAPTER 26

Tuesday, March 8
Bandera, Texas · Early Morning

Bootsie slipped in beside Roger. "We are 15 minutes out from Aguila. Our plan is to land there and spend the night. You still good with that?"

"Maybe. I need to talk to my father as soon as we land. After that, I'll let you know how fast we have to move."

"Fast is my middle name. I'll radio in and ask your father to be ready. What about Butch?"

"Yeah, I guess both my brothers should be there."

"Got it."

Bootsie turned and spoke into the squawk box.

"Hey, Bootsie. Have we heard from Luigi?"

"Yup. Two minutes ago. They found Dom and Andy and are bringing them back down the mountain. Dom's a little out of his mind from lack of water, but he's in good hands and will be well tended to."

"How are they getting out of Mexico?"

"We've got another bird on the ground at the evac site, and Luigi should have his team there by horseback in an hour or so."

"With Guerrera's men still all around will they have an hour?"

"That's the really strange thing. When the helo landed, none of Guerrera's soldiers could be found. It's like they vanished into thin air after we took off."

"Odd, but lets be thankful for small favors."

"One more thing. The Director of Homeland is sending someone high up, along with a contingency from the Secret Service, to take Michel back to Washington."

Roger nodded. *We'll see about that. I'm not sure Michel is going anywhere until I decide what's to be done with him.* They felt the helicopter slow and descend. Within moments, it bumped to the ground. Deacon covered his head with his big, muscled hands, ran to it, and jerked open the door. He looked in and spotted his two sons. He said a quick prayer of thanks and helped the men on board to the ground. When he got to Butch, he didn't know whether to cuff him or hug him. He jerked him forward, held him in a tight embrace and said in his boy's ear, "If you ever do something like this again to your mother and me, no need to hurry home. I'll find you and kill you myself."

"Thanks, Pops. Good to see you, too." Butch ducked down and squirmed away. He ran into the house, shouting, "Got to be something to eat in here."

Deacon ushered the others into the house. Bootsie held Michel by the elbow and asked where he should take him. Deacon looked startled, but suggested that Michel be placed in the small library to the right of the front door. "You can lock the door from the outside, though it doesn't look to me like this man's in any shape to run away. Why don't you park him there and get yourselves some food and drink. The spread is in the dining room. You remember where that is, I'm sure."

Bootsie nodded his thanks and pushed Michel up the porch and away from Roger as quickly as possible. Deacon waited for Roger to exit and took him by the shoulders, looking him hard in the face. "Son, I know you lost a good man out there. You did your best. Now, you can't let it eat you alive. There's too much left to do, and your mother needs you back in D.C. on the first flight we can set up for you."

"I know, Pops. I'm okay. I'll grieve another day. But there's more that you don't know about and I need to lay it out for you."

"Sure, son, Bootsie told me that you needed to get with me ASAP. But let's get you some food and drink first. You look like hell. How 'bout we reconnoiter in the upstairs study in 10 minutes. That'll give me time to see to the others."

"Yeah. All right. But no longer than 10 minutes, Pops. This can't wait."

"Just me and your brothers, right? I'll get both of them." Deacon trotted into the house wondering what the hell was going on now. Hadn't they dodged a big ol' bullet in Mexico?

Twenty minutes later, when Roger had finished giving the men in his family the rundown on Mexico and Martina's suspicions, Deacon kept trying to push down his anger so that he could think clearly. *Think. Think, dammit.*

"Okay, Roger. Are Martina's concerns credible? Who else can we talk to about this? Who knows anything about the drug that we can pull in immediately to help us? We no longer know whom to trust, do we?"

"All I can tell you is that Martina is convinced that mother is in real peril. And it's not just Martina." Roger went on to share what Hyler had added to the conversation. "They will do anything to help us, but she's a foundation president and he's a preacher."

"Well, let's go rip off that goddamn patch and ask questions later. Why are we standing here talking? She's got an army of people in the White House we could call right now. Or she can take it off herself, for Pete's sake." Deacon opened his cell and pushed a number on speed dial.

"No, Pops. Stop. Hang up. Martina's no expert but she's been in the world of pharmaceuticals her whole life and she has some concern that removing the patch prematurely might do more harm than good. Since I mentioned Michel, she suggested that we have an expert right here and should talk to him first. That is if we can trust the bastard."

Brother stood and massaged his neck, which suddenly had become as stiff as a frozen rope. "Roger, this is beyond us. Shouldn't you bring in the FBI and the Secret Service?"

"Yes, which I will do next. I wanted to tell you first."

Butch, the baby brother, usually listened without talking during these family pow-wows. His place was to be the reckless, devil-may-care sibling with the wicked grin and movie star good looks. He rarely offered suggestions in the company of his father and brothers, whom he considered to be towering intellects. But they were all missing something.

"Roger, I think you should take Martina's advice and talk to that dirtbag downstairs. After all, if he was the lead scientist on this before the shit hit the fan, I'll wager he could be of some help here."

"He was." Roger looked at his brother with new respect. "But I don't know. He's a murdering bastard and we can't trust anything that comes out of his fucking mouth."

Butch swallowed, his Adam's apple bouncing up and down. "Uh. You may be right. But...I'm not so sure. I had a chance to talk to him some. He hates his old man and wants to exact revenge on him. I think that he would do anything to help us, especially if he knew he could go and take care of daddy when we were through with him."

Deacon saw the sense of this. "Butch may be right, Roger. It's worth a try. What do you have to lose tonight? Tomorrow, you can put him under a maximum-security prison if you want to. Let's use him. See if he can give us some inside information about the patch or, at least, tell us where to look."

"But, Pops. It was his explosives that blew up Vice President Franklin's car. We can't ever forgive that."

"Son, I would forgive the devil and have dinner with him in the fiery furnace if it helped your mother. C'mon. Let's go down and join Bootsie and this man, Michel, in the library. I'd like to have a word or two with him."

Deacon cracked his knuckles and marched out of the room. His boots made a loud, thumping sound on the stairs. His sons looked at each other and back at the door. They jostled to be the next one behind their father. Roger won.

CHAPTER 27

Tuesday, March 8
Mexico City • Morning

The unmarked Blackhawk that evacuated Emilio and de Franco from Santa María del Oro touched down at Army headquarters. The pilot, a Ranger, had reluctantly agreed to circle the capital before landing so they could get a feel for what was happening on the ground. Though it was dark, they saw the sharp light of gunfire and flashlights running in a chaotic array of directions.

At Zumpango, campfires and tents with lanterns spread even more light. The General looked up when he heard the Blackhawk rotors, a distinctive sound among helicopters. He momentarily wondered who was flying over the capital at this time of night, but forgot as soon as his aide broke into his thoughts.

"General."

"Yes, Captain."

"Would you like me to leave the overnight report?"

"Yes, but go ahead and give me a quick update."

"One of our biggest problems is the looting going on across the city. People are on a destructive rampage, burning buildings and beating each other with baseball bats, and they are getting in our way."

"Why? Just shoot them. This was to be expected."

"Most are unarmed, General."

"And your point is?"

"Yes sir. As you know, forces loyal to Castillo have taken back one of the two television stations that we occupied."

Vilas nodded and sighed deeply. "That will do him about as much good as it has done me, with communications blocked for God knows what reason. What about de Franco's men? Have they reached the airport? What is the situation there?"

"Yes, about 1,000 of his men are in place."

"How did they get through our lines? I was assured an hour ago that we had the airport completely surrounded."

"De Franco's son was able to bribe our own General Sanchez to look the other way."

"Son of a bitch. I want him shot immediately. Do you hear me?"

"That might be easier said than done. Seems the good general let in de Franco's men and also joined them."

"We must secure the airport. Otherwise I can't fly in reinforcements from the south."

"I understand General, but we won't be able to fully engage until daybreak, when our troops from the occupied TV stations will arrive at the airport."

"What about the rest of de Franco's soldiers? Do we know where they are right now?"

"They have been seen north of the center of the city. But this information is spotty at best. With communications so disrupted, we must rely on couriers."

"We've been blown back to the fucking dark ages."

"Yes sir, something like that."

"What about Guerrera's men? Any word on when they will get to the capital?"

"No, and that's a matter of increasing concern for the staff. They should have been close enough by now for us to have received word from the countryside."

Vilas stood with his hands behind his back and looked out into the night. He was gradually being left with one option – to get to Los Pinos, one way or the other, and eliminate the son-of-a-bitch Castillo himself. "You realize that, without those men, and without control of the airport, we are outflanked and outnumbered."

The captain decided that silence was the most prudent response.

Without turning to face the man, Vilas said, "The airport is now the key to our success. With it under our control, we can fly in reinforcements from across the country. Without it…well, then, order the attack on the airport to begin immediately. We can't wait for sunrise. And alert me the minute you have any news."

As the morning turned to day, Castillo's troops returned control of all three stations to his government and continued the pitched battle at the airport. De Franco's forces managed to help shift the balance of firepower, but even with that, Castillo's Secretary of National Defense, Hector Ramos, knew this could not last long. Ramos could rally a few troops as long as the situation looked like it could go either way. Plus, if Guerrera's men reached the capital, even with de Franco's troops, the outcome was still far from certain. President Castillo had to rally the country, too, and the way to do that was to communicate with them.

Ramos left Federal District army headquarters, with all its silent radar and radio equipment, and joined Castillo at Los Pinos. He entered the Presidential office and stood at attention, every hair of his thick buzz cut appearing to stand up straight for the Chief of State. Though not a tall man, he exuded animal energy and power. Castillo had been his friend since college days, but today was not a day for familiarity. The man was his boss and his country's legally elected leader. That would not change under Ramos' watch, if he had to die to prevent it.

"Mr. President, I have two items of good news for you. You know that the television stations are back under our control, of course. But you may not know that de Franco's men are helping us to restore civilian order. And they are doing it well, with minimal casualties or further property damage. I must say that these are highly trained men. They follow orders and seem to understand that their loyalty is now to us primarily. I am surprised at this shift."

"To what do you attribute their cooperation?"

"The main thing seems to be de Franco's son. Emilio, right? He has command presence and has proven to be more than a diplomat."

"This comes as no surprise to me. Where are Emilio and his father now? Haven't they been here since the early hours of the morning? I expected them at Los Pinos."

"We prepared a bunk for them at Army headquarters. They asked to be near central command, and I saw no reason to prevent that. So far, they have been assets. I anticipated De Franco to be a brutal, ruthless man. And perhaps, he can be that, but he has an amazing grasp of military strategy. I have actually learned a few things from him. And he has been very helpful in integrating his men into our command structure."

Castillo laughed. "People are usually more complicated than one expects. I am glad that he came through for us. I know the son to be a fine man, who shares none of his father's craven desire for money and power. I believe Emilio to be a patriot.

"Hector, you said two items of good news. What else?"

"There are unconfirmed reports from eyewitnesses in the small towns north of the city that Guerrera's men are turning back."

"What?"

"Yes, we have received messengers from several outlying areas that very few of Guerrera's are marching in the direction of the city."

Castillo's face relaxed and he managed a smile, his first in many days. "Well, now. That could turn the tide for us." He wished that Martin were here to learn of this change of fortune. He felt a stab in his heart. But he forced the smile back on his face and walked over to Hector, clapping him on the back. "That is good news. How soon can you confirm these reports?"

"That brings me to my next point. We simply cannot make further progress with this carrier pigeon system we have cobbled together. We have to restore our communication network. I know that we've been able to thwart the enemy by crippling their ability to command and control, but, ironically, we've done the same thing to ourselves."

"We have to put it off as long as possible, at least until dark. More people will be off the streets and the police have initiated marshal law, with the help of de Franco's people, so we can still maintain civil order."

"I wish for it sooner, but I take your point. I realize that you need to make a call to Washington, and I assume that particular line is in place."

"It is."

"Shall we tell them 9:00 PM? It's dark by then. And it gives us enough time to set everything up. Do you wish to speak to the public from Los Pinos? It's safer for you not to move around the city. We can't give you much protection with the streets full of people and homemade barricades."

"Yes, Los Pinos is fine. I would like to speak from my desk with you and as many members of my cabinet as we can round up standing behind me. We have to appear calm and united."

"Yes, Mr. President. I will do whatever you need."

"As you always have, my friend. We must convey that we have the strategic advantage when we go on air. I would like to be able to announce that the airport is in government hands and is fully secure. I'd also like General Sanchez to be standing behind me when I make my speech."

"That should not be a problem. There is more news. Before midnight, my aides tell me that the power grid will be restored to our control. Then, we can select the nodes that serve Zumpango and choke them down even more."

"The General has woven his own rope. Now let's hang him with it."

CHAPTER 28

WEDNESDAY, MARCH 9
WASHINGTON AND BANDERA • MORNING

"**3**2 to 5."

Those numbers bounced off the walls of Room 2141 of the Sam Rayburn Building, which sat at the corner of Independence Avenue and Capitol Avenue like a massive Buddha.

"Order, order. There will be order in this room." Even the basso profundo voice of the Chairman of the House Judiciary Committee could not be heard over the eruption of applause and shouts. People stood and clapped. Some stomped their feet. It was a cacophony of sound, appropriate for this historic day, one seen three times in the annals of the Republic. Everyone present appreciated that they now had a place in the mythology of the United States of America. They had voted to recommend a confirmation to the full House of a new Vice President.

The Chair started to pound the gavel again, but stopped in mid-air as he caught the eye of the Majority Ranking Member who sat to his right. He looked over to the Minority Ranking Member. Both men shrugged their shoulders as if to say, don't stop them. Let them enjoy the moment. The Chair quietly placed his gavel on the dais.

He remembered back to times in which this room was used for more somber occasions – an impeachment inquiry against a sitting president or a House sub-committee meeting on crime, terrorism, and Homeland Security. Today's meeting was far more genial.

He looked at the far wall of the imposing hearing room at the eagle in bas-relief. The eagle faced its right talon, in which it gripped an olive branch, so that it always looked with hope for peace. In its left talon, symbolizing readiness to defeat an implacable enemy, it held sharp-tipped arrows. He wondered about David Richter, the man they voted to recommend as Vice

President. Would this largely untested Senator be able to do both of those things and lead with fairness and impartiality?

In one of the hearing room's coveted seats allotted to the Speaker of the House, sat Valerie Sandermann in a blue funk. She kept a pleasant enough expression on her perfectly made-up face, but inside she felt murderous rage. Her hopes to delay Richter's confirmation were completely dashed. The timetable moved inexorably forward in a way that was out of her control. The full House would vote on Friday, followed by the Senate confirmation for the new Vice President on Saturday.

Valerie tried to calm her racing mind. *Hadn't Preston met with the President yesterday? And hadn't he mentioned that Kate wanted me to know that the patch seemed to be working perfectly? And hadn't she been very appreciative of that?* Well, okay. Saturday will still work. Yes, the patch will be off by then and should have done its damage. The confirmation vote by the Senate will begin at noon. The clock is still in my favor. She turned to the wife of the Minority Leader and plastered a smile on her face. All would be well.

In Bandera, Martina was spinning from the speed with which Homeland Security had whisked her from Denver to Texas. Deacon had asked her to be there because she knew Michel best and could gauge his responses as either honest or, as Roger feared, worth a bucket of warm spit. She sat with her knees touching Michel's knees. They were alone in one of Aguila's second floor bedrooms. She wanted to be as close to him as possible.

When she arrived earlier that morning, she listened to a synopsis of the events in Mexico and then took her turn to tell them of the suspicions held by herself and Hyler about the patch. Deacon was innately skeptical about anything that came out of that "blowhard televangelist's" mouth. He remarked that the sure way to know if Hyler were telling a lie would be to observe if his mouth were moving. But the man had been kind to Kate at the prayer breakfast and she seemed to have believed him. He would try to take that into account.

Lawrence Chou, the assistant director of Homeland Security, kept his counsel. His boss had sent him there to listen and observe.

"I don't get it. Why don't we rip the damn patch off right now and be done with it? If you have a snake on your arm, you shake it off. You don't watch it crawl up to your head and bite you on the face."

"I know, Deacon. But this isn't a snake. It's genetics. I trust Peter Tate. He urged us to leave it on because there could be dire consequences if the genetic process isn't completed. Genes could be damaged. I don't understand it very well, either. That's why we need to talk to Michel."

Roger's voice was strained to the point of breaking. "No, he is a terrorist, Martina. No. Are we really willing to put ourselves in the hands of the man who assassinated our Vice President? Wasn't the mission to kill my mother, as well? That makes me think that everything he tells us will be to further that aim, not to help her."

"Roger, we're talking in circles now. The man is a genius in his field. He wasn't at Valentine when the patch went FUBAR. We don't have time to find a person who could possibly interpret the data the way that Michel can. He's it. I will know if he's lying. I'm ready for him."

Deacon had heard enough. He held up his hand to stop Roger from responding. "Roger, I know that you are the Chief of Staff to the President. And Mr. Chou, I know that you are second in command to the Director of Homeland Security. But I am making this decision. Martina is going to talk to Michel."

"Martina, what else do you need from us before you see him?"

"A little time to go over my notes."

"Fine. It is about 1:45 PM. I will come to your room in 30 minutes and walk you upstairs. Gentlemen, I will call us back together when Mrs. Valentine is done. Thank you."

At 3:30, Martina sipped on cold lemonade as she recounted the conversation with Michel for Deacon, Roger, Chou, Brother and Butch.

"So, that's it, then? You are satisfied that he can help us?"

"Yes. I am also quite certain that he no longer has anything but hatred for his adopted father and the cause that evil man espouses. But Michel highly doubts that Hezbollah had anything to do with the patch. He's more than willing to cooperate, but with one condition."

Chou jumped in. "What condition? I'm not of a mind to make any deals today."

Martina stared directly at Mr. Chou. "You're going to have to trust me on this, for now. Believe me. What Michel is going to request will be something you will agree to readily."

Deacon reasserted himself into the conversation, preventing any further objection from Chou.

"All right. He will fly back with you to Denver, accompanied by Mr.

Chou and his team. Mr. Chou, are you set to leave as soon as we clear it with Director Sanchez?"

A slight bow was Chou's response.

"Dad, I would like to accompany Martina. One of us needs to be eyes-on in Denver and you need to get back to mother. You are the one person who can tell her about the patch and keep her from yanking it off of her arm."

Martina jumped in. "What about Valerie?"

"What about Valerie?" Deacon was ready to get back to Kate.

Roger answered Martina. "We need to tread lightly here until we have some irrefutable proof of her involvement. Can you imagine if we make an accusation against the wife of the Speaker of the House and it turns out that we are wrong? The shit wouldn't just hit the fan, it would knock it over."

Chou spoke up. "I've already alerted my boss as to the fears about Mrs. Sandermann. We are looking into her activities on our end. If she has chipped a fingernail in the last few months, we'll know it soon. At this point, we can't rule anything out. Ms. Valentine stated that Michel believes that Hezbollah had no part in the patch being dispensed, but we're not certain of that. There is a possibility, however remote, that Mrs. Sandermann is involved with Hezbollah. Perhaps her role was to be a backup measure in case the IED didn't work."

"Holy crap." This became too much even for Brother, a wily courtroom lawyer, to absorb. "Look she may be a bitch, but she's the wife of the Speaker and a loyal Democrat at that. She has no obvious motive and I can't imagine that she has contacts in Lebanon. Get real."

Roger walked over to his brother. "'Real' doesn't apply any more. Whether or not she is involved, and whether or not she is working for Hezbollah, she does have motive. Remember, mother beat out her husband for the nomination. People have killed over less."

Deacon agreed. "All I can say is that skinny woman has always seemed unhinged to me. She's strung as tight as catgut. Martina, you're her stepmother. Do you think she's capable of something this dark and complex?"

That question caught Martina off guard. "I'm not sure how to respond, Deacon. I guess the truth is that I don't know her all that well. David is a good man. Could his daughter have gone so far off the rails? I don't know."

Deacon walked to the window and looked at the fields that would soon turn to a solid carpet of bluebonnets. He turned back to Brother and Butch. "Fellas, we have got to pursue this Valerie thing to see where it takes us. And I have to get to your mother. Aguila is in your hands. You need to help the Rangers get packed and out of here and try to get this place back to some semblance of normal. Butch, the Ranch will be yours soon enough. Time to knuckle down."

Both boys held their hands behind their backs, like being at parade rest. The old man had passed the baton to them.

Deacon looked at Martina firmly in the eyes. "Martina, does it work for you for Roger to accompany you to Denver?"

"Deacon I have no problem with Roger going with us, as long as he can keep his animosity towards Michel in check. Can you do that, Roger?"

"Goddammit. The woman in question is my mother. She saved my life. I'm not a fucking schoolboy. I can do anything I need to do in service to her and my country."

Chastened, they all hurried out of the room.

CHAPTER 29

WEDNESDAY, MARCH 9
MEXICO CITY · SUN-UP TO SUNDOWN

President Castillo smiled to himself when his thoughts turned to last night's address to the nation. Army and Air Force units that had been either standing down or unreachable were reporting in to the Ministry of Defense in a near avalanche of support for his government.

Suddenly Cabinet Ministers were available when he called. Order was gradually being restored in the streets of the Capital. And most satisfying of all was his late night call to Kate informing her that there would be no need for American Marines to land on Mexican soil to help stabilize the situation.

The final blow to the coup came shortly after midnight when control of the power grid returned to Government hands. Power was immediately restored to most sections of the city, but was cut to Zumpango. And without power, even with restored communications, Vilas couldn't hold out much longer.

Castillo's top Generals had joined him at Los Pinos prior to the address, as did de Franco and Emilio. The Generals urged a show of force and insisted that they launch an attack as soon as possible on Vilas's forces at Zumpango, but Castillo urged caution.

"We don't know exactly how many men have remained loyal to him or their disposition. Until we get additional intelligence, I suggest we try for a little rest. Let's deal with General Vilas in the morning."

De Franco held his tongue, wishing to avoid undercutting the President in front of his own men. But he felt Castillo's replenished army, with the assistance of de Franco forces, could hit Vilas immediately and put an end to this foolishness.

De Franco cleared his throat, as he looked across the office at all these Generals, in their starched uniforms with medals covering their chests.

Now that it appeared that the coup was failing, they stared at him as though he were pariah.

"Perhaps, Armando, we could have a moment in private."

It wasn't lost on anyone in the room that de Franco had addressed the President by his first name.

"Yes, of course."

As the others withdrew from the President's office, de Franco signaled for Emilio to remain.

"Armando, I think the generals make a solid case for hitting Vilas before he has a chance to reorganize and bring in reinforcements."

Emilio understood better than his father why President Castillo appeared to equivocate. "Father, I think the President would like to find a more diplomatic and perhaps graceful way for General Vilas to withdraw from public life. An offer of exile rather than a blood bath might serve the nation well."

Castillo looked fondly at Emilio. "Thank you. I couldn't have put it more perfectly. Federico, you have your ways of dealing with traitors. And while I'm not for a moment second-guessing your methods, I have to think about the country as a whole. It is lost on no one that Vilas garnered impressive support, which gives me pause. It is clear that there are legitimate grievances that must be addressed."

De Franco waved his hand, palm down. "Echhh... Politicians and diplomats. I hope you both know what you are doing. And lest we forget, once you've dealt with Vilas, we still have Guerrera to contend with. I assume that an offer of exile doesn't extend to him?"

Despair hung in the damp, night air at Zumpango. Men huddled against the chill and spoke in low whispers. The excitement and laughter that filled the field hours earlier, when success seemed within their reach, was replaced by eerie quiet now that all seemed lost. An occasional cough broke the wall of silence. Most of Vilas' top staff remained loyal to him, but there was grumbling from junior officers.

"Gentlemen," Vilas began an urgently called staff meeting well past midnight, "don't look so downtrodden. We have one more move on the chessboard before you lose your king. With communications re-established I have learned that Castillo has ordered his Generals not to start an assault on Zumpango until after sunrise."

What difference does that make? The General who had that thought decided not to say it out loud. He liked his head right where it was – on top of his neck.

"You may not be aware that, over the past four hours, I have been moving as many men as possible to forward positions outside of Los Pinos. Within the next two hours, we should be able to mount a surprise attack on Castillo's residence. If luck is with us, we will catch the President off guard."

There was a low rumble among those assembled. Bowed heads snapped to attention. Shoulders straightened.

"I plan on personally leading the attack and when I find that gutless son of a whore, I will kill him with my own hands."

In unison, all in the room shouted. "Viva El General!"

Years later, historians would write that the siege of Los Pinos was one of the bloodiest battles in the country's history. Mexican against Mexican to the death. So much blood was shed over the course of two hours that thick red rivulets of it ran across the beautiful landscaped pathways and splattered walls and ceilings.

"Did you hear a noise, Carlos?"

"No, just the sound of you pissing yourself. Relax, the coup is all but put down."

The young, handsome cadet, mustered in from Mexico's military academy, didn't have the reassurance that the older CISEN Secret Service agent did. "I'm sure I heard...."

Before he could complete his thought a bullet came ripping out of nowhere and entered his neck, cutting his vocal cord, as he half turned toward Carlos, and fell dead to the ground.

"Pablo, did you say something?" And before another bullet would take his life, Carlos looked up to see hundreds of General Vilas regulars swarming over the outer perimeter of Los Pinos.

The initial advantage lay with General Vilas. His men, superior in number and well trained, with the added advantage of the element of surprise, quickly overran the outer defenses of Los Pinos.

Had Vilas been able to launch his attack an hour earlier he would have been able to subdue the entire compound within 30 minutes. But in war as in many things, an hour can be an eternity. And this particular hour was the time that Federico needed to have 400 of his best and most loyal soldiers airlifted via helicopter from the airport to the Presidential Residency.

After the first 50 yards, Vilas soldiers were deep into the woods surrounding the grounds and administrative buildings. Resistance was sporadic and Vilas' confidence built with each inch of ground covered.

But as the first wave of his men entered the formal gardens, resistance developed, seemingly out of thin air.

Vilas' second-in-command, General Lopez, was shot between the eyes in front of Vilas. And two other officers were also struck down. Someone must have given the order to take down the officers because with the head cut off, the body would surely fall.

Vilas was dismayed to realize that the resistance was coming from more than young cadets and CISEN Agents. While he had expected stiffer resistance the closer they got to the Residency, this was more than even the well-trained Presidential Guard could muster. *Where was all the fire coming from, and from whom?*

As if reading his mind a young Lieutenant reported in to General Vilas that several dozen helicopters of the Mexican Air Force had been seen landing and taking off shortly before the attack commenced.

"You idiot. You tell me this now. Why was I not informed of this before we started the attack?"

"But your Excellency, you specifically gave the order for radio silence to maintain our element of surprise. I got to you as quickly as I could."

"Not quickly enough." Vilas pulled out his sidearm and shot the young lieutenant at point blank range in the chest. "I won't suffer any more incompetence." Turning to one of his remaining aides he ordered the reserve of his forces called up and for the attack to continue.

Over the next hour of hand-to-hand combat, de Franco's men and the Palace Guard fought fiercely for Castillo's government and gave ground with their own blood. Vilas could understand the Palace Guards' commitment, but once he fully understood that de Franco's soldiers were part of the resistance, he couldn't fathom why they battled with such dedication. Why would cartel soldiers fight to the death for the pig Castillo?

What Vilas didn't know was that these men, many of them with Federico for over 30 years, had sworn a blood oath of loyalty to him. When de Franco gave his allegiance to the President of Mexico, he gave his men to Castillo, as well, without protest from even one of them.

Slowly, with the support of his reserves, Vilas progressed toward the Executive Office Building. Though his numbers had been greatly diminished, he was within 50 feet of the building's rear balcony, where two weeks ago President Castillo had sat while on the phone with the President of the United States.

De Franco and Emilio understood that, unless they could hold off Vilas until additional reinforcements arrived from the airport, they were as good as dead. Emilio tore through the building, organizing a last ditch defense using the few exhausted men and diminished resources that remained. President Castillo was about to join in when Federico grabbed him by the shoulder and pulled him back into his office.

"Armando, we don't need a dead President, no matter how heroic he might be. You must realize that our reinforcements are starting to outflank Vilas. He is left with one option - to move forward and do so quickly. We must prevent that and secure you. If he can break into the residency and capture or more likely kill you, he wins. By the time your loyal reinforcements arrive, he could be sitting behind your desk, wearing the Presidential sash."

"Then I fear, old friend, that you and your son may have forfeited your lives for a lost cause."

"Perhaps, but if that is the will of God, then so be it." Castillo was surprised by de Franco's religiosity. "But at least we will have died loyal Mexicans, not traitors."

Emilio, now armed with an Uzi that he had liberated from a downed CISEN Agent, burst into the President's office with about half a dozen well-armed men careening in behind.

"Close the doors and block them with one of the credenzas." Emilio snapped the orders as if he had been born to command.

"No, I will not be boxed in like a caged mouse." President Castillo now sitting behind his desk with de Franco standing at his side, calmly overruled Emilio.

"Emilio, I know you mean well, but if I am to die today, let no man say I cowered behind a credenza at the last. Close the doors, by all means, but do not block them. Our fate now lies, as your father says, in the hands of God."

Emilio had never thought that President Castillo was capable of such assurance and courage. As if a calming euphoria had swept over the entire room, all the men's breathing became less labored. Perhaps, soldiers who know that death is imminent can feel such a thing before the moment arrives, if provided the example by their leader.

The trance was broken when they heard shots and screams from the outer office. It was a matter of seconds before General Vilas' men would break through.

Vilas, walking through the outer office with the swagger of a conquistador, saw that inlaid wooden doors stood between him and victory. How many times had he walked through that door as a subservient? How many times had he felt humiliated by that incompetent Castillo? Well, now he would have his revenge, sweet revenge.

The order was given to break through the doors, but not to touch or harm Castillo. That honor belonged to Vilas and Vilas alone.

The first surprise was that the door was not locked and that no round of fire greeted them. All they heard was a lone call from President Castillo for every man in his office to put down their guns. Enough blood had been spilled for one day and, if by sacrificing his life, he could put an end to the death of his countrymen, then that would now suffice.

Vilas, dumbstruck, entered the Presidential office and walked towards Castillo. Castillo ordered the General to put his sidearm on the desk and obey his commander-in-chief.

Several of Castillo's guards surged forward to come between him and Vilas, but Castillo ordered them to stand down before Vilas' men opened fire.

"A wise command and probably your last, Armando." Vilas' face was a mask of scorn.

"I gave you an order and you chose not to obey it. At least I die knowing who I am. All you are is a traitor and a fool."

"Who you are? That's a joke. The country has been going to hell for years. You and your likes have done nothing but look the other way, or worse, enriched yourselves further by doing business with the drug cartels."

With that Vilas lifted his side arm and took aim at President Castillo. In a whisper that would later roar throughout Mexico, de Franco jumped in front of Castillo. The bullet, without conscience, guile or favor, found Federico's heart instead of Castillo's head.

What happened next is still a matter of conjecture, like the five witnesses to a traffic accident who each tell a slightly different version of the truth. What was certain was that Emilio screamed one word, "Father." He fired his Uzi and severed the General's neck from his shoulders, bringing to an abrupt end one of the most inglorious moments in Mexico's history.

Some reported that the General's head was affixed to the outer gates of Los Pinos for several hours until President Castillo ordered it taken down.

Others reported the General's surprised visage was marched on a spike throughout the capital city. In truth no one knows what happened to the head of the ignominious General. It was never found.

Few saw Emilio place the weapon on the desk and run to his father. Few saw him fall to the floor and touch his father's face. Few saw Emilio whisper something in his father's ear. No one but Federico de Franco heard the promise that Emilio made that day. But Federico died feeling the love of a son he had thought to be lost to him, knowing that the son would avenge the father.

CHAPTER 30

THURSDAY, MARCH 10
WASHINGTON · NOON

Monroe, the chief steward, delivered lunch to Kate and Lucy in the private quarters. Kate had finished out the morning in the Situation Room and had spoken at length with Emilio. Nothing she could say would dissuade him from hunting down his father's nemesis. And she hadn't been able to track down Roger, but she assumed that he was on his way back and would talk to her in person. She had avoided a conversation with Butch, but would call him back later. Now, food seemed a good idea, although she had lost her famously prodigious appetite, even for the chicken salad, for which she usually requested seconds.

Monroe stood by, until Kate looked up from the small dining table and smiled, asking him to come back later for the dishes. "Ma'am? Miss Lucy? Isn't there anything else you all need? As my grandmother would have said, Madame President, your eyes look like two burnt holes in a blanket."

Lucy laughed and looked at her mother. "I agree. Those circles around her eyes are getting pretty dark, aren't they? We would like to have known your grandmother."

"Listen you two, I'm a little tired, but I thank you for your concern. Been a long few days is all. Mr. Jefferson is right outside the door, so why don't you take yourself out into the Rose Garden for some fresh air, Lucy, and I'll see you back here in a bit. Thank you, again, Monroe, for the lunch."

Lucy leaned down to kiss her mother on the cheek. "Mom, you really don't look well. Is something else going on with you? Physically, I mean. I'm worried."

Kate patted her daughter's cheek. "Lucy, it's just the fatigue that comes with this office. Let me get a little nap in while you take a walk, or call your long suffering husband. I'll be fine."

Lucy looked hard at her mother, but left her alone. She knew that her mother was a stubborn woman, and was finished answering any questions about her health. She shut the door quietly behind her, but the nagging concern remained.

Kate threw off her shoes and leaned back on the comfy sofa. She smiled when she thought of Lucy, who never gave her a moment's grief. *Thank God for homebody daughters.*

Before her head touched the cushions, she was in a fitful sleep. Somewhere in the midst of being chased down a dark hallway, she felt Deacon's presence before she was fully awake. He stood over her and had the most puzzled look on his face when she opened her eyes. "Deacon, my God. You could have scared me into an early grave. Why on earth are you standing there like that? For Pete's sake, come sit and give me a kiss."

"Sugar, that's the best request I've had in days." He lifted her to her feet and held her tightly. Finally, she pulled back and looked him over.

"You look none the worse for wear. I swear you must have the constitution of an ox, Deacon."

"Naw, I just cleaned up good."

"I see that. And you even pressed a crease in your jeans. Nice." She sat back down and patted the cushion next to her. "Okay, catch me up, especially on the boys. You've been with them. Tell me the truth. How have they handled all of this? Really."

"You'd'a been proud of them, Kate. I think that Butch grew up by years over the past few days. He saved his big brother's ass out there on that mountain road in Mexico. You know that whole story. They started calling him Wild Bill for showing off on his motorcycle, but they would have been in a hard hole without him. I know you feel like they poked you in the eye with a sharp stick for putting themselves in such danger, but I don't doubt their judgment in this case."

"I know, Deac. I'm not going to belabor the point with any of them. What can I do? They're all men now. But I do wish that, at least once in awhile, they'd remember I'm not only their mother; I'm the President."

Deacon, ignoring that last remark continued, "And don't forget, honey, that they all love you more'n' anything and haven't gotten over the fact that you came close to being killed. You can't fault a son for that, right?"

"It's okay, Deac. You don't have to worry about me not letting them off the hook."

"Then why haven't you called Butch?"

"I wanted to be better composed, so I didn't make an emotional fool of myself. That wouldn't do him or me any good."

"Well, don't wait too much longer, Kate. He needs to know that it's going to be okay with you."

"I will. Before I go back downstairs."

"All right, then." Deacon sighed before he could catch himself.

"What is it, Deacon?"

"Okay, honey. You have to listen to me real good right now. And you have to do exactly what I say. How often have you heard me tell you that?"

"Once. When that 'rattler was on the front porch as I opened the door. You're scaring me, Deac. Spit it out."

"It's complicated, Kate. And while I'm talking, you sit there and think about that 'rattler. I mean it. Here goes. You know that patch you've got on your arm. That quit smokin' thing?"

"Of course." She began to roll up her sleeve to show him.

"Stop, dammit. Don't touch it."

"Deacon McIntyre, what in the hell is wrong with you?"

"Sorry. Let me start again."

Deacon told her about the possibility that the patch might be doing her harm, that Martina and the preacher man, Hyler, had their suspicions about Valerie Sandermann being the culprit, and that she couldn't remove it or touch it.

Kate knew her husband was dead serious and she listened to him without comment until it came to the Speaker's wife. She jumped up and began pacing in front of the huge, circle window that dominated the room. "Deacon, that is plain crazy. That woman is no friend to me, but the idea that she is a cold-blooded killer is…"

Kate searched for the right word…"bizarre. Crazy. I don't understand how Martina or Hyler could even think such a thing."

Deacon put his hands on his knees and leaned forward, then decided to go over to Kate. He took her hands and held them in front of her. "I know, honey. But Martina and Hyler are convinced that something is going on. Valerie brought you the patch, right?"

Kate nodded and said, "But…"

"Hang on. Let me finish. So, they think that patch is from a box that may be an earlier prototype taken out of production. Where is the box, by the way?"

"In my dressing area. Do you want to see it?"

"Yes, but not right now. We'll put it in the hands of the scientists and let them run their tests on it."

Kate pulled her hands away from Deacon, a gesture that was not lost on him. She resumed pacing. "If there's even the remotest possibility that it's dangerous, I don't understand why I can't take it off. The scientists can run their tests and I'm none the worse for wear. Don't forget, I have my OWN scientists and they are down the road at the NIH. Why can't they handle it?"

"Kate, I know that this is an impossible situation. Martina is standing by to try to walk you through it."

"Through what?"

"Apparently, genetic engineering might cause the patch to do more harm if we remove it before you complete the full cycle of wearing it for fourteen days. She and Roger are in Denver waiting for David to return from Shanghai. They hope that he will be able to supply some answers to what's going on."

Kate stopped pacing and looked back at Deacon. "Hold on. Roger went to Denver? I thought that he was on his way back to DC."

"He wanted to go with Martina to provide any help he could."

"She doesn't need the help of a political genius. She needs another kind of genius. What's the real reason?"

"He didn't want to let Michel out of his sight."

"Michel? I thought that Michel was under lock and key until Gabriel's team has a chance to question him. He brought the explosives over the border from Mexico, right? Now, you're telling me that he's not in jail but in Denver? Geez, Deacon. Has everyone gone mad?"

"Gabriel is waiting to talk to you about that. But the long and short of it is that Martina thinks only Michel can figure this out in time. They needed him in Denver. The guards are on him like a sticker burr on a bare foot and he won't get to pee without someone knowing and reporting it back to you."

"Stop. Back up. You said that Gabriel is waiting for me? Where? Here?"

"Yes. He wants to go over every detail with you. And Martina and Roger are waiting for you by a secure line in Denver."

"So, what does that make you?" Kate sat heavily on the winged back chair next to the couch and stared ahead.

She finally looked up at her stoic husband, standing in front of her. He was steeled to take whatever she needed to say. Instead, she had a tiny hint of a smile on her face. "Ahh, I think I get the picture. They sent you to talk to me first so that – what? – I wouldn't shoot the messenger? You drew the black bean, didn't you?"

"Somethin' like that."

"Lemme' get this straight. I'm wearing what is essentially a time bomb. Nobody knows if it's really dangerous or who's behind it. We've let a terrorist go on a field trip to Denver. And Roger is in the middle of it all…again."

"That about sums it up."

"Well hell, Deacon. Do you think you could have come in here and told me something any more complicated and weird than this?"

Kate closed her eyes and let herself indulge in the fantasy of being anywhere else but in this place, hearing this confounded story. "I might as well get to talkin' to people. Let's find Gabriel. I'd just as soon meet with him right now.

"And I tell you what, Deacon. Roger might be the death of me before this damn patch can do it. That boy…"

"It's 'cause he loves you, Katy girl. Wants to protect you."

"I know. I know. After I speak with Gabriel, we'll call Martina and Roger. Needless to say, you and Gabriel should be part of that conversation."

Kate knew that all these good people were trying to act in her best interests. But at that moment, she felt that events were escalating out of anyone's control, and that she might, somehow, be beyond protecting.

CHAPTER 31

THURSDAY, MARCH 10
DENVER • LATE MORNING

The shock wave from the wind caused by the landing helicopter almost knocked Martina off balance. Fortunately, Roger was quick on his feet and caught her before any harm was done. For the past two hours they had been going over the facts and suppositions they were going to present to David and Jackson Baines when they got a call that the bird was about to land.

Martina knew that David would be fatigued, but that any tiredness he felt would be overcome by the righteous indignation and anger he would have over the array of accusations leveled at his daughter. Martina's profound moments of doubt almost made her lose faith in the effort, but Roger persuaded her to press on. He was a man possessed.

Michel was allowed to be on the grounds of the company because he could be of great help to them, but he was secured in a conference room under the close supervision of a number of guards from a variety of agencies. Seemed that everyone wanted a piece of the man.

Jackson exited first and jumped down, holding the door open for David. When Martina saw her husband's handsome, but weary face, at the door of the helicopter, she forgot everything except how she had missed him and needed all of this not to be true. He managed a wan smile and small wave when he spotted her. Despite the torrent of wind still coming off the blades, she ran toward him, wanting to feel the comfort of his arms around her. She stopped for a moment and put her hand above her eyes to keep out the dust and debris. Later, she would realize that this one protective gesture is probably what kept her alive.

The powerful concussion rolled over her, knocking her facedown on the roof. Her side felt on fire and blood gushed out of a gaping shrapnel wound. Amid deafening explosions, she vaguely heard Roger calling her name and felt hands on her back and side. One pair of hands turned her over and kept yelling for her to stay awake. She opened her eyes and saw Roger, followed by dozens of other people rushing by. She wondered where they came from. She closed her eyes, trying to block out the sound and the pain.

"Martina, open your eyes. Look at me." Roger knelt beside her and placed his hand hard against her side. She startled awake.

"What happened? Where is David?"

Involuntarily, Roger looked at the place where the helicopter had been, now a burning pile of crumpled metal. Martina strained to raise herself up and follow Roger's eyes, but she fell back down. Roger still had his hand on her side. "Uh, let's get you moved. The security team is here with a gurney and we'll get you on another helicopter and to the hospital."

"Roger, where is David? I need to see him. Take me to him."

Roger looked at the broken concrete beneath his feet, rather than at her. "Roger, no. David? Is he…"

Martina screamed, an unearthly sound from somewhere sound isn't supposed to be made. Roger forced himself to look at Martina. "Marti, we have to go. Now. We'll talk as soon as you have been attended to." He motioned to the men, who gently placed Martina on a stretcher and ran with her to the other helicopter that was firing up its engines.

Even though his ears were ringing from the missile's concussion, Roger could still hear her screams as they lifted off.

With the economy of motion born of years of practice, Jad Farrah folded up the missile carrier and slipped down from the roof of the nearby parking garage. He had, at last, accomplished his primary mission for that camel turd in Beirut. Now, he could receive the balance of his payment. Michel and David Valentine were as dead as one Stinger missile could make them. It had been a hit in the middle of a bull's-eye. As to the other something the Sheikh wanted him to take care of. *Well, that would be on the house, a final farewell present to his Beirut employer.* He imagined women in their skimpy bikinis, as many women as he wanted, and rum drinks that never went dry on a secluded island in the Caribbean. About time.

The flames were too thick to get much closer to the rubble, but Roger peered into the smoke, looking for answers, knowing all on board or nearby were dead. He turned to one of his security detail.

"Please report this immediately to the White House. This can't be a coincidence. I heard the distinct sound of a Stinger missile overhead and then the explosions. We need a team here ASAP to go over what remains as soon as the heat dissipates. And I need to go to a secure room to call the President."

"Yes sir. The White House already knows. A team from Homeland is on the way from their Denver office."

"That was head's-up thinking. Thank you."

"They should be here in about 15 minutes. Meanwhile, no one will come near this place. We're locked down tight. Right now, I need to get you out of the open. We have deployed men to the surrounding rooftops, though this is a pretty isolated spot. I'm sure that the shooter is long gone. But we may find traces of him that will help us know who is behind this."

"I've got my own ideas about that. But first, the President."

The men who had been surrounding Roger ran with him in the middle, one on all four sides.

As they neared the stairway down, Roger realized that they needed Michel now, more than ever, to save his mother's life. The other two people in the world who had any kind of answers for him were charred piles of flesh and bone, burned into the tarmac.

PART III

MURDER + POLITICS = ASSASSINATION

CHAPTER 1

Thursday, March 10
Mexico City/Sabinas · Late Morning

Los Pinos was a smoldering ruin. Most of the magnificent pines now had the look of a forest after a volcanic eruption. Buildings that were still standing were mostly empty shells. The Presidential Residency and Executive Office building remained, as if by some surreal wave of a magic wand, unscathed.

But the stench of blood and sinew was still fresh to the nostrils. What had hours ago been the center of Mexican democracy were now killing fields. The President refused to abandon this symbol of the Republic, so army tents and hastily assembled shelters now functioned, if one could call it that, as the seat of the Mexican government.

It would take days for all the bodies to be identified and removed for burial, but President Castillo insisted on conducting the work of government as though nothing out of the ordinary were happening all around him.

Army officers and cabinet ministers used cell phones and every other type of wireless devices to keep in contact with their respective departments. Even a few aides and secretaries were now at makeshift desks trying to restore order. Slowly a semblance of normalcy was returning to the capital.

News of General Vilas' death had ended the armed resistance to the central government. And none of Guerrera's soldiers were within a hundred miles of the capital. The Ministry of Defense quickly analyzed the American SAT photos, which showed Adán's army in full retreat and in a state of disintegration.

Headlines on the network's morning news and in the few papers that made it to press reported on a complete victory for the central government of President Castillo. Some referred to Federico de Franco as the next

Pancho Villa, suggesting that he should enter the pantheon of Mexican saviors.

Behind this backdrop of restoration, a firestorm was brewing between President Castillo, Hector Ramos, and Juan Marcos. Both Ramos, the Minister of Defense, and Marcos, the head of CISEN, were out for blood. Hundreds of army cadets had been slaughtered during the siege and almost every CISEN agent in the capital was either dead or wounded. Emilio remained silent.

He couldn't seem to form a coherent thought. He had seen his father give his life to save the President. He couldn't shake the picture of General Vilas' head being detached from his body. And he felt the onset of exhaustion that everyone in the room experienced.

"Emilio, you, more than any of us, must have an opinion. What do you think our next step should be in dealing with Guerrera?"

Emilio tried to compose his thoughts before offering any insights. "Personally I'd like to kill him with my bare hands. But I agree with Armando, I mean President Castillo..."

"Emilio, no need for formality now. Armando will do fine."

"Well, my personal feelings are not the issue. President, I mean Armando, is right. We have suffered enough bloodshed as a nation. If there is a less violent way to deal with Guerrera, I think we should explore that option."

"Option! You diplomats are all alike." Ramos and Marcos roared in a strange unison.

Marcos continued. "We have them on the run. Los Rojas is in chaos and we will have Guerrera's compound at Sabinas surrounded by the end of the day. Why the fuck don't we finish what he started?"

Armando was too exhausted to respond. He looked to Emilio and Emilio roused himself out of his stupor and responded. "Because taking Adán out will not be as easy as you think. He still has thousands of armed men in the vicinity of the compound. Yes, the Army will ultimately prevail, but at what cost? We were willing to offer Vilas the option of exile and I think now we should do the same with Guerrera. With him out of the country, he will no longer be a threat and his cartel will be quickly dismantled.

"Gentlemen, this is a new Mexico. The killing has to stop. The remaining cartels have to be destroyed. And let us not forget that General Vilas, for all his treachery, did bring voice to what many Mexicans were and are feeling…a total estrangement from the government that is supposed to represent their interests."

Ramos interrupted, "Fine, even noble sentiments, but the Army will never agree to cutting a deal with Guerrera, as long as I am Minister of Defense."

Armando shot Ramos a look that reminded the Defense Minister that he served at the President's pleasure. While no decision had been made, anyone who worked for the President would support the President's course of action.

"Hector, Juan, I've never pretended to be a great reformer. I've been complacent about the status quo. But too many men have died today fighting for liberty...on both sides. It is time for a new way.

"I've made my decision. But before I share it with you, I'd like to add a thought. No one has mentioned Hezbollah's involvement in our internal affairs. For too long we have looked the other way while they helped these cartel wolves eat into the marrow of our society. They, even more than Guerrera, must answer for what happened here today.

"I've asked our Ambassador to the United Nations to call for an immediate Security Council session to condemn Hezbollah specifically, and Lebanon more generally, for allowing this disgusting organization to thrive and plot on our soil. I have declared that each person on the staff of the Lebanese Embassy in Mexico City is persona non grata. Depending on Beirut's response, we will make the further decision to break off diplomatic ties or not.

"I have spoken with America's Secretary of State Jordan, and she fully supports us as to our actions at the UN and with our actions concerning Beirut.

"Now, back to my decision about Guerrera. I think we will try diplomacy first. Emilio, I hate to ask this of you, but you may be the one person in Mexico who can convince Guerrera to accept the offer of exile."

CHAPTER 2

Thursday, March 10
Denver • Mid-Afternoon

Roger perched on the edge of his chair in the waiting room of Broomfield's Cleo Wallace Hospital Center. It was a small but well equipped local hospital less than ten minutes from Valentine Pharmaceuticals. He would have preferred that Martina be seen at one of the larger medical facilities in Denver, but Lawrence Chou from Homeland had already taken charge of the situation and insisted on the nearest facility.

"Roger, I appreciate your concern, but until we know what we're dealing with here, we need to keep a lid on this. One of the doctors at Valentine says that Martina's injuries look worse than they are."

Roger, a little shaken from the impact of the blast, decided not to argue.

Chou continued. "We have secured the hospital and informed the emergency room doctors that a minor explosion of unknown origin injured Mrs. Valentine while she was inspecting one of the production facilities."

Martina's injuries turned out, as expected, to be minor, especially in light of the violent nature of the attack. She had a mild concussion and a puncture wound near her two broken ribs. Forty stitches and intravenous pain medicine later, her doctors released her into Roger's care.

He knew that she was in shock and had not yet grappled with the death of her husband, but that would come in a rush later. For now, he needed her to concentrate on his problem – the patch and its potential to kill his mother. Grieving could wait.

A nurse wheeled Martina out and Roger struggled not to gasp at her appearance. She was gray and even a little green surrounded the deep black circles above and below her eyes. Yet when she looked at him, he knew that she was fully alert. God, she was strong.

After they had moved her gingerly into the backseat of the town car,

Roger nodded at the agents in the front seat to pull out. Two cars led them out and two cars followed. They drove in a security box. Roger took her hand. "Marti, are you sure you're up to returning to headquarters tonight?"

Martina gave him a dry, brittle laugh. "We don't have a choice. Time is running out and we've got to crack into those files. I'm afraid that David…"

She sucked in her breath…"had all of that locked in his brain, for what reason, I don't know. Michel might be our last hope. And can we trust him?" Martina's shoulders slumped. It all seemed impossible right now. David was dead. Roger's mother was in grave danger. And a terrorist who helped kill the Vice President of the United States was at Valentine Pharmaceuticals to work with them. The world had evidently gone mad. She wondered when that had happened.

They drove through the waning light, past security and pulled up to a now darkened building. Inside, Homeland, the FBI, the FDA and half a dozen other government agencies had commandeered offices that faced the central courtyard. To the outside world the building looked like it did every night. A few lights were on but there was no indication of the activity therein.

A certain pecking order had already been established while Roger and Martina were at the hospital. Overall coordination on the ground was squarely in the hands of Lawrence Chou of Homeland. Peter, as the senior official most familiar with SST, coordinated Valentine's efforts. He was the one who had thought to contact the FDA. Kate's team decided in Washington that the FBI would take the lead chair in investigating the explosion, with the CIA and NSA supplying any additional intelligence that might be helpful. But the primary focus had to be on opening up Valentine's computer security system. The fate of the President depended on it.

Gabriel, Edgar and Deacon realized that they could run a covert operation like this from DC for only so long before word leaked out that something big was happening in Denver.

The agents leapt out of the car and opened both back doors at once. They walked as fast as Martina's injuries would permit, moving them out of the danger of open spaces.

While Roger was at the hospital, the team leaders representing all the agencies involved had gathered in the large conference room where David had conducted his last board meeting. They made three lists. One was what they knew was true. The other was what they had good evidence to believe. And the third was what might be possible.

They knew that an unknown assailant killed David and Jackson in a missile attack. They did not know the motivation, but there had to be a reason. They did not know exactly the intended target. Was it Valentine? Baines? Martina? Roger? They were all on that roof and in harm's way.

Until they knew the 'who', it was hard to determine the 'why'. They speculated about the reasons. Was it coincidence or did it have something to do with Kate and the patch? Valentine Pharmaceuticals was the eye of the hurricane right now, and few people at their level of training and cynicism believed in coincidences.

Every person in the room was monumentally frustrated. Chou, slammed his hands on the table and pushed his chair over as he stood. "Dammit, people. We have got to get into these blasted computers. David Valentine and Jackson Baines had the codes and they used 256-bit nano-encryption algorithms for their file storage. Even Henry…" Chou nodded at Henry Becker, Homeland's security guru, "hasn't been able to get in."

"No, sir. There are an infinite number of combinations with nano-encryption, so without the key, we are spinning our wheels." Becker was mortified by his lack of results. He wasn't called the Guru for nothing.

"Okay, people. Any ideas?"

Becker swallowed. "What about that man downstairs? Michel Hayek?"

Everyone looked up at the sound of the doors and Roger's voice. "Yes. What about Michel? Why isn't he in this room? We need his mind and his experience at work for the President."

Martina followed Roger in the room, avoiding any eye contact.

Chou blanched. "Roger, I wasn't sure that we should let him in on these deliberations. I thought his time would be better spent at the computers. Do you not agree?"

"Oh. Well, sure. But are you giving him complete access to all the information? Are you giving him help? I see Henry Becker here. Henry, have you worked with Michel on accessing the data?"

"Yes sir. Side-by-side. This is a reporting meeting."

"And so far, you all are treading water?"

Becker nodded.

Roger stepped outside to take a call from Deacon. "Hi, Dad. How's mom?"

"Roger, she's about to go crazy with that patch on. And the news from Denver didn't help. It's her life on the line here and she's not one to stand idly by. I don't know how much longer I'm going to be able to prevent her from ripping the damn thing off. So far, Lucy has kept her distracted and Gabe and Edgar are pretty much living at the White House. But I need your help, son. You've got to get to the bottom of this...quickly."

"I know, Dad. But Michel said that she shouldn't take it off under any circumstances. That it could be immediately fatal because of some mutation."

"Yeah. We've heard all that."

"Hey, shouldn't you all be in bed now, or watching a movie? You've got to distract her long enough for me to get into these damn computers here."

"Distract your mother? You're kidding, right? Actually, she went to bed a few minutes ago. I'll check on her when we're done talking."

"Dad, we have a mess here. With David dead..."

"Oh, Roger, I forgot. I'm so wrapped up in your mother. How is Martina? She must be in deep shock."

"Yes, that about sums it up. She hasn't begun to deal with David's death. She is trying to concentrate on the patch for now. She does have to tell Valerie about David soon. That's going to be a tough call."

"Well, tell her how sorry your mother and I are that he was killed. Any leads yet on your end?"

"No. And I take it you don't know anything either."

"No. Nothing. But it can't be a coincidence. The assassination and the attack on David have got to be tied together somehow. Anyway, you started to say something about David."

"Oh, yeah. Only David knew the security codes for this nano-encrypted security they've got around here. It's unbelievably tight. I don't know how we're going to break through. Homeland's head tech guy is working relentlessly, and he hasn't made a dime's worth of progress."

"Son, I wouldn't know a nano-encrypted code from a grape Popsicle, but I do know one thing. You've got to involve this Michel guy. He worked there. He's trained in the research. Hell, he did the basic research for the patch, according to what I understand. For now, his knowledge is the most important thing about him, not what he did in bringing weapons across the border. Are you hearing me on this, Roger? Michel is the key. I know it."

"You're right, Pops. And I've told all the people here that Michel is to be read in on everything. This is all I care about, too. Any other disposition on Michel can wait."

"Hang on."

"Pops, dammit. I'm agreeing with you."

"No, not that. You said some word…'nano' right? That's a word that Edgar Frazier used to name his company, Hibodyne Nano Technologies. Right?"

"Yes, but…"

"Nano technologies. I bet Edgar's company has a wizard in that field. Maybe it would apply here. I'm going to ask Edgar right now. He's on leave from his company, of course, but he would make it his business to keep up with the best people who work there. Okay, Roger. Get with Michel. I'll call when I've talked to Edgar."

The phone went dead. Roger looked at it for a minute. If America knew his father the way he did, they'd elect him president next. Better they don't know.

Roger got himself another cup of coffee and walked the interior circumference of the building to get his mind back on track. When he entered the conference room, his phone beeped. He looked at the caller ID. "That was fast, Pops."

"Yep. Like I thought, Edgar has a fella' he thinks is the best in the world at encryption codes. He is putting him on a company jet from Texas. The guy's name is Harold Uretsky, but Edgar said they call him the blind Ukrainian. Dunno' what that means. Anyway, he should be there in less than three hours. Edgar is arranging for a car to meet him at the Executive Terminal of the airport near wherever the hell Valentine put his headquarters."

"It's west of Denver. Town is called Broomfield. Did you say the blind Ukrainian? Great."

"Listen, Roger. Get off your ass and go talk to Michel. Maybe only the two of you at first. Put him at ease. He thinks that you're going to blow his head off. Why don't you make him feel a little more secure? He might think better."

Roger laughed despite himself. Deacon often had that effect. The guy was special.

"Son, we are hanging on the edge of a terrible cliff. Everything, I mean everything, is irrelevant except finding out how to save your mother. Overcome your pride and hostility."

"Wilco. I've heard you loud and clear."

The phone went dead again. Deacon had to hurry up and make one more call, one he never imagined making. Hyler Ellison answered on the first ring.

"Deacon, what is it? Has something happened to the President?"

"You could say that something is happening to the President. And I need you to do something for her."

"Anything. I'm still in D.C. Do you want me to come over there?"

"No, preacher. I want you to go to Valentine Pharmaceuticals."

"Now?"

"Yes. Right now. I remembered that you were the first person who picked up that there might be something wrong with the patch. You were right. There is something wrong. Really wrong. And the President's life is at stake. At least, that's the working assumption. Until we know otherwise we have to assume the worst. You heard some conversation between Valentine and a couple of other people, right?"

"Yes."

"Okay, then. Would you go to the headquarters and piece that conversation together for all the investigators and spooks on the scene. They can't find a way to unlock the information about the patch on the computers."

"Wait a second. Martina told me that David was flying home early from China to get to the bottom of this. He's the one who knows how to find all the information. He should have been there hours ago."

"Hyler, I hate to give you such bad news in a rush like this, but David is dead."

"What in heaven's name…Dead? How?"

"We don't have time to go into it, but there aren't many details anyway. He was killed on the roof of his headquarters by some kind of hand-held missile."

"Deacon, for God's sake. This is madness."

"Sure as hell is."

"But there's that other person. Jackson Baines. That's it. He's the researcher who was in the conversation I overheard. He would know how to access the data."

"He was killed in the strike. He and David were getting off the helicopter that brought them in from the airport."

"Oh my God. What about Martina? Did she see this? Was she hurt?"

"Yes and yes. She saw her husband go up in a ball of flames. She sustained some injuries, which have been treated. She's back at headquarters, trying to help as much as she can. She's a brave girl."

"Deacon, how do you want me to proceed?"

"I'll have a plane waiting for you on the tarmac at Edwards and I have already dispatched a car to pick you up. How fast can you move?"

"I'll be ready when the car arrives."

"Hyler, thank you. You may be the only living witness who can offer a clue about the patch. Maybe something is locked in your brain."

"I'll try, Deacon. I'll try."

Deacon got up from the family's couch and stretched. He walked lightly to the door of their bedroom and looked at the still form of his wife. Despite the drama and her obvious angst, she was still able to sleep without an aid of any kind. She always called that her secret weapon. He figured that she slept because she was that rarest of creatures, a politician with a clear conscience.

Martina picked up the phone in her private office that she kept at the company. She put it down again and studied the diamond ring on her left hand. She looked at a picture of David with her, taken on their wedding day. Their carefree and excited smiles made it appear that having money and looks and education and ambition made them invincible.

It was time. She dialed the phone. She heard Valerie's voice on the other end. "Valerie, this is Martina. Is Preston there with you? Please get him. I have some bad news…"

CHAPTER 3

Thursday, March 10
Washington • Late Afternoon

The large clock on Senator Mutnick's desk beat the rhythm of the seconds and minutes ticking by. The Senator glared out at the assembly of his colleagues. He was not accustomed to waiting, especially on momentous occasions. His Senate Committee on Rules and Administration was scheduled to vote on the recommendation for confirmation of Senator Richter at 3:00 pm. But it was well past 4:00 and Senator Mutnick still didn't have a quorum.

Those damn Nationals and Mets. Scheduling a pre-season charity game was one thing, but not on my committee's time.

Mutnick stood and joined six of his comrades pacing about the ornate room as one-by-one the recalcitrant senators crept into the Caucus Room of the Russell Building. Once he had ten senators in his clutches, Mutnick would have his quorum. But because of the historic importance of this vote, he had promised his baseball-devotee colleagues that he would be a little more flexible as to the time of the vote.

When 4:30 PM finally rolled around, 17 of the 19 members of the committee were in their chairs. Reporters, many of whom had also rushed back from National Stadium, were frantically setting up their cameras and trying to find space in the now tightly backed room.

In his famous sonorous tones, Senator Mutnick called the committee to order.

"As you all know we are here today to vote on the recommendation to the full Senate for the confirmation of Senator David Richter to be the next Vice President of the United States. Without objection, and with the approval of the ranking majority and minority members, I will now call the question."

"Excuse me, Mr. Chairman, but I have an objection."

"The Chair recognizes Senator Langford of Ohio. What is your objection?"

"Mr. Chairman, I have no doubt as to the outcome of the vote that this committee will take and I do not plan on delaying it any longer than necessary. But I want to be on record that I most strongly object to the way this committee has handled the nomination, both its majority and minority members. I remain unconvinced that we have done adequate due diligence regarding Senator Richter's finances because we have moved too hastily to satisfy our impatient President."

"Your objections are duly noted. Now, unless another member has something else to add, I, again, call the question."

One of the reporters from the Washington Post whispered to his friend from the Times, "Well, the ol' fart seems to have retained his stage presence. I bet he was up half the night practicing his lines."

"Oh come on, give the old guy his due. He's been here, not in the spotlight for, what, 40 years or so, and he's right. We are about to make history."

"Since when did you become such a tight ass?"

Before the Times reporter could respond, Mutnick's voice rang out, asking for a show of hands in favor of the nomination. 14 shot up in the affirmative; then, 3 opposed. Senator Langford immediately called for a voice vote, as was the prerogative of any committee member and the committee clerk called out the Senators' names, recording their vote for the record.

When the clerk completed his task, Mutnick asked him to announce the final tally. And, again, there were 14 votes to recommend and 3 opposed.

"The people have spoken. By an overwhelming majority, the Senate Committee on Rules and Administration refers the nomination of Senator David Richter to the full Senate for a final confirmation vote, which is scheduled to take place at noon on Saturday, the 12th of March.

"With no further business before this committee, I move that we be adjourned." And with the ringing sounds of his voice and his gavel echoing throughout the room, Senator Mutnick's longevity had finally allowed him to become, albeit in a minor way, a part of history.

Valerie couldn't exactly understand what she was feeling as she returned the phone to the cradle. Her father, her indomitable father, was dead? The thought almost made her laugh out loud, it was so implausible. But where were her emotions? Sadness? She tried to access something heartfelt, but could find nothing there.

Martina had pointed out to her that she needed to come to Denver to hold an emergency meeting since Valerie was now Chair of the Board of one of the largest pharmaceutical companies in the world. Did that mean that she would have that title and be First Lady at the same time? Actually, she realized with a start that she would rather be a captain of industry than a titular person who held tea parties. Oh well. Too late to worry about that now.

"Valerie, I think that you should take a few days to be with Preston before trying to come to Denver. We are both in shock. And the building is swarming with people from the FBI, Secret Service and Homeland who are investigating the attack. There's not much either of us can do here for a few days."

"You're right, of course. But I'm trying to think what my father would do. Don't you believe he would want me there?"

Martina had to think on her feet. The last thing they needed was for one of the chief suspects in a crime against the President to be underfoot. "Yes, he would want you here, when you could actually do something to help. I am going to be leaving here in a few minutes and let them do their work."

Valerie bit. "Okay. I can see the logic in that. But I have a question. Did I hear you say that the Secret Service is there along with other investigators? Why on earth is the Secret Service involved? No one in government service was attacked."

Martina had to improvise again. "The way they explained it to me is that the Secret Service is looking into any strange event that could be a terrorist act. A stinger missile apparently qualifies as that possibility."

Valerie sighed inwardly. "Okay. Well, then. I need to give Preston the details about what has happened, Martina. Thank you for calling me."

Martina thought that Valerie might as well have been thanking her for a birthday present, the tone in her voice was that detached.

"Oh, Martina, I should tell you how sorry I am for your loss, too. He was your husband. Though you can have another husband, and I can never have another father, I still know that you are suffering."

The only response that came to Martina's mind was something like, 'bite me, bitch'. So, she said nothing.

CHAPTER 4

Friday, March 11
Sabinas · Wee Hours of the Morning

Adán stared out the leaded glass window across the wide expanse of his lavish living room. He was impatient for President Castillo's representative to make an appearance. Patience was never one of his strong suits and, while his usual nerves of steel were starting to wear thin, he still felt he held enough cards to safely negotiate his way out of the mess in Mexico City.

Most of his army was in full retreat, but not back to Sabinas. Scattering like a swarm of ants that had been hit with scalding water. Still the hacienda was well protected and he didn't give his personal safety a second thought.

Actually he considered President Castillo's surprise call a sign of weakness. Why offer to negotiate when you have already crushed your opponents? Adán wondered which lackey Castillo was sending to do his dirty work. Well, it didn't matter. If they wanted him out of the country, it was going to be a very cushy exile. Of that he had no doubt.

Emilio had agreed to go on the condition that Guerrera not be informed of his identity until they actually met. He convinced President Castillo that the element of surprise was the only advantage he would have once he was inside the compound. Castillo, grateful that Emilio would risk his life on what might be a suicide mission, offered no objection. Guerrera was a psychopath, making him unpredictable and dangerous under any circumstances.

Finally, around 2:00 AM, Garza, now back in Sabinas, sent word that Castillo's representative had landed at the airport in Sabinas and would be arriving in about ten minutes. Adán started to pour himself another drink, but then thought better of it. *Best to be as sharp as possible, at least until I know with whom I will negotiate.*

Garza searched Emilio as soon as he deplaned – orders from Guerrera who did not want any surprises. Emilio immediately recognized Manuel Garza from the confrontation at Santa María del Oro, but surprisingly Garza showed no sign of recognizing him.

Emilio had examined his own motives. Did he want to negotiate with this warlord or just kill him? Capi, the CIA Station Chief at Eagle Pass, had asked him that very question when Emilio called him a few hours earlier. Satisfied that he knew the answer, Capi began placing a series of secure phone calls.

Garza must have signaled ahead, because as the car approached the massive gates to the main house, they swung open as if by magic. The all-terrain vehicle came to a jolting halt at the imposing front door of the hacienda, which opened, also by itself.

Garza called out to Guerrera, who answered, "Sí. Estoy aquí."

Emilio followed Garza into the room, his senses on high alert, his heart pounding in his throat. His father's nemesis was a few feet away.

Guerrera stood by the limestone fireplace, carved with snakes and lions wrapped in an eternal struggle. He looked at Emilio for a long moment and felt that there was something familiar about the shape of the face and deep-set eyes. Emilio walked forward, with Garza remaining behind.

"You were sent here to negotiate on behalf of Castillo? Why did he insult me by sending me an unknown lackey?"

"Why don't you ask the President?"

"Ah, perhaps I will. Forgive me my lack of manners, speaking of names. I am Adán Guerrera de Marza. Welcome to my humble home." Guerrera did not offer his hand.

"I know perfectly well who you are." *You are a bully and a coward.* "And I am Emilio...Emilio de Franco, to be clear."

Guerrera's pupils widened, registering surprise and then he laughed. "This is an unexpected pleasure, indeed."

"For me, it is no pleasure."

Garza nodded to himself. Now he remembered where he had seen Emilio's face...in the door of the helicopter as they fled Santa María del Oro.

Guerrera looked over Emilio, reassessing the situation. Not one to be caught off-guard, Guerrera was impressed by the temerity of this man. To come to the belly of the beast, without aid or back-up, took some big ones.

"It would seem you have your father's belief that you are invincible. Oh, that's right. Your father was wrong about that, wasn't he? He is quite dead, as I understand it. My condolences."

Emilio bristled at this crude reference to his father's death, but suppressed his response.

Guerrera's eye caught the beautiful figure of Estebán emerging from the shadows of the dining room. "Ah, what excellent timing. Estebán, please bring us some coffee and Irish whiskey. We have a special guest with us."

Estebán nodded and glided out of the room, his delicate features a mask.

"You were saying something about my father, I believe. Were you finished?"

"Yes. Shall we get down to the business that brought you here? I am correct, yes? You are here to negotiate my exile from Mexico? I am prepared to give you my requirements."

"Of course, you are. However, if I could have a moment, I would like to freshen up. Would you please direct me to the bathroom?"

"Again where are my manners? Estebán." And then a little louder, "Estebán!"

Estebán returned from the kitchen holding a tray of coffee and whiskey. "Estebán are you deaf? I called for you twice."

"I am sorry, Señor."

"Put down the tray and show our visitor to the..." a pause as Guerrera tried to think of a more appropriate word than toilet, "...guest powder room."

"Sí, Señor."

Guerrera turned to answer his cell phone, as Emilio followed Estebán down a long hallway beyond the dining room. Emilio was glad for the distraction so he could more closely study his surroundings.

Guerrera snapped the phone shut. "It is as I thought, Manuel. My contact in Castillo's office has confirmed that they do not mean for me to leave Mexico. I do not know how they intend to accomplish this, but as soon as the bastard's son returns, blow his fucking head off. Two de Francos dead in less than 24 hours…that is a great thing."

Garza removed his .357 Magnum and checked it. He wrapped his fingers around the weapon, savoring its heft. He was ready.

"On second thought, Manuel, blow his kneecaps apart and let me talk to him for a few minutes before he bleeds to death. I want to watch his eyes as I tell him that his father was nothing but a fraud and a fool, that I dance on his father's grave. I want to be the last thing he sees before he joins Federico in hell."

Garza smiled.

Emilio left the bathroom after throwing some water on his face and slowing his breath. In his right hand, he cradled the gun that Capi's inside source had planted in the bathroom's linen closet. The extra clip was in his left pocket. He crouched along the wooden floor; the muscle memory from years of training returned to him in an instant. He avoided the dining room and turned left into the grand foyer. They would not be looking for him in that direction; at least, that's what he hoped.

At the 12-foot wide archway into the living room, he slowly stood, utterly silent. The pistol in his hand felt cold and hard, like his heart. As he rose, he quietly said, "For my father. For my country."

He fired rapidly, dropping Garza immediately. Guerrera was faster. He turned toward the foyer and slid behind the huge sofa. Emilio saw that Guerrera was bleeding from a hit to his left shoulder, which meant that he could still shoot with his right hand.

Emilio dashed into the room and overturned a six-foot long stone table. He knelt beside Garza and felt for a pulse, finding none. He reloaded and leaned over the table's top edge, scanning for Guerrera. He caught a slight movement behind the sofa and to his right. Guerrera was still alive, but had to be losing blood at a pretty good rate.

Now or never.

He scuttled to the sofa and rose at the moment that Guerrera rose. Both men looked like statues, guns at point-blank range. Who was quicker? Emilio pulled back on the trigger, but saw the top of Guerrera's head burst open before he could get off his shot. In stunned disbelief, Guerrera fell back, his mouth open and his eyes searching the ceiling before his world turned black.

Emilio whirled to the sound of the shot, holding his gun in both hands, arms outstretched in front of him. There was Estebán. His gun clattered to the floor. He leaned over and vomited, then fell down. When he looked up, Emilio was kneeling over him, placing strong hands under both arms. Estebán stood, guided by Emilio.

Through gulps of air, Estebán pushed out a few words. "I had to, Señor. He was a monster. He raped my mother and she killed herself because of the shame and sorrow."

"You saved my life. It was you. You did the right thing for me…and for the many people that he hurt. Thank you, Estebán. We'll talk more later, but for now, we need to get out of here."

Emilio and Estebán turned to the sound of a familiar voice.

"Hey, fellas."

"Capi!"

"Uncle!"

"I got here as fast as I could, but it looks like you didn't need me after all."

Capi hugged Estebán. "Your mother would be proud of you, son. I wish she could have been here to know what you did to avenge her death."

"I was ready, Uncle. Señor de Franco gave me the courage."

Emilio looked at Capi, the question on his face.

"I know that I should have told you, Emilio, that Estebán is my nephew. But I thought that it might get in the way. He is the son of my dead sister. She fell under Guerrera's spell when she was a girl, and we couldn't save her. We planted Estebán here years ago and he has endured unspeakable things at the hands of that mad man. I kept trying to get him to come out, but he wouldn't leave. He was determined to get the job done."

"I look weak, Uncle, but I am strong."

Emilio shook his head. "Nothing weak about you, Estebán. Now, can we get out of this hell hole?"

As if on cue, men dressed in black from head to toe stormed through the front door. "The compound is secure, Capi. We have placed Guerrera's men in the vans, and the Range Rovers are ready to drive us to Eagle Pass. Let's get a move on."

"Right. Emilio, Estebán, you're with me."

Capi pushed them to the door. Emilio turned and saw three of the Rangers pulling the bodies out behind them. He put his foot out and stopped the body of Guerrera. He spit on Guerrera's now stone-dead face and walked into the darkness before dawn.

CHAPTER 5
Friday, March 11
Denver · 9:00 AM

The ambient light from the screens of four computers gave Harold Uretsky's face a ghostly sheen. The deepening circles around his eyes looked like they had been drawn on his skin with a charcoal pencil. His back was bent and tired from leaning over the keyboard, but he wouldn't stop. Not for anything. Michel hovered over Harold and Harold wanted to reach back and send Dr. Frankenstein into the next century.

Harold didn't enjoy being hovered over; it slowed him down. He had spent the last 12 hours in this room because the President of the United States, a woman he greatly admired, needed him to break through the damn security. He didn't require constant interruptions and reminders, especially from some molecular biologist, of how important it was. No one knew that better than he.

Michel sensed Harold's growing irritation, but this was Michel's old office, now reconfigured as a state of the art computer lab by Homeland, and they might have questions. Michel moved away from Harold's workspace and walked across the room to check on Homeland's computer genius, Henry Becker. Henry looked up at Michel and simply shook his head, a gesture that spoke volumes. Michel glanced at the large wall clock. Minutes became hours and the faint ticking sound became like a gong.

Michel picked up the secure line to the conference room.

"Mr. Chou, you asked for a report, but I don't have anything new to tell you. We are having a devil of a time breaking through the firewalls. They are ingenious – technology I have never seen before, although Becker recognizes some familiar patterns. He can't put it together yet."

"Dammit to hell. I would like to know what sonofabitch designed this thing. Do we know? We could bring him here."

"I don't know. We don't have anybody on staff who could have done it. Mr. Valentine went to great lengths to protect the secret. You might ask Mrs. Valentine again if she can remember David mentioning a security expert or cutting edge encryption technology."

"Will do, but so far nothing has come to her."

"When we do break into it, we might see a signature of some kind that will tell us the designer. Keep that in your hip pocket for future reference. But for now, we need to concentrate on those familiar patterns that Uretsky seems to have picked up on and see where they take us."

"Speaking of him, how are the computer gnomes doing? Do they need a break? Some food? Rest? We don't want them to stop, but we don't want them to drop dead, either."

"I don't know what it is with these techie types, but they don't ever seem to need a pit stop and the food groups they crave are caffeine and donuts."

Harold and Henry had already become famous in the hours they had worked side-by-side, or rather back-to-back, in the bowels of the Valentine building. They argued like maiden ladies about everything up to the hole in ozone layer, but they had made a competition of it, which was good for the President. Their hands flew over the keyboards and numbers, symbols, and words came and went in a blur across dozens of screens.

Harold, the blind Ukrainian, was not about to be outdone in the nickname department and decided on a moniker for Henry --Tiresias the blind prophet of Thebes. It didn't make any sense to the rest of the team but computer geeks had language and humor unique to themselves. Roger picked up on the possible source of the reference. Besides being blind, Tiresias was also a clairvoyant and if they were ever going to break the codes, that might come in handy.

Upstairs, Roger felt that same clock ticking in his head, except this one sounded more like the drums in a funeral march. He had set up a command post in an office near the conference room and stayed in constant contact with his mother, father, the White House staff, and Homeland. The mounting frustration in every call was palpable.

His mother tried to comfort him. "I'm not dead yet, honey. Calm yourself down and go help those computer geniuses keep their shoelaces tied so they don't trip over themselves. I trust you, Roger. You've never let me down and I don't think that you're going to start now. I'm taking it easy. I cancelled all but my most essential appointments and have mostly put my feet up today. I'm being smart. You go be smart, too."

She handed the phone over to Deacon and let the anxiety and fatigue wash over her. The last thing that Roger needed was to hear fear and resignation in her voice.

"Okay, son. It's 5:00 in the afternoon, your time. We know that your people there were able to extract some raw data about the modification to the gene behind the SST that corrected the problem. Right? That's a huge leap for us."

"Yeah, Pops, but that was over three hours ago. Now they're stalled again." Roger remembered the excitement and relief that they experienced when Michel broke through to some significant raw data concerning the six women who had died. But when they cross-referenced that data with the FDA, they hit a blank wall. His frustration and anger were starting to get the better of him.

His mother's face entered his mind. She was crying and she receded into a filmy light. She waved until she disappeared. He awoke when his head fell over and bounced against the desktop, as his cell phone buzzed. That was sleep he'd rather avoid.

"Yes, Michel. What do you have for me?"

"Not much, Roger. You know how the deaths occurred in women and how some kind of modification in the genetic code was able to fix that."

"Yes. Yes. We've known this for a few hours."

"Well, we've been trying to figure why only women, and why so few. There had to be common denominator to these women, but it is buried deeper than the seventh level of hell. So far we haven't even been able to identify their names. Is there anybody else to talk to around here who might have the faintest clue?

"And Roger there's something else."

"What?"

"Harold and Henry seem to have hit another wall. One that they've never seen before. Some kind of biometric coding that makes absolutely no sense to them. But if they can't figure it out and quickly…well, I'm not even going to go there."

"Michel, I'll be right down."

"Roger, what is it?"

"Tell you when I get there."

"Martina, I have to go speak with Michel and the geeks for a minute. Why don't you take one more stab at Hyler? There has to be more than he's been able to remember so far. Maybe if you reconstruct the scene of the board meeting for him, it will strike a chord."

"Roger, I'll do what ever you ask, but Hyler has been over this at least 50 times."

"Maybe 51 will be the magic number."

While Roger headed for the elevator, Marti walked across the hall to the office where Hyler had crashed about an hour ago.

By the time Roger reached Michel's office, he was sweating like he had sprung a leak, not from physical exertion, but from adrenaline. *It couldn't be that simple.* "Michel, Harold, Henry, stop what you're doing and listen to me for a moment.

"Henry, you keep saying you see familiar patterns but you can't quite put your finger on it. Michel, at its most basic, Valentine Pharma is a molecular and genetic engineering company, correct?"

"An over-simplification, but yes, I guess so."

"And David Valentine would be very familiar with the science of both?'

"Correct."

"Don't you see?" *David you sly fox.* "I'll wager the patterns that looked familiar to Henry are DNA strands turned into code."

The three men in the room turned to Roger as their jaws dropped.

"By God, I think you're right. There it was in front of me all the time and I didn't see it.

"Henry, don't be hard on yourself. Neither did I."

Michel took the lead chair. "If Roger is right, we need to narrow down to what strand of DNA was used, or else we might as well be back at square one. And I have an idea of how we can do that."

Now it was Roger, Harold and Henry's turn to stare at Michel. "Look, Valentine Pharmaceuticals uses biometrics for its security system. Some systems use retinal scans and some use palm scans, but our state-of-the-art security actually has a copy of each employee's DNA. Why not try crosschecking the firewall access code with our security system's DNA database. Maybe we'll get lucky and find a match."

By midnight, Roger, Hyler and Martina felt desperation set in. Roger had been right about the DNA sequencing firewall, and the boys found a match. It turned out to be Valerie's DNA that David, or the program's developer, used. But being into the system and making heads or tails of thousands of bits of data was still a nightmare, and time was running short. They sat alone in Roger's office while Homeland and Secret Service personnel snacked in the conference room.

Martina looked at her watch for the 1000th time that day. "Hyler, I have to ask again. Is there anything from the day of the board meeting that could help us? An odd or misplaced word? A reference to something out of context? Let's go through the day minute-by-minute."

"Marti, I'll do it again. But, what could possibly be left in my brain that we haven't examined? Roger, you weren't there. You don't have a biased view. Can you think of a different question to ask?"

Before he could answer, Hyler was again going over, detail by detail, what he remembered of the board meeting. When he got to the part about returning from the bathroom, after the board meeting had adjourned, and overhearing some of the conversation between David, Jackson and Valerie, Roger, who was listening with his eyes closed, sat bolt upright in his chair. It clanked against the floor. "Wait. Wait, Hyler. Say that last word again."

"What word? What? What did I say?"

"Marti, what word did Hyler just say?"

"Roger, you're freaking me out. He was talking about the same event we've heard about for hours. It's after midnight."

"Please, Marti. What word?"

"Okay, he said that David mentioned that they had buried the…what was it? Agent? No, co-agent. That's it. Co-agent."

Martina couldn't breathe. Words caught in her throat. She croaked out, "We have never once contemplated a co-agent."

"What does that mean?" Hyler blanched. He was upset and confused. Was this something he should have remembered earlier?

Martina found her voice. "It's okay, Hyler. A co-agent is some kind of separate substance that introduces a response to the drug. Like if you drink alcohol and take some prescription drugs, it can cause seizures or even death. A co-agent, in the case of the patch, has nothing to do with the patch itself, but the patch interacts with it. With the SST, something made it have a deadly consequence for those few women who died."

"So, the co-agent is necessary to be introduced to cause harm, right? Well, what the hell is the co-agent?"

"Roger, it's something benign, something that the women ate or that was somehow absorbed by their bodies."

"Absorbed by their bodies. You mean like hand lotion or soap?"

Hyler jumped up. "Quit talking about it. Call those people downstairs and tell them about a co-agent. Now. Now."

Roger was already running out of the room, calling over his shoulder, "Get Chou and the others. Meet me downstairs."

He passed the elevator and took the stairs, sliding on the handrails and leaping down whole flights. Roger kept repeating over and over, we're looking for a co-agent, a co-agent. Maybe that one word would open up the data to them. There was time. Barely. The fourteen days were up later this morning. The course of the patch would be done. It might take a few more hours, but this was it. This was it. It had to be.

Find the co-agent. Save my mother.

CHAPTER 6
Saturday, March 12
Washington DC · White House · 6:30 AM

Ezra's cell rang as he was spreading a bagel with cream cheese from his stash in the White House ground floor kitchen. He was about to sit down in the small Secret Service office next to the refrigeration room. It had been a calm morning, with roll call and the day's schedule set.

Now who the hell would be calling this early?

"Ezra?"

"Yes"

"It's Roger." After an interminable pause adding, "Veritas."

Before Ezra could respond Roger asked, "Are you outside the President's bedroom?"

"No sir."

"Then run."

Ezra, already on autopilot, was in a high sprint that his superb conditioning allowed. As one of the oldest agents, he wanted to be faster than the others, all of whom started to scramble in behind him as they saw him run by.

He tore around the corner of the center hall, up the lower level of the Grand Staircase, using the polished banister to pole vault ahead three steps at a time.

"Roger, what is going on?"

"Ezra, the President's life is in your hands. It would take too long to explain, but she's been slowly poisoned. If she uses her normal perfume this morning, nothing, I repeat nothing, will save her life."

From anyone else, Ezra might have considered this a bit melodramatic. But from Roger, never a drama queen, Ezra had no doubt that the life of Kate MacIntyre now rested in his hands.

Passing the entrance to the Grand Hall, he bounded up the next set of stairs, now making four steps at a time, careening diagonally across the center hall of the second floor private residence, coming to the door outside Kate's bedroom in under 60 seconds. Eight agents trailed behind him, none knowing the source of the emergency. But all knowing something big was happening.

He pushed through the agent on guard and flung open the door to see Deacon standing there with a towel wrapped around his waist. Deacon stared at Ezra like he had gone mad.

"Where is the President?"

"Ezra, what the hell?"

"Deacon, I don't have time…where is the President?"

"Still in her dressing room."

Ezra rushed past the First Gentleman with the other agents on this tail. He turned right and bore down on the President's private dressing area.

At the door, his deep ebony face went ashen. Shadows formed under his eyes. There was Kate sitting at her dressing table with a bottle of perfume in her hand.

But was she putting it down or picking it up?

He responded, all the years of training coming into play – the moment all Secret Service agents prayed would never come, the moment he would take a bullet for his boss. For a split second, time froze.

Ezra sprang forward, right hand outstretched.

CHAPTER 7
Saturday, March 12
Washington DC · Senate Chamber · 1:00 PM

The Senate chamber was almost full. The vacant seats belonged to Senator Richter; the late Senator Peveto who had died unexpectedly last week and for whom the Governor of Missouri had yet to name a replacement; and Senator Baylor of Mississippi, now 92 and the oldest member of this august body. He attended the Senate if his vote were needed.

The galleries, on a mezzanine level that surrounded the room on all four sides, were jammed. The press gallery was so tight that cameramen were hanging over the railing. Diplomats had packed their own gallery and the seats reserved for House members and Senate guests had long ago been claimed.

Valerie and Preston were seated front and center in the ornate Senate Chamber, directly opposite the podium. The royal blue and gold tones of the carpet and wall panels bespoke of elegance and authority. Valerie selected a suit that was slightly darker than the royal blue. She was meant to be there.

"Senators, the question has been called. Without objection, we will now call the roll."

Senate Pro Tem Chester Harwood, according to custom, sat at the elevated podium. He had seen much in his life as a United States Senator, but, even with the outcome a foregone conclusion, this might be the most dramatic moment of his 89 years.

The Chief Clerk of the Senate began to read the roll of Senators alphabetically.

"Senator Aaron…"

"Aye."

"Senator Aaron votes Aye. Senator Allen…"

And so it went, with a few Senators choosing not to respond, as the usual game began of who would have the honor of pushing the nominee over the top. To Preston, this felt like the dance of the tigers, natural enemies warily embracing and pulling apart in a never-ending cycle.

Valerie was nervous and jumpy, incessantly clearing her throat and tapping her fingers. She couldn't take her eyes off of her watch.

Preston noticed her fidgets. "Valerie, I appreciate your concern, but really, do you have to look at your Rolex every 30 seconds?"

"Sorry, a nervous habit, I guess."

Preston knew there was something not quite right about Val's behavior over the past two weeks and it had worsened as the confirmation hearings proceeded. Now, she had become ridiculous.

About half way through the roll call, the gallery responded to the first 'no' vote from an obstreperous old Senator from Ohio and a Democrat, at that. No surprise, Senator Langford had announced his intentions after the news broke of Richter's supposed relationship with Valentine Pharmaceuticals. Langford declared that he would oppose the nomination and no amount of cajoling would change his position.

"I'll have order. There will be order in the Senate Chamber." Chester banged his gavel and was secretly relieved to have a little something to do while the clerk continued the roll.

"Senator Mallory of Nevada." The clerk needed to address the fact that the Senate had two Senators named Mallory.

"Aye."

"Senator Mallory votes aye. Senator Mallory of Pennsylvania."

They reached Senator Nelson of New Jersey.

"Senator Nelson."

No response. Again the clerk, according to form, called out "Senator Nelson."

Again, no response. But this had been pre-arranged so that Senator Northcutt, the senior Senator from North Dakota and a member of the minority, would have the honor of being the vote that pushed his fellow Senator's confirmation over the top. *Heck, he may be a Democrat but he's North Dakotan, first and foremost.*

"Senator Northcutt." A hush fell over the entire gallery. They were aware of this prearranged bit of political theater.

"Mr. Senator Pro Tem, it is with great pleasure that I cast this vote to confirm the next Vice President of the United States of America, Senator David Richter of the great State of North Dakota."

The galleries and the Senate Chamber burst into applause. The rest of the vote was now a technicality. For all intents and purposes, the United States had a new Vice President, continuity was reestablished, and Washington could slowly return to the life that the past two weeks had shattered.

Valerie's heart sank. What had gone wrong? She looked at her watch once more. The President must be dead. Wasn't Preston, at this very moment, supposed to be informed that, since the Vice Presidency was still vacant, he had succeeded to the Presidency? Somebody at the White House must be playing tricks in order to allow David Richter to succeed to the Presidency. That must be it. How dare they.

As she tugged on Preston's sleeve to get his attention, an usher walked down the center aisle of the Senate Chamber, up to the podium, and handed Senator Harwood a note.

Valerie sat up straighter. Maybe it wasn't too late, after all. The vote had not been officially cast, and Preston might still be President.

The entire Senate and all the galleries now focused on the Senate Pro Tem. It was impossible to get a read on what was happening because his body language revealed nothing.

He lifted the gavel. The bang that followed split the gavel in half.

"Senators, if I might have your attention. And Mr. Jamison, please stop the roll…"

Murmurs filled the Chamber. Heads turned in dismay. It was unheard of for the presiding officer to stop a roll call before completion, let alone with three more Senators to go. The Pro Tem must have news of such import that it would warrant this breech of senatorial decorum.

Valerie fought the urge to jump out of her chair. This was her moment. Preston had no idea of what was occurring. And the entire press corps had awakened from the stupor caused by the preconceived nature of this event. They had thought that there would be no surprises today.

As Chester began to address the Chamber, doors across the room crashed open and Secret Service agents secured every exit.

Valerie looked back and saw three agents walking down the stairs towards her and her clueless husband. Yes. Her plan had succeeded. The patch had done its work. She was the new First Lady.

"If I might have the Senate's attention. This is most unusual. I have a note from the Chief Usher of the Senate informing me…"

The agents reached Preston and Valerie. Valerie assumed that one of them would immediately inform Preston that he was the President of the United States.

Madame President

The agents squeezed behind the Speaker and one of them leaned over to speak. Preston snapped his head toward Valerie, as the agent, whom he now recognized as Clint Hollingsworth, the head of the Secret Service, whispered in…

Chester continued. "My fellow Senators, Distinguished Guests and Visitors I have the…"

…Valerie's ear. He placed his hands on her shoulders. "Mrs. Sandermann, would you please be so kind as to stand up slowly. Do not make a scene."

Preston put out his hands to stop them.

Senator Harwood announced, "distinct pleasure to welcome…"

The barreling voice of the Chief Usher of the United States Senate interrupted Harwood. "Mr. Senator Pro Tem, Senators, Distinguished guests, Ladies and Gentlemen…the President of the United States."

Kate strode into the Senate chamber. Agents escorted Valerie up the stairs of the visitor aisle, with Speaker Sandermann in tow, demanding an explanation from the Director of the Secret Service.

Every eye in the room fixed on President MacIntyre as she walked the 75 feet to the podium. Astonished Senators' jaws dropped. Pages knew they were about to be a part of history, but didn't know why. The press stood rigid, pens in midair, as though the Hindenburg had just exploded.

"Members of the United State Senate, Distinguished Guests and my Fellow Americans," Kate was aware that the proceedings were being fed live to all the news outlets. "it is with no joy that I come here this afternoon, but, at least, our dark days of uncertainty are over."

Epilogue

The dry, fragrant wood popped out sparks in one of Camp David's stone fireplaces, this one in the comfortable living area in the main lodge. The entire family, with the addition of Martina and Emilio, and even Hyler and Beryl, gathered there over the kids' fall break in late September. Kate's health had returned to her in full force, especially since she no longer smoked, and she even played a game of touch football, as the quarterback, of course. She learned as a girl how to throw a football with a decently tight spiral.

The cool fall air in the Catoctin Mountain Park invigorated everyone and appetites were prodigious. They kept the Navy cooking staff busy from sunup to after sundown. This was the place where Kate felt almost as good as she did at Aguila. Camp David had the added advantage of being about 60 miles from D.C.

Kate asked Deacon, Emilio, Roger, and Martina to join her for after dinner drinks around the fire. She included her other adult children. There were no secrets about this now among family and they all needed to close a few loops after the harrowing events of spring.

Kate noticed that Roger and Martina were never too far apart and the occasional hand brush betrayed their growing relationship. Heat came off the space they tried to keep between them. Kate knew.

"Roger, how is the Ranger's widow doing in the months since Andy was killed? We don't want to forget her and the baby."

"She's a strong woman, Kate. She has a good family behind her, but, you know...it's hard."

"I spoke with her only that once. I know that this isn't the usual situation, but I really do want to be kept informed about her and her little boy."

"Absolutely."

"Martina, are you satisfied that your stepdaughter was treated fairly by the government?"

"Fairly? Oh, much more than that, Madame President."

"Kate."

"Yes...Kate. She was not prosecuted under the terms of your generous deal, and she is receiving better than adequate care at the federal facility where she will spend the rest of her life."

"I hated to have to label her an enemy combatant under the Patriot Act, Martina, because no official tie between her and Hezbollah was established. There was no other way to remove her from the spotlight before she could cause further damage to the country."

"It is better this way. In exchange for not being charged with treason, she agreed to sign over all her shares in Valentine to me. She spends most of her time in a fog, coming in and out of reality. She really did have the complete nervous breakdown, for lack of a better phrase, that the papers reported. Some days, she demands to see Preston, and others she cries out for her father. She is an empty shell of a person. Poor Preston is quietly pursuing a divorce and is trying to decide whether or not he wants to continue in public office. We'll see."

Deacon's heart went out to this young woman. She had a world of responsibility on her slim shoulders. "What about the company, Martina? Has everything been settled with the FDA?"

"We negotiated the final deal last week. You know how big business, along with the federal bureaucracy, can be. Looks like the patch will be allowed to remain on the market because the results are too miraculous to lose. Valentine had to agree to give up the patent on it, resulting in untold losses to the company – all entirely appropriate, I should add."

Roger inched closer to Martina on the couch. "She's a great boss for the company now. She is steady at the wheel and her people are healing. They were traumatized, too, you know."

Kate nodded. "Of course. Everyone involved was thrown by the attack on David and Jackson, by Michel's double life, and Valerie's craziness. And we're still not sure who the actual target was."

Roger made a last minute decision to tell the group about something that had remained the secret of a few. "We do have some new intelligence on that score from our Israeli friends. They are pretty sure that the assassin was after Michel. Only the quirk of nature – the fact that Baines could have been a double for Michel – saved Michel's life."

He looked over to Martina. "David was, I'm sorry to say, collateral damage."

All the murmuring and side conversations stopped. This was sensitive material but Kate decided to let Roger continue.

"There is a man in Beirut, Sheikh Nasrallah, who is well known to our security forces. We now believe that he hired the assassin. We also discovered earlier that Nasrallah is Michel's adopted father.

"Well, I don't care who his father is. He should fry for what he did, or go to an 'undisclosed location' where he can suffer real punishment." Butch was not much in a mood to forgive.

"Butch is right. Why should we give a damn?" Brother felt like he must be the only person in the room who didn't know the whole story.

Roger understood his brothers' anger, but didn't acknowledge it. "Briefly, Nasrallah killed Michel's parents and then took the boy to raise as his own since he and his wife couldn't have children. He made sure that the boy was saturated, almost from infancy, with anti-American rhetoric. And when Michel found out the truth about this man he had once loved, he jumped in and helped us figure out what was going on with the patch."

Martina inserted, "We couldn't have done it without him, Brother."

A companionable silence followed that understatement. Butch was curious about the new Vice President because he had never had the chance to talk to him personally. "Mom, how do you think Vice President Richter is doing now that he's had six months in office?"

"Remarkably well, Butch. He's still got a lot to learn, but we have time. I think he'll be ready when the time comes."

Deacon jerked his head toward Kate. "Honey, could you put that in a different way, please? Like 'when my second term is finished'... okay?"

She squeezed his hand and didn't let go. "Okay, Deac. He'll do fine in office when the Constitution says that I have to leave, and not a minute before. Now, I do have something I would like to say to Hyler."

She turned to him and held him in her gaze. "Thank you for saving my life."

Hyler waved it off. "No thanks necessary, Kate. I was glad that this old man could remember something that proved to be helpful."

Deacon weighed in. "It was more than that."

"Hyler, one time you told me that our philosophies are not so different. I didn't believe you. I do now. So does Deacon."

"Miracles do happen, after all."

Martina had one more question for Kate, something she had been wondering for months. "Madame President – Kate – I know that you can no longer wear your old perfume. Have you found a substitute?"

Kate laughed and the air in the room became lighter. "Oh, heavens, Martina. It was hard to give up "Mistral." You know that they make it at this tiny perfumery on the Left Bank, which has been in the same family for over 300 years. Louis XV gave it as a wedding present to his daughter-in-law, Marie Antoinette. Not a wonderful woman, but a wonderful fragrance. Good thing that it is relatively rare, huh? That's why only a handful of women suffered that terrible fate. I'll miss it, but the family of perfumers is designing a fragrance for me. Mistral will always be a reminder of the fickle nature of life and how lucky I am to still be here with all of you."

Unlike the chill in Camp David's air, Cancun's sun rose with an oppressive warmth and Abdel wanted to get in a swim before the heated sand burned the soles of his feet. He scurried to the clear, turquoise water, fell in, and let the waves tumble over him. He floated on his back and thought of his new friend back at the hotel. He usually wasn't attracted to Frenchmen, but except for the scar on his face, this man was quite sensual in a dangerous sort of way. Well, as the Americans say 'variety is the spice of life' and this was the life he deserved.

And that was his last fully formed thought before a bullet tore through the middle of his forehead. Back up the beach, hidden on the top floor balcony of the Le Blanc Spa Resort, Jad Farrah took his time taking apart and packing the standard tool of the trade, his sniper rifle.

How nice it was of that pervert Talal to choose such a fine hotel for his stay. It was almost too easy. Jad had met him in the hotel bar the night before, plied him with drinks and staggered with him back to his room. In the morning while he was showering, Abdel called out that he was going to take a quick swim before breakfast.

Jad snapped closed the carefully packed briefcase and walked out of the room to the bank of elevators. He was impatient to check out and fly to Beirut to tell Nasrallah in person that the job was done and was on the house.

In Beirut, the weather was still hot and miserable. The sheikh couldn't ever seem to cool off, even with the air conditioning blowing straight on him. Ever since Michel disappeared from Denver, Nasrallah couldn't rest. Jad had sworn by the beard of the Prophet that Michel was dead, but rumors had surfaced to the contrary. He tossed every night, replaying disorienting dreams about his son. The son he raised from an orphan child. The son who betrayed him and everything they had stood for together.

On a neighboring street, in a cramped apartment, that son stood over the still warm body of Talal El-Hussen. Michel hadn't talked to Talal or given the bastard a chance to defend himself. He simply knocked and fired his gun when he was sure that it was Talal who answered the door.

Michel walked the two blocks with the warm pistol in his right front coat pocket. He had reloaded it and made sure that the safety was off.

Nada stood by an open window, with a view of the street as she did most nights. Half seeking relief from the oppressive heat and half hoping that she would spot her beloved son, she kept vigil. After so many months without a word and still she watched and waited.

Nada gasped. She blinked her eyes in disbelief and put her hands over her mouth when she saw Michel walking toward their house. She padded softly to the door and opened it in a crack, waiting for Michel to approach. Her husband did not hear her or notice when she stepped out into the hallway. She threw her arms around her son, her precious son, and sobbed into his chest.

But after looking at him more closely, she wasn't so sure that he was truly alive. His eyes certainly emitted no light or warmth. He hugged her and took her hands, but he was as far from her as he was when he first came to them as a toddler – sad and lonely and afraid.

She placed her hands on either side of his face. "Michel, my son, I have worried about you. Where have you been? What has happened to make you so…so distant?"

"I know everything, mother. Everything. How my real parents were killed. What Nasrallah really is – a monster, a murderer."

Nada nodded but could say nothing.

"I do not blame you, mother. You loved me and kept me from a life on the streets. I would be nothing without you. You must have known what he did to my family."

She nodded again.

"You must also know why I am here."

"I fear I do. He is not worth the bullets you plan on putting in him, Michel. He is not worth you being killed by his guards. Go, Michel. Leave this terrible place. Choose life."

Madame President

Michel pulled the gun out of his pocket and shifted it from hand to hand while his mother spoke to him in soothing tones. She was always a beautiful woman, and that had not changed, despite years of living under Nasrallah's cruel hand. He started to move past her, but she surprised him. With shocking agility, she took the gun out of his loose grip and ran through the open door, slamming it behind her before Michel could intervene. She slipped the dead bolt into place while he pounded on the door.

Nada ran into Nasrallah's study and screamed, "You are filth. Living with you is worse than death, and I will not let you hurt my son. Go to hell where you belong." She raised the gun and fired six bullets into the sheikh's body. He rocked back with every shot until he fell onto the coffee table and slid to the floor. She looked at him dispassionately and then down to the gun in her hand. She whispered, "Run, Michel. I love you. Choose life."

The opposite door to the study burst open and Nasrallah's security guards swarmed the room.

Michel leaned out the window of the cab he had hailed, when he heard the rapid and unmistakable report of AK47s. He closed his eyes and tried not to picture his lovely mother, riddled with bullets. She had saved him.

He had committed to memory the address of the Mossad safe house in Beirut and started to give it to the driver. He stopped, looked back up to the old house, and he chose life. He had debts to pay. Maybe they would let him begin today.

"The American Embassy, please."

Acknowledgements

We sought the wisdom and counsel of many people in our journey of writing *Madame President*.

We received line edits from a number of serious readers, who took a great deal of their precious time to work with the manuscript. Their critiques helped us change direction when needed and made the book far better than it would have been without their ideas. They are Dawn Blobaum, Amy Sutter, Patti Skigen, Lewis Deaton, Harriet Kessler, Debra Jaret, Rosie Molinary, Mike Kessler, and Sally McMillen.

We had numerous first readers who provided general suggestions and who encouraged us to get this book in the hands of other readers. They are Vickie Firczak, Pamela Melnick, Irene Guttman, Keith Sutter, Patti Siegel, Andy Propst, Bonnie Lurie, Bob Merrithew, Jeanne Miller, Ed Harris, Polly Griffin, Susan Nelson, Boo Hess, and Brenda Goings.

Several experts in their fields helped us with research to attain believability in the scientific and military aspects of the book. Michael Chou is a molecular biologist. Mark Lester is a former Army Ranger and Shane Page is law enforcement official. Aaron Houck, a Constitutional lawyer, provided insight into the 25th Amendment.

Our publicist, Allison Elrod, used her genius to help us find our readers and she bouyed our spirits. Our thanks to Jim Sanders for his creative input.

Jyll Holzman and her husband, John Geddes, of the New York Times, read *Madame President* and, when we were on the verge of setting the book aside, insisted that it was worthy of being published.

Our children, Jeffrey and Ellyn Guttman, Amy and Keith Sutter, Ben Williams and Sun K. Park, and Daniel Williams gave freely of their spirited enthusiasm and love for the project and for us.

We are both blessed with extended families that are fun, witty, smart, and supportive. The matriarchs of both of our families, Robyn Oldham and Irene Guttman, are wise and kind and provide us tender comfort. Our sense of belonging in the world is due to the place they and our families make for us.

Without complaint, our spouses, Lewis Deaton and Bill Williams, provided us the time and space to write, understanding the demands of our work schedules and helping us overcome whatever doubts arose. Their belief in us is intrinsic to every page of this book.

The Authors

MARGUERITE WILLIAMS **JON GUTTMAN**

JON GUTTMAN is an award-winning media and communications specialist and the cofounder of Winslow Advertising Group/HVHM in New York where he served as creative director. A graduate of NYU, his extensive experience in the entertainment industry includes writing, directing and producing ads and radio spots for a wide variety of clients.

MARGUERITE WILLIAMS is a native of Texas and a graduate of the University of Texas where she earned degrees in English and Spanish. She is a widely published essayist and the co-author of two previous books, as well as a freelance editor and writing consultant. A long-time politician, Williams is a Senior Fellow of the American Leadership Forum.